"A hero to die for."

—Under the Covers

And praise for the Alien Huntress series

DARK TASTE OF RAPTURE

"A literal taste of rapture."

—Fresh Fiction

"Showalter consistently creates compelling and action-packed tales where alien creatures are intricately woven into a believable futuristic world. But *Dark Taste of Rapture* takes it up a notch. . . ."

—RT Book Reviews

ECSTASY IN DARKNESS

"A glued-to-your-seat kind of book . . . Showalter is a master of creating unique, fun, and super-sexy characters."

—RT Book Reviews

SEDUCE THE DARKNESS

"Imaginative and sexy, this story teems with nonstop action!"

—BookPage

"[A] compelling and entertaining story of lust, deception, intrigue. . . ."

—RT Book Reviews

SAVOR ME SLOWLY

"Takes the characters to their sensual and emotional limits—and beyond!"

—New York Times bestselling author Susan Sizemore

Also by Gena Showalter

Black and Blue

Gena
Showalter

Pocket Books

New York   London   Toronto   Sydney   New Delhi

Pocket Books
A Division of Simon & Schuster, Inc.
1230 Avenue of the Americas
New York, NY 10020

This book is a work of fiction. Any references to historical events, real people, or real places are used fictitiously. Other names, characters, places, and events are products of the author's imagination, and any resemblance to actual events or places or persons, living or dead, is entirely coincidental.

First Pocket Books paperback edition November 2013

POCKET and colophon are registered trademarks of Simon & Schuster, Inc.

For information about special discounts for bulk purchases, please contact Simon & Schuster Special Sales at 1-866-506-1949 or business@simonandschuster.com.

The Simon & Schuster Speakers Bureau can bring authors to your live event. For more information or to book an event contact the Simon & Schuster Speakers Bureau at 1-866-248-3049 or visit our website at www.simonspeakers.com.

Manufactured in the United States of America

10   9   8   7   6   5   4   3   2   1

ISBN: 978-1-4516-7160-5
ISBN: 978-1-4516-7162-9 (ebook)

Acknowledgments

To Lauren McKenna and Elana Cohen—
THANK YOU just isn't enough.
And Lauren, this book would not be the same without your insight, for which I will be forever grateful.
Working with you has been an honor and a privilege.

To three ladies who make my life better in
more ways than I can list:
Jill Monroe, Roxanne St. Claire, and Kresley Cole.
You carry my heart!

To Diana Peng and Sarah Lieberman for the
audio support! You guys are rocking it!

To Elisa Cavassi for the camera fun and
awesome photos at RomCon 2013.
Every time I think of you, I smile!

To Casey Harris-Parks and Sheila Hall for the
tremendous support. I had a blast, girls.

And to Nathalia Suelle for the amazing cover.
It's one of my favorites!

Black and Blue

Prologue

CORBIN BLUE TUCKED HIS girlfriend against his side, smiled his patented bedroom smile, and faced the cameras, playing the part of irreverent debaucher to perfection. As usual.

In reality, he was the World's Best Spy and Assassin (trademark pending), with the singular ability to kill everyone around him with only a thought. Too bad mass homicide was not tonight's orders.

Another round of flashbulbs nearly blinded him, and voices assaulted his ears.

"Blue! Noelle! Over here."

"Any wedding bells in your future now that the New World Order has legalized human-otherworlder marriages?"

"Blue, how did it feel when you broke the Mack's spine during last week's game?"

The crowd went silent, willing to wait for his answer this time.

"Like I should have hit him harder," he said. Football was his cover. And the Mack, well, he was the quarterback for the Strikers, the number two–ranked team in the National Otherworld Football League, and collateral damage.

Besides, it wasn't like the guy had suffered for more than a few days. He was an Arcadian, like Blue, and healed supernaturally fast. In fact, the arrogant prick was already back on his feet.

Noelle patted Blue's chest, her gray eyes twinkling mischievously. "Here's hoping for permanent damage next time," she announced in her I-just-want-to-be-naked voice.

While gasps of shock and glee swept through the paparazzi—the sharks had scented blood—Blue ushered Noelle into the crowded hotel ballroom that had been transformed into a twinkling wonderland. Multicolored flowers hung from the ceiling, and black velvet embedded with faux-diamond lights draped the walls.

A collage of perfumes scented the air, mixing with the effervescence of champagne and the aroma of smoked salmon on herbed crackers carried on trays by more than a hundred waiters.

The same conversations Blue had heard a million times echoed.

"Who are you wearing?"

"Did you hear about—" Blah, blah, blah.

Two minutes in, and Operation Lullaby was already boring him.

Come on, people. Let's try a new play on this field. He loved both of his jobs, and he was certainly great at them, but nothing challenged him anymore. Everything came so easily. From missions to ball games . . . to women.

Where was the fun? The excitement? The danger?

"After we've said our hellos"—Noelle swiped a glass of bubbly—"let's sneak into the bathroom and make out."

Can't sigh. He checked his watch. Ten thirty-four. Would he have time for a will-we-won't-we-be-caught quickie? No, probably not. Even though he expected tonight's plan to encounter zero problems, he knew it would be better to act as if the worst could happen.

"Sorry, Elle. That's a no go." To prevent any pushback, he said, "That's not the way we act in public, is it?"

She bowed her head, embarrassment coloring her cheeks. "I guess not."

And the Boyfriend of the Year award does not *go to Corbin Blue.*

He hated dishing the naughty child treatment to Noelle, but sometimes it was the only way to stop her from inadvertently ruining a mission.

She was a sweet girl, though she practically sprouted fangs and horns when anyone riled her temper. Despite Dr. Sweetness and Miss She-devil, which he actually liked, she wasn't his type. She had no idea she'd been handpicked by his boss and mentor, Michael Black, or that Blue worked for the government and he had stayed with her for the past year only for her connections. She thought they were in love.

Yes, he was a total douche for lying to her. He knew it, and tried to make it up to her with orgasms. "Just wait till we get home . . ." he whispered, hoping to soothe her. He kissed the hollow of her neck before maneuvering her through the crowd.

Smart people stepped out of his way. He had a reputation for causing "unnecessary bloodshed" in a sport lauded for its brutality, and as an Arcadian, one of the most feared races ever to cross a bridge of inter-world wormholes to live on earth, he possessed countless supernatural abilities. Not that the good citizens of the world knew about the majority of those abilities.

Like, say, the fact that he could propel the hotel through the sky if ever he unleashed the power frothing inside him. He could compel certain people to do anything he wanted with only a few spoken words. He could heal others with only a touch, though he had to take their pain inside himself. He could drain others just as easily.

He could do a thousand other things, but only a rare few could actually feel the energy humming inside him.

He scanned the sea of faces, searching for his crew. He spotted John No Last Name first. The golden-skinned Rakan despised crowds, but there he was, dressed in a waiter's frock, offering an older lady a glass of deep-red wine while the woman behind him gave him a good old-fashioned eye-screw.

Aaannnd . . . there was the big and monstrous-looking Solomon Judah standing in front of a set of terrace doors, acting as security. Not even Solo's closest friends knew his origins. They just knew to stay far, far away whenever his dark side took over. He made the Hulk look like a toddler who'd just had his paci taken away.

Blue, John, and Solo had met over two decades ago, after Michael rescued each one from a broken home. Or, in Blue's case, a darkened street. And though they had been given to different families, they'd come together every weekend to train, and quickly bonded. They'd worked together, killed together . . . and, in the end, saved each other. There was no one Blue loved more.

A low, sultry laugh drifted through the kaleidoscope of noise to caress his ears. The blood in his veins heated, surprising him. Interesting him. Muscles knotting with sudden eagerness, he searched the ballroom for the source—there.

Cue the slow-mo special effects. His surroundings blurred, a lone woman becoming the center of his focus. The only thing he noticed. She wasn't facing him fully, but had her side to him. Her dress was sapphire blue, the material clinging to her slender frame until flaring at her feet and trailing behind her like waves in the ocean.

The imagery fit. She was straight-up man bait, and he was already hooked and reeled. Her black-as-night hair curled down her back in long, shimmering ribbons. Pale skin with rosy undertones glowed as if she'd just rolled from bed—not completely satisfied, since she hadn't left *his*.

Five minutes alone with her. That's all he needed to take her from "not completely" to "utterly."

She was spectacularly animated as she spoke to a blond female in a red dress, her hands waving through the air. Then she turned in his direction, grinning, clearly searching for someone. Her gaze skipped right over him—what the hell?— as she pointed and the other girl nodded.

The force of her beauty hit him. Followed by her identity. His mouth dried the moment he realized he was lusting after none other than Evangeline Black. Michael's youngest daughter. Early twenties, lovely . . . and completely off-limits.

Blue had known she would be here, among the rich and famous, celebrating eighty years of peace between humans and otherworlders. Earlier, Michael had shown him a picture of her.

Look out for her, but don't touch her, he'd said, his tone sharp. *I didn't get to be a father to her while she was growing up, so I'm making up for it now. She is never to be a conquest.*

Defile the offspring of a man he respected? Never.

In the picture, she appeared innocent and pretty, so he had no problem assuring Michael of his pure intentions. No problem meaning what he said.

In person, she appeared wanton and gorgeous, and Blue was having trouble catching his breath. Defile? *With pleasure.*

Apparently, she spent most of her life overseas with her mother, and the last two years secretly training with her father. Tonight was her final lesson. Michael wanted her dropped into the middle of a mission, with only the barest of facts, having only seen photos of her team.

"Oh, no. My mother just spotted me," Noelle muttered, reminding him of her presence. "I've got to hide before she corners me and tells me all the ways I've disappointed her. Join me?"

"I've got to say hello to Michael's daughter," he said, tearing his gaze from the dark-haired girl.

Noelle cringed. "I think you've got it worse. Good luck."

Worse than the devil's twin sister? "Wait." He took his girlfriend by the shoulders. *Exactly. You have a girlfriend. Remember that.* "You know her?"

"We met the last time I was in Westminster. Let's just say she's unforgettable and leave it at that. Why ruin the surprise?"

Unforgettable wasn't a bad thing. "Outsassed you, did she? Well, I doubt I'll have the same problem. I happen to know how to charm the ladies." A flicker of guilt accompanied the words. If she only knew half the things he'd done . . .

She grinned with wicked anticipation and gave him a little push in Miss Black's direction. "Go charm her, then. Give her everything you've got. You can tell me all about it when we get home—after you've nursed the Blue Ranger and his berry good friends back to health."

No one could be as bad as Elle was leading him to believe.

As she raced away to avoid her mother, Blue homed in on Evangeline. He felt like a hunter who'd just spotted the tastiest of prey. At her side, he noted the scent of honey and almonds wafting from her. The fire in his veins sizzled and smoked.

"—bloody hot," she was saying to the pretty blonde, her accented voice rich and smooth, as much of a caress as her laughter. "I mean it. At least ten guys have mentally stripped you out of your knickers. I'm only surprised you haven't been ticketed for indecent exposure."

The girl giggled behind her hand.

Seizing the opportunity, he said, "Miss Black. I'm—"

She sucked in a breath, the action so inherently sexual his body responded as though she'd stuffed her hand down his pants and gripped his length. *Careful.*

As her smile melted away, she turned in his direction. Their gazes collided, locked, and he experienced an instant shock of awareness. Her eyes were a rich, chocolate brown, and the longer she looked at him, the more her pupils dilated.

A sign of attraction.

I'm in trouble.

"I know who you are," she finally said, her tone giving nothing away. "You're Corbin Blue. Breaker of spines and hearts. A legend on and off the field. And an absolute, total tool."

A tool. As in strong, reliable. Able to fix any problem. He would assume that's what she meant.

He ran his tongue over his teeth. *Charm.* Taking her hand—not that she'd offered—he pressed a kiss against her knuckles. Her skin was surprisingly calloused and scarred, yet deliciously warm, and for the first time in his life he actually tingled from contact with another person . . . as if he were a woman overdosing on sappy romantic comedies. He mentally berated himself.

"Please," he gritted. "Call me Blue."

Rose infused her cheeks as she jerked from his hold. "I suppose you may call me Evie."

Formal tone, but oh, that blush . . . or was it a flush of deeper attraction?

Either way, instant hard-on.

You can't go there with this one, remember? Even though Blue was only using Noelle, he had never cheated on her—except when the job had demanded it. He wouldn't start now. Especially with Michael's precious.

Eyes narrowed, Evie hitched her thumb at him and said to the blonde, "He's exactly the type of male I warned you about. Lovely on the outside, poison on the inside. Stay far, far away."

Irritation was like a hook in his chest, snagging several other darker emotions. She didn't even know him and yet she dared speak about him like that? *You read this one wrong. No way she's attracted.*

The little blonde was a few years younger than Evie, probably no more than eighteen, as well as shorter, curvier, and not nearly as confident. She peered down at the black-and-white-tiled floor as she said, "Wonderful to meet you, Mr. Blue. I'm Claire."

He arched a brow at Evie.

She elaborated, her expression softening. "Claire is my sister. From my mum's side, not my father's."

Clearly she adored the girl.

He reached for Claire's hand, but Evie moved between them, blocking him. Taking Claire by the shoulders, she said, "Darling, I'm having a chat-up with Blue, so I'm going to leave you for a few minutes. Will you be all right?"

Claire offered a wide, assuring smile. "Yes, of course."

After kissing the girl on the cheek, Evie turned and hooked her arm through Blue's, practically dragging him through the throng of laughing, chatting partygoers. The heat she radiated seeped through the fabric of his tux, stroking his skin. Felt good. Too good. He swallowed a mouthful of curses.

"I'm going to do you a solid and always be honest with you, no matter how cruel it may seem," she said, nodding to an acquaintance across the room. "I'll start with this little nugget of truth. I'm not interested in making nice with you. We're here for a reason. Let's get on with it and go our separate ways."

It took him a moment to realize she was serious. Women just didn't talk to him that way. They fawned. They flirted. They teased. "Did I kill your cat or something, and just don't remember? What's your problem with me?"

"Where to start?" she said on a sigh. "Oh, I know. How about the fact that you're a he-slut? Or do you prefer the term 'man-whore'?"

His sense of irritation grew. No wonder Noelle had warned him about the girl.

"Have you lived your life so perfectly you've earned the right to judge me?"

John stopped in front of them and held out a tray of crab cakes, golden eyes bright with determination. "May I get you anything, sir?"

Blue wanted to say "A rack and flogger," but didn't. John would have found a way to get the items for him. "Not yet," he muttered, dragging the girl toward the terrace.

"Are you daft?" she demanded, picking up their conversation as if it had never lagged. "Everyone but your girlfriend knows about your affairs. Have you ever dated a woman you *haven't* cheated on? Wait. Don't answer that. If my opinion of you dips any lower, I'll be tempted to murder you—just like I'm tempted to tell Noelle what you're doing to her. I happen to like her and think she deserves better."

All right. So. The worst had happened.

Through gnashing teeth, he managed to say, "You know why I've done what I've done."

"Yes, and at any time you could have told Michael no. My guess? You like sharing your love juice behind your girlfriend's back," she said.

Love juice? What, were they fourteen?

Before he could comment, she tripped over her own feet, surprising him with her clumsiness when she'd been so graceful before, and bumped into—

Their target, he realized. The wife of a government official. A woman who had no idea she'd been caught selling her husband's secrets to the highest bidders.

"I'm so sorry," Evie said to her. "The big oaf hasn't learned to share the walkways."

Blue worked his jaw in an effort to release tension. The attraction he'd first felt for Michael Black's daughter had been in the process of withering, and this just finished the job. He moved his arm to her waist, locking her against him, just in case she decided to bolt from the coming wrath.

The curves of her body fit perfectly against him. The heat of her burned his palm in the best way. Not that he noticed.

"Do you have any idea what you just did?" he snarled softly.

"Of course I do," she replied, using the language Michael taught all of his agents. A language of his own invention, ensuring no one else understood. "I took care of things. Our target will be dead within the next five minutes."

He shook his head, but it only intensified his confusion. "What are you talking about?"

"I stuck her with my ring." She raised her hand and wiggled her fingers. A walnut-sized sapphire twinkled innocently.

"*You what?*" he shouted. The people around him cast dark frowns his way. Lips pressed tightly together to silence a stream of curses, he hauled Evie past Solo and the terrace doors.

Solo sealed them outside, giving them a moment of privacy.

When Evie faced him, Blue was ticked to realize his attraction hadn't died like he'd thought. In the moonlight, the woman was a goddess, and he was momentarily struck dumb. Her pale skin glowed, making her look like a priceless pearl trapped in a dark sea.

Then she opened her mouth and ruined everything. "You heard me," she said, her tone snotty. She raised her chin. "I just did your job for you. You're welcome, by the way."

Harpy! "Your arrogance is unprecedented."

"Thank you." She fluffed her hair, as if he'd just given her the best of compliments.

"And undeserved," he finished with a snap. "It's going to get someone killed."

Her brow furrowed adorably. "Isn't that the point of tonight's entire operation?"

"Someone. As in you," he corrected.

"Are you jealous? Is that what this is about?"

He snorted. "Jealous? Please." Maybe a little.

Her smile was as sharp and cold as a blade. "Liar. But I'm afraid you've got a hard truth headed your way. I only get better. A lot better. I'm as good at defense as I am at offense."

Can't kill her.

She's Michael's daughter.

You respect Michael. Love him.

If he had to remind himself a thousand times, he would. And how foolish was he, to have craved a challenge? Challenges sucked. "Just so you know, I will be writing a review of your performance, Miss Black."

"Great. I will pretend to care."

Michael isn't *that* good a friend, he decided. "You aren't as superior as you think you are. You have no real experience." A slight gust of wind danced a lock of hair over the deep V of her dress, drawing his gaze to her cleavage. Little teacup breasts, perfectly displayed. His hands fisted. "The target's death was supposed to seem natural."

"And so it will. I used a potion of my own creation. Completely untraceable."

"Nothing is completely untraceable."

"You haven't seen my work. Yet."

He scrubbed a hand down his face. He wasn't going to get through to this girl, was he? "I should put you over my knee."

She snorted. "A spanking? Really? That's your solution?"

"To start." He wouldn't contemplate the way he wanted to finish.

"Why are you so angry, anyway? It wasn't like you had many choices. You couldn't shoot or stab her. Your only real option was to sex her to death."

I think I hate this girl.

"Look," she said on a sigh. Dark eyes softened, revealing . . . a hint of vulnerability? "I admit I was predisposed to dislike you, John, and Solo because—well, it doesn't matter. It's my problem, and I'm trying to deal. I'm sorry I've been so harsh with you, but I *needed* to make this kill."

Blue had always been able to sense the emotions in others. In fact, at the start of each new day, he purposely deactivated all things empathic. Only, Evie's emotions were so strong they penetrated his shields. He felt her bone-deep hurt. Raw anger. Gut-wrenching fear.

Why?

He was desperate to know.

Desperate? Him?

Never.

He stepped away from her. *End this. Now.* "Apology accepted," he said. "For future reference, you made two critical errors tonight. You didn't work with your team—and the plan we already had in place—and you allowed arrogance to direct you. That's the best way to make the worst decisions. You won't be the only one killed."

"Is that so?" Her narrowed gaze slid past him, taking in the party still in full swing beyond the doors. "I calibrated the poison to the target's specific body mass and chemistry. If my calculations are correct, this mission will be over in three, two, one . . . ."

Someone screamed.

Frantic footsteps sounded.

Evie grinned, all hint of vulnerability gone. "The target is now bagged and tagged. All thanks to me. Good luck next time, Mr. Blue."

"Work with Evangeline Black? I'd rather be slit open from navel to nose."

—CORBIN BLUE

"Good thing I always carry a knife."

—EVIE BLACK

One

FOUR YEARS LATER

*W*HAT'S WRONG WITH ME?

Evie Black executed her fiftieth lap in the long, rectangular pool that consumed half of her backyard. The sun shone brightly, heating her skin as well as the water. Very precious water. Expensive. During the human-alien war, a good portion of the world's supply had been contaminated.

But then, she was obscenely rich and wanted for nothing.

She also had a fantastic job. At twenty-six, she was the youngest surgeon at St. Anthony.

It wasn't the life she once envisioned for herself, but it was a good one all the same.

So why did she feel so utterly unsatisfied?

Fifty-one.

Her heart thumped against her ribs. Her muscles burned from the strain.

Fifty-two.

Something had to be missing. Not a man. She didn't have time to date. Besides, there wasn't anyone she *wanted* to date. Her hormones were in hibernation, and had been for years.

Fifty-three.

Ever since Claire had—

No. No, no, no. Not an acceptable thought path.

Fifty-four.

"Eden Black, requesting video conference," a computerized voice announced.

Perfect. A distraction.

"Granted," Evie said, and swam to the pool steps. As she emerged from the water, her sister's hologram appeared in front of her.

Eden Black was a beautiful woman. One of the rare Rakans to walk the earth, with golden skin, hair, and eyes. Adopted by Michael, trained as an agent. One of the best. Respected as much as John No Last Name, Solo Judah, and—as much as she hated to admit it— Corbin Blue.

The males her father loved as if they were his own flesh and blood.

That had always been a sore point for Evie, who had not met Michael until her eighth birthday. And for ten years after that, she had seen him only a handful of other times. Yet, he couldn't seem to function without the Dynamic Trio.

Why does no one want to keep me around? Was she really so terrible?

Whaa, whaa, whaa. Baby! Stop whining.

She blamed No Daddy Syndrome. For most of her childhood, she'd assumed Michael hated her, and it gutted her. Even now, knowing that wasn't the case, she struggled with self-esteem issues. But at least she was on the road to recovery. Step one: admission of a problem.

"Look at Miss Hot Stuff in her teeny tiny bikini," Eden said, wiggling her brows. "I'm so freaking jelly."

Evie stalked to the chaise longue to grab her towel, her sister's hologram moving with her, so that they were always in sight of each other. Before drying off, she struck a pose and said, "Thank you, thank you. I try."

Eden rolled her eyes. "Goofball."

Hardly. Everyone else called Evie spoiled and haughty, a party girl without a filter, who let daddy's money buy her a career she didn't deserve. Uh, try honest to a fault. And never mind the fact that Evie hadn't been to a legit rager in years.

"Headed for another job?" she asked, rubbing her hair between folds of the cloth.

"Yep. Michael wants me to do a little recon from inside a Shanghai prison. I'm set for transport tomorrow morning, and I don't know how long I'll be there."

"Dude."

"I know." Eden pouted for a moment, then brightened. "Hey, hop on the jet and join me. We can tag team the inmates hard-core."

She didn't even try to hide her shudder. "I'd rather be cut up and sold for parts."

"Come on, Evie. It's been three years since—"

"Don't go there," she rushed out. Looking back hurt. Hurt bad.

Unfazed, Eden said, "You have to forgive yourself."

Have to? No.

Would she ever? No, again.

Well, hell, why not look back? she thought then. She deserved the pain.

Once, Evie had been desperate to prove her worth to Michael. To outdo his favored boys. To be strong like Eden. And at first she succeeded. But with every mission, every victory, her confidence grew, and her arrogance intensified—until *boom!*

Blue's prediction came to pass.

She led the worst kind of criminal straight to Claire's door. Sweet, innocent Claire. Brutalized. Murdered.

Dead.

Acid churned in Evie's stomach, splashed through her veins, scorching.

She quit Michael's agency, and spent the next few months spiraling out of control. Then Eden charged into her life and quite literally knocked some sense into her, and she'd straightened up. She'd even fast-tracked her residency at the hospital.

Her father still used her on the occasional job, but only as an asset, when he needed to get another agent inside a high-class establishment or party. He never used her as an assassin.

"Fine," Eden said on a sigh. "Stubborn girl. I'll suffer through the mission all by my lonesome."

"Like you're really going to suffer." Evie stalked into the house, her sister's image remaining at her side. Cool air kissed her bare skin as she bypassed the leather couch, glass coffee table, and forty-inch holovision screen. "Guaranteed your boyfriend will be sneak-

ing into the prison to secretly satisfy your every desire."
Lucius Adaire was an agent, too, and lived to make
Eden happy.

"True." Eden's smile was dreamy. "Speaking of boy-
friends . . . are you dating anyone?"

Evie stopped in the kitchen to pour a glass of wine.
"You ask that question every time we're together, and
the answer has never changed. What makes you think
today will be any different?"

"Because you aren't the coldhearted bitch you pretend to be, and one day you're going to snap out of this
funk and want some guy to give it to you good and
hard."

"No way."

Not so fast.

An image of Corbin Blue flashed through her
mind. Though he had the white hair and lavender
eyes quintessential to his Arcadian race, everything
else about him was all his own. At least six and a half
feet of pure, raw strength, he had a body layered with
the mouthwatering muscle he'd earned playing football. Such a silly name for the sport. He had the face
of an angel, so beautiful it sometimes hurt to look at
him. He also had the smile of a devil. Wicked. Total
temptation.

And power—wowzer, but that man crackled with
power. Standing next to him was enough to raise the
fine hairs on the back of her neck. At their first meeting, Evie had been gobsmacked by her up-close-and-
personal sighting of him and had scrambled to put up
impenetrable defenses. Not only had he been the boy-

friend of an acquaintance, but he also had the reputation of a gutter rat.

Becoming just another one of his conquests held no
appeal.

At least Noelle Tremain wised up and dumped the
cocky bugger soon after the peace gala. Not that he'd
cared. Over the years, he'd dated too many women to
count—all blond, all stacked, making it perfectly clear
Evie had never been and never would be his type.

Then he met Pagan Cary. Blonder and more stacked
than any of the others. The two had been together for
several months and were now engaged. To be honest,
their relationship baffled Evie. Blue had been caught
cheating on Pagan at least a dozen times. News sta-
tions loved to blast elicit pictures of his trysts.

Man-whore!

And yet, Pagan stayed with him. The girl never
seemed to care what he did. Actually, the girl had been
linked to several other men.

Evie would have castrated him. To start.

Although . . . she got why women fell under his
spell. She really did. That knickers-melting smile . . .
when he flashed it your way, you felt as if you were the
only female alive. The lover of his most erotic dreams.
The other side of his heart.

I'm pathetic.

But, unlike other females, she knew he was a savage, unbound by any kind of moral code. He was hardened, detached, and lived by his own set of rules—but
even those he sometimes ignored. And he was calcu-

lated. No one would ever be able to shake him from his endgame, whatever that endgame happened to be.

No, thanks.

So why am I shivering?

Because it's cold. Yeah. That's why.

"Hello. I'm still here, you know. I've been telling you all about the guys I've got lined up for you. When the time comes, of course."

Eden's voice pulled Evie from her thoughts, and she blinked into focus. She leaned against the bar in the kitchen, her glass of wine raised midway to her mouth. "Sorry," she muttered. "I wasn't listening."

"Clearly. You're flushed, and I know my descriptions weren't *that* entertaining," her sister said, her tone suddenly sly. "Just what . . . or who . . . were you thinking about, hmm?"

Evie plucked a grape from the temperature-controlled bowl in the center of the counter and threw it at her sister. The little green fruit sailed through Eden's now laughing image.

"That salacious, huh?"

"Good-bye, Eden," she said drily.

"Bye, Eves."

They smiled at each other a split second before the hologram disappeared.

With a sigh, Evie pressed the Power button on the TV remote, and the screen in the kitchen lit up.

A young, pretty reporter stood in front of utter chaos. Smoke billowed through the air, creating an eerie backdrop for absolute carnage. Homeowners lingered on their front lawns, watching as firemen and policemen dug through piles of charred debris.

"—unknown male was rushed to the nearest hospital," the reporter was saying. "We're told he's in critical condition, and yet, somehow he disappeared five minutes after his arrival. No one seems to know what happened to him."

An address flashed across the screen, and Evie gasped. Michael's house.

Trembling, she set her wineglass aside and reached for her cell. "Michael Black. Father." The line rang, a screech in her ears.

She went straight to voice mail.

She never went straight to voice mail.

Unknown male . . . hospital . . . disappeared . . . Had to be her father. If he'd been injured and carted away by civilians, his people would have swooped in, stolen him, and taken him to *their* medical facility. That's the way black ops worked.

Okay. Okay. So. If the reporter was to be believed, Michael was critical but alive. If Evie hurried, she could reach the facility in half an hour. She could help him.

As quickly as possible she gathered her things and jumped in her car. The sun was hidden behind clouds as she soared down the highway at a speed cars were not supposed to be able to go. But then, most people could not rebuild the sensory system as she could, nor did they know they could disable preset maximum speeds.

You can take the girl out of the agency, I guess, but not the agency out of the girl.

Thankfully, black-market shields kept her from being noticed by any nearby cops.

The farther away from her home she got, the fewer buildings and shops appeared, until they stopped appearing altogether. Finally, her destination loomed ahead. A metal blockade surrounded a sprawling structure with dark concrete walls and shield armor rather than windows. Bright halogens glared down from the steepled roof, chasing away every shadow.

She stopped at the front gate. An armed guard—human—stepped forward to bang on her window. She lowered the partition and flashed the ID she'd never shredded.

He shook his head. "I'm sorry, Miss Black, but no one gets in tonight."

"I'm just here to see my father and—"

"I'm sorry, Miss Black, but you'll have to turn around now."

Gah! She tried again. "Bloody hell, my father—"

"I'm sorry, Miss Black, but no information is to be given out. Not to you. Not to anyone."

Can't kill him. Was Michael inside?

Surely. Why else would the guard act like this if not to protect her father from further harm? "Can you just tell me—"

"No," he said, one hand motioning for her to back up, the other curling around the handle of his pyre-gun. "Now, I suggest you leave before I'm forced to make you."

"I'd like to see you try," she retorted. With the press of a button, she could pepper him with bullets. "But let's save our tussle for another time, shall we?" She threw the car in reverse, spraying gravel in his face.

At home, she would gather the supplies she'd locked in her basement three years ago. Then she would break into the facility and unleash all kinds of hell. No one kept her from the people she loved.

No one.

Two

A FTER AN HOURLONG MEETING with Michael, Solo, and John, Blue received a new assignment: Operation Dumpster Dive. A new target: Gregory Star. And a new female to seduce for information: Tiffany Star.

Blue's fiancée, Pagan Cary, had no idea he lived a double life, but she would find out what went down with Tiffany. The entire world would find out. Blue no longer tried to hide his "affairs."

Did you seriously just put that word in mental air quotes? You do actually have affairs.

Yeah, but the one-night stands still aren't for my pleasure. They're for my job. Therefore, they don't count.

Tell that to the Black Plague. His nickname for Evie. Actually, he had a lot of nicknames for Miss Evie. "Honey Badger" was his second favorite.

Don't think about her or your anger will cause a power surge.

At the very beginning of his relationship with Pagan, he'd told her there would always be other women. She hadn't cared then and she wouldn't care now. She stayed with him for his body, his money, and his fame, and not necessarily in that order.

He was fine with that, because he stayed with her for the convenience. A wife would stop targets and assets from planning a future with him.

Hard-core? Maybe. But, in the end, far more merciful.

"I have a bad feeling about this mission," Solo muttered.

"That's because it's going to suck," John replied, just as quietly.

"What are you guys complaining about? I'm the one who has to do the actual sucking," Blue said as he led the pair to the front door of Michael's office. He twisted the knob, prepared to exit.

Boom!

A violent blast of wind lifted him off his feet and threw him backward. He wrecked through a wall. A terrible high-pitched ring vibrated in his ears, his world shrank to only a tiny bubble, and everything hazed with black and white. He managed to draw a breath into his partially deflated lungs, and instantly regretted it. The air burned and blistered, igniting a bonfire.

Lava flowed over him . . . pressure squeezed at his limbs, his chest . . . something hard fell on his arm and leg, snapping the bones, and everything proved to be too much, pain rolling over him, consuming him, melting him, then pulling him apart piece by piece.

He drifted in and out of consciousness, his muscles too heavy and knotted to even twitch. The ringing in his ears eventually faded, allowing him to hear the crackle of flames mixed with little bits of conversation.

"—with this one?"

"—fetch a decent price."

"—this one?"

"—ashing him."

"—last one?"

"—keeping him."

Blue blinked open his eyes, a nearly impossible feat. His lids were like two pieces of sandpaper that had been glued together. A human male loomed over him, one he'd never before met.

Medical personnel?

A thick cloud of smoke surrounded the man, shielding his features.

What the hell had happened?

Blue opened his mouth to ask, but rather than words, something warm and wet gurgled out and trickled down his cheek.

"Stupid alien," the man muttered, splashing cold water over Blue's body. No, not water. The pungent aroma of accelerant stung his nostrils. "I have double or nothing riding on your next season. Without you, the Invaders are going to blow it, and I'm gonna lose a fortune."

A match was lit, the flames immediately capturing his attention. Yellow-gold, flickering, growing taller and taller . . . quite lovely . . . falling . . . landing . . . *on Blue*.

What was left of his shirt acted as kindling, feeding the flames a delectable treat, and Blue's already decimated skin bubbled up and liquefied, drip-dripping . . . over his sides, leaving only muscles . . . but even those began to fry.

An agonized roar burst from his throat as he forced his petrified, aching limbs into action, and sat up. A chunk of plaster skidded away from him—had it pinned him? Whatever. He batted at the flames until they died, only to stop and gaze with horror at the condition of his body. His left arm ended in a stump, his hand missing. The rest of him was a mass of blood and meat. He could see several bones peeking past charred muscle.

The man stumbled backward, gasping, "You're alive."

A surge of fury activated Blue's Arcadian power, and he was able to lumber to his feet. Dizzy . . . swaying . . . so much pain . . . And yet, fueled by ragged animal instincts he usually kept on a tight leash, he managed to stomp forward and grab the man by the neck, using his remaining hand, squeezing and lifting.

"Who. You?" Blue's thoughts were coming swiftly, too swiftly, then breaking apart before he could sort through them and speak coherently. "Why. Kill. Me?"

Choking sounds. No words.

His fury magnified, and Blue squeezed harder.

Skin shaded to the color of sapphires . . . violets . . . eyes bugging out . . . lips opening and closing . . . then the man's spine snapped, and his head lolled to the side.

Silence.

Mistake.

Irritated, Blue tossed the limp body to the ground.

He scanned his surroundings, surprised by what he found. Fires here and there, walls toppled and torched, furniture in shambles, debris everywhere, but no sign of John. No sign of Solo. *Please.* No sign of Michael, either.

Taken away? They wouldn't have willingly left without him.

Can't stay.

Had to heal. Find them. But where could he go?

If one of Michael's houses was destroyed, it was safe to assume all the others were compromised. For the moment, Blue had to operate as if the person responsible knew the names and occupations of the three agents he'd just tried to kill, because only someone who had been welcomed into Michael's house could have gotten a bomb inside.

Blue had to avoid his own homes, then. Maybe even Pagan's.

Pagan. Was she a target, too?

He'd have to track her down and find out.

He climbed out from the rubble and smoke. Ignoring the agony of his body, he entered the daylight. Sirens blared in the distance, blending with the panicked murmurs of onlookers. The two houses next door had suffered extensive damage.

A frightened scream erupted behind him.

Blue spun, the action nearly knocking him off his feet. His dazed stare landed on a human female. He recognized her. She lived across the street from Michael. Was forty-eight years old. Had two children. Always hosted a holiday party at Thanksgiving.

The information hit him like bullets, one fact after the other. All useless.

She clutched her stomach, gasping, "Monster."

Monster? Him? Probably.

Can't stay, he reminded himself.

Authorities would arrive any minute and try to question him. They would demand to know who he was, why he was here, what he'd been doing, and in this compromised state he might admit to something he shouldn't.

Blue tripped forward, heading down the street, staying as close to the shadows as possible. Anyone who spotted him gasped with horror and jumped out of the way. No one asked if he needed help. Good. He didn't.

Tucking his ruined arm against his chest, he kicked into super-speed, running as fast as his broken body would allow. It was difficult to do, every step jostling him, agonizing him, but he'd trained for every eventuality over the years, even something like this. No one would be able to get a lock on him.

He passed a busy shopping center—but not before he caught a glimpse of his reflection in one of the store windows. His hair was gone. Even his eyebrows were gone, and one of his eyes drooped onto his cheek. He had a patch of flesh on his left side, but that was it. Everything else was raw and red.

Hideous.

Whatever. He'd had worse injuries. He would heal. Would even grow a new hand.

There was Pagan's house. A three-story restored brownstone he'd bought for her. How much longer could he stay on his feet? What little strength he possessed waned with . . . every . . . second. . . .

The laughter woke him.

Blue jolted upright, hissing as a stark, burning anguish claimed him. A black crust had formed over his exposed muscles, cracking with his movement. Each of his bones felt brittle, ready to shatter at any moment.

He looked around, taking stock. Dark red walls, a black sink and toilet. He'd made it inside Pagan's home, he realized, but he must have passed out in the guest bathroom, thinking to clean up before confronting her. How much time had passed?

"In three months, I'm going to be Mrs. Corbin Blue," Pagan crowed. "Can you believe it?"

"He's so beautiful. All that silky white hair . . . those lavender eyes . . . and oh, those lips! So lush and red. I'd say they were better suited for a woman, but they look too good on him."

Her sister's voice.

"I know," Pagan said with a giggle. "He's absolutely perfect."

"But aren't you worried about his . . ." the sister continued somberly.

"His what?" Pagan prompted.

"Well, his infidelities."

His fiancée scoffed, and his admiration for her tripled. "He and I have an open relationship. He tells me when he's going to be with someone else, and I extend him the same courtesy."

"What! You've been with other men?" the sister gasped out.

"He thinks so, yes."

"But you actually haven't?" the girl insisted.

"No."

"But . . . why would you want him to think so? Isn't he jealous?"

"First, men want what other men want. Second, no, he isn't."

Was that bitterness in her tone?

"But what if he falls in love with one of his affairs?" the sister asked.

"Blue? Fall in love?" Pagan snorted. "No matter how much he smiles and teases, that man is emotionally shut off. But, okay, let's say he does the impossible and falls in love. So what? I'll be his wife and the mother of his children. He'll never leave me."

A crack in the door allowed him to peer into the living room where the girls sat, sipping wine. Pagan wore a skintight dress that stopped just below the line of her panties. If she was even wearing panties. Most nights she wasn't. Her voluminous breasts practically spilled from her halter top, just the way she knew he liked. Her skin was a perfect golden brown, bronzed by a reverent sun. Sexy. A chic crop of platinum hair framed a face most men would only ever see in their wet dreams.

She wasn't under attack, as he'd feared. He should leave. If he revealed himself, she wouldn't recognize him. Who would? He might be able to convince her of his identity, but she would insist on taking him to the hospital. He couldn't risk it.

Right now, the person responsible for his condition might assume he was dead. It would be better for Blue—and Pagan—if that person continued to assume so.

Should have thought this through first.

Now, at least, he knew Pagan hadn't been targeted.

Where could he go?

Who could he trust?

Who had tried to kill him? And why?

And where were his friends? Had they survived?

They must have. He wouldn't believe anything else.

Darkness . . . weaving through his vision . . .

He had to get somewhere, and fast, before he once again lost consciousness. There was a good chance he wouldn't be waking up anytime soon.

No one playing for the Invaders knew of his other job. Only Michael, John, and Solo did—no, that wasn't true. Evie knew.

Would she help?

Would he harm her when she irritated him? Because she would definitely irritate him. If he lost control of his abilities . . .

No other choice.

Blue labored to his feet, moaning as the agony became too much.

He heard a startled gasp. "Who's in there?" Pagan called, sounding worried.

Without a word, he climbed through the window into the daylight.

Three

———

*E*VIE STOMPED INTO HER bedroom and threw her purse in the general direction of her closet. Key to the basement, that's what she needed. But where had she put the bloody thing?

"Light on," she said, the darkness instantly chased away by the overhead lamp. She—

Screamed, and reached for the blade she always tucked inside her pocket.

A hideous creature sprawled on her lovely king-size bed. Whatever it was, it was male, and big. *Really* big, both wide and long, its feet hanging past the edge of the mattress. Its skin was red and black—no . . . that wasn't skin. That was blood and charred flesh. Its body was sliced to ribbons, and it was missing a hand. Several bones stuck out in the wrong places.

The scent of smoke wafted through the air, stinging her nostrils.

"Evie," the creature said on a moan. "Blue."

Shock slammed through her. He spoke with Blue's voice, and even mentioned his name. And . . . and . . . he was peering at her with Blue's eyes. That gorgeous lavender, usually framed by long black lashes that made him look as though he always wore eyeliner.

"Blue?" she gasped out. No way. Just no way.

"Didn't know . . . where else . . . to go."

Hesitant, she approached the side of the bed. He watched her every movement, reminding her of a predator getting ready to attack. What would he do when she was within reach? Because it *was* him, she decided. Same height, same body mass. Same crackle of power so unique to the football playboy. A crackle that had rendered her blind to anything but lust for a few seconds of their first meeting.

"I must say, Mr. Blue, you've looked better."

He might have snorted. Hard to tell while he was gurgling blood.

"How did you get in here?" An alarm should be screeching right now.

"Window. Disabled . . . security. Inside and out. Sorry."

She craned her neck, zeroing in on the interior ID box. Sure enough, the lid had been pulled from the wall and the wires exposed, obviously cut and realigned. "That's going to cost a fortune to fix." But only because she would be doing the labor, and her time was mega money, and oh, wow, she really needed a moment to process what was going on.

"Bill . . . me," he gritted. "First . . . help me."

"Sure, sure," she said. "I'll ring the Arcadian chief of medicine at St. Anthony. Nice guy. Usually a three-month waiting time to see him, but for me he'll make a house call. You will, of course, be responsible for your bill, as well as owe me a huge favor." *Stop babbling.*

"No. You."

She got what he was trying to tell her, but wished she hadn't. For a year straight, this man had screwed with her anytime they were forced to work together. Nothing overt, and nothing that would compromise the end result of the work—his work, that is. He'd left her behind. Told her wrong places to meet, stuck her with all kinds of paperwork. Worst of all, he'd *always* written a review of her performance.

The gist of every review? Miss Black stinks like arse.

She'd seen him a few times since Claire was killed, when she'd acted as an asset. He'd always ignored her, as if she were unworthy of his attention, and made a big deal of making out with his date. Whoever that happened to be.

The suckwad treatment cut to the quick, even though she hated the guy. Like she really needed another male to drive home the point that she wasn't good enough—for anything! And for a conceited man-whore to do it? A male willing to hump anything that moved? Bloody humiliating.

"Ignoring?" he said now. "Typical."

I should make him beg. "Fine," she huffed. "I'll help you." For Michael. And information. "Just be warned. Arcadians are not one of my thousands of specialties, and I *will* be keeping track of your behavior. Expect *me* to write a report." *Babbling again.*

She dragged her gaze over him, medical eye assessing the massive amount of damage, her mind at last computing just how weak he must be. His nostrils were black. He could have inhaled a lethal amount of smoke.

She might have to place a tube in his trachea. It would deliver a higher concentration of oxygen to his lungs. Also, resuscitating fluid would definitely have to be dispensed. He might even need a transfusion. Clearly more than ten percent of his cells had suffered hemolysis, and that could lead to kidney malfunction.

If he were human. But he wasn't. Blimey. She truly had no experience with his race.

"I'm assuming you weren't playing Throw Another Arcadian on the Barbie but were in the explosion that decimated Michael's house," she said, walking to her dresser and withdrawing her box of "home brew," as she called it. Drugs she'd . . . tampered with.

"Yes. Woke up. Michael . . . gone. Everyone gone."

Great. He knew as much as she did. So much for trading her services for info. "You'd fare better in a hospital, you know." Once more at his side, she stuck him in the arm. "That should take the edge off your pain."

"No hospital. Please . . . no. Too . . . dangerous. Star . . . bomb . . . could still . . ." He went quiet, his head lolling to the side.

Unconscious? Or dead?

Had the anesthetic harmed him?

She felt for a pulse, frowned. He had no— There! It was too slow, too light, but there. Relief flooded her.

Evie rushed into the bathroom and drew a bath. She gathered everything she would need—or, rather, everything she had that would work. Scissors, IV tubes, and fluid bags she'd once used to practice, as well as a medicinal liquid soap usually only loaded into an enzyme shower, and a bottle of antibiotics she kept on hand.

She would treat Blue as she would treat a human, and hope it worked.

She stuffed one of the pills under his tongue, praying it would dissolve and help prevent sepsis. Then she cut away what remained of his clothing, and removed his shoes.

When he was stripped to—*well, can't say* the skin—raw meat, she loudly stated, "Blue, I need you to wake up now."

His eyelids blinked open, and he moaned.

"Don't be a crybaby," she said, being merciless to be kind . . . maybe. "I have to get you into the tub, and while I may be strong, I'm not a crane and can't carry you." She slid her arm underneath his shoulders, intending to help him rise, but he flinched away from the agony of the contact.

"Don't touch!" he roared.

Don't shout! Despite her calm appearance, she was kind of a mess inside and he was only making it worse. "Be a dear and stand up on your own. I need you to walk into the bathroom."

Blue lumbered to his feet and stumbled toward the tub. She couldn't fathom the enormous amount of strength required for him to remain in an upright position while his leg was broken, and tried not to be impressed.

"Good boy. Now climb in the tub," she said.

Wheezing, grimacing, he slowly sank below the waterline.

"Guaranteed this isn't going to be the sponge bath of your fantasies," she said, crouching beside the stone tub to wash him with the soap and minimize the possibility of infection, "but I have to do it."

"Whatever . . . necessary," he hissed.

Her grin was devoid of humor. "Give me a few minutes. You'll probably regret saying that."

Time ceased to exist for Blue. He lived only in moments.

There were moments he was utterly alone, lost to pain and darkness. There were moments he was trapped in a nightmare, when the meeting with Michael finished and he stood with John and Solo and they walked to the door, unaware their lives were about to be forever altered. There were moments a woman stroked him, and muttered to him, her honey-almond scent saturating him and her raspy voice delighting him.

He loved those moments.

"It's been a week," she said now, "and you've already grown a new layer of skin—unscarred, of course, because you're the gold standard every man is measured against, and flaws aren't allowed to stay. Gag. You grew a new hand, and a new head of hair." Soft fingers shifted through the strands. "It's sickening."

He wanted to lean into her touch, her warmth, but his body refused to obey the mental command.

He hated his body.

"You need a scar. You're too pretty. Why won't you wake up?"

I will. For you. And then I'll strip you and take you, and you'll scream my name, again and again, and I won't stop until I'm sated, and you're too exhausted to beg me for more.

"And how are you causing my furniture to levitate? Stop that!"

His power must be seeping out. He would have to do a better job of controlling it.

Who was she?

He'd gone to Pagan's . . . and his fiancée had been with her sister. Yes. He remembered that much. The two talked about him, and Pagan mentioned becoming a mother. He'd thought she'd understood kids would never be part of their arrangement.

Humans and otherworlders could procreate, but it wasn't easy. Still, Blue had taken measures to ensure it never happened. Plus he always wore a condom. He didn't need protection from disease, since humans couldn't pass anything to him; but in his early days, too many girls had come forward citing a rubber broke and pregnancy was the result. A lie on both counts, but the claims had scared him. No way did he want to raise a kid with a one-night stand. Or worse, a target. A simple little surgery negated the possibility of children.

Need to have a talk with Pagan. He would make her understand kids were out of the question, or they would part ways.

But the woman with him wasn't Pagan, he thought. Her scent was richer, and her voice sexier. She was thinner, yet somehow softer. Her tone wasn't as gentle, and he was glad. He wasn't easily breakable.

"Yesterday I hacked into Michael's database and read your updated file, you know. And by 'read' I mean skimmed. I wasn't *that* interested. Still, you've done some pretty impressive wet work."

Hells yeah, he had. He'd taken down his first target at the age of thirteen.

A male never forgot his first.

Blue had actually butchered the job, an up-close-and-personal grab-and-stab, getting himself grabbed and stabbed in the process. Somehow, even with his injuries, he'd found the strength to pull through and finish. It hadn't been pretty, but the victory had tasted, oh, so sweet.

He'd learned a lot since then. Now his victims never saw him coming.

And maybe he'd been born for this type of work, because he wasn't like Solo and John. He'd never felt a moment's regret for doing what he considered a public service. The equivalent of a human taking out the trash.

"So my question is, why have you allowed Michael to leave you in the hobaggery department?" the female continued. "You rock with guns, blades, and even swords. You're amazing in hand-to-hand. Compared to anyone but me, of course. And I was particularly impressed with your undercover stint as a cage fighter. Taking down six Bree Lians at the same time? Delish."

He wanted to pound his chest with his fists. She was impressed by him. For some reason, that mattered.

"Ugh. Why am I complimenting you? You've already got an overinflated ego. And I bet that's because no one has ever told you how much of a pain in the arse you are. No female wants to offend the man responsible for her orgasms. Or are you a selfish lover? Do you forget all about your partner's pleasure?"

I'll never forget yours. He wanted to tell her. Tried to tell her. Failed.

"No response? No witty comeback? Come on, Blue! Talk to me." The mattress tilted on one side. The covers rustled. The scent of honey and almonds intensified, and his mouth actually watered. Heat wafted from her with furnace-like intensity, enveloping him. It was exquisite, better than exquisite, and he was suddenly as hard as a steel pipe.

"I hate yammering to comatose Arcadians, I really do. I'm giving you a few more days to wake up, and then I'm dumping you right out the window, just see if I don't. Because you, Mr. He-slut, are a freaking cover hog, and I'm tired of it."

He-slut . . .

The word reverberated in his head, irritating him. Who would call him—

In a split second, he remembered sneaking into a fancy two-story belonging to . . . Evangeline. Yes. Evangeline Black. Evie.

His caretaker's identity stunned him. Angered him a little, too. Here he was, pussing up over the Black Plague and actually feeling affection for her. He'd even considered pleasuring her. Was still freaking hard for her! What kind of madness was *that*?

Maybe the explosion had fried the wires in his brain.

"When this is over," she muttered, "I'm probably going to need a tetanus shot. The proverbial *they* say that inviting a man into your bed is the same as inviting all of his previous lovers. That would explain why I feel so freaking *crowded* right now."

The anger sharpened and clawed at his chest. He was desperate to strike back at her. But though his muscles twitched—finally, movement!—he remained in place.

He wasn't worried about his inability to act. His body was in the process of re-creating itself, and was now in the final stages of the healing. Sometime soon, an electrical current would rush through him, bringing new nerves and cells to vibrant life. He would be back to his . . . old self and . . . he would make Evie . . .

Her insistent warmth drugged him, lulling him deeper and deeper into darkness. . . .

Evie sighed into her pillow. The past week had passed in a blur of activity. She worked at the hospital. She took care of Blue. One night, she finally scouted the military compound where she suspected her father was being kept, but didn't break in. They'd beefed up security, and she was out of practice. She couldn't risk getting caught while she had a two-hundred-and-fifty-pound manimal to feed.

What would happen when he woke up? How would he react? He couldn't—

A massive burst of energy swept through the room, electrifying the air. Goose bumps broke out over her skin, and her adrenaline spiked, every cell in her body waking up to say hello. She gasped, startled.

"Smell good," Blue muttered.

They were the first words he'd spoken since the night she'd found him, and his voice snapped her out of her shock. Excitement slithered through her. Was he finally coming around? Would she soon be rid of him and the annoying sense of awareness his mere presence elicited? Never had she been more conscious of her breasts, or the quiver in her stomach, or the ache between her legs than she had these past few days. And she didn't like it!

Before she could turn over and check on him, he threw a heavy arm over her middle and tugged her into the hard curve of his body, spooning her. Warm breath tickled the back of her neck . . . and, blimey, she melted against him. *So good.*

"Uh, Blue," she said, embarrassed by the tremor in her voice.

"Mmm, you feel even better." As he rubbed his erection into the cleft of her bottom—no way was that thing as big as it seemed to be—his fingers reached around to slide under her T-shirt. Suddenly she was skin to heated skin with her greatest enemy. He cupped one of her breasts, purring, "Sweet little teacup. Can't wait to put my mouth on it."

Her nipple beaded, craving exactly what he promised. Mouth, with tongue and teeth.

More.

"Blue," she gasped. "Stop." *Don't you dare stop.* "I'm not one of your women, and I'm not here to service your every whim. You're engaged to another woman." That's right. Oi. Shame beat through her. "And while I know that doesn't mean anything to you, it does to me."

"My woman." He tweaked her nipple and kissed her nape, his tongue flicking out to taste her. It was ecstasy. It was agony.

It was wrong.

Reaching back, Evie grabbed Blue by the hair and yanked. "I said stop."

"Ow," he yelped, his hold on her at last loosening.

Though it nearly killed her, she rolled from his heat, moving on top of him and pinning his shoulders to the mattress with her knees. "I think it's time for us to chat, yeah?"

Four

$\sim\!\!\sim\!\!\sim$

BLUE SNAPPED OUT OF the most spectacular sensual daze of his life. Used to having to think and act fast, he took stock of the situation in an instant. Moonlight filled a spacious, femininely decorated bedroom.

Evie Black's bedroom.

Every piece of furniture hovered over the floor, even the bed.

With a sharp mental command, every piece crashed into place. The bed shook, and Evie almost tumbled over the side. He grabbed her by the waist to steady her—such a slender, perfect waist. His palms flamed at the contact.

He'd noticed their fit before. Somehow, it was better now.

She slapped at his wrists with enough force to let him know she meant business, just not enough to actually break his hold. He released her of his own volition. But rather than reward him for good behavior, she glared at him.

"What's going on?" he demanded. He'd been living

with her, he recalled, and she'd been taking care of him. "Why are you on top of me?" Why was his body already aroused to a fever pitch?

"You made a pass at me," she spat at him. "Put your hands right on my wee breasts."

Horror filled him. Horror . . . and a more intense arousal. "No way."

"Yes way. Want me to write up a review of your performance? Done. First line: Mr. Blue's rendition of Grabby Hands did *not* earn a standing *O*."

"*O* as in orgasm?" Annoying baggage. "You're lying."

"Are you suggesting you *did* give me an orgasm?"

"Filthy-minded girl. No." *But I'd like to.* "I'm saying I didn't grab you."

"Let's look at the evidence. You have a python between your legs, and it's poking at me right this very second."

He bit the side of his tongue. To keep from cursing or laughing, he wasn't sure. A python? *Thank you.* "That's not evidence I touched you. That's evidence I'm a man. What disproves your grabby hands theory? You aren't my type, and my fingers aren't suffering from frostbite."

For a moment he felt the sting of rejection and frowned. She hadn't rejected him, so—

Her sting of rejection, he realized. He tried to turn off his empathic ability, but still the sense of rejection remained, hurting *him*. But . . . she was an emotionless harpy, concerned only with the destruction of all mankind. Nothing he said should bother her.

"Well," she announced, her tone now flat. "I can honestly say that's the first time I've ever been rejected for being too awesome. Because your type sucks. Blondes with breasts so big they can be used as flotation devices, and heads so filled with air they're comparable to balloons. Cliché!"

Yes, he did prefer that type of woman. Even though one had never turned him on the way Evie did. And why the hell did he want to beg for her forgiveness? She'd dished worse to him.

And damn it, why was he now focusing on her perfect teacups, practically salivating, definitely desperate to draw her hard little nipples into his mouth? As if her "wee breasts" were the sweetest treats he'd ever had the privilege of touching.

They were. He knew it soul deep.

All right. So there was no denying he'd touched them . . . or that he wanted to touch them again.

Danger. He gripped her by the knees and shoved her to the side of the bed, away from his mouth, and, worse, his throbbing erection.

"Lights," she said, and golden light cascaded from the overhead lamp.

He sat up and looked himself over. He was completely healed and dressed in a pair of large sweatpants. Men's sweatpants.

To whom did they belong?

His gaze arrowed to Evie, and his chest constricted. She wore a pink tank top and a pair of men's boxer shorts.

Did the boxers belong to the owner of the sweatpants? A . . . boyfriend?

For some reason Blue suddenly wanted to punch a wall.

Odd reaction. One he didn't fully understand.

She tucked her long, slender, and so lusciously pale legs around her, sitting in that crisscross way only a female could manage. Hair of the deepest jet hung wildly around a face he used to tell himself wasn't really pretty, as he'd first assumed. But he couldn't tell himself that anymore.

Maybe, after their first interaction, he'd never let himself look past her attitude; but now, in this moment, that prickly layer had been peeled away and he could see her, really see her. Large velvety brown eyes drew him in and refused to let go. Lush porcelain skin flushed to the most erotic shade of pink. Heart-shaped lips red and deceptively kiss-swollen, practically begging for more.

He had to fist his hands to keep from reaching for her.

Arousal he could comprehend. But straight-up attraction? To *her*?

Really, Blue? Really?

The very idea appalled him.

Michael was more than a boss. Even more than a mentor. Blue considered the man a surrogate father. Michael had found him at his lowest, picked him up, given him friends, a purpose. A reason to go on. And he'd never forgotten Michael's warning to leave Evie alone.

What father would want his daughter to be with a man like Blue? Not a good one, and Michael was better than most.

It stung to be considered completely unworthy, but

that's just the way things were. The way they would always be. He got it.

Blue wouldn't destroy his relationship with the man just because his treacherous body wanted to spend a bit of quality time inside the Black Plague.

More than that, Blue hadn't suddenly started liking her.

And more than *that*, he was engaged, and Evie wasn't a job.

"Update," he demanded.

She gaped at him. "Seriously? After everything I've done for you, you can't start with 'Thank you'? Instead, you have to bark a one-word order as if I'm a robo-dog that's just supposed to obey?"

Could she never just let things roll? Did she have to make everything a freaking challenge?

"Thank you," he gritted.

"You *aren't* welcome," she reported—and, strangely enough, it doused his irritation.

Despite everything, she sometimes amused him. The little spitfire was as unpredictable as a storm.

She crossed her arms over her chest. "I'd like an update, too, you know."

"I'll tell you everything," he said with a nod. "But me first. Please." He had to know.

Her eyes narrowed with suspicion as she said, "I have a feeling you say 'me first' to a lot of girls. And in this case, I doubt you know anything, anyway. But, fine. I haven't heard from my father, but I do know a man was found at the explosion site and taken to the nearest hospital. That same man was soon moved out without any civilians knowing how, why, or where."

"You think that man is Michael?"

"Yes. I also think he's at a government-owned medical facility—"

"I know the one," Blue interjected. "If he was taken there, he wouldn't have stayed long, because he wouldn't have known who to trust. The moment he was stabilized, he would have found a way out."

She pinched the bridge of her nose, a wave of despair drifting from her. "I haven't let myself worry about him—much—because I know he's wily and strong and unbelievably determined, but it's not like him to leave me in the dark."

Yeah. That didn't bode well. "Have you heard anything about John and Solo?"

"No. I'm sorry."

She sounded sincere.

He nodded to let her know he'd heard her. Then he told her everything he remembered about the explosion. As he spoke, she turned her face away from him, as if she couldn't bear for him to see whatever emotion shined there. He didn't tell her that he could feel her sadness.

Was she thinking about her father in pain?

"So how's the security here?" he asked, changing topics as an act of mercy.

She drew in a deep breath, and when she next met his gaze, he thought he saw a hint of gratitude. "It's amazing. Of course. You haven't been ambushed once, have you? You're welcome, by the way."

Don't respond. You'll only encourage her. "What do you use?"

Her shoulders squared with pride. "A system of my own creation."

So . . . she was a skilled killer and a surgeon as well as a wire tech? Why was that so sexy? "Honey Badger, you're clearly not as good as you think you are. I managed to get through your window without any problems."

"'Honey Badger'? Did you just call me 'honey badger'?" She waved her fist at him. "Do it again and I'll cut out your tongue to wear as a charm on my necklace. And I've already fixed the flaw that allowed you to break in."

"So there *was* a flaw. Meaning . . . what? Say it with me. You're not as good as you think you are."

Her gaze threw daggers at him. "Anyone on Michael's payroll was flagged in the system as permissible, just in case someone ever needed to come in and hide while I was away."

A bona fide act of kindness. He didn't want to think of her as the caring type, but did so anyway and responded accordingly, expression and voice softening. "That's an excellent excuse for a subpar system," he teased.

She hissed as if he'd stabbed her. "How dare you sink so low and insult my software! You take that back."

Wow. She actually looked capable of murder just then. He realized he'd just found the line she'd drawn. The one he wasn't ever to cross. Or bad things would happen. "Fine. I take it back."

A moment passed before she got herself under control. "You may live."

"Thank you." He meant that. "Now, would you mind if I had a look around, checked things out?"

Though her expression remained blank, he felt a thrum of anger radiate from her. "Do what you want. But I'll expect breakfast and a full report about how impressed you are when you're done."

"Breakfast I can do. I guess I owe you."

"You *guess*?"

"And a report . . . why not? I just hope you can handle an honest critique—since you certainly know how to dish them."

Hot color spread across her cheeks, and he once again had to deal with a throbbing hard-on.

Gotta stop reacting to her. Especially over stupid crap like that.

He rolled from the bed—and what the hell. It was difficult to leave her. First he swept through the entire house, inspecting it for cameras and bugs as well as any indication an uninvited guest had come through unnoticed. All was well. And, okay, all right, he had to give Evie props. Her system was utterly badass.

So was her home. There were four bedrooms and an office. She preferred bold colors, antique furniture, and modern finishes. She had hung pictures of her father, her sister, Claire, and her adopted sister, Eden, all over the walls. Blue had always considered Eden one of the most gorgeous women in the world, but just then he would have said Evie was the sexier of the two. By far. Something about the fragility of her bone structure, the humor lighting those mysterious, dark eyes. The mischievous curve of her smile.

A mischievous curve never more apparent than in the photos of Evie and Claire. . . . The girl died three years ago, yes? Yeah, he thought. Three years. Shortly after, Evie left the agency to work at the hospital.

He'd always wondered why.

Michael kept details about Claire's death hush-hush, so Blue had no idea what had happened. And he didn't like that he didn't know, he realized.

Frowning, he turned away from the pictures and entered the game room. There was a pool table and a poker table, a dock for a large-screen television, and a huge sectional couch. The smoked-glass door in back led to a massive greenhouse.

Lucky girl.

From what Blue understood, the earth was nearly destroyed during the human-alien war. Plant life was compromised, animals were almost wiped out, and huge bodies of water either dried up or turned to sludge. Now all three were expensive commodities.

Had Michael paid for the greenhouse, spoiling his precious princess just a little more, or had Evie? As one of the most skilled surgeons in New Chicago, she had to make bank. Not that he'd kept track of her career or anything. He'd just saved a few articles. In case Michael wanted to read them. No big deal.

"Agent Dallas Gutierrez requesting an interview," a computerized voice said over an in-house intercom system.

Blue exited the game room and headed toward the bedroom. Evie, in the process of anchoring the length of her gorgeous hair in a high ponytail, met him in the hallway. She'd pulled on a long-sleeved tee and a pair of figure-hugging jeans.

Hello, erection.

He looked down at the Python. *Keep it up, I dare you, and I'll hack you off. I won't even hold a funeral. Because no one would . . . come.*

One day, I've got to mature. "What's going on?"

"The agent is at the door," Evie said, pink color flooding her cheeks.

Had she checked out his package? Wished for a special delivery?

Idiot.

"Any idea who he is or what he wants?" she asked.

Was her tone breathless? "Who he is? Yes. What he wants? No."

"Come on, then." She led him back to the game room and flipped on the TV. "Record and reveal from the living room cameras."

"What—"

"Not you," she muttered, as if he were a few brain cells short.

No. Her tone was not breathless.

A large holoscreen appeared above the dock, the air crystallizing to reveal a picture of the living room he'd just searched. "By the way, I'm ready to give my report," he said. "Cool."

She rolled her eyes. "One word to describe my home's utter magnificence? You're usually more eloquent. But I shouldn't be surprised, I suppose. Sentences hard for caveman," she said, banging her chest like a gorilla. "Just . . . stay here. Watch and listen. And who knows? Maybe you'll learn something."

The little witch always had to have the last word, didn't she. Well, not this time. "You might want to take a breather before you face the agent, Miss Black. The more time you spend with me, the harder your nipples get. I'm beginning to think you don't hate me as much as you've always claimed."

Five

T RYING NOT TO TREMBLE—STUPID nipples, and stupid Blue for noticing!—Evie opened the front door, revealing a tall, handsome man with dark hair, dark skin, and freaky eyes so pale they were almost devoid of color.

He wasn't Arcadian, but he crackled with a muted version of Blue's power.

"Miss Black?" the agent said.

She nodded. "The one and only."

The corners of his mouth quirked up the slightest bit. "I'm Agent Dallas Gutierrez, and I'm with AIR."

Alien Investigation and Removal. "Interesting, but irrelevant. I'm human and therefore not under your jurisdiction."

"Well, that depends on certain circumstances, doesn't it?"

She peered at him steadily, refusing to back down. "Do tell."

Far from intimidated, he said, "I'm here to ask you a few questions."

"About?"

"Your father."

Heart suddenly racing, she moved back, allowing the agent inside. "Next time, don't bury the lead." After she'd shut and locked the door, she showed him to the living room. And it was weird, knowing Blue was upstairs, watching her every move, listening to her every word. Weird and exciting. Almost . . . arousing.

Stupid hormones. Now that they'd woken up, they were determined to gain her attention.

Let us have Blue, just once, they shouted, *and we'll go away again. Promise.*

Liars!

I would rather give myself to an Agamen. The males had poisonous horns and barbs at the ends of their penises. She'd heard tales of human women dying within seconds of orgasm.

"I'd offer you a beverage, but I don't want you staying any longer than necessary, so let's get to it, shall we?"

"Let's," Dallas said as he settled on the couch.

"You mentioned my father."

"I did. It's funny, but as wealthy and successful as he is, not a lot is known about him."

Okay, not a great start. Where was he going with this? The world knew Michael as an arms dealer trying to go legit.

She eased into the chair across from him. "He's a businessman who owns half of New Chicago, as well as a few other states." The typical spoiled-girl response. "Who cares about anything else?"

No quirking of his lips this time, just a cold, hard stare eerily similar to the one she'd received from Blue only a few minutes ago. She wasn't sure what it meant. Well, she had some idea—nothing good.

"When did you last speak to him?" Dallas asked.

"The day before his house went *boom, boom*. Why?"

Tone just as cold as his stare, he said, "How about *I* ask the questions, all right?"

How about . . . not.

"Have you ever met Gregory Star?"

She thought for a moment, recalling Blue's first night here, when he'd mentioned a bomb and a star. Could he have been referring to a person? "Yeah," she said. "I've met him. Several times." Then, just to be contrary, she added, "Why?"

He ignored her question. Of course. "Where did you meet him?"

"Social events. I don't remember when or where. Our conversations were limited to the usual hello, how are you, how have you been. Oh, except for the time I told him to brush his teeth, because he had coffee breath. And now I'm done talking, Mr. Gutierrez, until—"

"Agent Gutierrez."

"Whatever. I'm done talking until you've explained why you want to know about my father, why AIR cares about Mr. Star, and whether or not Mr. Star could have played a part in the explosion."

Smart questions, Blue thought. Maybe he shouldn't have given her so much crap over the years.

Why *was* AIR, rather than the local PD, interviewing Evie about the bombing? Some kind of otherworldly evidence must have been found at the scene. Something to implicate Gregory Star, the very man Blue, Solo, and John were suppose to investigate for the disappearance of seventeen people—two of whom were AIR agents, and one a U.S. senator.

Had Star set the bomb?

Star was a fifty-three-year-old self-made billionaire. He'd grown up dirt poor in a part of town known as Whore's Corner. Speculation was rampant about what he'd had to do to survive. The front contender: black-market organ sells. If that was true, he'd had to slice open his victims while they were still alive. Talk about hard-core.

Over the years, the male earned the ear of some of the world's greatest leaders. He developed an eye for the pretties, and a weakness for gambling. He changed mistresses as easily as Blue changed underwear. He dabbled in recreational drugs—the snorting and the selling—and he would not leave his house without armed guards.

What reason would he have to harm Michael? How could he have known about Michael's real job?

He couldn't have. Right? So . . . what if the bombing had nothing to do with the case? What if the culprit—Star, or someone like him—simply hoped to get rid of a business rival?

Made sense. But that wasn't enough for Blue. Because, as much sense as it made, it failed to explain the coincidences. And Blue didn't believe in coincidences.

As Evie showed the flustered agent to the door—

guess the male had never come across anyone like the Black Plague before—Blue returned to her office and logged on to her computer. Priority one: finding his friends. They had to be alive or he would . . . he would . . . He banged a fist against the keyboard, cracking the casing, and cringed.

Deep breath in. Out.

They were alive.

Evie came up behind him. He didn't have to see her to know she was there. He sensed her. The heat of her. The scent of her. Every muscle in his body tensed.

"Good job, pudding pop," he said, trying to keep things light. "He got nothing out of you, but you got a few things out of him."

"I know. And don't call me 'pudding pop' or I'll empty out your scrotum and make you enjoy it."

He covered a laugh with a cough. The little fire-cracker had these moments of utter hilarity. Although she wasn't as animated as she'd been four years ago. She no longer used her hands to punctuate every word. He wondered what had changed. Because honestly? He'd liked the hand gestures and kind of missed them. "If I'm going to enjoy it, I might as well keep calling you names. Like 'pinkie pie.'"

She waved her fist at him. Okay, so that was a hand gesture she hadn't lost. A habit?

He hoped so. One day he might grab that fist, jerk her into his lap, and—

Nothing.

He'd do nothing.

"What are you doing in here, anyway?" she asked.

"Looking for clues."

"Oh, well, I'm one step ahead of you. As always." She jimmied open a secret drawer he'd missed and handed him a digital reader. "Check out the most recently downloaded articles."

He did. Apparently, a body was found at the explosion site, one burned beyond recognition. Testing was done, and though the identity was unknown, it was clear the bones belonged to a Caucasian male with a broken spine—who was not Michael Black. *Has to be my Fry Guy.*

Michael Black was missing. Assumed abducted.

Two days ago, his former assistant had been found dead in her home. Drug overdose.

Blue knew the woman. Three months ago, at the age of forty-one, she quit working for Michael to become a stay-at-home mom. If she'd had a drug problem, he would never have sex again.

Blue inhaled a waft of honey-almond and nearly snapped the e-reader in half. Guaranteed, he was having sex again.

Just not with Evie Black.

Right. Right?

Michael's former assistant must have been killed, the death made to appear accidental. But why kill her?

Perhaps she came to see Michael, spotted the killer, and was eliminated as a precaution. Or perhaps she aided the killer for money? After all, stay-at-home mothers made less than slave labor. And if she'd aided the killer, she would have been eliminated as a possible witness.

Her aid would explain how the killer had gotten the bomb inside Michael's.

He turned to the computer, and typed in "Corbin Blue." He needed more data.

"Oh, you're going to like this," Evie said, her arm stretching over his shoulder. She pressed a fingertip against the holoscreen, selecting a gossip website. "This is a particular favorite of mine. Fascinating stuff. Really delves deep into the past and current antics of the world's most famous Romeo. But who knew the press could actually print the truth?"

Can't choke the life out of her. No longer so amused by her, Blue scanned the website's report. The writer listed every female Blue was thought to have bagged over the years, and claimed he had panicked about his upcoming nuptials and was hiding out in Bangkok, sleazing his way through the female population.

Pagan had to be foaming-at-the-mouth worried. Not because of the women but because of his absence. On all of his football trips and all of his out-of-country missions, he'd always kept in touch with her.

"Just . . . shut it, Evie." He swiped his hand over the text until the screen went blank. "Not another word out of you."

"Word."

He rolled his eyes. "Real mature."

"Thank you."

He threw a file at her.

"Are you on your period or something?" she said, her

tone snippy. "First you looked ready to laugh, and now you look ready to commit murder. Your mood swings are a wee bit out of control, yeah."

He was not the one with a freaking emotional disorder! "There's nothing wrong with sleeping around," he gritted. He'd just never wanted to do it, had always craved monogamy. He knew how precious it was.

"There is something horribly wrong when you've got a partner."

"I *know* that. Cheating isn't what I meant."

"Besides," she continued, "no one likes a himbo."

"Actually, everyone does."

"Yeah, for the whole five minutes they have of his attention."

"I promise you, I grant my women more than five minutes of my time."

She opened her mouth to comment and he decided he'd had enough.

"Instead of obsessing about my sex life, princess," he said, "why don't you get one of your own?"

She backed a step away from him. "First, I am *not* obsessing about your sex life. Second, who says I don't have one?"

"Do you?" He tensed all over again as he waited for her response.

She never offered one, and he could only wonder what that meant. That she didn't have a man and was embarrassed, or that she did—as the sweatpants and boxers suggested—and wanted him kept out of agency business . . . kept safe.

The thought ticked Blue off, and it had nothing to

do with wanting her for himself. He'd been sleeping in her bed. He simply didn't like the thought of sharing sheets with some lame asshole who was going to end up with a broken face the next time he put his skeevy hands on Evie Black!

You want to fight the guy now? Seriously?

He forced himself to get back to work, and searched for articles about Solomon Judah and John No Last Name. There wasn't a single mention of either male. But then, neither had ever led a public life. When Solo wasn't working, he spent his time at some hick backwater farm without any kind of modern convenience (shudder). And John . . . well, Blue wasn't sure what John did in his off time. The warrior had secrets, and Blue and Solo never pressed.

I have to find them.

When a friend's life was at stake, he had to question everything and everyone. Nothing could be overlooked. Every piece of information had to be verified.

Blue leaned back in the chair and ran a hand through his hair, swiveling to face Evie. Beautiful, irritating Evie.

"John and Solo are out there. They need me."

Her expression softened, and she nodded. "Believe me, I know how you feel. My father is out there, too."

He was struck by the most insane urge to pull her into his lap and hug her close. To offer comfort . . . and to take it. "I won't stop until all three are safe. You have my word."

"Good," she said. "Because I won't stop, either. I'm officially on the case."

Uh, what now? "Counteroffer. You go back to the hospital and let the big boy do all the heavy lifting. I'll report in at least once a day. You'll never have to wonder what's going on."

She shook her head, ponytail dancing. "My counter to your counter. Go screw yourself."

"I have. It's not actually half-bad."

Her eyes narrowed. "Pig."

"Prude."

"A name I'll wear with pride. But take a moment to think this through. As Michael's daughter, I'm your superior. What I say goes."

Please. "Give me an order. Let's see what happens."

Looking ready to spit nails, she said, "I'm helping, Blue. Got it?"

"No. You're not an agent anymore. You'll only get in my way." And possibly get one or both of them killed.

Anger sparked in those chocolate eyes. "News flash. You're either going to work with me, or against me. One way or another, I'm investigating. But before you decide, maybe think back and remember what happened to the people who got in my way during my agenting days."

They'd ended up in the hospital, either physically ill or physically broken. "Coincidence."

Wow. Way to stand up for what you don't *believe in, Blue.*

Her grin was cold and certain. "Step one of my solo mission. Proving you wrong. I hope you enjoy raging diarrhea."

Fine. Why should he care if she got hurt?

Michael, that's why. Right. Not Blue's ongoing . . . attraction to her. There. He'd admitted it. It wasn't just arousal. Wasn't something he could tuck away and easily forget. Horror of horrors, some part of him found the moody woman appealing. And sexy. And sensual. And thrilling.

Arguing with her turned him on.

Who are you trying to fool? You've been turned on since the moment you woke up.

Maybe it was the forbidden aspect of their relationship. Yeah. That had to be it. He couldn't have her, so of course he craved her. Like the sugar he loved but couldn't eat, because it screwed the hell out of his heartbeat.

"What about your real job?" he asked, trying one last time to get rid of her.

She grinned again, but it was smug this time. "My father owns St. Anthony. Bought it just for me, in fact. So I can take off as many days as I want."

"My review of you as an employee?" He gave her a thumbs-down.

"I'm torn up inside. Really."

Was he ever going to win one of their disagreements?

"Give me a day to figure things out and make a plan. Plus I need to sneak home, check out my house, make sure no one broke in or took anything, and gather a few supplies. Tomorrow I'll know whether I should stay dead or miraculously come back to life, and we'll go to the explosion site together. It's the only place I know to start."

She thought for a moment, then gave another nod. "All right. Okay. But know this. If you're lying to me, trying to ditch me, I'm going to hunt you down and make you wish you'd actually burned to death."

If anyone could do it, he thought, it would be her.

Great. Something else to like about her. Follow-through.

He needed to get back to hating her. Like now. Otherwise, resisting her would be more difficult than it already was, and he didn't need difficult right now.

He needed answers.

Six

~~~~~~

THE WINDOWS IN EVIE'S car were tinted so dark, Blue didn't have to hide in back during the drive home. He sat up front, marveling that the world had continued on without him. It was morning, so people strode along the sidewalks, rushing off to work. Lines formed in front of the coffee shops. A team of pickpockets swept through the crowds, liberating wallets and jewelry.

For the first ten minutes, neither Blue nor Evie said a word, and he was glad. They'd argued all the way into the garage.

"Be on the lookout for tails," he'd said. "Before and after you drop me off."

"Duh. I do know what I'm doing, bluebonnet."

"And make sure you do a visual sweep of your entire property line when you return, just in case someone—"

"Dude! I know."

Now he was too busy battling his body to spar with her. Her honey-almond scent saturated the entire vehicle. He kept imagining easing her to her back and pinning her with his weight. Sliding his hands under her shirt . . . then her jeans. Touching every inch of her. Kissing and tasting every inch of her.

He cursed. He needed to buy her a new body lotion. Maybe one called Dog Crap and Old Sneakers. Or Locker Room Man-Sweat.

At the fifteen-minute mark, Evie broke the silence. "Hey, Sir Sexalot. We're almost there."

Thank God. Escape. "Notice I don't threaten *you* when you call me ridiculous names."

"Brilliant. Let me give you a medal."

He scowled at her. *Going to win one day.*

"But the difference is," she added, "the names I give you are steeped in truth."

"Well, then, why don't I just call you Judgmental Bitch from now on? That's about as truthful as I can get."

No response from her.

Finally. Victory.

But it felt kind of hollow.

He gave her the code to his security gate. "Park in the garage and close the door, sugar tush," he said in an attempt to lighten the mood. Any spying neighbors . . . or hiding paparazzi . . . or lurking bad guys . . . would just assume she came looking for him or even her father, the owner of the Invaders.

She obeyed without protest—or another smart remark. A true miracle.

Problem was, he was actually . . . disappointed.

"Tomorrow," he said, exiting the vehicle.

"Tomorrow," she confirmed.

Was that anticipation in her tone?

"By the way," she called. "Your new nickname for me? I like it. Because you're right. It fits. But I think I prefer JB."

And this round goes to Honey Badger as well.

He waited until she pulled out of the garage—why did it feel like he was losing an appendage?—before he slipped into the backyard, remaining in the shadows as he checked for tracks. He found none. His heart rate jacked up and his muscles tensed when he unlocked the back door and turned the knob.

Hinges creaked, but nothing exploded.

Still he didn't relax. He inspected the inside of the house for any signs of tampering. He'd always liked the place. It was three times as large as Evie's—*stop obsessing about her, moron*—and decorated with dark browns, like Evie's eyes, and pure whites, like her skin, and deep reds, like her lips, and if he didn't wipe that girl from his mind, his temper would get the better of him and he would start ripping the brick from the walls.

At least there was nothing out of the ordinary; the house was exactly as he'd left it.

He took a heated enzyme shower, the mist cleaning him more thoroughly than water, and studied his reflection in the full-length mirror. His skin had grown back, but he was now without any of his tattoos. He'd liked those tattoos. More importantly, women had liked those tattoos. For some reason, they'd enjoyed tracing the edges with their tongues.

To do: Get new tattoos.

What would Evie like? he wondered, then promptly cursed. What did he care what she liked? Wasn't like he'd ever give her a peep show. Or a taste.

Yeah. He wanted her to taste.

Enough!

After he dressed in a black tee and slacks, he sat at the desk in his office to watch the security feed. Pagan had come to the door about a thousand times and had even tossed a rock at the (unbreakable) window during her final visit, but the alarm had scared her off. No one else had so much as approached the property line.

So, again, the person responsible for the explosion either thought he was dead or never really had a beef with him.

He thought back. While lying broken and bleeding in the rubble of Michael's home, he overheard bits and pieces of a conversation. He hadn't recognized the speakers.

—with this one?

—fetch a decent price.

He'll fetch a decent price. Where, though? On the black market? As a sex slave?

—this one?

—ashing him.

Finish ashing him. That was Blue, no question. For sure, he was thought to be dead.

—last one?

—keeping him.

I'm keeping him. Or maybe: We're keeping. Or even: They're keeping him.

That meant one of Blue's friends had been sold and one had been kept.

Solo was unnaturally tall and cut with the kind of muscle earned only on the bloodiest of battlefields. When he was angry, his skin reddened and his bones thickened. He became the monster of grim fairy tales.

John was Rakan, like a priceless work of art come to dazzling life. He was just as tall as Blue, just as muscled, but exquisitely golden from head to foot. And, truth be told, he was the only man in this world or any other capable of making Blue look hideous in comparison.

Ego much?

Why yes. Thank you. Blue was certain his ego was as lovely as the rest of him.

Anyway. The culprit might have hoped to tame the gruesome Solo, perhaps use him as hired muscle. He definitely would have considered John the better sex slave.

John, who hated being touched.

Rakans were so rare, they were always top sellers.

Blue closed his eyes against the horrors his friends might even now be enduring. He had to find the pair. Soon. Then he had to punish the man responsible.

What did he know for sure?

AIR thought Star was involved. But was he?

There weren't many men with enough connections or cunning to bypass the security Solo had set up at Michael's. There weren't many men rich enough to pay someone to set a bomb in such a high-ranking commander's house, either, without fearing the consequences. Blue still figured that "someone" had to have used someone else—someone like Michael's former assistant, because that was the only way such a plan could have worked.

Star fit each instance. But then, so did a handful of others. *But then,* only Star had been a target for potential elimination.

What exactly did AIR have on the man?

Only one way to find out. Blue hacked into the AIR data system for information about Star, the explosion, Michael, the assistant's death, any recent black-market auctions for a Rakan male, as well as a male matching Solo's description. To his fury, he discovered a whole lot of nothing. Agent Gutierrez hadn't even logged his interview with Evie.

It was suspicious.

What was the best way to handle this?

If Blue returned from the dead to confront him, he could be placing a target on his back and giving up a very clear advantage. Although . . . the bomber might not even know Blue was involved. Michael had most likely been the main target, maybe even the only target. Then, when those two men had stepped into the scene—probably to ensure Michael was actually deceased—Blue was already unrecognizable.

But could he put his hopes in, well, hope?

No. So, for now, Blue would stay dead. There would be no confrontation with the AIR agent. Evie, though . . .

Yeah. Having a partner might actually come in handy.

One last task before he worked on a disguise. He deposited a million dollars in the account of the charity he secretly spearheaded, Safe Haven for Otherworlders, using one of his aliases. SHOW was a place where children living on the street could go for long-term food and shelter. The money should last until he returned to the land of the living, and could continue his weekly support.

Blue strode to his private bathroom, and dug through his hidden stash of emergency supplies. Hair dye made specifically for his race. Colored contacts. A voice modifier chip. Studs for facial piercings. A serrated blade that would cause temporary scarring in an Arcadian.

Why deal with makeup that could wash away? Blue preferred authenticity. Also, he thought he remembered Evie telling him that he needed a scar.

He'd never had one, and he'd never imagined a woman would desire one—or that he'd want to cater to her.

Tomorrow, he would test his new look on her—the only person he currently trusted. If she failed to recognize him, he'd know he was good to go.

This could actually be fun.

The next morning Evie made her rounds at the hospital as usual. Then she talked to the chief of staff about taking an open-ended vacation. As expected, there were no arguments. Her coworkers would think she was taking terrible advantage of her status, as Blue had said, and she would have to agree. She totally was. But this was life and death for the only man she had ever loved, and she wasn't going to feel guilty about it.

At home, she strode straight into the kitchen, slammed her purse on the counter, and poured herself a much-needed glass of wine. When would Blue get here?

And he had better get here. If he'd tricked her just to get rid of her . . .

She drained the glass, barely tasting the hints of

plum and fig, and poured another. The air was still charged with electric power, she realized, from when he'd been here before, the fine hairs on the back of her neck rising—liquid heat rushing through her.

When would it freaking end? She was tired, so very tired, of the rush of sensations he caused, whether he was there or not. The tension in her lower belly. The heat in her veins. The ache . . . oh, criminy, the ache.

"Do you always drink like a sidewalk bum when you get home from work?" The deep, gravelly voice caused every nerve in her body to come alive. The reaction was familiar, though the voice was not. Not really.

In a lightning-fast move, she whisked the pyre-gun from her purse, turned, and aimed. A second later the gun was ripped from her grip, only to hover in the air just out of her reach. But it was never aimed at her. Either the guy was a suckwad criminal, or he meant her no harm.

He'd bypassed her security. He wasn't suckwad.

Mr. B and E stepped from the shadows, and she stiffened.

He was tall—Blue's height. He was muscled—Blue's build. He even smelled like Blue, champagne and fresh-plucked strawberries. Odd for a man, but no less addictive. And yet, he had short, spiked black hair, and eyes to match. Thick kohl rimmed his eyelids, altering the shape. A jagged scar ran from his hairline to his chin. Both of his eyebrows were pierced, and so was his lip. Could be him. But could also *not* be him.

"Let me see your hands," she demanded.

For a moment he gave no reaction. He was too busy

peering at her as if he actually saw her, rather than through her. Blue always peered through her. This man's stare was intense. Steady. Almost . . . magnetic. She couldn't even bring herself to blink.

Finally, he lifted his arms, palms out.

She knew those hands. She'd cleaned and bandaged one, then watched the other grow—and she'd enjoyed having both on her body, cupping her breasts.

Had secretly prayed they would move lower.

Leaning against the counter, relaxing, she said, "So. You kept your word, bluebird. I'm impressed."

He blinked in surprise. "You recognize me. How?" As he spoke, the pyre-gun floated back to her purse.

His affront amused her. "Hello. Trained agent. I notice details the average Joe misses."

"No, it's more than that." He studied his hands in the light. "You didn't know for sure until you looked at these. But why would—" His gaze jolted up, landing on her, heating with black fire. "Because you liked when they were on you. A woman never forgets pleasure."

She straightened as though yanked by a cord. "Don't be ridiculous. I forget all the time." Gah! "I mean, I've never experienced pleasure from you."

Where's your brutal honesty now, girl?

Silent amendment: *Except when he was grinding on me.*

Trying again. "Maybe you have distinctive sunspots."

That wasn't a lie. She'd said "maybe."

"I don't." He watched her for a long while, whatever thoughts danced through his head hidden from her. His expression gave nothing away. No, that wasn't true. His features had softened, oh so slightly.

If he tried to prove his theory, she might not have the strength to resist.

She gulped.

"What do you think of my scar?" he asked, rubbing the raised tissue.

It gave him a savage edge, as if he couldn't decide whether to hack you to pieces or give you the hardest sexual ride of your life—and only time would reveal the answer. He was the bad boy every woman yearned to taste, but only the bravest ever dared approach.

Must regroup.

"Nothing to say? You disappoint me, princess." He walked toward her, placed his hands—those big, strong hands—on the counter, caging her in, *thrilling* her. "Or, maybe your silence speaks for you."

Red alert! "What the bloody hell do you think you're doing, blue balls?" she demanded, hating how breathless she sounded.

His gaze dipped to her lips—and stayed. "What would you like me to do, princess?"

Kiss me. Hard.

No!

"I'd like you to move. Now," she said. Unfortunately, her voice was still raspy with longing.

"Someone's forgotten her own rules, I think. Just like she claims to have forgotten her pleasure." He nuzzled her nose, the contact innocent and yet somehow all the more erotic for it. "You sure that's what you want?"

No, she wasn't sure. He affected her in a way no one else ever had. He made all her naughty bits tingle, and she liked it. Her breasts felt heavier, ready for his hands . . . his mouth. Her nipples hardened and throbbed. Her legs trembled, and at the apex of her thighs she was warm and wet. Her knees threatened to buckle under her slight weight, a reaction guaranteed to land her in the strength of his arms. And probably on her back, on the receiving end of a good snogging. Or more . . .

Yes, please.

She hadn't had sex in three years, since she'd spiraled after Claire's death. And before that, her last sexual encounter had happened at the ripe old age of seventeen. Back then, she'd given herself to too many, desperate for male approval and attention.

The curse of those bloody daddy issues.

But she wasn't a needy little girl anymore, and she wasn't going to be some guy's bang and bail ever again.

"You might be a cheater, Professor Hit It and Quit It, but I am not." She shoved him, and though he could have resisted and remained in place, he moved backward. A scowl marred the rugged beauty of his new face. A scowl . . . and maybe a little hurt.

I am a judgmental bitch.

"Look. I'm sorry I was mean," she muttered. "Let's just forget the last five minutes." She reached into her purse and grabbed the paper she'd stuffed there. "Here. This is your bill for your stay at Chez Black."

She expected him to comment on her apology. He didn't. He acted as if he hadn't heard it, and she wasn't sure what to think.

As he read over her notes, she moved to his side to make sure she hadn't left anything out.

Security system, parts and repairs: $8,000.

New window: $2,000.

New sheets: $1,000.

Water: $10,000.

Time and mental anguish: $3,000,000.

No. Nothing left out.

He eyed her with a strange mix of amusement and exasperation. "Do you accept orgasm? Because that's my preferred method of payment."

She puckered her lips, knew she looked like she'd just sucked on a lemon and didn't care. "I'm sure. And no. I do not accept orgasms." *But I'd like to.* "Lucky you, I can get you started on a stellar payment plan. Meaning you have one month to pay or I'll break both of your kneecaps. Now, are we going to search the explosion site or what?"

Seven

E VIE APOLOGIZED TO HIM, and she liked having his hands on her soft, sweet body. Blue was having trouble getting past those two little facts.

He gave himself a mental slap. First, she apologized for being mean. Not for what she'd said. Because she thought it was true. Thought he liked screwing anything in a skirt. Or breathing.

Can you blame her? You've been acting like Dr. Happy with a life-and-death vitamin Dick injection to impart.

True. Deep down, he knew he deserved her rancor. He'd done horrible things to his women. Things he could have said no to.

And so what that she'd enjoyed his hands on her. He wasn't going to do anything about it.

He lived his life by one simple rule: *Never mess around unless it's job related.*

After his breakup with Noelle, he'd added a second: *Always let the girlfriend know there will be others.*

He'd kept those rules. Until Evie.

Not that they'd done anything. But the intent was there, and that was just as bad. He was just as guilty.

Michael would kill him.

If you find him.

He would. Soon.

Blue waited in the living room as Evie changed out of her purple scrubs. Did she have any idea how adorable she looked in them? Probably not. The girl seemed utterly unconcerned about her appearance. But then, she didn't need to be. She was a natural beauty.

Seriously. How had he ever gotten away with telling himself she wasn't pretty?

Five minutes later she stood in front of him, this time wearing a shirt that read "Dear Math, I'm Not Your Therapist. Solve Your Own Problems." A pair of tight, hip-hugging jeans encased her lower half. Old tennis shoes covered her feet. Her hair was now anchored in a high ponytail, her face scrubbed clean of makeup. She looked young and fresh—still so freaking gorgeous his chest hurt.

Jaw clenched, he forced himself to look away from her. "I put my stuff in one of your guest rooms." The one closest to her room, but whatever. Details weren't important right now. "Since I'm supposedly dead, I can't stay at my place. I need to stay here."

"That's fine." No change in her demeanor. "You ready to go?"

He nodded, taken aback by the ease of her acceptance. "We have to use one of your cars." He had a few vehicles the public hadn't seen, but for what they were about to do, they needed hers. No one would think it strange for Michael Black's daughter and her grungy friend to dig through the rubble of his home.

She offered no protest as Blue hustled her into the

garage. "I know you're a sports car junkie, but I think we should go with the sedan," she said.

"Sure." The sedan had two major wins: it would blend in with all the other cars on the highway, and the windows were smoked glass. With Evie, he never knew what he would do or how he would react to something. Privacy was best.

She let him drive, but as he eased into the driveway she barked an insistent "Stop!"

He did, palming a weapon, and she hopped out. A little boy playing in the front yard of her neighbor's house spotted her and bounded over.

The sun was a bright little bastard, reaching out with fiery fingers to stroke over Evie, giving her pale skin the same pearlescent glow that had struck him dumb at their first meeting.

You're staring at her. Don't be that guy. Look away!

"Dr. Evie!"

"Hey, Drew," she said, giving him a hug. "Did you handle that wee problem we discussed?"

Blue returned his weapon to the sheath at his waist.

"I sure did. I waited for you earlier but Momma told me I had to come in and eat and then I cleaned my plate so fast she said her head was spinning and then I rushed back out 'cause I wanted to tell you I popped Bobby so good. I think I broke his nose. There was blood."

"Oh, that's wonderful. I'm so proud of you!"

Condoning schoolyard violence? Interesting. And kind of hot.

You think everything about her is hot.

Not everything. When that viper's tongue called him a whore, he wanted to cut it out.

Drew's gaze slid past her open door, catching on Blue, and widened.

Blue tensed. Had he just been made by a prepubescent?

"Are you gonna kill me?" the kid asked.

Kid definitely didn't know who he was. There would be fawning.

Wait. He looked *that* scary?

Grinning, Evie said, "Nah. You've got nothing to worry about, squirt. Mr. Brothario is a lover, not a fighter."

Blue glared at her.

Drew flipped him off before rushing inside his house, probably to hide.

"Aw, how sweet," Evie said, settling in her seat. "I think he was trying to warn you against unleashing your dreadful wrath on sweet, innocent me."

"If the poor kid thinks you're sweet, I have to fear his home life."

"Ha-ha. You are hilarious."

"Thank you."

Like Drew, she flipped him off.

Grinning, Blue programmed the car to head to Michael's, sat back, and tried to relax as the sensors did the driving for him. Problem was, Evie's honey-almond scent saturated this vehicle as well. His shaft—which hadn't shrunk since the counter incident—throbbed, and the hum of his power cranked up the volume, screaming for release.

Not here, not now.

But if he wasn't careful he would levitate the vehicle and everything around it.

He needed a distraction. "Encouraging jailhouse justice on the preschool playground, sugar muffin?"

She glared at him, and it lightened his mood. "Encouraging the end of a bully's reign of terror."

Ah. "I approve."

Smirking at him, she said, "You do realize you just set yourself up for a horrible insult, right?"

He leaned against the door and faced her. She didn't wilt under the intensity of his stare, and didn't look away. She met him head-on, completely unfazed. He had to admire her fortitude.

Had to? Hell, he already did. He'd never met a woman like her. All bark *and* bite.

"Let's call a truce," he said. The moment the words registered, he realized he liked them. He and Evie had never been on sociable terms, and he was curious to know what that would be like.

"I thought we already had." She rubbed at the goose bumps on her arms. Cold? "I mean, we haven't killed each other."

Good point. He tried again. As he turned down the air with a single swipe of his power, he said, "Let's be friends." He'd never had a female friend before, had never thought he'd want one; but this one had saved his life, and no matter how he felt about her, he kinda sorta owed her. "After all, you're the only person I can trust right now, and you're determined to work with me, so we're going to be spending a lot of time together."

Her color was high, just the way he liked it, and her dark eyes were luminous as they searched his features. Her lips were so soft, so red, and already parted; he experienced a sudden urge to lean into her, to breathe her in and taste her, and what the hell was he doing? *Stop.*

"We're not good for each other," she said.

"Because we let our own issues get in the way. We all have baggage, princess. Let's ditch ours and move forward."

"What would this friendship entail?" she asked.

"For starters, we need to always tell each other the truth."

"I already do that. Are you saying you don't?"

God save me. "Also, you'll need to guard my back rather than stab it."

She took no offense, surprising him. Then she nodded, surprising him even more. "I could give that last one a try, I suppose. I'm not making any promises, though," she rushed to add.

He rolled his eyes. "Just do your best."

A pause as she fiddled with the strap of her purse. "So, do you really think we're going to find anything at Michael's? I'm sure the agency has already sent people to search through the rubble."

"They aren't me," he said simply.

"And you're the best?"

"Indisputably."

Now she was the one to roll her eyes. "I seem to remember a certain agent telling me arrogance would get people killed."

The moment the words left her mouth, her amusement faded. Her expression fell and her shoulders hunched in. Great waves of regret and sadness rolled off her, slamming into him.

What the hell?

He thought back to their first meeting and how much he'd wanted her even then. How shaken he'd been by her attitude. How, when the smoke of his injured pride had cleared, he'd been impressed by her. She'd taken a three-man mission and simplified it down to the bones, all on her own.

"I was wrong," he admitted. "Your arrogance was deserved."

"No. No, it wasn't."

Something about her tone . . .

He frowned. He couldn't think of a single mission she'd botched. "Why did you leave the agency?"

"I don't want to talk about it."

"Evie—"

"I mean it, Blue. Leave this alone."

He wanted to push. Her regret and sadness were intensifying. But she was the type to push back, and as he'd proven, he didn't always come out ahead with her.

Challenges more than sucked.

"Suspicious behavior detected," a computerized voice suddenly announced.

He was amazed only for a moment. "Your security system?" he asked.

"Yes." Evie twisted to peer out the back window. "Modified to record and decipher the habits of nearby drivers."

Extraordinary. And seriously hot.

On alert, he scanned the mirrors and found the culprit. Three cars back was a dark sedan with windows as smoky as theirs. Evie punched a few buttons and a small screen appeared on the console in front of Blue.

"We're definitely being followed," she said.

With another punch of the buttons, the camera that was anchored to the back of the car honed in on the sedan. An image appeared on the console screen.

"Can you give me the make and model of the car?" he asked.

Evie was not the one to answer. The computerized voice gave him the details he wanted, adding, "The vehicle has been modified to allow for manual steering. There are automatic assault rifles anchored to both the left and right side."

Gotta get me one of these. "Can you see past the window tint and tell me how many bodies are inside?"

"Checking . . ." the computer replied. Several tense seconds ticked past. "Body heat indicators suggest four adult males."

He liked those odds.

Eight

"**W**E COULD BE DEALING with the men who bombed my father's house," Evie said. "Maybe they're here to end you for good."

"Maybe," Blue replied, "but I'm presumed dead, and this isn't my car. *You* are a more likely target."

She shook her head, so close to him the end of her ponytail brushed his arm. "Your body was never found. You're not presumed dead."

"No one saw me go into my house. No one saw me go into yours, either."

"No one that we know about."

She had an answer for everything.

"I'm sure, Evie," he said, his tone flat. "I would have sensed if I was being followed. I'm never not aware."

"I'll ignore the double negative and agree with you." She released a heavy breath. "So say I *am* the target. What's the motive? Why now?"

Why indeed. "Because the AIR agent came to visit you and you're now a liability? Because Michael is missing and the bad guy wants to use you as bait? Should I go on?"

"No," she grumbled. "Those two did the trick."

Well, what do you know? He'd won another argument. And this time victory *was* oh, so sweet. "Are the occupants human?" he asked the computer. "Or otherworlder?"

"Unsure."

Too bad. "Any New Chicago PD posted along the road?"

"Checking . . . Yes. The nearest patrol unit is ten miles north."

He knew the area to avoid, then.

"How do I put the shields up?" he asked Evie. "Assuming you have shields."

"Like I would ever own a vehicle without shields. And the method is kind of complicated, so pay close attention." She cleared her throat, then said, "Engage shields. Now."

Clear armor came out of hiding, wrapping around the car to protect it from enemy fire.

He shook his head in exasperation—and, okay, a little amusement. "Program the operating system to accept my voice commands."

All she said was "Accept Blue. All access."

"Engage manual steering panel. Now," he said. The moment he had the wheel in hand, he switched lanes, careful to maintain the same speed—for the moment.

The sedan remained where it was, playing innocent.

With only a thought, Blue could force the cars around him to swerve into the vehicle's path, but that would put innocents in danger, maybe even cause a few deaths. He had *some* scruples.

"Are you okay with me putting a few dings and scratches in your car?" he asked Evie.

"Strip her to the studs. I don't care. Just nail those bloody bastards to the wall. I'd like a chat-up."

Perfect answer, and sexy as hell, her excitement making her accent thicker.

He wanted to kiss her.

You can't ever kiss her.

"You mean a conversation?" When dealing with Honey Badger, it was best to be clear.

"That's what I said."

Well, all right, then. "Here goes." He yanked the car to the right and slammed his foot on the gas, shooting off the highway. The sedan gave up all pretense of innocence and followed. Tires squealed as the sensors on the cars around them engaged, automated systems performing deep swerves to avoid a collision.

Evie dug through her purse, withdrawing the modified pyre-gun she'd brandished earlier. "Get me the angle I need and I'll disable the car," she said, dialing the internal crystal to its highest setting.

I think I'm turned on—again.

"I want to get to a less populated area first." An intersection loomed ahead, the light red. There were three lanes. Two were clogged with traffic. One was open, but for right turns only.

Pop! Pop! Pop!

"Shots fired," the computer stated calmly.

"Blimey," Evie cursed. "Obviously our shadow doesn't care about hurting others."

"They'll get theirs." Blue increased his speed, staying

in the turn lane, even though he wasn't going to turn. He flew through the intersection, jerking the wheel this way, then that way, stopping oncoming traffic and directing the cars out of harm's way. "You have my word."

Rather than keeping to the side roads, Blue zipped back onto the highway.

"They're about to fire again," Evie said.

Pop! Pop! Pop!

"Shields can only withstand two more rounds before failing," the computer announced.

Great. Blue revved the turbo-booster and shot into warp speed, weaving through traffic, searching for the perfect place to—

There.

A bridge. Very little traffic in front, only the tail in back.

"Incoming," Evie warned.

"Almost there."

Pop! Pop! Pop!

"Get ready, moon tart," he said, pressing a button to lower the passenger window. Violent wind blustered inside the car. "Don't try to get the men, just try to blow their tires."

"Duh. This isn't my first rodeo, cowboy."

He really hoped she was a good shot.

"You'll have less than a second to—" the computer began.

"I know!" Evie growled. "Shut up."

Pop! Pop! Pop!

The moment Blue crossed the bottom edge of the bridge, he threw the car into a spin. Suddenly, Evie was facing the other vehicle. She found her target and squeezed off a single shot. A bright yellow laser blasted out, slamming into the vehicle's front left tire at the same time another bullet hit her door.

The shield had been damaged beyond repair, and the bullet shot through the metal to embed in the console directly in front of her.

So close to hitting her, Blue thought, trembling with sudden rage.

"Nailed it!" she said, happy.

He straightened out the car and slowed, watching in the rearview mirror as rubber melted and the sedan began a tailspin of its own before flipping over and rolling, the roof crashing into the road, then the tires slamming into the road, then the roof, then the tires, until finally stopping on its belly.

Smoke wafted through the air as he came to a halt. Clasping his gun, he jumped out and raced toward the crash site. He was halfway there when a brutal gush of molten wind shoved him backward, lifting him as if he weighed no more than a feather. A piercing boom scraped at his ears, making them ring. He landed with a hard *thunk*, a door handle dropping from the sky and clanking beside him.

Been here, done this shit already.

As he stood, he watched flames engulf what was left of the vehicle.

That had been an intentional blast. Most likely, whoever sent these men to nab—kill?—Evie hadn't wanted anyone caught and questioned. Planting a self-destruct bomb would have been easy.

Blue's rage exploded with the same viciousness, and he struggled to rein it in as he marched to Evie's car.

She stood in the passenger doorway, her hand braced against the open window. Her hair had come loose from the ponytail and framed her soot-streaked face in tangled waves.

"Well, that sucks," she said.

No smart remarks. No recrimination directed at him.

He stopped. Just stopped and tried to catch his breath. She was beautiful and here and alive, unharmed, the knowledge battering at the desire he tried so valiantly to deny. He wanted her. More than that, he needed her. Inside, his Arcadian power tugged at a flimsy leash. He'd been too worked up lately. Too agitated, too hungry, too angry, with zero release.

Each one magnified his rage.

"I am *so* pissed off right now," he snarled.

"Uh, I can tell," she said, not sounding worried. "Your eyes are glowing."

Glowing past the contacts? That was bad. Very, very bad. Soon a surge of pure energy would leave his body, frying everything around him. Unless . . . No. No, he wouldn't. "You need to leave, Evie. Get in the car and drive away. I'll meet you at the ruins."

"As if!" The foolish girl approached him. "What's going on with you?"

"Evie!"

"If we're friends, you'll tell me," she insisted. "Maybe I can help."

Low blow, using the friendship he'd insisted on. "I

have more Arcadian abilities than anyone knows. I'm more *powerful* than anyone knows." He'd never told anyone the full scope of his badassery, not even Michael. Humans feared what they didn't understand, and he didn't want his friends to fear him. "Sometimes that power builds up and requires an outlet."

She thought for a moment. "Kind of like the world's worst temper tantrum with deadly results?"

He nearly choked on his tongue. She wasn't afraid of him, and clearly she never would be. "Yes."

"What kind of outlet?" she asked.

"A physical fight." He paused, watching her expression for the minutest change. "Sex."

No horror. Only interest.

The interest nearly slayed him.

"In that case . . ." she said. She punched him once, twice, three times. "Better?"

Each of the blows knocked his head to the side. Blood trickled into his mouth, and sharp stings registered.

Amusement doused the hottest threads of the rage—but not his sexual hunger. He spit out the blood, his desire for her *even worse*. "Amendment. *I* have to do the beating."

"Oh. Well, my bad. I'm going to decline on that one."

"That one will never be offered to you."

"But the other . . ."

Yeah. The other. Sex. He noticed she didn't move away from him but stayed right where she was. Her gaze locked on his lips, and she began to pant.

Thinking of kissing him?

Maybe. Her adrenaline must have skyrocketed. He knew his had.

He stepped closer, unable to resist.

She did the same.

And then he was on her, wrapping his arms around her and jerking her into the hard line of his body. His tongue thrust into her mouth, demanding a response. She gave it, kissing him back with a passion he'd never before encountered, as if she had been starving all her life and he was her first meal.

Desire burned him from the inside out, sparking a fire in his blood, driving him torward the car. He lifted her to the trunk and forced her legs to spread and cage his hips. With his hands on her lower back, he yanked her against him and directed her into a hard, fast grind against his erection.

Hell yeah!

She groaned, and it was the most delicious sound.

The pleasure of her . . . it was almost too much. . . . Her breasts rubbed against his chest, and he could feel the stiff peaks of her nipples. All the while, he continued to feed her a down-and-dirty kiss that mimicked exactly what he wanted to do to the rest of her. Hard, almost punishing. Taking. Demanding.

He couldn't get enough of her. The honey of her taste was a drug. Beyond addictive.

Necessary to sustain life.

Power seeped from his pores, and he suspected Evie could feel it, because little moans kept rising from deep in her throat, and her fingers kept brushing up and down the exposed skin on his arms . . . until her hands were tangled in his hair, her nails digging into his scalp; she angled his head just the way she wanted it. He liked that. Liked that she demanded and took with the same fervency he used.

She sucked the piercing in his bottom lip, and a low growl reverberated from him.

More. He needed more. He needed all. He needed her naked, and open. He needed to graze her nipples with his teeth. Needed to devour her between her legs, then pound inside her, deep, so deep she would feel him for days afterward. He needed to hear her cries of rapture.

Yes. He reached for the hem of her shirt, ready to tear the thing off her.

A siren wailed in the background, and Evie stiffened.

"Wait. Stop." She drew in a deep breath and shoved at him. She wouldn't meet his gaze. "This is wrong."

Wrong? No. He—

Wasn't kissing his fiancée.

Yes. This was wrong.

A tide of disgust rolled through him, and with a step back—physically and emotionally—he increased the distance between them.

Evie stood and did the same, then wiped her mouth with the back of her hand as if she couldn't bear to deal with his taste a second longer. "That shouldn't have happened."

"I know." He wasn't in love with Pagan, true, but he'd given her a ring. He had rules. Rules he should have followed.

He was ashamed.

He had just betrayed Michael in the worst possible way. Michael, who had done so much for him throughout the years but had only ever asked for one thing in return. That he leave his daughter alone.

I'm scum.

Correction, I'm worse than scum.

Blue had disrespected the man, and for what? Momentary pleasure.

Perfect phrase. *Momentary pleasure.* That was all Evie could ever be.

She wasn't like Pagan. She would never accept the fact that he had to be with other women, no matter the reason for his actions. She would murder him, and perhaps even murder the female, totally unwilling to concede that what he did was a necessary evil of the job.

He—

Liked that, he realized, a little dazed. Wanted a woman to fight for him. To desire him, and him alone. To crave his unerring devotion and insist upon it.

Who are you?

"It was the moment," Evie said, her voice hollow. "The rush of surviving the chase and explosion."

Was it? "I know," he repeated, his own voice just as hollow.

He didn't know.

He'd been attracted to this girl from the beginning. Maybe she'd been attracted to him just as long. Maybe it had happened only recently for her. But the fact remained. They were into each other, no matter how wrong it was.

They'd have to be careful.

"Are you good now?" she asked.

Was he? The leash on his power was reinforced, but his mind was in turmoil. Never again taste that honey? Never again feel those teacup breasts smashed against his chest? Never again rub between her legs?

Never thrust his fingers deep?

Impossible.

"I'll be fine," he gritted. "Let's go before the cops arrive."

They returned to the car, settled inside.

As he reprogrammed the GPS, he said, "As soon as I rise from the dead, I'm telling Pagan it's over." He'd just cheated on her for real. Yeah, he'd told her there would be other women, but this was different.

This had been of his own volition.

He really was a he-slut.

There was no way to make this right. No way to reclaim his honor, but he *could* do an honorable thing. He could set Pagan free, allowing her to find someone else. Someone deserving of her.

"I hope you're not doing that on my account," Evie said, peering out the window, hiding her expression. "That was our first and last kiss. It's never going to happen again."

He'd just thought the same thing—and yet, it still irritated him to hear her say it. "Don't worry, flower petal. Getting involved with you is the last thing I want to do."

Nine

❧⤳⤝❧

I'M IN SO MUCH *trouble.*

Before, Evie had only been able to speculate about Blue's sexual prowess. She'd told herself that all the women flocking to him were fools, and his skill completely overrated.

Now she knew better.

His skills were seriously *underrated.* He hadn't just kissed her. He'd screwed the hell out of her mouth. And all the while, waves of his power had cascaded over her, heating her, making it feel like a thousand hands were concentrated on her naughty bits.

She'd never been so swept up in a moment, or so lost in sensation.

How close she'd come to letting him take her in public, out in the open, for anyone and everyone to see. How close she'd come to being used—and discarded.

I'm not going to be another conquest. I'm not!

From now on, she would be more careful around him. Although . . . maybe she wouldn't have to be.

Getting involved with you is the last thing I want to do, he'd said, and even though she'd agreed with the sentiment, the words had still managed to cut at her.

How pathetic am I? she thought. *I can't even get the world's most promiscuous man to want me unless he's desperate to release a little power.*

Whatever. It didn't matter. Nothing mattered except Michael, John, and Solo. She wouldn't forget again. And if she did, she might just give herself a lobotomy.

While Evie set up an external perimeter around the rubble of Michael's decimated house, creating invisible walls that would keep everyone and everything out, including prying eyes, Blue tossed charred boards out of the way by using his power, clearing the biggest pieces of debris before picking through the section where Fry Guy had tried to cook him for dinner.

He wished he could use his favorite ability. Or rather, he wished he could use a tweaked version of his favorite ability. Blue could stand in one location, any location, and force the last ten minutes to replay. He could watch everything that had transpired, like a movie unfolding across a television screen, whether he'd first borne witness or not. But the explosion had happened over a week ago, too far in the past for this capability.

There was another talent he could use here, however. One he'd always considered useless. An azure glow began to seep from the pores in his hand, and he ran his palm over bits and pieces of scorched wood, metal, and paper, the char disintegrating to reveal whatever was hidden beneath.

The glow could clean anything—except his dirty

thoughts. His desire for Evie hadn't faded in the silence of the drive. Had only grown.

He was more appalled by the knowledge with every second that passed. He was also extremely ticked.

How had he gone from total dislike of her to this . . . seeming obsession?

"Cool trick," she said, coming up beside him.

He steeled himself against her honey-almond scent, saying, "Just one of many."

She placed her hand at her heart. "So humble."

"I seem to recall your aversion to lies. Or has that changed?"

Ignoring the question, she said, "What, exactly, is it that you think we're going to find?"

"Not sure yet."

"Ah. This is a we'll-know-it-when-we-see-it mission."

"Yes. Now zip it and help."

"Sir, yes, sir."

The response was unexpected—where was her anger?—and he barely stifled his laughter. There'd never be a dull moment with this girl, that was for sure.

She worked alongside him for ten . . . twenty minutes without a word, but his awareness of her never dissipated. There was something about the grace of her movements that continually drew his eye.

Why did she have to be Michael's daughter?

"Just say whatever's on your mind," she finally growled, her good humor gone. "I don't like the way you're watching me."

Noticed, had she? "And how am I watching you?"

"As if you'd like to eat me."

I would. I so would. Breakfast, lunch, and dinner. Then again for dessert. "Why don't you do us both a solid and get over yourself, butter buns." The best defense was a good offense and all that jazz.

"Butter buns? That's the worst of the lot!" She threw a piece of wood at his head.

He stopped it midway with only a slight thread of power, letting it hover a moment before he sent it flying to the side. Of course, she used his distraction against him and threw another. This one pelted him in the chest, nearly deflating his lungs.

"Do that again," he growled. "I dare you."

"Dare accepted." She did it again.

Like the first time, he stopped it and sent it flying. "I'm warning you, Evie."

"Oh, yeah? What are you going to do to me, huh?"

She was panting, he realized, and so was he. They were staring at each other, just as they'd done after the explosion, looking for an outlet for their anger . . . and awareness of each other. Only, this time nothing had happened to provoke such a response. If they kissed, they would only have themselves to blame.

He almost didn't care. His mouth watered for her. His hands ached for her.

"Never mind." Her cheeks flushed as she stomped away from him. He thought he heard her mutter the word *lobotomy*. "We're here for a reason. Let's concentrate."

How aggravating that Evie Black had become the voice of reason in their relationship.

"Miracle of miracles, you're right." He returned his attention to the pile of ash, and his gaze snagged on a small cigarette lighter. The metal had melted, but after a quick cleanup the unique logo became visible. A naked blonde straddled a male that was half white knight, half black unicorn.

The logo represented the Lucky Horn. A strip club he may or may not have visited . . . countless times.

Was it Michael's lighter? Or could it belong to Fry Guy?

"Ever seen this before?" he asked, holding it up for Evie's inspection.

She looked it over, shook her head. "No. And to my knowledge, Michael has never visited the Lucky Horn."

How'd she know the logo?

"Like he'd really tell you if he had," Blue quipped.

"Like he wouldn't. He doesn't think of me as a daughter but as an agent. Well, as a doctor now."

Threads of deep inner pain stroked over him, cold and stinging. They'd come from her, he realized. When would he stop being astonished by that? "What are you talking about? Of course he thinks of you as a daughter. He's always spoiled you rotten, letting you get away with crap he would have killed other agents for." And it had always bothered Blue, though he couldn't seem to work up any kind of indignation at that particular moment.

Her expression turned pensive as she mulled over his words. A few seconds later she said, "Why did he leave me in Westminster with Mum, then? Why did he visit me so rarely?"

She thought . . . what? That Michael had never really loved her? Ouch.

But she couldn't be more wrong. Hurt was coloring all of her memories.

He had his own experience with that. He couldn't remember his biological parents, only his three older brothers and two older sisters. They'd lived on the streets, his brothers stealing every scrap of food and clothing, and his sisters . . . he didn't want to think about what they'd done. But then they all got sick, dying one by one, until, at the age of four, Blue was on his own. To survive, he ate out of trash cans.

A sweet old homeless man noticed him and tried to take care of him for a while. But it wasn't long before Blue's pretty face drew the notice of the wrong kind of people. The homeless man was stabbed and killed, and Blue shoved into a car.

That's when power first bonded with him and activated.

Frantic, scared, he somehow caused the car to levitate and crash into a building. And when the survivors tried to drag him out, he caused *them* to levitate and crash into the building. Alone once again, he hid in the shadows.

Michael found him two days later.

After feeding him, cleaning him, and clothing him, Michael ensured that Blue was given to a good home. One with lots of children, so that he would have brothers and sisters again.

At first, the parents included him in the family meals. He protested, wanting to be alone with his grief, and they finally stopped asking, allowing him to remain in his room. It was then that Blue decided they didn't really like him, and that they were glad to be rid of him.

After that, every interaction was strained.

Looking back, without the pain of loss, he could see the couple had only been trying to help, doing everything possible to let him heal.

"Why don't you ask Michael why he did what he did the next time you see him?" Blue said, using his gentlest tone. "The answer might surprise you."

Dark eyes probed him, as if searching for answers he couldn't give her. She offered him a small, sweet smile. "I will. Thank you."

"Welcome." He got back to business before he did something stupid, like pull her into his arms. "We need to find out everything we can about the Lucky Horn. If the lighter belongs to Fry Guy instead of Michael, we might be able to ID him."

"I'm assuming Fry Guy is the man who tried to torch you."

"Yes. If we can ID him, we can link him to friends. Friends who might know where Michael, John, and Solo are."

She heaved a sigh of dread. "I have a feeling that includes a personal field trip."

Blue nodded, astounded by the amount of dread building inside *him*. For once, he had no desire to be pawed by naked strippers. He just wanted—

Nothing.

"Let's go," he snapped.

Five hours later, Evie invaded the Lucky Horn, claiming a table just to the side of the stage.

Blue was the club's newest stripper.

They'd found out the place was hiring, and he insisted she apply.

"Screw that," she'd said. "*You* want someone on the inside. Therefore, *you* are responsible. I shake tail for no one. Besides, one of us has to pry information out of the patrons, and the more people look at your face, the more likely they are to recognize you. And let's be honest, up on the stage, no one is going to be looking any higher than your groin."

He'd only huffed and puffed for a few minutes. "Someone is trying to either abduct you or kill you. Meaning you need a disguise. What better disguise than stripper?"

Nice try. "Give me one hour and I'll show you a better disguise."

And she did!

Right now, her hair was so blond it was almost white, and streaked with pink. Her eyes were bright blue and her chest hugely inflated by a silicone-infused bra.

Blue had taken one look at her and shaken his head in disapproval. Disapproval she didn't understand. No one would recognize her *and* she fit his preferred type of female.

But on top of the disapproval, he displayed zero

hints of arousal. And the lack, well, it disappointed her.

Lo. Bot. Omy.

Even with his scar and piercings, Blue was hired at first sight. No one had a body quite like his. Cut from granite. No one could move quite like he did. Every action was a sensuous mating call.

Now, hoping she appeared awed by her surroundings, she scanned the club. Dark walls, dark carpet. Dim lighting, except onstage. At both sides of that stage, women dangled from wires, their naked bodies sparkling as they twisted and turned into different sexual positions. In the center, glitter rained from the ceiling, sticking to the exposed skin of the half-naked bumping, grinding brunette currently teasing the audience with the removal of her G-string.

One of the patrons shoved a bill in her box—and, no, *box* wasn't a euphemism. Men weren't allowed to touch the goods until they'd paid, stuffing their money inside an actual box at the edge of the stage. The bills disengaged the shock line, allowing the girl to stroll up to the patron and settle a high-heeled boot on his shoulder, giving him the perfect money shot.

A topless waitress arrived and asked for Evie's drink order. "Beer in a bottle. Don't pop the cap." There was no reason to think anyone would try and poison her, but she wasn't taking any chances.

The brunette finished her show, and a husky voice spilled from the intercom. "And now, ladies and gentlemen, we are proud to introduce the newest addition to the Lucky Horn family. Give it up for the hard and horny . . . Jack Hammer!"

This was it! Unable to contain her excitement, Evie clapped her hands and bounced in her seat. Sometimes agenting had its perks.

The curtain at the back of the stage parted and out strode Blue, wearing nothing but a scowl and a pair of black leather underpants.

Blimey. She lost her breath. She'd expected to be amused by his situation, but she was inexplicably aroused. He had muscle stacked upon muscle. His skin was pale, like all Arcadians', and yet, there was a shimmery golden undertone, as if he'd showered in fallen angel dust. He looked wild. Dangerous.

And, okay, quite livid.

The waitress arrived with the beer, and Evie waved her away. "You're blocking my view."

As always, power radiated from him. Did anyone else feel it?

He stood still as a statue as the music played. Someone booed. Someone else threw a chip at him. *Gonna blow his cover.*

"Let's see your best moves, Mr. Hammer!" Evie put her fingers in her mouth and whistled. "Yeah, baby. Yeah! Show Momma what the good Lord gave you!"

Somehow he found her in the dark and glared. Then, from one moment to the next, the tone of the glare changed. From anger to anticipation.

Uh-oh. What just happened?

He sauntered in her direction, and her hands began to sweat. At the edge of the stage, he tugged a bill from the waist of the underpants—*if some skank backstage put it there, I'm going to . . . nothing*—and stuffed it in the hot box, lowering the shield.

He hopped off the stage. The crowd watched, awed.

Surely he wouldn't close the distance between them.

He did.

Leaning into her, he braced his hands on the arms of her chair. "How about a lap dance, sugar plum?"

Bloody hell. Shivers cascaded down her spine.

"Your nipples just beaded for me. I'll take that as a yes."

No way he could tell. Her bra was far too thick.

"I can," he said, as though reading her thoughts. "I can *feel* your reaction."

Her eyes widened, and her response died as his hands encircled her waist. He lifted her to the tabletop, better aligning their bodies. He forced her legs to part and the apex of her thighs to cradle his—

Oh, bless me. His massive erection.

Then he danced. Slow and steady, grinding against her sweet spot. Ratcheting her desire to an earth-shattering level. A place where fires raged. She couldn't stop her hands. They roamed over his chest, glided over the scar on his face, tangled in his hair.

If the patrons cheered or booed, she didn't know it. She was utterly focused on the man in front of her, hyperaware of his every move. Of his power, stroking her with the mastery of a thousand hands. Of his scent in her nose, champagne and strawberries. Of his gaze, boring deep into hers—perhaps seeing into her soul. Of his erection, pressing where she needed him most, retreating, pressing again, and—*oh, keep going, please.* A moan escaped her. The pleasure . . . too much . . . not enough . . . *Give me more. Give me everything.* Eden was right. The day had come. Evie wanted some guy to give it to her good and hard.

Press, retreat. Press, retreat. Liquid heat pooled between her legs, the crease in her jeans just making everything worse. Press, retreat. Or better. Press, retreat. No, definitely worse.

Her head swam with the force of her arousal. A dangerous pressure built inside her, coiling, readying. If he kept going, he was going to make her come. Right there. In front of everyone.

Dismayed by the thought, she dug her nails into his bare chest. Felt the heat of his skin, and gave another moan.

"Don't," she whispered, panicked. "Please."

Just like that, he stopped.

He was panting, his lips thinned and pulled taut against his perfect teeth.

He turned away from her and returned to the stage, quickly disappearing behind the curtain.

This is being more careful around him? her good sense screamed. *Really? Stop threatening that lobotomy and actually do it!*

Evie tore the cap from the beer and drained the contents. Then she signaled for another and drained it, too.

Once her body had calmed, she pretended to have a nice buzz going and tripped her way to a table of older gents who looked to be regulars, very familiar with the lay of the land. Over the next hour they hit on her and teased her about the we-swear-you-were-having-sex dance Jack Hammer had done with her. Trying not to blush like a stupid schoolgirl, she bought them several lap dances—not from Blue, because he was still backstage, probably searching the offices and cursing Evie's very existence—and they finally stopped hitting on her, instead treating her like one of the guys. That's when she paid for a round of drinks for everyone in the club.

Eventually, all of the patrons came over to thank her and ended up staying to talk. She learned far more than she'd hoped.

Mr. Gregory Star and his entourage visited the club at least twice a month, and they always migrated to the back to speak with Timothy Mercer, who had worked at the Lucky Horn for three years. Two weeks ago, Timothy just up and vanished. No one had seen or heard from him since, or had any idea what might have happened to him.

Star, thrown into the mix once again. No question, the man was involved in her father's disappearance. It was just as certain that Timothy was the man who'd set Blue on fire.

Eager to verify this news with hard evidence, Evie excused herself under the guise of having to pee and stumbled away as though snockered, heading toward the backstage entrance. The moment she cleared the corner, out of everyone's view, she dug a shielder out of her purse and threw it behind her, the tiny black device creating an invisible wall upon landing. Until she disabled it, only she and Blue would be able to bypass it, since they were the only ones with a scrambler on their phones, an app designed to disrupt the shielder's signal.

She tripped her way toward the armed guard at the end of the hallway.

Frowning, he gripped the handle of his gun. "I suggest you turn around, ma'am. No one's allowed in this section of the building."

Ma'am? Did she really look like a ma'am?

Ma'ams had at least sixteen robo-cats, wore muumuus, and never took the rollers out of their hair.

Did he *want* to die?

She stopped in front of him, a familiar surge of excitement hitting her. *Don't you dare get used to this kind of work.* It was a onetime gig. As soon as her father and his boys were found, as soon as Star was taken down, she was going back to her nice, normal life.

But honestly, the last time she'd experienced anything this high octane, she'd been on her last mission, and Claire had—

She locked those thoughts down.

"Is this not the bathroom?" she asked, making sure to slur her words.

"Turn. Around. Now. You won't like what happens if you don't."

"Okay, okay, you don't have to be so rude about it," she grumbled—then rammed her knee into his groin.

With a strangled bellow he hunched over, struggling to breathe, and she lined up at his side to slam the back of her elbow into his mastoid process. His body went limp as his brain tissue rapidly compressed, and he collapsed onto the carpet, well and truly out for the count.

"Sorry, bloke, but you picked the wrong side. And you called me ma'am!"

She peeked through a crack in the door. Half-clad dancers sat in front of a row of vanity mirrors, checking their hair and makeup. No one paid a bit of attention to the entrance as she slipped inside the employees-only area.

To her right was a closed door with the name Timothy Mercer in the center. Brilliant. Evie strode forward and twisted the lock. It held. After a quick glance behind her—still good—she pulled the necessary tools from her purse and got to work.

"Hey, what are you doing?" a female snapped from behind her. "You're not supposed to be back here."

Evie pasted a bright smile on her face before turning and facing the brunette who'd been Blue's opening act. "Hi. I'm Chlamydia Jones, the new stripper. Hired only a few hours ago." *Too chirpy, Black. Dial it down a notch.* "I was told to speak with Mr. Mercer."

Green eyes narrowed with suspicion. "Mr. Mercer isn't in."

"Dang. That sucks." *I tried to do this the nice way.* Evie had worn three rings, just in case. In the center of each, under a jewel, was a needle she'd loaded with poison of her own creation; they'd once been trademarks of her mission work. She thumbed the diamond from Wrath, her most-used toxin, and clasped the girl's hands. "Can you please—"

"Ow," Brunette said, just before yanking free to clutch her stomach.

"Are you all right?" Evie asked, faking concern.

The girl shook her head. As her skin turned a putrid shade of green, she ran as fast as her feet would carry her to the nearest receptacle, where she vomited the entire contents of her stomach . . . and maybe even the stomach itself.

Behind Evie, the door swung open, and a hard hand seized her arm, wrenching her backward. The moment she was inside the office, the door closed, sealing her inside. With Blue.

She recognized the hum of his power.

Slowly she pivoted. He wore a T-shirt and jeans, all hints of Mr. Hammer eradicated, and yet, as soon as their eyes met, there was a suspended moment where all she could remember was the feel of his erection rubbing between her legs, and the sharp, desperate need of her body.

All she could think was *More*.

"Stop staring and tell me what you're doing back here," he demanded.

O-kay. So he didn't feel or think the same. Flushing, she said, "I came to give you a review. After a shaky start, you—"

"We will *never* speak of this again. Do you hear me?"

Can't laugh. "Consider this blackmail material." She told him what she'd learned.

"Confirmation that Star is involved." He nodded. "We'll have to search his house. Among other things."

Missionspeak. Good. The best way to get back on track. "Found anything in here?"

"Not yet." He stomped to the desk and tapped away at the computer keyboard. "I'm loading the club's security feed for the past three weeks onto a flash drive and erasing today's activities."

Thank God. Replaying Jack Hammer's debut—and her reaction to it—would have been humiliating.

"All right. Done," he said, removing the flash drive.

"So we're ready to leave the club?"

"Yes. And if you can get me out without letting anyone grope me, I'll admit you're the better agent."

She snorted—then inwardly cursed. Did the man have to be so witty *and* likable? "Deal."

Ten

decorative divider

*E*VIE KEPT SURPRISING HIM.

At the club, she'd handled the patrons and employees with equal skill. Hell, she'd even handled Blue.

He'd lost himself in the pleasure of grinding on her, forgetting their goal, their audience, until she reminded him.

She'd begged so prettily.

Begging. Completely unlike her. It had startled him back to his senses.

Mentally and physically, he couldn't seem to control his reactions to her.

Can't worry about that now.

They'd had to ditch her car. Whoever had ordered the earlier chase—hit?—was still out there, and Evie was now . . . no longer Evie. She was Miss Blond Boobies, and he freaking hated it. When he wasn't grinding on her, of course. He much preferred her luscious dark hair and slender curves.

Concentrate. Going back to her place would have been stupid, giving away their identities, no matter what they looked like, so he'd offered no protest when she stole a truck and drove him to a safe house she swore no one knew about.

And why would he protest? Watching Evie steal a car was like watching sexy female auto-mechanic porn on set. He was still hard.

You've been hard for two days.

"You quit the agency. Why did you keep a safe house?" he asked as he cased the place. It was small but virtually undetectable, hidden underneath a middle-class neighborhood where all of the homes above it were the same shape and color. There was only one entrance, and that was concealed in a darkened alcove next to the district enzyme tower half a mile away.

Evie had reinforced the walls with alien metal that could withstand a nuclear attack, and hung countless monitors, all watching the surrounding area from different angles. The only furniture was a bed, a chair, and a desk cluttered with a computer, papers, and mechanical parts and equipment he didn't recognize.

"I like to be prepared," she said with a shrug.

He was the same. He collected safe houses the way other men collected sexual mementos, ensuring he had someplace to go in every corner of the world. Maybe one day he'd give Evie a tour and impress the hell out of her.

He stiffened. Give her a tour? Impress her?

Seriously? Michael, John, and Solo weren't even aware of half of his holdings, and he wanted to share with *her*?

Scowling, Blue settled at the desk and booted up the computer. Opening the contents of the flash drive would take a while.

"I'm going to make a sandwich," Evie said, pressing a few buttons on a small black remote. In front of her, one section of the wall opened, revealing a fully stocked fridge. "You want one?"

He masked his bafflement with a muffled "That'd be great, thanks."

"Brilliant. I'll leave out the bread and peanut butter so you can make yourself one."

Now, that was more like the Evie he knew and . . . liked. He rubbed two fingers over his mouth to hide a smile. "Have you always been such a ballbuster, baby bear?"

She shook her fist in his direction. "Stop calling me by those ludicrous names. And, yeah, I guess I have been. But then, I've had to be." She dug a knife from a drawer hidden in the island. "Otherwise Mum would have broken me."

She had never willingly offered information about her past, and he found himself leaning toward her, as eager to hear more as he usually was to make a kill. "Tell me about her."

As she put two sandwiches together, she said, "She could have been a general in the army. Everything had to be a certain way. Her way. And then it had to meet her exacting standards. Meaning nothing was ever good enough."

Little Evie, under a military-like regime. He frowned, not liking the image. Had she ever gotten to act her age and play?

"I'm not sure what Michael ever saw in her, to be honest."

Adorable, the way she added an *-er* to the word *saw*. "Does she look like you?"

"Yes. I've been called her carbon copy, actually."

Well, there you go. Michael hadn't been able to help himself. "No good times?"

"Not until Claire came along."

Happiness coasted over him, followed by sorrow. Both emotions sprang from her. Clearly Claire's death destroyed her, and she was still dealing with the pain.

Breaking my heart. "What's your favorite memory of your sister?"

She thought for a moment, then smiled. "Claire made me watch romantic comedies, romantic tragedies, romantic . . . everything," Evie said, and her smile faded. "I used to tease her about the horrors of heartfelt emotion, only I called it heartfelt crap, and she used to say I was fooling no one, that I already had that crap in my blood, and then we'd laugh about the word 'crap.'"

Blue suddenly wished he'd never allowed dislike of Evie to keep him away four years ago. It would have been fun to watch her and Claire together. The fire-breathing dragon and the shy princess somehow finding a way to happily coexist.

"I had siblings, too," he admitted. "I was only four years old when they died, but they'll always have a place in my heart." He remembered how, before his brothers and sisters died, each placed a hand on his chest. Warmth had then spread throughout his entire body.

He hadn't understood at the time, but Cade, Caell, Cameron, Caymile, and Candice had bequeathed their powers to him. They were the reason he survived the sickness they did not. They were the reason he was as strong as he was.

And he would never get the chance to thank them.

For a moment Evie was still and quiet. Then she walked over and, expression carefully blank, handed him a sandwich. "Here." She sat at the edge of the desk, not caring when she pushed supplies to the floor.

They ate in silence, and for that he was grateful. The more she spoke, the more he liked her.

And he shouldn't like her while she was nearby . . . affecting him. Bad things happened. Proof: already he was tense and aching. Ready for sex. Hard, pounding sex. Dirty sex. The kind neither one of them would ever be able to forget.

What did she prefer? To be touched gently? Or firmly?

Did she like to be licked? Or bit? Or both?

How did she feel about oral?

He wanted her mouth on his shaft, her dark hair spilling over his thighs.

The power began to writhe inside him, and both the chair and desk wobbled before lifting into the air. Her eyes—those dark, rich eyes—widened. She'd removed the contacts, and he wanted to howl with gratitude.

"Blue?"

He didn't care that her hair was currently blond and not his preference for her. He could still wrap the strands around his hand and fist. He could guide her into the rhythm he wanted her to set. Afterward he could strip her and return the favor.

He flattened his hands on her thighs. Big hands.

Delicate thighs. She sucked in a breath . . . but didn't push him away.

"Push me away," he said. The heat of her skin was so intense, he could feel the burn of her through her jeans.

"Blue, I—"

A muffled buzz stopped her.

Frowning, she pulled her cell from the purse still draped across her middle and read the screen. Shock curled from her, slithering around him and tightening like a noose.

"What's wrong?" His desire instantly cooled. The desk and chair settled on the floor.

Her gaze met his. "I think . . . I think my father just texted me."

U KNOW WHERE SUNBEAM

That was the extent of the coded text, and yet the shock lifted and Evie knew. Her father was responsible.

Sunbeam was his nickname for her. And she did indeed know where. About a mile out from Lake Michigan. Michael had planned for something like this—one of them being chased, needing a secluded place to stay—and had told her where to go if ever he contacted her.

She and Blue left the safe house and stole another car. They drove to the dock, doubling back a few times to make sure they weren't being followed. Then, with the rerouting of a few wires, the "spare parts" her father kept in multiple slips drew together like magnets and metal to create a small boat.

After pulling on protective bodysuits, she and Blue

climbed inside the craft. This was going to be fun. Not. The bacteria in the lake constantly mutated. With Blue's Arcadian blood, he was probably resistant. But even though her immunizations were up to date, she could sicken.

Finally, they were speeding along.

"Don't get your hopes up." Blue had to yell to be heard over the roar of the engine. "This could be a trap."

"It's not," she yelled back. Strands of hair slapped at her cheeks and filled her mouth as she valiantly tried to grab them and hold them at her nape.

He cast her a grim look. And it wasn't fair. The sun was in the process of setting, providing a majestic pink and purple backdrop, making him more beautiful than ever. "I hope you're right."

She drew in a breath and promptly coughed. The air was thick with the scents of rot and mold.

Calming, she realized Blue watched her with concern. She had to look away.

When was her desire for him going to fade?

They'd almost kissed. Again. She'd known it was about to happen, and she hadn't planned to stop it. Had actually planned to *encourage* it.

What was wrong with her?

Maybe . . . she should just give in, she thought now. *After* he broke things off with Pagan. The poor dear. No matter what Blue said, Evie played a part in the demise of his relationship with the girl, and she felt terrible about it. Terrible and guilty and ashamed.

I need to ask for her forgiveness. But that wasn't going to make a difference, was it. If anyone ever kissed Evie's man, "anyone" would die. No questions asked. No apology accepted.

You don't have a man all your own. You've never *had a man all your own.*

One day she would. And when that day came, she wouldn't share.

So . . . what should she do about Blue?

First up, she had to rid her body of its craving for him. Until she did, she wouldn't be interested in anyone else—and now that her hormones were awake, she wanted to be with someone, she realized. Wanted to have a real relationship. With a doctor at the hospital, maybe.

Second, she had to—

Go back to step one.

Oi. The only way to rid her body of its craving was to give it what it wanted. Blue. After she had been sated, she could forge ahead with new plans for her future. No harm, no foul.

"Nearing a dock," Blue said, drawing her from her musings.

She raised the night-vision binoculars and scrutinized the area. There were no other boats stationed at the small, floating post. No bodies hiding behind the poisonous trees and plants thriving in the dry, acidic atmosphere. About fifty yards back was a seemingly dilapidated shack with no lights glowing from the inside to indicate someone lived there.

"We're good," she said.

Trusting her, Blue parked and tied the boat to the dock. When she tried to step up and out, he stopped her by clapping a hard hand on her upper arm. Then he applied pressure, urging her to lie down.

"Now is not the time to make out," she said, hating how breathless she sounded. Especially since it wasn't the first time.

He glared at her. "Sex is not always on my mind, you know."

"You're right, I'm—"

"At least, it didn't used to be," he muttered, his anger draining. "Now, stay down and you won't be hurt." Done with the conversation, he straightened and closed his eyes, forcibly breathing in . . . and out . . . until his usual hum of power became a screech.

She cringed against the violence of it, and her pain receptors actually vibrated. What was happening? How was he—

A glowing blue ring shot from around his waist, widening as it moved, soon sweeping across the entire expanse of land. But as suddenly as it started, it stopped. Everything stilled, quieted.

He'd once told her he had countless abilities. She hadn't taken him literally, but she probably should have.

"What did you do?" she asked.

He smiled down at her. "If anyone was hiding nearby, they are now paralyzed, and will remain so for the next few hours."

"What about Michael? If he's in that house—"

"He could have been in the way of the blast, yes, and if so, he will be paralyzed. It's a small price to pay for our protection," he said, helping her to her feet. "He'll understand and agree that I made the right call. Eventually."

Okay. "I can live with that."

His smile returned, widened . . . enchanted her. But when her gaze lowered to his mouth—that lush red mouth any woman would probably kill to have all over her—his amusement died a quick death. He angled his body toward hers until their chests were almost brushing with every breath they took . . . breath that was suddenly coming faster.

Tension sizzled between them, hot and hungry.

Not here. Not now.

But soon.

"You are a nifty little toy to carry around, you know that?" she said with only the slightest tremor.

He held on to her hand, refusing to let go. "Interesting choice of words. Toy? You thinking about playing with me, bunny boo?"

Gah! Stupid names. There was no way to answer his question—and save her pride—without lying. But she'd told him she would never lie to him, and she'd meant it. Not counting the few times she had, in fact, lied to him.

"Enough." She jerked free and shouldered him out of the way. As she stepped onto the dock, his palms flattened on her arse and gave a little push. She fought a grin as she whirled on him. "You wanting to lose a hand, Mr. Hammer?"

"Please. Like you're really going to do anything. We both know you like what I do with my hands." He eased up beside her, tall and strong and everything she longed to devour.

Again she had to turn away, because again she had no response.

They stripped out of their bodysuits, then maintained the same pace as they stalked to the door of the shack. Blue kept a pyre-gun trained dead ahead. Something was odd—she didn't feel the hum of his power, she realized.

"What happens after you expend so much energy?" she asked softly.

"I have to recharge."

"So you are without Arcadian abilities?"

"For a few hours, yes."

"I'll just have to guard you, then." She dug inside the purse draped across her middle and removed a tube of lipstick.

"And you're going to do that by freshening up your makeup?" he asked. "Wow. I've never felt safer."

She twisted the tube until it morphed into a pair of wire cutters. "How about I freshen *your* makeup with these, huh?"

"What else do you have in there?" he asked, trying to grab the bag.

She slapped his hand away, saying, "Pray you never find out." An ID panel was hidden behind a piece of rotted wood. She removed the lid and scanner to fiddle with the complicated interior. "Only one person has entered in the past three days. No one for weeks before that."

"And you know that how?"

"I read the data entries. And now I'm programming myself into the system."

"If this is Michael's place, shouldn't you already be programmed in?"

"Like he'd really make it that easy." The front door opened with a click and a whoosh.

"Easy enough," Blue muttered.

"For me, yes. You? Not so much."

"Are you trying to say you're smarter than me?"

"Trying? Ha."

"Well, I'm stronger, so suck it." Suddenly he was all business, pushing his way inside.

Evie followed close on his heels, watching as he scanned and aimed, scanned and aimed.

"Stay here," he commanded, disappearing around the corner.

"You might want to come back," she called. "There are—"

"Ow!"

"—traps," she finished with a flinch.

He stomped back into the foyer, a frown tightening the scar running through his lip. A scar that was thinner than it had been a few hours ago. Was it not from makeup? Had he actually cut himself?

For some reason the thought of him bleeding and in pain bothered her. *Need to kiss it and make it better.*

He held up his leg, revealing the antique metal claw now biting into his ankle. "What are we? Barbarians? This is how we do things now?"

"Apparently. Let's get downstairs and I'll patch you up," she said, doing her best to hide her amusement. Bother her, yes—but come on, this crap was funny.

She must have failed in her endeavor because he said, "Is this a joke to you, chuckles?"

"Well, yeah. Only a moron falls for the old 'Step here' trick."

"Zip it. I don't need any patching. I'm already healing." He removed the claw and stalked toward her—or, rather, limped toward her.

Laughing, she crouched down and rewired a second ID box. A crack opened in the concrete, just wide enough to allow a body, and revealed a staircase.

When she looked up, she realized Blue had stopped his approach midway to stare at her with a bemused expression.

"What?" she asked.

"You laughed."

"I know."

"I mean, you really laughed."

"Uh, yeah, I know." His point? "So I ask again: What?"

"Nothing," he muttered, finally looking away.

Not nothing, but she wasn't going to press. She descended the stairs, following a trail of golden light. At the bottom she saw plush carpets and soft couches that led to a chef's dream kitchen. Around the corner from the stainless steel fridge was an office with an entire wall of computer screens.

"Evangeline Black. About time you showed up," a voice said.

Evie's heart raced with joy as she plowed toward her father, who clearly hadn't been in the path of Blue's power. He stood in the doorway of the only bedroom.

He sported multiple bruises and his shoulders were stooped with fatigue, but he was alive and well, and that was all that mattered.

Rather than hug him, as she wanted, and potentially bruise him further, she grabbed hold of his hand and held it close to her heart. Warm tears trickled down her cheeks. "I am so angry at you right now, I could shove a fishing rod down your throat and hook your organs one by one. Except for your intestines. That would just be gross."

He gave her a wry smile. "I love you, too, sunbeam."

He'd said those same words many times before, but she'd never really believed him. This time she wasn't looking at him through a veil of hurt feelings. She was too relieved to see him. She actually *saw* the affection in his eyes.

I'm such a fool for ever doubting him.

"Where have you been?" she demanded. "Why did you stay in hiding so long? Do you know where John and Solo are?"

A muscle ticked in his jaw, a sign of irritation she knew wasn't directed at her but at their circumstances. "One question at a time." His gaze strayed to Blue. "Son."

Though his lips thinned, Blue nodded in greeting. What was up with that?

"I'll want a full report on how the two of you came to be together," Michael said.

"Sure, sure," she said before the agent could respond.

Michael led her to the couch and sat down, urging her to take the spot beside him. "I suspected there was a traitor in my midst, and I was right. I stayed away, letting the world think I was dead, because I didn't want you used to hurt me. But, of course, an attempt was made."

"The chase this afternoon," Blue said, claiming the chair across from them.

Evie avoided looking at him. At the moment she wasn't sure she could guard her expression. She was just too raw, too overcome. And she didn't want her dad to know she'd . . . softened toward the agent. He'd flip.

Women fall for Corbin Blue every day, he'd once said, after she'd ranted and raved for an hour over Blue's treatment of her. *Tell me you're too smart to be one of them.*

Duh. I totally am. But I have to confess, I'm a little surprised by your warning. You adore the man.

I do. He's like a son to me, and I love him, faults and all. I just don't want those faults anywhere near my daughter.

"Yes," Michael said now. "Speaking of, I've been monitoring AIR feed, and they have already spoken to witnesses and watched traffic cams, so they know you were involved, sunbeam. You'll soon be contacted and questioned."

Another round with Agent Gutierrez, she thought with a sigh.

"About Solo and John," Michael said to Blue. "I have searched and searched, but found nothing. I'm sorry. I thought I had a solid lead on Solo, and flew to his home, but there was a woman claiming to be his wife—"

"Wife?" Blue burst out.

Michael dug a phone from his pocket and tossed it. "I have pictures."

Several minutes passed while Blue studied the images. When he finished, he handed the phone to Evie. She gave him a grateful half smile before flipping through the photos. In them, a sweet-looking blonde was pulling weeds in a garden . . . feeding horses . . . pigs . . . goats. She appeared harmless, but then, appearances never meant jack.

The woman who'd sliced and diced Claire had—

Shut that crap down.

"Her name is Vika," Michael said, "and she told me Solo survived the explosion, that he was sold to her father's circus and later returned to his home planet, with no way back."

True? Or a great cover story for his murder?

Blue massaged the back of his neck. "So, Solo was the one sold?"

Michael's brow furrowed with confusion. "What do you mean?"

"I overheard a conversation between two men at the bomb site. They planned to sell one of us, and I assumed it was John. They planned to keep one of us, and I assumed it was Solo. They also planned to burn one of us. And since a guy doused me with accelerant, I'm clearly Mr. Battered and Deep Fried. So, if Solo was sold to the circus, that means . . ."

"John was kept, not sold," Evie said. As a sex slave? The same fate he probably would have endured anyway. *Oh, John. Don't give up hope. We're coming for you.* "But where?"

Blue gripped the arms of the chair in an obvious bid to control his rising anger. "I will find him. Find them both."

"We'll go to Solo's farm," she suggested, "and chat up the girl. Maybe she knows more than she told Michael, maybe she doesn't. I was always good at interrogation." If *good* was the new word for *mediocre*. For some reason, people did not respond well to her. No matter how much force she used. "I'll take a crack at her."

He rested his elbows on his knees and dipped his head. She knew he was hurting deep, deep inside and knew he'd hoped to learn John and Solo were okay. She wanted to go to him and put her arms around him, to assure him everything would be all right.

The desire confused her. Yearning for his kisses she understood. Offering comfort? Not so much.

"I would stake my life on the fact that Vika was not involved," Michael said.

"Would you stake John's?" Evie asked.

A confident nod. "Trust me, this is all Gregory Star's doing."

Blue stiffened. "There's no room for error in this. Doesn't it strike you as odd that there's so much evidence pointing to him, yet he's been so careful to hide his tracks in the past?" He paused to ponder, as if the thoughts were only now coming to him. "This could be a setup, or a misdirection. We—"

"No setup, no misdirection. I saw him there, at the house," Michael said. "I woke up, and saw all three of you on the ground, motionless. I fought my way free of the debris and stumbled toward you. Then I heard voices and wasn't sure if they belonged to friend or foe. I hid under the rubble, intending to find out and strike if necessary—I still had a gun on me—and got a look at Star and another male, but passed out before I could do anything about it."

A gleam of determination and hate darkened Blue's eyes. "Okay, then."

Definite target in sight now.

"He's gotten cocky, I guess," Michael said. "He messed up. It happens."

Yes, it did.

"What was his motive?" Blue asked.

"That," Michael replied, "I'm not sure about."

"Why don't we snatch Mr. Star, torture him for answers, and then kill him?" Evie suggested.

"Snatching him will be a problem," Michael said. "He's too well guarded. And if we failed and he retaliated . . . No, we'll have better luck with stealth."

She could do stealth. "He has two kids. Tyson and Tiffany. We can abduct one or both and offer a trade." That was stealth, right?

Michael shook his head. "I've done business with him. He isn't the type to cave to demands, even to save the lives of his children. He's the kind to hurt John to prove a point."

Blue lifted his head, his determination undaunted. "Do you have eyes and ears on him?"

"Unfortunately, no," Michael said with a sigh. "That's why I need you to go public, Blue. I have a plan."

"Wait," Evie said.

Michael held up one hand for silence. "I don't think Star knows you work for me, Blue," he continued. "I've taken down several of his guards in the past few days, and your name has never been mentioned. If I'm wrong, and he does, you'll find out pretty quick."

Meaning, he would be bait. "Are you sure that's the wisest course of action?"

"Yes," Blue said. "And I'm fine with that."

"Well, I don't agree," she replied.

He shrugged his wide shoulders. "I'm still going to do it."

"Michael," she said.

"Danger is part of the business," her father said. Supporting his boy. As always. Gaze on Blue, he added, "As soon as the world knows you're in town, arrange an accidental meeting with the daughter. Star no longer goes out in public. He stays in his country estate, always surrounded by armed men, both human and otherworlder. Tiffany might be your ticket to a face-to-face with Daddy dearest."

Blue nodded. "Consider it done."

"Before we go that route," Evie said, unsure why her body was now so tense, "we should break into that country estate and have a look around, plant a few bugs. We can get in and out without anyone realizing. B and E isn't the same as trying to haul a body out, yeah."

Her father met her stare, nodded. "All right. Break in. Snatch Star if you've got a green light. But don't you dare get caught. Afterward, if Star isn't in custody, you'll move forward with my plan."

A concession. She took it gratefully. "What about you?"

"I can't go public yet. I'm not strong enough to defend myself from a full-on attack."

"We can protect—"

"No," he said, cutting her off. "I have something else in mind. I want you to take over Black Industries, sunbeam. That way you can set up a preseason exhibition game between the Invaders and Strikers to honor my precious memory. And *that way* you have a legitimate reason to contact Tyson Star to rent out the roof of the Star Light Hotel for a victory celebration."

"I don't know about that," Blue spoke up. "I'll have the Star kids covered with Tiffany."

The competitive spirit she'd once hated peeked from the shadows, and Evie smirked at him. "Two is better than one."

"No," Blue said again, with more force this time.

"Yee-ess," she replied in a singsong.

Michael looked from one to the other and frowned. "It's your turn now. How did you two hook up?"

Hook up. A poor choice of words. Her cheeks flamed.

Blue gave nothing away. "After the explosion, Evie was the only person I could trust," he said, his tone just as bland. "I snuck into her house and she patched me up. It was as simple as that."

Smiling, Michael reached out to ruffle her hair, just as she'd always wanted him to do to her when she was a child. "Thank you for taking care of my boy."

His boy.

And there was the jealousy she used to feel, a companion to the competitiveness; she tamped down both. Michael loved his "boys," yes, but that didn't preclude his loving Evie, too.

One day she would gather the courage to ask him why he'd left her in England.

Although . . . if he'd taken her away from Claire, she would have hated him. So maybe he'd actually done her a service.

"Now, what are we going to do about taking care of my girl?" Michael said. "The car chase has me spooked."

"I've already had to move in," Blue said. "We planned to keep it secret anyway, so my coming back to life and going after Tiffany won't change anything. No one will know I'm there, and yet I'll still be able to protect her. It's a win-win."

Evie shook her head. "I was okay with a move-in when you were dead to the world, but not now. People will be watching you. Sneaking over will be difficult. You *will* be caught. So, no. You won't be staying. You'll be moving out. I won't be the girl responsible for your newest breakup."

Too late.

Oh, yeah.

I'm a horrible person.

She couldn't even fall back on an I'm-going-to-leave-him-alone-from-now-on cushion. She had decided to sleep with him.

And that right there was another reason playing house with him was no longer an option.

"We won't try to keep my presence a secret, then."

"I won't be the girl you cheat on with Tiffany," she retorted.

"She's right," Michael said, his tone just as sharp.

Blue raised his chin. "I don't care what the world thinks. I'm ending things with Pagan the moment I go public." His gaze bore into Evie. "But if you want everyone to think Tiffany is the reason for the breakup, rather than my move-in with you, and that I'm seeing *you* behind *her* back, that can be arranged."

"No. I don't want that." How big of a douche would she be, letting another woman take the heat for her actions? Besides, she didn't want him with Tiffany *at all*. Not even in the mind of others.

Gah. She was already acting like a live-in girlfriend.

His gaze never strayed from her. "I'm spending the evenings in your home one way or the other, princess. Pick the other and I'll make sure you regret it." He turned his attention to Michael. "I'll be sleeping in a guest room. Right now I'm the only person you can trust with her safety."

Michael scrubbed a hand over his weary features. "Now he's the one who's right, sunbeam."

What!

"Before you protest," her father added, then sighed, and it was clear he was fading fast, his eyelids drooping, his shoulders pulling in, "don't protest. If anything happened to you . . ."

She squeezed his hand, his concern washing away her next objection. "Fine. Blue can stay at my house, but first I need you to tell me you know I'm well able to take care of myself."

His smile was sad. "I do. I've always known. But one thing you have failed to learn is that it never hurts to have backup."

Eleven

BLUE RESTED FOR A few hours but got up early to shower and clean the dye out of his hair. He threw away the contacts and removed all of the piercings, happy to be Bad Boy Chic again. He still had a line of scar tissue, but it would be gone in another day or two.

If Evie asked, he'd give himself a new one.

He dressed in a black T-shirt and slacks. Spares of Michael's. Blue hadn't expected to stay the night, so he hadn't brought any extras. He headed to the kitchen.

Evie had beaten him there.

She leaned against the counter, sipping at a steaming mug of coffee. The sight of her arrested him. She had such long lashes. And were those faint little smudges on her nose freckles?

How had he never noticed them before?

She puckered her lips to blow on the coffee, both top and bottom red and deliciously swollen, as if she'd nibbled on them all through the night.

She, too, had found the necessary supplies to return her hair to its normal dark luster, the wavy locks flowing freely. She'd ditched the silicone bra, her breasts once again a perfect teacup shape.

Creeper! Stop eyeing her like you want to eat her.

Mmm . . . I want to eat her.

Cursing, he bit his tongue until he tasted blood. He hated challenges, he decided. Because he wanted Evie, desperately, and her parentage was one challenge he could never overcome.

If she were anyone other than Michael's daughter, Blue would carry her to bed. Here. Now. But she was his daughter, so he couldn't.

Gotta have sex soon. His body couldn't take much more frustration without causing a worldwide power surge.

And yet, the thought of being with anyone else left him . . . hollow.

No one else would taste as good. Or feel as soft and warm. No one else would give back as good as she got and take whatever she wanted. No one else would satisfy him.

"Michael's still sleeping," she said, breaking the silence.

Perfect. No way Blue would be able to hide the raging party in his pants.

"I checked him over. His vitals are stable."

"He'll be in prime shape before you know it." He confiscated the mug from her and drank before she could protest. "Listen, I'm going to arm up and head out. I want to case Star's house before I go in."

"Before *you* go in? I think you mean *we*."

Hardly. But he had to tread carefully here. With

Evie, he couldn't use old faithful: *It's too dangerous, sugar dumpling, so let the big, bad man go and save the day*. She would empty out his liver and fill it with rocks.

"Honestly, buttercup?" he said. "No matter how skilled you are, you'll just get in my way. To get in and out undetected, I'll have to move at a speed you won't ever be able to match."

Her lips thinned as she peered over at him. He held her stare without flinching—and, somehow, without grinning. He should be frightened rather than amused. If anyone could kill him and bury the evidence, it was this woman. But then, he was only just beginning to realize how much he liked the strong, fierce firecracker and her diabolical mind.

"I need you here," he added, "at the computer, watching my back." Literally. He would have a night-vision camera attached to the back collar of his shirt, streaming live feed. "It's a job John and Solo have done many times in the past, not something meant to keep the little woman home safe. I promise."

Her eyes narrowed with suspicion. "You're lying."

"We don't lie to each other, baby doll. Remember?"

The fight drained out of her, and she nodded. "All right. But you better come back free of injuries, or I will slice off your favorite body part, name it something filthy and wrong, and sell it to the highest bidder."

Again he wanted to grin. With those words, he realized Evie Black didn't just desire him with the same fervency he desired her—she also liked him as much as he liked her. Something he'd noticed: she only threatened people she cared about.

I'm in trouble with this one, aren't I?

As the sun set on the horizon, shadows began to thicken. Blue was able to place ten small cameras on the perimeter of Star's country home, a huge compound surrounded by an iron gate, armed guards, and a forest of fake green trees.

"Done with the outside," he whispered. He was roughly thirty yards from the mansion, hidden by a massive trunk. Not to mention the fact that his clothing had tiny microchips woven throughout, causing the fabric to blend with his surroundings every time he moved.

"I've disabled the laser sensors," Evie said through the piece in his ear. "Avoid the middle of the gate and you should be fine."

"'Should'?"

"Let's find out together."

Funny. "I'm about to go in."

"Your six is clear."

"All right. I'm moving in." For protection, he had a pyre-gun, an image cloak, and a few daggers. For surveillance, he had a single sheet of microbugs—twenty-five peel-and-stick tabs to place throughout the home. "Unless you see something, I need you to be quiet from now on." Her sexy voice was a distraction he couldn't afford.

"Roger that."

Deep breath in . . . hold . . . hold . . . As he released

it, he surged forward, out from the shade and into the waning sunlight, moving at such a swift pace the guards would only register the slightest blur. He climbed the gate. As he placed a bug on the north, east, south, and west walls, he searched for the best entrance into the home. No one shot at him. No one cried out a warning.

"See something. Three giggling women in lingerie just snaked a corner behind you," Evie said, her voice a caress in his ears. "Please tell me you didn't accidentally stumble into a harem . . . oops. Shutting up now."

Can't laugh. A guard exited a side door. There. He slipped inside, unnoticed, as the metal began to close, and found himself in . . . a break room. Eight men. All armed. Some playing cards, some watching monitors that displayed the house grounds. He couldn't slow; he would give himself away. He had to keep going, even though he didn't know the layout.

When he reached a hallway with only one guard, he seized the opportunity. Finally slowing . . . stopping, Blue placed a hand over the male's nose and mouth, and pinched his carotid, cutting off both of his airways. It wasn't long before the guy sagged in his arms, a deadweight. He dragged the guy into a nearby storage closet.

"While we've got a moment, let's revisit the lingerie," he whispered to Evie. "You ever wear any?" Working as swiftly as possible, he switched off the chips in his clothing and held the image cloak—a small black band with a camera in the center—at the top of the guard's head and scanned all the way to his feet.

"Actually, I prefer to go commando," she admitted.

He moaned. How was he supposed to keep his hands off her now?

Michael, that's how.

But Michael would understand if he caved. Surely.

As soon as the guard's identity registered, Blue snapped the band around his own neck, and the guard's hologram was cast, front and back, shielding his identity. "Here goes. Radio silence again."

Blue stepped into the hall and walked as if he were simply out on patrol. He reached around every door and, without pausing, placed a bug in . . . a sitting room . . . a bedroom . . . another bedroom . . . He marched downstairs, took a corner. People buzzed around in the kitchen, preparing the evening meal. He anchored another bug.

In a perfect world, he would find John locked in a room. Or down here, in a cell. And Solo would burst through the entrance to help him. Together, they would free John.

In a less-than-perfect world, Blue would find something to point him to their locations.

In a crappy shithole of a world, he would find nothing.

He was in a crappy shithole.

He'd been so hopeful. Frustration poked at his power, and that power expanded inside him until his skin felt taut, ready to rip apart at the seams.

Keep it together. One last room to bug. The most important.

Blue searched until he found Star's office. The doors were closed and locked, and he would bet Star was inside, working. He could sneak inside and try to use voice compulsion, forcing Star to lead him out to safety and then to tell him everything he wanted to know. But there were two flaws in that plan. One, guards would come gunning for him and he couldn't hold them all off at once without emptying himself. And if he emptied himself, he couldn't carry Star away—or save John and Solo, if they were nearby. Two, half the population was immune to the compulsion. Star could be one of the immune.

"You've got two males coming in hot," Evie announced.

Great.

"Marco," a deep voice said.

Blue placed the last bug on the office door. No way could he get in without blowing his cover. He turned. As promised, two males were barreling toward him, both frowning.

"Marco. What are you doing down here?"

"I think you're Marco," Evie prompted.

Yeah. Probably. But Blue couldn't say a single word to the guys—he wouldn't have Marco's voice. That meant he had to go with plan B.

He released a small ring of power. Not enough to render Blue completely useless afterward, but enough to weaken him as he disabled the guards. The two grunted and jerked before slumping to the floor.

He considered the consequences worth the reward.

"Nice," Evie said, "but you better get out of there before they're found and an alarm is tripped."

Blue kicked into high gear—which wasn't as high as it had been before—propelling outside. He raced across the lawn . . . no alarm . . . he climbed the iron gate . . . no alarm . . .

He jumped into his waiting car and sped down the street, constantly glancing at the rearview mirror to see if he was being followed.

"How long before you're back at the boathouse?" Evie asked.

He thought he heard the words she didn't say: *How long before you're safe?*

"Missing me already, princess? How sweet."

"Blue! I'm being serious."

How adorable was the pout in her voice?

Dude. You've got it bad.

And it was only getting worse.

"I'll be there first thing in the morning," he said, more sharply than he'd intended.

"Morning? Tell me you're kidding." The pout was replaced by a growl. "I have no intention of taking the evening off. I need to pay a visit to AIR headquarters to discuss the car chase and pump Agent Gutierrez for information."

The words *pump Agent Gutierrez* hit him the wrong way, and he gripped the steering wheel with so much force he cracked the metal. "Does Michael have another boat?"

"Yeah, but if I take it, I'll leave him stranded."

"I seriously doubt that. He's a plan B, C, and D man. Take the boat."

She sighed. "You're right."

"Aren't I always?"

"Ha, ha."

"So listen. Tonight I have to rise from the dead. I'll sneak over to your house as soon as it's done."

A sharp intake of breath. "So . . . you're ending things with Pagan?"

"Yes. It'll be done by midnight."

Utter silence.

Man, he wished he could read Evie better, but when she wanted to be, she was a master at disguising her reactions. And without her nearby, he couldn't sense her emotions.

Funny, but the empathic ability he'd once despised was now one of his most beloved and well used.

"Just so you know," he added, "I'm not going to sleep with her." He didn't owe Evie the assurance; they weren't dating and had made no promises to each other—and, damn it all, they couldn't be together.

None of that stopped him, however.

"I didn't ask, did I?" There was no emotion in her tone. "Besides, sleeping with her before and/or after you've broken her heart would be a total douche move."

His jaw clenched. "Look, until you, I always told her before I was going to do something with someone else. Not why, just that it was going to happen. She never minded, and that's part of the reason I stayed with her. If it weren't for the job, I would have been faithful. I *want* to be faithful."

Again silence.

He wanted her to see him, the real him, he realized. And he wanted her to tell him she thought better of him. Even though he sometimes didn't think better of himself.

"Do you know what it's like to seduce someone you're not attracted to?" he gritted. "Or worse, someone you despise? Do you know what it's like to hear their cries of pleasure and wish you were hearing cries of pain? Do you know how dirty something like that can make a person feel? *Do you?*"

"No," she whispered.

"Do you know what it's like to have sex with someone you know you're going to have to kill? Or to know just how badly your actions are going to hurt someone you care about?"

"Blue—"

"Would you mind if I *did* sleep with her?" he snapped. He didn't want her to see him now. Some part of him just wanted blood.

Another sharp intake of breath. Then, very softly, she said, "Yes. I would mind. Just . . . try to end it by eleven, yeah. I'll be waiting for you."

Waiting for you.

What did that mean?

He knew what he wanted it to mean. Because as much as he wanted blood, he still wanted *her.* If she'd let him, he'd take her and deal with the consequences.

"I'll hurry," he said.

The piece in his ear shut off, spilling static.

Blue called Pagan from the road and told her he would come by her place around ten for a chat-up, as Evie would say, then hung up when she rapid-fired questions at him.

Non-man-whore move: he wasn't going to destroy her dreams and aspirations over the phone.

Besides, there was nothing he could tell her that would make her feel better about what was about to happen.

He stopped at Evie's safe house to grab the laptop and Lucky Horn flash drive, then went home to get his favorite SUV and let his neighbors know he was back in business.

Finally the moment of truth arrived.

He checked the perimeter of Pagan's house for any surveillance equipment—found none—and made his way to the door. She answered before he had a chance to knock, and a hard fist of guilt pummeled him. She wore a slinky red dress that hugged her voluminous curves, and her blond hair framed her perfectly made-up face. She'd gotten dolled up for him.

She was beautiful and stacked and everything he'd once thought he wanted—but nothing he truly did. Seemed he had a taste for a certain slender, dark-haired, doe-eyed girl and only she would do.

I'm sorry, Michael.

I'll be waiting for you, Evie had said.

Be naked, he should have told her.

Pagan motioned him inside, and as he passed her she said, "Where have you been? Why didn't you call? Who were you with? I have a right to know!"

He turned to face her, hating himself more than ever. *Just get it over with.* Tone gentle, he said, "I'm sorry, Pagan, but this isn't working for me."

Shock registered a moment before a nervous laugh

slipped from her. "I know I'm acting like a witch right now. I've been worried about you, that's all. But you're here now, so I can relax. Let's have a drink and we can discuss something else."

Witch? Evie would have shot him in the face and called him a whore. And as much as he always despised when she used the word, he kind of preferred that kind of response to this. Acceptance.

Pagan took one of his hands and urged him forward. He planted his heels and clasped her other hand, holding her in place.

"You're asking questions you have every right to ask," he said, "and if I was a good man, I'd answer them. But I'm not, and I'm sorry about that, too. You deserved better than I gave you and you deserve better than you're getting."

Paling, she released him to twist the silk of her dress. "What are you trying to say?"

"I'm saying . . . we're over. I'm sorry," he repeated.

"You're serious," she gasped out.

"I am."

"But . . . but . . . is there someone else?"

He gave her the hard truth. "Yes." He owed her that much at least.

She threw herself at him and gripped his shirt, clinging. "Who is she?"

"Does it matter?"

"Tell me. Tell me right now. Is there more than one?"

"Pagan. Don't do this to yourself."

A moment passed, then two, and all she did was breathe heavily. "You're right. I don't care who she is."

Her hand trembled as she hooked a lock of hair behind her ear, her gaze never leaving him. "Get her, or them, out of your system. I don't mind. Then come back to me."

He pried her fingers from his T-shirt and kissed her knuckles. As tenderly as he was able, he said, "No, Pagan. This is good-bye between us."

"But . . . but . . ." Tears welled in her eyes and trickled down her cheeks. "Blue. Don't do this. Please."

Maybe he should have done to her what he'd done to Noelle Tremain, and given *her* a reason to break things off with *him*. That way he could leave her with her heart intact.

No, he thought next. The guilt of what he'd done to Noelle still haunted him. This was the better way. The honest way.

The right way.

Sometimes the truth could tear a person apart piece by piece, but at least the pieces could be welded back together, stronger than before. With lies, the pieces went up in flames before they ever hit the ground, and there was nothing left to patch.

"I'm sorry, but I'm not going to change my mind about this. And, Pagan? You should be happy that I won't. You're far better off without me. You want a family. I don't."

"But I don't have to have a family," she rushed out. "Besides, I don't even want one. Not without you."

"Don't say that. Don't change your heart's desires for me or any man."

She pressed on. "Take some time to think about this. It's late, and you've been gone, so you're probably tired right now. Yes. You're tired, that's all. Get some sleep and we'll talk again."

"No," he said, shaking his head. "I'm not going to change my mind."

"Yes. You will. You must."

He tried again. "You're a beautiful, passionate woman, and someday a man will come along and put you first. But that man isn't me."

"I don't have to be first. I just want to be with you. Please, Blue. I love you. Love you so much."

He'd never considered the fact that she might actually love him. He wouldn't have stayed with her this long if he had. "You'll get over me," he said softly. "One day you might even thank me for this." Then he stalked out of the house, feeling like a total tool because the breakup was over—and all he wanted to do was go to Evie.

Twelve

B LUE BROKE SPEED RECORDS to get to Evie's house, hid his car, and swiftly snuck his way to her back porch, out of sight of her neighbors. Then he pounded on the door with enough force to bend the entire structure.

For the first time in their acquaintance, he was single.

A minute passed. Two. She didn't answer.

He knocked harder, leaving an indentation. If she wasn't here . . .

If she'd changed her mind . . .

He could have disarmed her system—again—but he didn't want to give up his advantage or add to the bill he still hadn't paid. She hadn't yet realized that no matter what improvements she made, she would never be able to keep him out. His power could fry the wires in mere seconds.

Finally, she opened the door. His heart kicked into an uncontrollable rhythm. Unlike Pagan, she hadn't dressed to please him. She wore a tank top and shorts, and she wore them well, her slender body on perfect display. Her hair was loose. Fistable. Her eyes were unreadable, but that was okay, because he could feel the emotion pulsing from her.

White-hot, consuming desire.

His own, always there, roared to the surface.

"I'm sorry for what I said earlier," she muttered. "For what I've said throughout the years. For what I've called you. I was wrong and I was cruel. I was a judgmental bitch, just like you called me. And I know these words aren't good enough. I know I owe you so much more, and I'll understand if you can't forgive me."

Something clenched in his chest. She saw him. In that moment he realized he'd never stopped hoping for this. "Princess, I've done bad things. I get why you said what you said. Yes, I can forgive you."

Relief bathed her expression. "Thank you."

He nodded.

She nibbled on her bottom lip. "You did it, then," she said. "You ended things with Pagan." It wasn't a question.

He answered anyway. "Yes."

"Good." She had her arms wrapped around his neck a second later, her lips mashed against his, her tongue thrusting deep into his mouth, demanding a response. He lifted her off her feet, his hands firm on her ass to hold her against him. Now that he had her, he wasn't letting her go.

Gentle. You'll break her.

He stepped deeper into the—kitchen, he noted— and kicked the door closed, then walked to the wall and slammed her against it. Screw gentleness. The kiss became a wild thing, so down and dirty he couldn't stop the little growls rising from his throat, his mouth pressing harder, insisting on more from her. Everything. All.

"Any idea . . . how good . . . you taste?" he asked between sucking and nipping at her.

"Don't talk. You'll ruin our truce."

His chuckle was dark and hungry.

His hands tangled in her hair, such silky, soft hair, and he fisted the strands the way he'd always wanted. He angled her head for better access, needing more, desperate for more. He was like a starving man at a buffet, taking, taking more, taking all that he could get, doing to her mouth what he wanted to do to her body. Possessing. Branding.

"You wet for me, baby?"

"Soaking." She jerked at his shirt even as she arched her hips forward, back, rubbing her core up and down on his erection, creating the most delicious kind of friction.

He removed her tank with a single tug. Her nipples poked through the thin fabric of her bra, and abraded his chest. He was so desperate for her, so hard. And his power was tugging at its leash. Beside him, several pots and pans floated in the air.

"I'm going to play with you for hours," he rasped. He wanted to tongue her nipples while his fingers thrust into her, pushing her over the edge once, twice. He wanted his mouth to descend and devour, and push her over a third time. Then . . . finally, then . . . he wanted to lift up and slam home.

"Don't bother," she said, biting his bottom lip. "Just do it."

The words startled him, and he frowned. No fore-play? "Why the hurry? You got somewhere to be?"

She licked her way across his jaw, then delved lower to suck on his neck. "Just want to . . . reach the . . . fin-ish line."

Finish line? A quick in and out? So they could both get off, and the wanting could stop? So they could both walk away and forget it happened?

She didn't want to want him, did she.

Maybe he'd been wrong before. Maybe she didn't see him or like him, even in the smallest way. Because, despite her apology, she definitely didn't respect him.

Anger mixed with his arousal.

No sex, then. Not yet.

Not ever—Michael's daughter!

Yeah, but that was starting to matter less and less. Right now, it was her attitude he couldn't get past. But he had to take *something* from her. Otherwise he'd have a power surge.

Sure. That's why.

He scooted her higher up the wall, nuzzled her bra aside with his chin, and sucked on a pretty pink nipple. A broken groan left her. He tunneled a hand under her shorts, palmed the very heat of her, thrilling when she shouted with relief and pleasure.

"Yes!" The back of her head hit the wall. "Going to . . . oh, so close already . . ."

So beautiful. So mine.

"Grip me," he commanded.

Her eyelids flipped open, and passion-drugged eyes stared at him. "What? No. You'll come."

That was the point. "Do it."

"But—"

"Do it or I'll remove my fingers from between your legs. Tonight, we're going to make each other happy with a hand job. But that's as far as we're going to go."

"Why?"

"Because I said so. If you've got a problem with that, we can stop right now."

Her gaze fumed as she did as he'd commanded. She would never know how thankful he was for her capitulation—or how close he'd come to begging. She reached past the waist of his pants to clasp his length, and hell. With that one touch, she almost unmanned him.

"You're so big," she breathed. "Are you sure you don't want to put it in me?" She nibbled on his earlobe. "I think I'd come with the first thrust."

Killing me. "Lick first," he commanded.

She licked his ear.

"Not there."

Understanding, she pouted for a moment, then removed her hand. He swallowed a moan as she licked her palm. Then, while her skin was wet, she clasped him again. The moist heat provided a smooth glide.

"That's not good enough," he said. He took her hand, forced it under her panties, between her legs, and let her rich wetness coat her skin. Then he returned her grip to his shaft.

"Harder," he said, "and I'll give you a finger."

She squeezed, slowly pumping her hand up and down. Her cheeks flushed with pleasure. This wasn't what she'd wanted, but she wasn't going to be able to stop herself from enjoying it, he noted with pride.

And when her clasp tightened, he sucked in a breath, doing as he'd promised and sliding one finger deep inside her. And, oh, he almost wished he hadn't. She was tight, hot, and *soaking*, just as she'd promised. He had to get in her soon.

"Faster, baby," he instructed, "and you'll get another."

Her speed increased, enough to wring a deeper moan out of him. So he gave her a second finger, stretching her. How long since she'd had sex? As tight as she was, he'd have to guess years. The idea filled him with a heady sense of possession, and he decided to reward her, working his thumb in a circular pattern at her apex.

"Blue!"

"You feel so good. When I finally get inside you, I'm going to pound so hard, take so much, you'll swear you're dying. Later, you'll beg me to pound even harder, to take more."

The dirty talk sent her over the edge. Her broken cry echoed as her inner walls clutched around him, again and again, holding him close and wringing every drop of pleasure she could from him.

Knowing she'd climaxed sent a white-hot lance up his shaft, and he exploded in a rush, pumping into her grip until the last of his shudders faded.

It took him several long minutes to come down from the high, and when he did, he heard her breakfast table crashing to the floor, followed by the pots and pans. He removed his hand from her—maybe the most difficult thing he'd ever done.

No. Wait. Not tasting the moisture on his fingers was the most difficult. But if he did it, if he gave in to the craving, he would next be on her. He wouldn't be able to stop himself.

He bent down and grabbed his shirt, then used the material to clean her hand. "One day soon," he said, "after we've both had a little time to think, we're going to talk."

She eyed him warily. "And what will our topic of conversation be?"

"Expectations."

A roommate.

A single, sexy male roommate.

A single, sexy male roommate who'd just given her an earth-shattering orgasm.

The thoughts rolled through Evie's mind, unstoppable. She'd attacked Blue the moment she'd found out he was single. He'd been just as frantic to be with her . . . but he hadn't wanted sex from her. Just a hand job.

She wasn't sure what to think about that. Or the fact that he wanted to talk about expectations.

What kind of expectations? His? Hers?

She knew what his were—no strings. He could see other people and she couldn't complain.

But what were hers?

She didn't want to think about it. She thought she might actually cry.

Apparently, for now, they were just supposed to pretend they hadn't had their hands in each other's pants.

"We've got work to do," he'd said, moments after dropping the chat bomb. "Go and get dressed in something that covers you from neck to toe, then meet me in your office. I want to watch the video feed from the club and listen to audio feed from Star's house. After that, we can figure out the best way for me to run into Tiffany."

Tiffany.

Gah. He had to charm the girl. Maybe more.

Evie wanted to kill her.

See? This is why you can't get involved with someone like Blue.

"I protest only one detail of your work plan," she'd replied, trying to act calm. "Let's do our watching and listening in the living room, not the office."

Now, dressed in a pair of flannel pj's, she hooked her laptop to her giant holoscreen TV, allowing them both to view the Lucky Horn video feed from the comfort of the couch. Blue already reclined there, gorgeous and shirtless, wearing only a pair of loose slacks.

He was allowed to show skin. So unfair.

She wanted to lean into him as she settled beside him. Thankfully, she had a big bowl of popcorn clutched tightly to her middle, preventing her from making a fool of herself.

She forced herself to concentrate. On the screen, Timothy Mercer, the man who'd tried to burn Blue alive, wandered throughout the Lucky Horn, shaking hands with a few of the patrons, leering at the girls as they paraded past him, and even slapping a few on the ass.

"Pig," she said, tossing a handful of popcorn at the screen.

"Good to know I'm not the only one," Blue muttered.

She stiffened as she read between the lines. He claimed he forgave her, but clearly he hadn't yet forgotten. "You're not a pig. I was wrong to call you one, and I'm sorry."

No response.

Fine. Back to the video, before she became a needy bag of pleas. *Please tell me you've truly forgiven me. Please don't be mad at me. Please like me.*

After hours and hours of watching Mr. Mercer repeat the same routine, she began to feel as though she were on a merry-go-round.

Finally Blue pressed Pause, the image freezing. He scrubbed a hand down his face. "We're friends, right?"

Yes. No. Maybe. After what had happened in her kitchen . . . "Right."

"Can I tell you something without getting a lecture about my whoring ways?"

He'd slept with Pagan after all, and *that's* why he hadn't wanted to go all the way with Evie. "What did you do?"

His eyes narrowed. "It's not what I did, it's what I feel."

Oh.

Her guilt became the white elephant in the room. She had to stop thinking the worst about him. He wasn't a bad guy. He was actually a *great* guy. And bottom line? She had absolutely no room to judge. It was just easier to acknowledge his faults and ignore her own.

"Tonight was hard," he said.

A pang cut through her chest. "With me?"

He threw a pillow at her. "No, smarty. I hurt Pagan pretty bad."

Finally she understood. The breakup. She released a breath she hadn't realized she'd been holding. "You feel bad."

"Yeah."

"Even though you did the right thing?"

His gaze was stark. "Yeah. Even though. She cried."

A serial bang-and-bailer wouldn't care. He was so much more than Evie had ever given him credit for, wasn't he. "Do you love her?" she asked, tensing.

"No."

"Then you gave her a small hurt now to prevent a big hurt later on. Sometimes you have to be cruel to be kind, Mr. Blue. I think I told you something along those lines at our first meeting."

Their eyes locked, neither of them willing to look away. The air thickened with awareness, always that awareness, and waves of his power brushed against her skin. Why? Why was this happening? She'd climaxed once tonight. She shouldn't be gearing up for another.

Blue jolted to his feet and backed away from her, toward the exit. "I'm tired. I'm going to bed. We'll figure out a plan of action in the morning." With that, he turned and stomped from the room.

Thirteen

ORNING SUNLIGHT WASHED THROUGH the bedroom, splashed on the bed . . . on Evie, who was sprawled across the entire mattress. And she'd once accused him of being a bed hog, Blue thought with a wry smile.

He peered down at her, his entire body buzzing with energy—and need.

It wasn't going away.

Surrounded by wisps of white lace hanging from the posts of the bed, and the pale blue fabric of the comforter, she was Snow White after she'd eaten the apple. Or maybe Sleeping Beauty waiting for her prince . . . and a kiss. *I've had my hands in her hair. I've had my face pressed against hers. I've moved my lips against hers.*

I almost had that pale, soft skin completely bared . . .

He fisted his hands to stop himself from reaching for her.

Last night, shortly after leaving her in the living room, he almost said to hell with it and jumped her. The heat of his desire practically scorched his soul. But first he wanted her to want him with the same ferocity he wanted her. Because if he took her, he would disappoint a very good man; a man he loved. He could even lose his job.

That was a lot to deal with, just for a casual affair.

Too much, really. And he wasn't going to do it, he decided.

Things with Evie had to be platonic from now on.

For the best.

Blue gave her a gentle shake. "I need you to wake up now, dewberry." Unable to sleep, he'd spent the entire night listening to the audio feed from Star's house. Finally, a few minutes ago, he'd heard something worthwhile.

She blinked open her eyes, her irises a deep, rich brown with striations of gold. He'd never noticed the gold before.

He really liked the gold.

Great start there, Platono.

"Blue?" She batted his arm away and grumbled, "What the flip are you doing in my room? And did you just call me 'dewberry'? Because I am fully prepared to castrate you with a dull spoon."

He grinned. "Get up and get dressed. We have a lead, and I know you want to tag along."

"A lead? What lead?"

"Star's guards have information about someone matching Solo's description. Apparently, he was spotted at an abandoned warehouse in No Man's Land, and they plan to gather the troops and go in guns blazing at dark, since they don't have the stones to face him in broad daylight. That means we can beat them there."

Blinking, she jolted upright. Dark locks tumbled down her shoulders and arms, and he had to force himself to back away from her before he did something stupid.

He strode to her dresser and pawed through the drawers, throwing a pink T-shirt in her direction, followed by a pair of socks, a bra, pink, like the top, and lace—*nice*—and a pair of pink panties. Lace as well. *Really nice.*

His stomach clenched as his craving for her intensified.

You respect Michael. You want to keep your job.

How many times would he have to remind himself?

She caught every item.

"I know you like to go commando some of the time, but today you're going to be a good girl and wear proper undergarments." He'd never be able to concentrate otherwise.

"Fine."

He strode to her closet and selected a pair of jeans. "How soon can you be ready to leave?"

"Five minutes. And that's not girl code for an hour." She padded to the bathroom, shutting the door behind her. A second later he heard the whirl of the enzyme shower's motor.

He needed something to do with his hands or he was going to go balls to the wall, strip, and join her in that stupid shower. In the kitchen he made a pot of coffee and filled a travel mug for her.

Mr. Domestic. That's me. He couldn't remember doing anything like this for anyone else.

The creaking of wood snagged his attention. He turned, watching as Evie marched down the stairs; damn it, she was once again so beautiful his chest began to ache. She'd pulled her hair into a ponytail, and her cheeks were bright from the heat of her shower. She wore the garments he'd selected, and looked young and innocent and—

Not for him. Never for him.

MICHAEL. JOB.

He gripped the kitchen counter with tense fingers.

"What?" she asked, adjusting the purse strap crossing over her middle.

"Nothing," he croaked. To distract himself, he used his power to tug that strap over her head, allowing him to grab hold of the bag.

"Hey!"

He dug through the contents. "A headlamp, compact, eyedrops, pyre-gun, superglue, brass knuckles, wet wipes, four rings, a mini flare gun, and a whistle." As he spoke, he held up each item. "Some of this stuff I don't even recognize."

"Give me that," she said, snatching the purse away and returning it to its rightful place.

"Why a headlamp?"

"Why not?"

Fair enough. He pushed the travel mug in her direction.

She arched a brow, suspicious. "You made this for me?"

He returned to gripping the counter, the granite cracking, and nodded.

"Well." Her frown had nothing to do with anger but everything to do with confusion. "Thanks. I guess."

"Not a morning person, sunshine?"

A glint of contrition in her eyes. "There are people who would tell you I'm not an anytime person."

"Well, those people just don't know you."

Her jaw dropped, and she gazed at him with astonishment.

Yeah. He'd just astonished himself, too. Time to move on. "You ready?"

"I need one more minute to send Michael everything we've acquired from Star's, and the Lucky Horn," she said. "I know he plans to stay at the boathouse another day or two, and he's got nothing but time on his hands. He can let us know if he finds anything else that's useful."

When she finished, Blue led her to the garage.

"Let's take my SUV," she said. "It's not registered in my name, so it's my in-case-all-hell-breaks-loose vehicle. A must-have for any agent of our generation."

"Perfect."

During the drive, he remained on alert for any tails, and even took several wrong turns, doubled back, and went in circles. No one attempted anything nefarious.

If that changed, the car's sensors would know and alert him. More than that, the windows were made of shield armor, and the metal body was impenetrable. He could relax. If only for a little while.

"How did yesterday's conversation with Agent Gutierrez go?" he asked.

"It didn't. He wasn't there. And rather than deal with anyone else, I left."

"Good call."

"Yeah." She twisted her jeans at the knees. "Hey, Blue?"

"Yes."

"Why didn't you tell me you created SHOW?"

He stiffened. He didn't like that she knew. Hadn't wanted to alter her opinion of him that way. "How did you find out?"

"You checked the website from my computer and the data streamed to my phone."

"So? I'm not mentioned on the website."

"Maybe I did a little digging."

He forced his body to relax. "It's no one's business, Evie."

"I know." A suspended pause before she whispered, "I'm Anita Huginkis, a longtime donor."

He was surprised. He was impressed. He was heart-warmed. His foul mood suddenly lifted. "I *knew* that was a fake name, but I checked Miss Huginkis out, and her background seemed legit."

"Yep, I'm *that* good." Preening, Evie fluffed her hair.

Grinning, he admitted, "I'm Justin Sider."

She snorted. "Just inside her? Nice. A few years ago, I was Sherwood Lovett."

"Holden Mylode."

"Nealanne Licket."

"Iva Woody."

She burst into laughter, and he marveled anew at the beauty of her. Eyes bright. Cheeks aglow. She was the epitome of radiance, flooding the dark places inside him with light.

Need to make her laugh every day for the rest of her life.

Rest of her life? *Don't be ridiculous.*

When she quieted, the tension was so thick, he doubted a knife could cut through it. He was turned on, verging on desperate.

"Ever been to No Man's Land?" he asked, changing the subject.

"No. You?"

"Yeah." There, the air was sharp from ongoing acid rains, and stung the skin and nostrils. Humans had moved into the city, out of the country lands, decades ago, so several alien races had then moved into the abandoned areas and taken over. "I would have guessed you'd worked out here with Eden. You guys are close, and Michael's always sending her on the worst jobs . . . Can I ask you something personal?"

After a slight pause, she said, "Sure. But that doesn't mean I'll answer."

Here goes. "What happened to Claire?"

Sadness and remorse filled the vehicle. "Blue . . ."

"Still not ready to talk about it?"

"I'm not sure I'll ever be," she admitted.

The wind began to beat against the car, even throwing pieces of gravel into the hood. Grime thickened the air outside as the paved road gave way to dirt.

Unsure why he was so determined to get her to open up to him, especially now that he'd decided to keep things friendly, but unwilling to back down, he said, "Why did your mom and Michael split?"

"She used to work for him."

He nearly swallowed his tongue. "Michael dated a subordinate?"

"Yes, and it was quite the scandal in their day. She got pregnant and he refused to marry her. I think deep down she wanted to punish him for it. So she packed up and returned to her family in Westminster."

"What about Claire's father?"

"I was a year old when she married him, and Claire came two years after that. He stuck around till just after my sixth birthday. I was devastated by his abandonment. He was a good man, sweet to Claire and me, and our only real source of doting."

"He never came around after that?"

"No."

Then he wasn't a good man, Blue thought darkly. He'd kiboshed his kids. He was a bastard.

Blue had done a lot of shitty things in his life, but ripping out a kid's heart wasn't one of them.

And now he hated that he'd once called Evie spoiled rotten. She wasn't. Not at all. She'd faced rejection time and time again, and had built a wall around herself. Probably the only way she'd been able to survive.

"How about you?" she asked. "What about your parents?"

"I don't remember my biological parents. I was adopted at the age of four."

"Were your adoptive parents good to you?"

He'd never talked about this with anyone, not even Solo and John. Still, he found myself saying, "They tried to be."

"Tried?"

"I wouldn't let them." He told her about his brothers and sisters, how they'd saved him. "I was so broken up about losing them, I shut everyone else out. When my new parents tried to hug me, I threw a tantrum. When they asked me to come eat at the table with them, I turned my back and went silent."

"You were an emotionally traumatized kid. I'm sure they understood and hold no grudge."

"You're probably right, but I can't ask them because they're dead."

She reached over, squeezed his hand. "I'm sorry."

He breathed a sigh of relief when a town came into view. "We're close to the warehouse." He wasn't sure how to respond to this kind, generous side of her.

With spotted fur and catlike movements, the Bree Lians looked like animals stuck on human legs. The Cortaz were far more delicate in appearance, with glittery skin and bright lights seeping from their pores.

Everyone stopped whatever they were doing—shopping, selling food from wheeled carts, talking, and laughing—to watch as the car passed through. Blue gripped the handle of a pyre-gun, ready, just in case. But no one chased after them as they turned one corner, then another and another, leaving the center of town and entering a deserted area.

Finally, the vehicle stopped at the entrance of a metal building that looked as if it had been beaten by wind and weather, and seemed to bend at several odd angles.

Any other time he would have parked farther away, but he wanted the car as close to his location as possible.

"We're here."

"You think Star's men are nearby?"

"No. They were pretty adamant about not coming to the area until dark, because they were afraid to face the otherworlders that live here, as well as Solo himself—if that's who is actually here. But we're still going to act as if they're surrounding the place."

"You going to power surge?"

"No. Too many innocents. We're doing this the old-fashioned way. With guns." He checked his pyre's crystal. "Here. Put this on." He handed her a black leather mask with clear, malleable plastic in the eyeholes.

After she pulled the thing over her head, he gently untangled her hair from the ear hooks. She went utterly still, as if anticipating his next move, and the moisture in his mouth dried.

He couldn't dare a next move. His arms fell away.

He threw a pair of gloves at her. "These, too."

She yanked the material over her hands, and withdrew the pyre from her purse. "Don't you need a mask?" she asked, dialing the weapon to its hottest setting.

He did, but he'd only been able to find the one. "I'll be fine."

He held his breath and exited the vehicle in sync with Evie. They raced inside the building together, and in the short time it took, Blue's face was pelted with thousands of stinging grains of dirt. As he shut the door to the warehouse, blocking the wind, Evie trained her weapon on the space behind him.

"Clear," she said.

He removed her mask for her and set it aside for the return trip. "Fresh air is being fed into the vents by an outside source." He wondered who owned the building. Because although the entire structure looked ready to collapse, that was reinforced steel on the walls. The place was probably strong enough to withstand any kind of storm, natural or artificial.

"Blue, you bloody wanker!" she suddenly belted out.

He blinked in surprise. "What?"

"You lied!" She dug through her bag, withdrew a bundle of wet wipes, and cleaned the curve under his eye.

He let her, caught up in the blood-heating, gut-wrenching pleasure of her touch.

"I didn't lie. I said I'd be fine, and I am. I'm already healing," he muttered gruffly.

"Well, I'm still ticked."

"Do you want to rip out my kidneys and stomp on them like you're making wine?"

"For starters."

Fighting a grin, he led her through a maze of empty halls and rooms. As expected, none of Star's men were here. However, in the far room, they came across a hooded man strapped to a chair. Beside him was a table littered with bloodstained weapons and syringes.

Not Solo. Too small.

Disappointment struck.

"Who are you?" Evie demanded, giving the guy's chair a little kick.

His body jolted in surprise. "Evangeline Black?"

Her shocked gaze landed on Blue. "Agent Gutierrez?"

No way.

Blue stalked forward and tore away the crimson-soaked hood to reveal an equally crimson-soaked man.

Swollen ocean-blue eyes took zero time to adjust

to the sudden flood of light, lasering in on Blue, then Evie, then back to Blue. "Free me. Now."

"Uh, I don't think we will," Evie said. "Not until you've answered a few questions."

"Free me," he insisted, "or I'll hurt you in ways you can't even imagine."

Fury wound around Blue as surely as a rope, dragging him into a hissing, snapping pit of malevolence. "Don't threaten the girl. You do, and I won't bother with threats of my own. I'll just start cutting."

Looking at the agent, Evie leaned down and said in a stage whisper, "My partner is very good with a knife."

Dallas ignored her. Focused on Blue, he grinned an evil grin; there was blood on his teeth. "Well, well. If it isn't the football star that once dated my partner's girl, Noelle Tremain. Funny seeing you here."

"Yeah. Real hilarious. Now, who tied you up and tortured you?"

Dallas's grin spread wider. In a silky voice the agent said, "You will let me go. You want to let me go."

It took a moment for comprehension to dawn, and when it did, amazement was right there, waiting. The man was human, and yet he had just tried—and succeeded—to use voice compulsion, an Arcadian ability.

Blue threw out his arm to stop Evie from moving, expecting her to try to obey the male.

She didn't. She growled with sudden outrage, obviously immune. "You actually thought it was a good move to force us to do stuff we don't want to do? Let's see how I react to that." Her fist slammed into his jaw, and the entire chair skidded to the side.

That's my girl.

No, not my girl.

"I mean it," Dallas said, this time sounding confused and desperate. "You want to let me go."

She hit him a second time. Harder. "If you aren't already brain damaged, you're about to be. Are you sure you want to keep running that road?"

"Let me try something." Blue decided to get down and dirty and pressed his booted foot between Dallas's legs. "How are you able to use voice compulsion?"

Gritting his teeth against the pain, Dallas said, "Your friend asked the same thing. By the way, he used the same methods. Ask me how well they worked. Not that I'll answer that, either."

"Friend?"

"Like you don't know."

"I want a name."

Dallas spit blood at him.

Whatever. Blue didn't care about his audience. This was too important. He pushed his power into his hands, and both lit up like rockets. Then he brushed them through the air in front of him, a screen of sorts forming. Colors appeared.

A scene took shape in the center. A scene from ten minutes before.

Blue watched as Solo—alive and well—pressed his boot between Dallas's legs. "What do you know about Gregory Star?"

"I get that you're a big, bad dude and all, but do you really have to keep me in the hood?" the agent said from the screen. "I already know who you are. We met at the circus, remember? And don't try to deny it. I recognize your voice."

"What the hell is going on?" real-time Dallas demanded.

Blue ignored him.

Solo pressed harder, and screen-Dallas hissed. "You're a friend of Kitten's, one of my cage mates, and that's the only reason you're still alive. But I'm looking for my friend, John No Last Name, and I will maim for information. Maim in ways that will make me a monster, and you a man with a death wish. So, you have—"

The screen went blank.

Blue almost couldn't contain his joy. Solo was alive and well.

"Forget what just happened," Dallas said. "Judging by the look on your face, I can tell you weren't aware your pal Solo snuck into my home, knocked me around, brought me here, tied me up, beat me up, and asked all kinds of questions I refused to answer."

He couldn't respond. Solo was alive and well.

Solo was alive and well and in New Chicago.

Solo was alive and well and in New Chicago, trying to find John.

Relief bombarded him, nearly buckling his knees.

He couldn't stay still. He turned to Evie and drew her into his arms. Her little body trembled against him, but she didn't hesitate to wrap herself around him, holding on tight. He buried his face in the hollow of her neck, breathing in the honey and almonds that seemed to be infused into her skin.

Maybe he was a pansy, because tears burned the backs of his eyes. He didn't care.

A moment to bask—fine.

More than that? No!

He had to force himself to release her, to return to the interrogation. "If you know anything about John No Last Name, Agent Gutierrez, I suggest you tell me. Otherwise, I will gut you where you sit and not feel a moment of remorse. Unlike Solo, I won't walk away and leave you for someone else to find."

That wasn't Solo's usual MO, either. So . . . was the agent a gift? Had the warrior known Blue would come?

If so, why not stay to greet him?

The corners of Dallas's mouth lifted in a parody of a grin. "I formally invite you, Solo, and even Miss Black to go screw yourselves."

Evie snorted. "You gotta give him credit. He's quite amusing, isn't he?"

Frustration ate at Blue. "You've been investigating Gregory Star, yet you haven't plugged your findings into a single database. Why?"

"Why don't you guess?" Dallas said, refusing to back down.

"All right," he replied, lifting a scalpel from the table and testing its weight in his hand. "You don't like Gregory Star for some reason—maybe because of that Kitten chick Solo mentioned—and you're planning to punish him old-school. You don't want him going to trial. You want him dead. How am I doing so far?"

Dallas paled and tried to cover the tell with a yawn. "I'm bored."

"Shall I question Kitten next?" Blue asked.

A mouthful of curses hurtled his way. "Leave Kitten out of this. She was horribly abused at that circus, and hasn't recovered."

Blue was the one to yawn this time.

The agent realized he was getting nowhere and tried a different path. "Does Noelle know you're black ops, Blue? Wait. Black ops. Blue. Black and Blue. And you're Black, too," he said to Evie. "How cute. Anyhoodles. I'm having dinner with Noelle and her man tonight. I'll make sure to let them know you said hi."

Blue had kept tabs on Noelle over the years and knew she'd joined AIR. Knew she'd gotten married. Knew she was pregnant with her first rug rat. He was happy for her, and hoped she wouldn't want to kill him when she learned the truth about him.

He wasn't going to try to stop Dallas from sharing the intel with her. At long last, he wanted her to know. She deserved the truth.

"All right, enough of this. I can make him talk without killing him, or even hurting him," Evie said, rooting inside her purse. "I hate to do it, because the side effects are so severe, but desperate times and all that. Aha!" Smiling, she withdrew a compact of loose white powder.

"Gonna make me up?" Dallas asked. "Make me prettier? No, please, no. Not that. Anything but that."

"At least use the flare gun on him," Blue said.

"You'll like this better, I promise. It's a truth serum I . . . played with."

Dallas frowned.

"Did we forget to tell you I'm good with poisons and potions?" she asked silkily.

The agent grew a bit uneasy, shifting in his chair. "Truth serum doesn't work on me. Solo tried it before you got here, and failed."

"Well, Solo didn't use this, now, did he?"

Dallas gulped. "What kind of severe side effects are we talking about?"

"Oh, you know. The uze. Growing man boobs. Total hair loss. Penile shrinkage."

Blue thought she was kidding and smothered a laugh.

"What!" Dallas bellowed.

Evie bent down, puckered her lips, and puffed the white powder in his face.

The agent coughed and hacked until his eyes glazed over and he relaxed in his seat.

"So, Agent Gutierrez," Evie said with a bright smile, "why don't you tell us what you know about Solo and Gregory Star?"

Fourteen

DALLAS TOLD THEM EVERYTHING.

"Solo was caged at the circus with my friend Kitten—she's AIR, you know, and all messed up now. I think she's hot. That's prolly why I've had so many fantasies about her. Real dirty ones, too, but my favorite is the one of us in the shower, because she drops—"

"What happened to Solo after the circus?" Blue snapped. "Who sold him?"

The agent nodded, all eager to please now. "Gregory Star sold him. Then, after we torched the circus, Solo disappeared with Vika, the circus owner's daughter. A real pretty little blonde I've had fantasies about. See, I'd like to bend her over a—"

"Do you know where Solo is now?" Evie asked, her tone dry.

"Nope. Didn't see him again until he showed up at my house. He threw his fists of fury around, and when I failed to answer any of his questions, he stomped off and said he'd let the owner of the building have me. That's Gregory Star, in case you didn't know. I've been following some of his men. Wanted to follow Mr. Star, but he's been holed up in the country, not even leaving for work. His employees have been coming to him."

"Why have you been following Star's men?" Blue demanded.

"Star's the one who sold Kitten and Solo to the circus. And I think he's the one that bombed Mr. Black's house, because, see, that woman, the one that used to work for him, came to me right before she died and said he'd done it and that he was now after her."

That woman. The assistant.

How could she have known about Star unless she'd helped set the bomb, as Blue suspected?

When the deed was done, she either experienced remorse, with a need to make things right, or fear, with a need to save her own neck.

Okay. Moving on. "How are you able to use voice compulsion?"

"Oh, that," Dallas said. "The king of the Arcadians fed me blood to save my life, and now we're, like, totally bonded. I was happy he did it . . . until I was mad. See, he's married to the current head of AIR, Mia Snow, and she used to be my partner. She wanted me to live and not die, and she didn't understand that I'd essentially become the guy's slave and that he'd know every time I had a fantasy about her."

Evie rolled her eyes. "Is there anyone you haven't fantasized about?"

"Prolly not. I dated Pagan long before Blue—did you know that?—and I'd be into a three-way . . . four-way . . . if anyone in this room was agreeable. And maybe we could have meat loaf, mashed potatoes, and black-eyed peas after. I'm kinda hungry. And dirty. I could use a shower. And maybe a new pair of briefs. Wait. I'm not actually wearing any underwear right now."

Blue cut the agent loose. "Discretion is your friend, Agent Gutierrez. I don't mind you telling Noelle about me, but I would prefer you not tell others. I'll just have to kill them. I also would prefer it if you stayed away from Gregory Star. I think he's the one holding John, and I will massacre anyone who gets in my way."

"If I had a dollar for every death threat I received, I'd be richer than Miss Hot Pants Black," Dallas said, rubbing his wrists.

What had Evie put in that truth serum? "You're on your own getting home. But I suggest you be quick about it, because Star's men plan to raid the building tonight."

Dallas remained in the chair and tried to catch a dust mote.

Whatever. Blue wrapped an arm around Evie's shoulders and led her out of the room. "Up next. The meet-and-greet with Tiffany."

She stiffened.

Why such a telltale reaction?

Thought he'd sleep with the girl?

He gritted his teeth. *Can't be mad this time. I mean, why wouldn't she think that? You haven't told her you'll be faithful.*

But why would he tell her something like that? They weren't even in a relationship! And he'd decided not to start one.

"About that," she said. "Tiff's a rich girl and grew up around powerful men. If you go about a meeting the usual way, you're just gonna be more of the same, and easily forgettable."

He stopped at the door to swipe up the mask. "Are you saying I'm going to strike out?"

"Was I not clear? I thought I was clear. Yes. You're going to strike out. That's why I need to go in first and prep her."

Prep her? "You've got to be kidding me, princess." He tried to fit the mask over her face, but she shook her head.

"You wear it this time."

A sharp pang scraped at his chest. She was . . . looking out for him. Putting his safety above her own. "No." He anchored the material in place and again tucked away her hair. "Returning to Project Tiffany Bang Bang. Madam Prude is actually going to help Himbo score?"

Eyes narrowing, she patted his cheek. "First, you're not going to score. The job doesn't call for that."

It didn't now, he thought darkly. But later . . .

No. He wouldn't think about that.

"Second, your gratitude is humbling."

"Well, I'm a spectacularly humble guy."

Just before they exited the building he thought he heard Dallas call, "Is it too late to get an autograph?"

Evie strode along the busy outdoor shopping strip, hands in her pockets, a bounce in her step. The sun glared hotly, making her sweat, but she didn't care. At a glance, she doubted her own mother would recognize her. Her dark hair was hidden underneath a short red wig, the strands kinky and straining under a ball cap. Dark aviator glasses wrapped around her eyes. Her stained and threadbare clothing had been purchased at a thrift store.

Finding Tiffany Star had been easier than expected, considering the lengths her father had taken to shield himself. But then, Tiffany was an up-and-coming designer, with a website to display her current clothing line. A little hack job, and *boom*. Evie had access to Tiffany's in-box, and discovered the girl had a meeting with the owner of one of these shops.

Only five minutes ago, Evie watched Tiffany struggle to find a parking space in the lot. A wave of excitement hit her. Excitement she quickly tamped down. Then, when the girl walked past her at the coffee shop, never glancing in her direction, Evie turned and followed.

Now they snaked a corner. Evie had only to wait for—

That. Blue.

At the end of the newest walkway, a crowd of people surrounded him, each vying for his attention. Tiffany picked up speed, drawing closer to him. . . .

Evie burst into motion, shoving people out of the way. When she reached Tiffany's side, she grabbed the girl's briefcase and, as the girl shouted, "Wait! Stop! That's mine!" she sprinted into one of the shops.

As she ran, she shed the top layer of her disguise— the ball cap, the red wig—and flipped the flannel shirt with half sleeves around, revealing a black business jacket. By the time she stepped through the back door, she looked like a new person entirely.

She walked at a leisurely pace and entered the empty shop at the corner, having already busted the lock. The windows were smoked, not allowing anyone to see inside as she emptied the contents of the briefcase on the floor, searching for anything that might point to John.

Sketches, sketches, and more sketches, but nothing important. Figured. As Evie put the case back together, Blue came through the door. As usual, goose bumps broke out over her skin and her lower belly quivered.

Was she ever going to get used to his power . . . or his appeal?

"Anything?" he asked.

"No." She tossed the case at him with more force than necessary. Though her aim was off, he leaned to the side and caught it without a hitch. "Now go be a hero and tell her how badly you roughed me up, just to save the day. She'll be all over you."

He paused, tensed. "I'm not going to let things go that far." He stood there for several more beats, just staring over at her as if there were something else he wanted to say. Then he was gone, and she had the strangest desire to call him back.

Or, worse, to say thank you.

Blue gave Tiffany his most charming smile, and she blushed. He almost sighed. He'd never met such a timid little bird, so he wasn't sure how to deal with her.

At five ten, she was taller than the average woman. She had straight blond hair she liked to hide behind, and pretty green eyes she kept mostly downcast. He wasn't sure why she lacked confidence. Unless she was embarrassed by her past? He knew she'd been a pretty wild teen, and more than a recreational drug user.

But it looked like she'd gotten her life together. Today she wore a yellow summer dress that screamed pedigree, style, and sophistication. There were no track marks in her arms, and a deep tan made her skin glow.

After he returned the briefcase, she was ecstatic and grateful and offered to buy him coffee once she finished with her business meeting. He played the attracted suitor and happily agreed to wait.

Now, an hour later, they were at a little outdoor café, sipping joe and chatting—well, he was chatting, she was listening. In the past fifteen minutes, he'd counted thirteen camera phones aimed in their direction, and he'd never been more thrilled by the public's obsessive need to know about his love life.

Star would hear about the encounter. Maybe decide to meet with the man who'd saved his little girl's briefcase.

"So," he said.

"So."

Awkward. Wow. This might be his first strikeout. And Evie was at home, listening.

Unreadable Evie. He wanted her more than he'd ever wanted any woman, and he knew how she felt about this part of the job. It must be throwing his game.

For John. This is for John.

"I've met your father a few times," he said. "He's a fan of the Invaders and used to come to all our victory parties." *You attended a few yourself.*

"Oh." Down went her gaze. She fiddled with the lid on her coffee.

"Nice guy."

"Y-yes."

Interesting. Was that fear he detected? "What's he up to nowadays? I haven't seen him around."

"Working. As always."

Uncomfortable silence.

Screw this. "Tiffany," Blue said, layering his voice with the barest hint of compulsion. Testing the waters. . . . "Pinch my arm."

Her eyes glazed over, and she reached out, pinching him as he'd ordered. He almost whooped with relief. She wasn't immune.

Using more compulsion, he said, "I'm going to ask you a series of questions, Tiffany, and you are going to answer honestly. Do you understand?"

"Yes."

Good. "Have you seen your father with a Rakan?"

"No."

"Have you *heard* about your father and a Rakan?"

"Yes."

"Have you—" Yes? Excitement built. He leaned forward, saying in a rush, "Tell me everything you've heard."

Utterly monotone, she said, "I will be punished for speaking of it."

He increased the amount of compulsion. "Tell me everything you've heard about the Rakan, Tiffany. Now."

"In three weeks, I am to create a line of clothing from his pelt."

Create, not debut. A line of clothing. From John's . . . pelt.

Realization struck, and struck hard. John wasn't being used as a sex slave, as Blue first feared. The male's golden skin was to be peeled from his body and given to Tiffany. Then, after his skin had regrown, it would be peeled again . . . and again.

He would be a never-ending gold mine. Literally.

If Star had once sold organs on the black market, as rumors claimed, he would have the right contacts . . . and he was just monster enough to do it.

Fury rode the tides in Blue's veins before spilling out, filling him up, consuming him. Behind him, chairs and tables toppled over. Glass shattered. People yelped and raced for cover. John did not heal as quickly as Blue and was probably still injured from the explosion, his skin unusable—hence the three-week wait. There was still time to save him.

"Anything else?" he demanded.

"A small patch of the hide has already been removed for testing. Ribbons were made. Those ribbons are being sold at auction tonight."

A part of John had already been skinned. Blue barely contained his roar. "Where is the auction being held?"

She rattled off the details.

No one—*no one!*—was going to own a piece of John. Blue would make sure of it. "Do you know where your father is keeping the Rakan?"

"No."

No. Then she was of no more use to him. For now. Before he destroyed anything else, Blue pushed to his feet. "I'm going to send you an invitation to a postgame party, and you are going to accept and do whatever's necessary to attend. Say yes."

"Yes."

"Good girl."

Blue leaned down, saying, "You will forget the questions about the Rakan, Tiffany, but remember the invitation and your acceptance. You will also speak to your father about me. You will tell him you are interested in me romantically, and you'd like him to meet me."

"Yes," she said of her own accord. "If he refuses—"

"You'll tell him again." Blue confiscated her phone and programmed in his number. "Call me when your father issues his invitation." He tossed the device on the tabletop and stalked away—before giving in to the urge to kill her.

Blue drove to Evie's house, careful not to be seen, his temper only escalating. By the time he found her in the office, every muscle in his body was locked tight on bone. Looking at her didn't help. Anger morphed into dangerous lust.

She sat at her desk, dark waves cascading down her back. Perfect white teeth nibbled suggestively at the end of a stylus. A red tank top displayed toned arms with small but definite ropes of strength. She was fit. He remembered how good she felt pressed against him.

Power seeped from him, the desk and chair lifting several inches above the floor. Gasping, she turned to face him. As she took in his battle-hardened stance, her eyes hooded . . . with desire?

"Blue," she said, her voice husky with, yes, desire. She dropped to her feet with the grace of a cat and slowly approached him. The sway of her hips transfixed him. "I know you're furious and frustrated, but you can't go to the auction this way. So take your emotions out on me. I can handle anything you've got."

An invitation.

One he would not decline.

Forget Michael and the job. He had to have this woman.

He grabbed her by the waist and spun her, slamming her face-first against the wall. He braced her hands over her head and kicked her legs apart, the need to dominate her overwhelming everything else.

"Yes," she hissed.

With his free hand, he tore away her top, but didn't bother removing her jeans or undergarments. Just ripped at the fastenings. Her bra gaped open, freeing her breasts. The jeans bagged on her hips.

Not sex, some part of his brain screamed. *Not yet. Not like this.*

Rational thought.

He heard and accepted—barely.

Needing flesh-to-flesh contact, he let her go to wrench off his shirt and meld his chest to her back; the heat of her skin drove him toward the best kind of mindlessness. When she rubbed her taut little ass against him, he pushed her jeans below the curve and his throbbing erection found its way between the cleft. He hissed at the pleasure. She squeezed at him and, oh, hell. He bit the cord of her neck. *Have to have my mouth on her.* Her groan of rapture filled the small enclosure.

His hands moved to her breasts, cupping and kneading, causing her nipples to harden into perfect little points. Points he pinched.

"Blue!"

He kissed and licked at the sting he'd caused in her neck, still rubbing . . . rubbing into her ass, unable to stop. Felt so good. His fingers glided down her belly . . . slid under her panties, and played for a moment at her small tuft of hair, before sinking lower.

He almost blew. "So warm and wet, baby."

"Always that way for you."

Killing me. "Shouldn't have told me. May not be able to keep myself off you now." He circled . . . circled . . . where she needed him most, and as she trembled, she followed him with her hips.

"Do it." A command she expected to be obeyed. "Please."

Always begs so prettily. He pressed the heel of his hand against her and thrust a finger in deep.

"Yes!" She groaned, her head falling onto his shoulder. "More."

As he fed her a second finger, she reached back and wound her arms around him, her nails digging into his ass. She urged him to move against her harder, faster, until he was practically grinding her through the wall.

"Kiss me." She turned her head and he angled his, their mouths meeting in a scorching tangle of tongues and need, possession and domination.

There was aggression in the kiss. His. Hers. He loved it. It was a claim. A branding. On both their parts. He'd never felt so . . . desired, so necessary, and it was a heady thing. He knew he'd need it again and again.

Would need this honey in his mouth, down his throat, intoxicating him. No one else had ever tasted as sweet, or wine-rich. It was as if she had been made for him, and him alone. A sweet little puzzle piece for his life . . . his bed.

She climaxed with the hard thrust of a third finger, clenching around him, and it wasn't long before he joined her, emptying his body of the fury and frustration, and filling it back up with unending satisfaction.

And fear.

He wanted her too much, and the craving wasn't going away. Wasn't even muting. He was falling for her.

Falling hard.

Fifteen

*B*LUE AND EVIE CROUCHED in the rafters of the old barn where the auction for ribbons of John's skin was to be held. They'd been here for almost an hour, still, quiet, waiting, hidden by thick wooden beams and moldy hay.

He held at bay memories of the aftermath of their explosive encounter . . . until the second hour, when they knocked on the door of his mind, demanding entry.

Uncomfortable silence as they'd dressed.

Evie unable to meet his gaze.

A murmured "Well, that was fun, thanks" from her before she strode from the room, leaving him alone with his thoughts. She hadn't claimed him, after all.

Didn't matter. *He'd* claimed *her*.

The time before, he'd felt horror that he'd betrayed Michael, and guilt. That time, he'd felt resolve. He wanted more. And so, more he would have. He couldn't resist her. Fighting the attraction had done no good.

Now he would go after her. Win her.

Finally, the back doors of the barn creaked, signaling they were being opened. A short, wiry human with thinning hair, a great-white-shark tattoo coming up the collar of his shirt, and a man-baby belly, strutted inside with two armed men at his sides. One had a rifle. The other had a pyre-gun. Both were human.

Behind them, another male carried a small lacquered box with the Chinese symbol for *revenge* lining each side. There was no sign of Gregory, Tyson, or Tiffany, but Blue didn't care.

This was happening.

"—gonna go crazy for these," Shark was saying. He swiped his arm across the items on the nearest table, scattering everything to the ground.

The male placed the box on the surface. He was an Agamen, with huge white horns protruding from his skull. Bona fide ivory towers. Seriously, a colony of fairies could live inside those things.

Hell, maybe they did.

"I'm to remind you that there's major heat on these," Horns said.

Shark nodded and rubbed his hands together. "Consider me reminded. Now show me what I'm gonna be selling."

Horns fiddled with the locks on the box. The lid was flipped open.

Blue saw three golden ribbons resting inside and nearly vomited. The pain John must have suffered . . . must *be* suffering. He had to swallow back a roar of fury, had to lock his power down tight.

"Pretty, aren't they?" Horns said with a crooked grin.

"Are you kidding? They're gorgeous," Shark exclaimed. "When the Star girl finishes her designs . . . people are gonna go *insane*."

Across the expanse of the rafters, Blue met Evie's gaze. Determination radiated from her.

"They die," he mouthed. "Hard."

Gripping two daggers, he dropped from the ceiling and landed on his feet. Evie did the same, and together they surged forward. The men noticed and reached for weapons—but they were too late. Blue threw both of his daggers, one finding a home in Shark's right eye, the other in his left. Howling with pain, the guy dropped to his knees. Meanwhile, Evie savagely knifed one of the humans across the throat, his skin ripping and blood spraying.

Horns tried to sprint out the door, but Blue caught him with a thread of power—an invisible rope—and dragged him back, kicking and screaming. When Blue reached out, intending to slice through the horns to take them as a memento, the male bucked in an effort to jab him with the poisoned tips.

A swift stab, stab, stab deflated all three of the Agamen's lungs. Alien anatomy classes came in handy sometimes. The male flopped forward, allowing Blue to break his neck with a vicious jerk.

The last remaining target managed to get his hands on a pyre-gun and fire a shot at Evie. She ducked, the laser soaring just over her shoulder. Blue closed the distance in a blink, grabbing the human's arm, twisting, breaking the bone, and swiping the gun. He fed the barrel into the man's mouth and pulled the trigger.

Yellow lights sparked from every orifice the human possessed, and blood quickly followed. He crumbled to the ground.

You think you can take out my woman? Blue spit on the body.

Your woman? Really?

Whatever. He spun, desperate to fight someone else, but the battle was over. He stomped to the table, and Evie tagged along. They peered at the glittering golden ribbons curling so prettily against the velvet.

"I'm sorry," she whispered.

He nodded to let her know he'd heard.

"We'll find him."

Yes, they would. They would never stop searching, never give up. He didn't care what they had to do or who they had to kill.

"Let's get the box to Michael," he said.

The next few days were packed with activities. Evie held a press conference to announce she was taking over Black Industries and that she'd set up an exhibition game for the Invaders and Strikers at the end of the week. She called Tyson Star and set up a tour of the Star Light Hotel, but he wasn't the one to give her the tour. His personal assistant did the honors.

She almost threw a tantrum.

Also, Tiffany had yet to call Blue and ask him to meet her father.

But at least no one had tried to kill him. Or Evie. It was safe to assume his cover was solid, he wasn't a target, and whoever had ordered the car chase had changed his—or her—mind.

Even so, Evie was a bit on edge. She and Blue had not had their chat about expectations and had not made out again. Was he done with her?

No. Impossible. Last time he'd been totally on fire for her. Flames that hot couldn't have just died out.

Really? Reeeally? Have you ever witnessed a fire burning? Flames die out all the time, moron.

She could hear him puttering around in the kitchen, and shivered. He'd snuck over a few hours ago. He'd snuck over every night, actually, secretly staying in the guest room, just as he'd promised Michael.

Have I lost my appeal?

No, she thought again. She wasn't a raving beauty like the women he was used to, and she had the wrong hair color . . . and the wrong boob size. . . . Hey. She frowned. What had he ever seen in her?

She didn't know. But she had not fallen from the ugly tree and gotten hit by every branch, thank you. Blue *had* felt an attraction to her, and it had been strong enough that he'd forgotten his dislike of her.

Maybe . . . the stress was getting to him? He worked constantly, and rarely slept.

To be honest, she was having trouble keeping up with him.

"Dinner," Blue called.

He'd offered to cook, and she hadn't even given a token protest. Her culinary genius was limited to boiling soup and thawing the frozen dinners her father sometimes sent over.

"Be right down." She had left him alone about half an hour ago; the sight of him preparing a meal, acting all domesticated, had nearly sent her into a euphoric state of shock.

Translation: she'd wanted to jump him.

Her phone buzzed in her pocket as she padded to the kitchen. She checked the screen, saw Michael's name, and grinned. "Hey, you."

"Hey, sunbeam," he replied. He called her once a day to check in.

"How are you feeling?"

"Better."

He offered nothing more, so she said, "Did something happen?"

"Nope. Just wondering if the exhibition game was set."

A lie. He knew it was. He watched the news. "In two days, as planned. I've finalized all details for the after-party as well." A party where Blue would probably have to seduce the pants right off Tiffany Star. Nothing else had worked.

He would always do anything necessary to get what he needed from a target, so maybe their aborted romance was for the best. Evie hadn't changed her mind. She would *never* be okay with her man bagging other women, no matter the reason.

"Good," Michael said. "That's good."

Blue stood behind the counter and, without moving a muscle, used his power to push a plate of spaghetti across the counter.

"Thanks," she mouthed—and had to force herself to

look away from him before she started drooling. Could the man never wear a shirt?

I've had that chest pressed against mine, but I failed to touch or taste it. Bad Evie!

It would be a lifelong regret.

"I wanted to ask . . . how things are going with Blue?" There was something odd about her father's tone.

"Fine," she said, grateful he couldn't see the sudden color in her cheeks. "Why?"

"Are you two . . ."

She stifled a groan. "Fighting? No."

"That's not what I meant."

"Too bad for you, because that's the only question I'm willing to answer."

"Sorry, sunbeam, but this is important. I love the man, I do, but he's not right for you."

"You think I don't know that? And anyway, what brought this on?" she asked.

"I keep remembering the way you looked at him."

How had she looked at him?

Blimey. Had Blue noticed?

Blue stepped around her, getting in her face, clearly concerned. He mouthed, "Something wrong?"

"My father is butting into something that is not his business," she said, loud enough for both men to hear.

Blue straightened with a snap and paled, confusing her. Had he guessed what she meant? Was he offended—hurt by her father's lack of trust?

The thought of Blue hurt . . . upset her.

Michael sighed. "All right. I'll let it go. I just . . . I care about you, want the best for you."

"Then why did you visit me only seven times while I was overseas?" The question left her before she could stop it, the neediness of her tone embarrassing her.

He heaved another sigh. "Your mom . . . are you sure you want to hear this?"

Mum had interfered? "Yes."

"She threatened to hide you from me, and she was a good enough agent that I knew she could do it. I took whatever scraps she let me have, and pounced the moment you were legal."

"Oh." *"Oh"? That's all you have to say?* Her entire outlook had just been turned inside out. Years of upset, for no reason. "Dad—" she croaked.

"No, it's all right. It's okay. I knew why you were holding me at a distance, and I couldn't blame you. I've often thought I should have risked everything and just taken you away."

She blinked away a prickle of tears. "Just knowing you wanted to . . . thank you," she said.

"Yes, well." He cleared his throat as if he were having a little problem with tears, too. "I trained you to be an agent so that I could have more time with you. And you far surpassed my expectations. You should come back to work for me."

"No." She hadn't changed her mind. When this was over, she was going back to her old life, where the lives of strangers rested in her hands—not the lives of loved ones.

"Stubborn," he muttered. "Look, I've been watching the video and listening to the feed you sent me. I found a clip of Star at the Lucky Horn the day before the explosion, but there's no audio, so I can only guess that's when the bombing was being planned. Then, in the live feed from his estate, I heard something interesting."

"What?"

"I'll text you the details. Tomorrow morning, you and Blue have a new mission."

The line went dead.

She set down her phone, scooped up her plate, and settled in at the table where Blue waited. He hadn't yet touched his food. Had waited for her like a proper gentleman. She would have thought him calm if not for the tendrils of power now falling over her.

They were strongest when he was upset . . . or aroused. Right now, they were *very* strong.

So which was he?

Trembling, she picked up her fork. He picked up his, and she was momentarily blinded to all but his long, blunt-tipped fingers. *I've had those inside me.*

"Tell me about Claire," he said, voice flat, utterly emotionless.

Instant mood killer!

Why did he want to know? Why was he pressing this yet again? "No," she said.

He stared at her, unwavering. "Have you ever talked about it with anyone?"

"No." And she wouldn't. Couldn't.

His nod of acceptance was stiff.

Silent, they picked at their food for a few minutes. He was a good cook, and that kind of sucked, because it meant he was good at everything he did. That he had no deficiencies.

Soon the tension got to her, his power still stroking over her, revving her up so much that liquid heat began to pool between her legs. Her voice was raspy as she said, "Are we ever going to talk about what happened in my foyer . . . and my office?"

"Yes. But not now."

What? Why? "When?"

"Soon. I hope."

Not good enough. She dropped her fork and glared at him. "Why wait?"

His gaze raked over her, and heated, the lavender darkening to a deep, rich plum. "Feeling needy, princess?"

Yes!

Can't lie to him. So, instead of answering, she hopped to her feet. "If you don't want me anymore, just say it. I'm a big girl and I don't need coddling."

He remained silent.

Figured. She stepped around him with every intention of storming off. But he grabbed her by the waist and jerked her onto his lap. Those thick, muscular thighs. But he didn't keep her there. He pushed the plates aside and set her on the table.

"I want you. I always want you." He unfastened her pants and tugged them and her knickers down her legs, leaving her bare from the waist down. "Now spread your legs."

She obeyed, but not quickly enough for his taste. He placed his palms on her knees, his skin so hot the contact burned, burned so good, and pushed her thighs apart, as wide as they would go. Exposing her. Making her vulnerable to his view.

He just sat there, looking at her. Heat in his glowing eyes. Expression taut. A charge thickened the air, and she found it difficult to breathe. She trembled, almost violently. Waiting was a beautiful agony . . . and then just agony.

"Please." Begging him again? Yes. If that's what it took.

"Oh, I'll give you something."

"Will you give me everything?"

"You're so pretty here," he said, ignoring her question. "I think it's time for dessert." And then he was on her, his mouth where she needed him. Hot and insistent, stoking her desire higher and higher with every flick of his masterful tongue. He licked up and down, from side to side, and all she could do was roll her hips and seek more.

Her fingers tangled in his hair. "Blue!" And then she was lying down, resting her feet on the arms of his chair, and he was reaching out, his hands cupping her breasts, as he ate and ate and ate. Pleasure spiraled through her, strong, insistent, demanding, building, building. She wasn't going to last. Had wanted him too much, too long.

A scream ripped from her as she climaxed.

Blue tugged her upright and stood. He tore at the button and zipper on his pants. His shaft, so long and thick, stretched past the material. The head glistened, proving just how badly he wanted her.

"Know how good you taste, baby? Never had anything like it. But now I need you to suck me."

"Yes." She dropped to her knees, with no hesitation, and took him deep into her mouth. He moaned her name, a plea, a curse, then moaned again, whatever he said next unintelligible. He was so big he hurt her jaw, but she didn't care. She moved on him, again and again, until his hips were pumping in rhythm with her mouth. Faster . . . faster . . . she pressed her tongue against his shaft with every upward glide, and when she reached the top she gave a little suck . . . again and again . . . and it was so good, *so bloody good.*

"About to . . . Baby, I want you to swallow me. Every drop."

Then they were on the same page.

She gave another suck, a harder one, and that was it, that finished him. He came, roaring with his satisfaction.

After she'd taken everything he had to give, she rose to shaky legs—only to realize she and Blue were floating in midair.

"Uh, do me a solid and ease us back down," she said even as she tensed, expecting a crash.

He tucked himself back into his pants and frowned. Then they were drifting to the floor, landing.

She pulled on her jeans and opened her mouth to say . . . what? *That can't happen again?* Or: *Why won't you just do me already?*

Her phone beeped, saving her from having to decide.

Michael's text. The new mission. "We're to intercept one of Star's employees tomorrow morning."

Blue nodded. Then, without a word, he stalked from the kitchen.

"I'm getting tired of watching you walk away," she called.

He offered no response.

What did he want from her? What were they to each other?

What would happen next between them?

Despite everything, she almost couldn't wait to find out.

He wasn't having sex with Evie until she trusted him enough to talk about Claire. The more he had of her, the more he wanted from her—and the less she offered. She had things backward, and it was time he turned things around.

Judging by the one-sided conversation he'd heard when Evie was on the phone, he suspected Michael knew something was going on.

Blue planned to nut up and tell the man all . . . just as soon as he knew what "all" encompassed. What, exactly, did he want from the girl?

What would she give him?

Right now, not much.

Would disappointing Michael be worth it? Should Blue change his mind about going after her *yet again* and walk away before anything else was added to his "all" tab?

His gaze strayed to Evie, who sat across from him in another unmarked sedan. She distracted him, obsessed him, angered him, frustrated him . . . delighted him. With her, he discovered a rare ecstasy.

He'd once considered her a momentary pleasure. But she wasn't. She was more than that. So he asked himself again: Would disappointing Michael be worth it, no matter how little Evie wanted from him?

Yeah.

So no, there would be no changing his mind.

Think carefully. His game was tomorrow, and the party the day after that. Which meant, in two days he would be turning up the heat on Tiffany Star. The thought left him cold, even disgusted, but he'd never been more determined to break a case.

His stomach twisted in a thousand tiny knots. In private, he could compel Miss Tiffany to do and think whatever he wished. Sex could be taken off the menu. But in public, he would have to play the part of besotted suitor. There was no way around it.

How would Evie react to, say, a kiss? End things with him then and there?

Would oral sex at dinner be nothing more than a fond memory?

He wanted to howl.

He would talk to her before the party and make her understand. And he would talk to Michael when things calmed down. He wasn't a coward. He would deal with everything thrown his way.

Concentrate.

He and Evie parked their car at the end of a neighborhood street, waiting for their target. Their windows were tinted. No one could see inside, but they could see everything outside. Blue was anxious to get the ball rolling. Apparently, an employee of Star's was supposed to deliver a message to a human named Tyrese Cooper, the owner of the house they were watching.

"Why hasn't Solo revealed himself to you?" Evie asked, probably to fill the silence. He'd noticed she always cracked after a few minutes, as if she couldn't bear to be alone with her thoughts. "I mean, he knows you're alive. The entire world does."

Blue had spent a lot of time mulling over that particular question. "Two possible reasons. He thinks he'll draw heat to us, or that we'll draw heat to him."

"Yeah, okay. That makes sense. I just wish he'd send a text, you know. You deserve a text at the very least."

She used her hands to punctuate her words.

Just as she'd done the night he'd met her.

He wanted to grin. It was as if she'd lost that part of herself, but now it was back.

But what had brought it back? Blue?

I want to be the reason.

"He has— Car!" Evie said, suddenly eager. "That's gotta be our guy."

His gaze landed on the SUV easing into Cooper's driveway. After parking, an Arcadian emerged. Oh, yeah. That was Star's man. "Stay here. We don't know what supernatural abilities he possesses."

Miracle of miracles, she didn't offer an argument. He exited into the light and heat of the day. Just in case anyone was waiting in the SUV, Blue wrapped a stream of power around it, ensuring the doors would stay closed. He also wrapped a stream of power around the Arcadian, trying to hold him in place, but the male easily broke free with his own power, whipped around, and searched for the culprit.

Their gazes locked. Lavender against lavender.

At first, the male appeared awestruck. He was seeing football legend Corbin Blue. Then the cogs in his brain started turning, and it was clear he'd realized a football legend would not be here, clearly armed and ready for war.

The male shot across the lawn, down the street. Superspeed. Blue used his own, following, closing in. Around a corner. Over a parked car. Evading several fake trees.

They were going around the block, Blue realized. Heading back to Cooper's. Guy planned to jump in his car, most likely, and grab a weapon or phone for backup—because there was no way the SUV could move faster than Blue.

Cooper's house came into view.

Closer . . . Blue released a stream of power to trip the male, but he dodged it. *Have to pick up speed—*

A shovel came out of nowhere, smashing into the male's chest. He ricocheted backward and landed on the street, air gushing from him in one mighty heave.

Evie dropped the shovel and withdrew a pyre-gun, aiming the barrel at the wheezing Arcadian. "All right, boys. Playtime is over."

Gorgeous, wily woman. Blue had never been so happy to see her. "Where'd you get the shovel, boo-boo?"

Grinning proudly—and ignoring his choice of nicknames for once—she said, "I have all kinds of fun things in the trunk of each of my cars. Pray you never find out firsthand."

Always prepared. Could she be any sexier?

Blue heaved his prize over his shoulder and stomped over to the SUV. There was no one inside. They closed in on Cooper's house and didn't bother ringing the bell, just burst inside.

A startled human sat in a chair in the living room, a bottle of whisky in hand. He was too drunk to care about the invaders.

"Stay," Evie told him, marching forward.

He stayed. And waved.

Blue tossed the Arcadian face-first on the dark shag carpet. He slapped a hand over the otherworlder's mouth, then ran a blade across the backs of his knees, silencing and hobbling him at the same time.

When the muffled screaming stopped, Blue turned him over and straightened, looking over his opponent. Bright lamplight revealed an otherworlder of average size. Meaning he was bigger than a human but far smaller than Blue. Typical Arcadian white hair and lavender eyes. Skin weathered from the harshness of the earth's sun. Extensively armed. Blue removed each of the weapons.

"I'm going to ask questions, and you're going to answer or you're going to suffer," Blue said, the seriousness of his tone making the guy shudder. "First up: Why were you sent to this house to see Mr. Cooper?"

"Message," the Arcadian moaned.

Good. There would be no messing around. "Tell me."

"Can't."

Or maybe there would. Blue raised his knife.

"I can't tell—I have to show you!" the guy said in a rush.

"Then show me. Just don't make any sudden moves or you'll lose an appendage."

Fat tears cascaded down the male's cheeks as he slowly dug into his pocket and withdrew a small IDC. An identification card.

Blue took it and pressed the button in the center. Inches above it, the air flickered with tiny blue lights, and the Chinese symbol for *revenge* formed. The same symbol had been painted on the box holding John's ribbons, as well as on the house walls of the seventeen people Star was suspected of abducting.

When Blue had first seen the symbol in the crime scene photos, he assumed it was either a mistake— too many people had gotten inked with symbols for constipation rather than, say, courage—or that it was meant to be deliberately misleading. What could Star have against all those people? People he wasn't linked to in any other way.

"Why were you supposed to give this to Mr. Cooper?" Evie demanded, picking up where Blue had left off.

"I—I don't know," the otherworlder said. "I wasn't told."

"Have you ever had to deliver this type of message before?" Blue asked.

"Yes."

"To whom?"

The male rattled off a list of names, all of the ones on the abduction list and several that were not. Interesting. Blue would have to check into the others and find out if the individuals were missing and just hadn't been reported, or if something else had happened to them . . . or if nothing nefarious had happened at all.

"Mr. Cooper," Evie said, her tone gentle now. She crouched in front of the homeowner. "Can you tell us what's going on? Why Gregory Star would want revenge against you?"

That's when the human began to sob. Great, heaving sobs, with tears and snot and slobber. He spoke, but his words were incoherent.

They'd get no answers from him anytime soon.

Evie met Blue's gaze. "Let's take him to Michael and get you to the stadium for your pregame workout or whatever it is you jocks do. Once Mr. Cooper has sobered up, he can be questioned further."

Blue nodded, then turned his attention to the Arcadian. "Does Mr. Star have a Rakan hidden somewhere in his home?"

"N-no."

"Are you lying to me?"

"No! I haven't seen a Rakan, I swear."

"Have you heard one?"

"No!"

Okay, then. Blue confiscated Evie's pyre-gun and squeezed the trigger. A bright white light lanced to the man's chest, burning through his heart in seconds. He was dead before he had time to panic or scream.

Blue had been ID'd as an agent. Maybe Star already knew, and didn't care. Maybe he didn't. No reason to take chances, and every reason not to—John could be used against him.

"You get Mr. Cooper to your father," he said to Evie. "I'll take care of the Arcadian."

"What about your practice?"

"I'll be on time, don't worry." Then: "You gonna come to the game tomorrow?" he asked, unable to help himself.

She closed the distance, took her gun, and peered up at him. "You want me to?"

He didn't need to think about his answer. "Yeah." He liked the thought of her eyes on him while he kicked ass all over the field.

The look in those dark, dark eyes softened. "Then I'll be there."

Sixteen

~~~

E VIE SAT IN THE owner's box at Black Stadium. She had invited Tyson Star, to thank him for renting out the roof of the Star Light Hotel to her the following night, but he'd declined. What was it going to take to meet the guy?

Secretive cur!

To place a cherry on top of an E. coli–infested sundae, she hated football. So far, Blue had endured eight major body slams. He had to have a concussion, among ten thousand other injuries. The Strikers were clearly determined to bag and tag him like a mangy animal.

There was one highlight, however. Blue ran the ball in for the first quarter's only touchdown. She cheered so loud she nearly shattered the armored window in front of her.

And okay, all right, fine. That wasn't the only highlight. Blue was sexy as hell in his black and gold uniform, and she was beyond turned on.

Like that's anything new.

It was just, she'd never met a man like him, and doubted she ever would again. He wasn't just beautiful on the outside, a fallen angel in an otherworlder's skin.

Or something out of a fairy tale. Like a prince/villain hybrid. He was beautiful on the inside. He treated her with respect, even when she didn't do the same to him. He protected. He amused.

She wanted him. Naked. In her bed. Not just for hand play, or oral, but straight-up sex. Hard. Fast. Rough. And then, when the first frantic wave of need was finally sated, she wanted him slow and soft.

Why wouldn't he give it to her?

And *why* did she want it from him and him alone? Why couldn't she just let him go and pick someone else? Tomorrow he might have to do things with Tiffany, in public . . . and in private.

No. No. Not this time. He hated that part of his job. Hated taking things so far.

That kind of crap stopped now.

She wanted him, and he wanted her. Therefore, she would have him—not Tiffany. He could get answers from the girl another way.

Evie would talk to him. He would either agree, or not. One way or another, she would have a solid answer, and she could decide her next move.

A one-time seduction . . . or more.

Because, at the end of the day, she trusted him. And, wow, what a difference a few weeks had made. They'd gone from hate and disgust to . . . whatever this was.

"I know!" a female voice proclaimed.

"Just isn't right," another said.

The voices snagged her attention. Behind her, a gaggle of the players' spouses and girlfriends talked and ran the gamut of emotion. Each female was tall, thin, and gorgeous, dressed in skimpy clothing meant to lure and tempt men famous for their feminine conquests. Somehow all of the girls were the "bestest friends ever."

Oi. Because Evie graduated so early, the only female friends she'd ever had were Claire and Eden, and as family they'd *had* to like her. She'd never made a friend on her own. Besides Blue. But he didn't have boobs so he didn't count. The mechanics of female bonding utterly baffled her.

At least she had the best seat in the box, the only one directly in front of the window. The rest of the women were squeezed behind her in rows of six.

"The entire situation is just so uncool. But I talked to Pagan last night and she told me they're just taking a break," one of the girls said in a stage whisper.

"Well, she lied. Her neighbor was interviewed this morning," another replied, using the same loud-hush tone, "and the guy told reporters he heard Blue tell Pagan they were finished forever."

"So brutal!"

Evie remembered how terrible Blue felt when it was over. No way he'd been brutal.

"Good riddance, I say. I never liked her."

"Me neither. Talk about sleazy. That girl would do anything with a penis. Supposedly, the day after Blue dumped her, she was seen making out with three different guys at Club Joy Ride."

"I can believe it. I caught her eye-stripping my man once. As if he would ever be desperate enough for the likes of her."

There was no response, and every moment of silence caused the air to thicken with tension.

Uh-oh. Bet her man *had* done Miss Cary at some point.

"What?" the girl demanded.

"Uh, nothing. Nothing at all."

"Well, I think Pagan had every right to seek comfort from other men so quickly. How many times did Blue cheat on her? Countless."

Evie's hackles rose. These women . . . they didn't know Blue. They didn't know his thoughts, feelings, hopes and dreams. They didn't know the situation or what happened behind the scenes. And yet they acted as judge and jury, as if they'd never made a mistake.

Once, I was just as guilty. But no more.

Besides, lovers went to Blue with their eyes wide open. They knew what they were getting. He told them. *Just like he'll tell me.*

The conversation tapered into another subject, saving her from having to throw a pimp hand around. After a while, even the newest topic lagged into silence. The girls turned their attention to the game. Unfortunately, the reprieve didn't last long.

"So, Evangeline. It's nice to see you here."

She turned to meet the gaze of the only redhead, and offered a tight smile. Though the girl's tone was friendly, there was a speculative gleam in her brown eyes. This was a gossip hunt, no question.

"Thanks." What was Red's name? The girlfriends came and went so frequently, Evie never bothered to learn.

The speculative gleam deepened. "I feel so bad that

so many of the players want out of their contracts now that Michael is gone. I'm sure it has nothing to do with you personally, though. I wouldn't worry."

What a sweet little backhanded compliment. Passive-aggressive behavior at its finest. Better to combat this head-on. "Anyone wanting out of his contract has only to ask. He'll be cut and replaced within a single day. And, actually, that's why I'm here. Now that I've taken over Black Industries, I want to give the boys a look-see." Then, just to be contrary, she added, "Might be fun to restructure and use new starters, don't you know."

Red flushed and said nothing else.

Break time. "Now, if you'll excuse me . . ." Evie stood and walked through the spacious room, past the long L-shaped bar surrounded by multiple padded stools. In the far corner, hidden in the dark wood-paneled walls, was the entrance to a private bathroom. She stepped inside, locked the door, and—even though she told herself not to do it—cranked the volume on the concealed mics in the box, multiple conversations filtering inside as she washed her face. She concentrated on one.

"—should take bets on Blue's next conquest," Red was saying.

A catty laugh sounded. "Whoever she is, she'll be blond and stacked."

Great. Like Evie really needed the reminder about Blue's preference—everything she wasn't!

"So, what do you think of Evangeline? I've never been a fan. She's such a bit—"

Okay. Enough of that. She cut the feed.

Bracing her hands against the sink, she leaned her forehead against the mirror. *I'm in way over my head, aren't I?*

Blue could be on the Bedroom Olympic Team.

Evie had experience. A lot of experience. More than she liked to admit. So much she was ashamed, often trying to hide behind a mask of propriety. *I can be honest with everyone but myself.* But all of that experience had come before the age of eighteen, when she'd desperately craved male attention. Whatever attention she could get. She'd learned from boys, not men. How was she supposed to seduce someone like Blue?

Uh, you haven't had trouble so far.

True. Three encounters with him, three earth-shattering orgasms. But what was it going to take to get Blue to go all the way with her?

Sighing, she left the confines of the bathroom and settled back in her seat. None of the women spoke to her. Wise.

Both teams rushed onto the field for the next play. Every member of the Invaders and every member of the Strikers was an otherworlder of some sort. From white-haired Arcadians like Blue, to big and meaty Ell Rollies, to thin and colorful Mecs, to catlike Terrans and Bree Lians, to Viking-like Targons.

Each race came with different abilities, which made the game a thousand times more dangerous . . . and exciting. There was only one rule. No using super-speed. Otherwise, spectators and refs wouldn't be able to track what was going on.

Evie watched the players explode into action, the

ball whizzing through the air, some men diving for it, some throwing others halfway across the field. After a particularly nasty tackle, the Arcadian known as "the Mack" shoved Blue, his hands exploding with a ball of light. Blue went soaring backward. A giant Ell Rollie pounded through the men forming a circle of protection around Blue, tackling him. Once again Blue soared backward . . . and yet still he managed to maintain a solid grip on the ball.

He rolled to his feet and launched into motion, slamming into the Ell Rollie and nearly splitting the man in two.

The crowd went wild, loving his use of brute force.

As the male writhed in pain, Blue grinned a cocky grin while lifting the ball and ending the play.

The third quarter concluded with no touchdowns.

In the middle of the fourth quarter, the other team finally managed to score, and she could tell Blue was ticked off royally. Then the . . . whatever his title was threw the ball to Blue and Blue threw the ball to . . . no, Blue faked a pass and now ran . . . and ran . . . and ran . . . until the Mack caught up with him. Rather than dodge, Blue grabbed him by the neck, twisted, and flung the limp body to the side. The Mack wasn't dead, but he'd be in pain for days to come.

Half of the stadium jumped to their feet and clapped as he sprinted . . . across . . . yes! He'd just crossed the finish line.

The Invaders scored their second touchdown!

Blue's teammates dog piled on him. Behind Evie, the women whooped and danced.

The game continued with two more plays, but the opposing team couldn't break through the Invaders' defensive line. When the final buzzer rang out, the Invaders were still ahead.

Victory belonged to Blue.

Utter chaos reigned on the field. As the other team jogged away to sulk, the Invaders, their coaches, and the fans closest to the action hurried together, cheering and hugging.

Blue stood in the middle of the storm, somehow set apart from it. He combed a hand through the pale hair plastered to his scalp. The black streaks painted under his eyes were smeared. Blood streaked his chin.

White-hot awareness held her in a tight clasp. He'd never looked more rugged.

He's mine.

For right now, at least.

He glanced up at the window where she waited and grinned slowly.

At her?

Heart thumping, Evie walked out of the box. She joined a group of reporters already congregating outside the locker room, and leaned against the wall to wait. A few eager beavers asked her what she thought of the game, but her answers must have bored them, because she was soon forgotten. An hour passed before Blue finally emerged, showered and clean, wearing a black tee and jeans.

She straightened as recorders were shoved in his face and questions were hurled at him. He ignored everyone, his gaze scanning the crowd. When he found her, a megawatt smile broke out on his face. Her heart skipped a beat and her blood heated.

He marched forward, and anyone stupid enough to stay in his path got mowed down. Then he was standing in front of her, thrums of his power stroking over her, making her tremble.

"As the new owner of the Invaders, what'd you think?" he asked.

She gave him a more colorful response. "A little tame, yeah. I expected rivers of blood stopped up by the occasional organ."

He barked out a laugh.

"I'll see you tomorrow night at Star Light, Mr. Blue." She left as reporters snapped pictures and threw more questions at him, but waited for him in the private parking garage the players and their significant others used.

He arrived a short while later. None of the others had made it yet, which led her to believe her man had rushed to get to her.

The thought warmed her.

As they walked side by side, he bumped her with his shoulder. "What'd you really think?"

"You should have broken every bone in the Mack's body, not just his scrawny neck."

His lopsided grin was too adorable for words.

A blond woman with tear tracks on her cheeks stepped from behind a pillar. Blue stopped abruptly.

"Pagan," he said, surprised.

Instant guilt.

"If I can't have you, no one can." The girl aimed a

.44 and squeezed off two shots before Evie had time to process what was happening.

Blue's body jerked once, twice before a crimson flood sprang forth, soaking his shirt. It looked like two valves had burst inside him.

Crimson. Blood.

Not Blue. Anyone but Blue.

Pagan sprinted off. Evie wanted to chase after her, *so badly*, but she wanted to see to Blue more. Concern coursed through her as she dug through her purse, searching for the first-aid kit she'd decided to carry only this morning, thinking Blue might have a few cuts and bruises after the game.

He pressed his fists into the wounds, then lifted his blood-soaked fingers to the light. Fury bathed his expression. "I'll be fine. Go get her. Bring her back. Mostly alive."

"Blue, you're—"

"Evie."

Fine. She tossed him the kit and launched into motion, following the path the human had taken. As she ran, she palmed her pyre, her gaze constantly scanning . . . there! The blonde shut the driver's-side door to a navy blue BMW. And she had clearly already programmed her escape route into the GPS, because the vehicle darted into motion.

I don't think so.

Evie aimed. Fired.

A stream of golden light arrowed to the back tire, and the vehicle slowed, stopped. That was the problem with preprogrammed systems. One little thing went wrong, and the entire vehicle shut down.

Evie closed the distance and jerked at the door. Locked. She aimed the gun at the window and said, "Open it and get out on your own, or I'll open it and drag your bleeding carcass out."

Wide, watery blue eyes stared at her for a long moment. Pagan's gun rested on the passenger seat, but she didn't reach for it. Her empty, trembling hands pushed the door out of the way.

"Slowly," Evie commanded.

Pagan straightened at a snail's pace, gripping the side of the door to remain standing as her knees knocked together.

Evie had once felt bad for this woman. And, okay, a part of her still did. But shooting Blue? Hell, no. That wasn't allowed.

"D-don't hurt me," Pagan stuttered. "Please. I'm . . . pregnant. With Blue's baby. Please, just let me go."

Pregnant? Hardly. Blue was smarter than that. "Don't be that girl. Now step away from the car, and drop to your knees."

Tears falling in earnest, Pagan obeyed. Evie moved behind her, dug a pair of laser cuffs from her purse, and fastened them around her wrists. When Evie pressed the center, the cuffs lit up, bonding to Pagan's skin. If she tried to break free, she'd lose her hands.

Evie helped her to her feet. A little push between her shoulders propelled her forward.

Blue hadn't budged. He'd removed his shirt and

strapped bandages over the wounds, but the cotton was already soaked in blood. Evie's anger revved back up.

"Knees," she commanded, forcing Pagan to the ground. Then she placed the barrel of the gun at the back of the girl's head. "I wouldn't try anything else, yeah. I'm already looking for an excuse to end you."

A sob bubbled from the girl. "I'm sorry. I'm so sorry, Blue. I didn't mean to kill you, I just . . . I'm so sorry. I wanted you to hurt the way I'm hurting."

"I know," he said, and his gentle tone surprised Evie. "But you could spend the rest of your life in prison for this, Pagan."

Her head bowed. Her body shuddered.

"Tell him what you told me," Evie snapped.

"I'm . . . not," the girl said, her shoulders hunching in. "I lied."

"About?" Blue asked.

Evie met his gaze. "Pregnancy."

His lips pressed into a thin, firm line.

"I'm sorry," Pagan said again.

He sighed. "I'm going to let you go."

"What?" the girl gasped.

"Yeah," Evie said, baffled. Mercy from a hardened agent? "What?"

"Go home. Get some help. Don't approach me again. Don't approach Evie. You do, and I'll consider you a threat and act accordingly."

"Yes, yes." A stream of rapid nods. "All right. I promise."

He looked to Evie, his expression granite hard. "Release her."

Though she wanted to argue, she removed the bands. Pagan drew her wrists to her chest and rubbed at the sensitized skin. "Thank you, Blue." She stood, saying, "I'm sorry for what I did, I really am."

"Go," he said.

She didn't have to be told twice. Off she scampered.

"Well, that was stupid," Evie said, disappointed, relieved, and a thousand other conflicting emotions. "She'll try again."

"No. It's out of her system. And besides that, it was deserved."

Hello self-recrimination. "Blue—"

"No," he said. "Don't say it."

"I will say it. What happened *wasn't* deserved."

He gave her a small smile. "Let's go home and get these damn bullets out of me."

"Fine. But this conversation isn't over."

Seventeen

~~~~~~~~~~~~~~~

*E*VIE WASN'T SURPRISED THAT Blue remained conscious during the drive. There was no man stronger. But she was concerned by the amount of blood he was losing, and the way he was staring straight ahead, his breathing choppy, his heartbeat too hard and too fast every time she checked.

"Distract me," he said.

"How?"

"Talk to me. Tell me about your life."

No way she could refuse. "Well . . . I tested out of school, and attended university at the age of thirteen. I majored in chemical engineering, my first love, but Mum made sure I took private classes on weapons technology and security."

He frowned. "You were too young."

"Yeah. Believe me, I know. Kids never let me forget. No friends, but lots of teasing."

"No wonder you're so guarded."

"Guarded? Me?"

He snorted. "You know you are."

Maybe. Okay, definitely. Letting people in was tough. Caring about someone other than yourself made you vulnerable. Left you wide open for all kinds of hurt. And if you lost a loved one? You would never be the same.

No pain no gain, though. Right?

Ugh. Stupid cliché. But, okay, she got the gist. Letting people in also came with great rewards. You'd have someone to rely on. Someone to protect your back. Someone to pick you up when you were down.

"How did you become a doctor?" he asked.

"Medicine was already in my wheelhouse. When I worked with people in drug trials, I realized I enjoyed the fruits of one-on-one contact, making individuals better. I switched my focus, and pharmacology became a hobby." The NOW—New World Order—allowed students to dive into their chosen field without retaking subjects they'd mastered in high school. "However, I opted not to take a residency and instead came to the New States to be with Michael. He trained me for two years before sending me on that first fateful mission."

"I knew you were young when you started working with him, but wow. Only twenty."

"How old were *you* on your first mission?"

"Mission, twelve. Kill, fourteen."

Blimey! "Now *that's* bloody young."

"Yeah, but I trained with Michael since the age of five. He'd found me on the streets and placed me with my human family. He paired me with John and Solo. He gave me a purpose."

No wonder Blue loved her father so much.

No wonder her father loved him. They'd been together a long time. *Relied on* each other a long time.

"I was jealous of you, you know. During our first meeting."

He shook his head, as if he'd misheard. "Jealous of *me*? Why?"

"For the entire two years I spent with Michael, he talked about you and your magnificence. 'Blue's so good at this. Blue's so good at that.' What a privilege it was to work with you, blah, blah, blah. It was quite disgusting. I'd waited my whole life to be with him, only to see his devotion directed at someone else."

He gave her a small, sad smile. "That explains a lot."

"Yeah. But it wasn't your fault, and I'm sorry for the way I treated you."

"You keep saying that."

"Because it's true. I am."

"If I can get past it, you can, too. Stop apologizing."

"Are you, though?" she continued softly. "Are you past it?"

He reached over to smooth a lock of hair behind her ear, grimaced at the smear of blood he left behind, and dropped his arm. "I really think I am."

Think was far better than *no*.

"But even if I wasn't," he added, "you wouldn't need to apologize again. You said it, you meant it with all your heart. If that's not good enough for me, the problem is with me and you'd be better off dumping my ass."

"I—"

"Don't dump my ass," he rushed out, and she smiled. "The only thing I'll ever make you beg for is pleasure."

They reached the house before she could question

him further. Her beautiful redbrick home had three sets of windows on both stories, everything lit up by strategically placed night-lights. At the side of the house, she went down, down, down the ramp into the basement garage.

She parked and rushed to Blue's side to offer her body as a crutch. He refused, linking their fingers and leading her inside. He-man, she thought with a shiver. *Such strength.*

He took her straight to the top floor, to the suite of rooms she'd turned into a woman's paradise. There were plush couches and chairs made of real leather and drapes of velvet, plus gilded mirrors, and cherrywood furnishings. Her favorite? The huge bed with marble posts, swathed in ice-blue fabrics.

"Sit," she commanded. In the bathroom, she grabbed her medical bag from under the sink.

He was in the same place she'd left him. Standing.

"I told you to sit."

"No way. The moment I bleed on your sheets, you'll stick me with a bill for a couple thousand dollars."

True. "You can afford it."

"Not if I continue to hemorrhage cash at Chez Black."

Their arms brushed as she moved past him, and she gasped as bolts of white lightning flashed through her. Flushing, she set the bag on the nightstand and dug through the contents, removing everything she would need. Bullet extractor, hand sanitizer, two syringes of cell regenerator, bandages, and wet wipes. All packaged and sterilized.

"I'm surprised you didn't have these supplies in your purse," he said. "Speaking of, have you added anything new?"

"Here." She lifted the strap over her head and handed the entire bag to him. "Have a peek."

As she spread a plastic tarp over the bed, making sure the protective cover draped all the way to the floor, he said, "A moon rock, a glass eye, a retractable blade, a socket wrench, and 3-D glasses." He grinned at her. "You have to tell me. Why a glass eye?"

"I thought you might lose a real one during the game and didn't want to stare at an empty socket. Now, lie down."

He both laughed and hissed as he stretched out on the mattress.

"Here," she said. "Let me shoot you up with—"

"No. No drugs. Want to stay awake and keep a clear head."

"You'll hurt."

"I'm not afraid of pain, princess."

She cleaned her hands and removed the bandages he'd applied. There were two wounds, both the size of a quarter and still leaking blood. "I've done a little research on Arcadian anatomy since the last time we were in this position. You'll find I'm a better doctor this go-round."

"You were great before."

A compliment? Injured Blue was sweet. She'd have to remember that. "Ready?" she asked, placing the cups on the extractor over both wounds.

"Do it."

With the press of a button, the cups adhered to his chest, the camera mapped the best course for exit, and the suction slowly pulled the bullets out of his body. He cursed only eight times.

"Not better," he gritted. "You are definitely not better."

Don't grin. "Need another distraction?" she asked. "Because what happens next is going to feel a thousand times worse."

"Yeah. Distract me."

She lobbed her first question. "Are you truly attracted to me?"

He blinked up at her. "Are you kidding me?"

"Dead serious."

"You actually have to ask?"

"Yes. I'm not even close to being your type."

He ran his tongue over his teeth. "So, your real question is whether or not I'm using you for something. Thanks a lot."

"You couldn't be more wrong. The question had nothing to do with your reasons and everything to do with my own insecurities. There haven't been many men interested in inserting themselves into my life, not for long anyway, yet here you are and I just don't get what I have to offer you."

The faint lines around his eyes softened. "I am truly attracted to you, Evie Black. And it's a strong attraction. The strongest I've ever experienced. Even though I've tried to fight it—and that statement has nothing to do with any kind of type."

The strongest he'd ever experienced was with *her*? *Watch Evie melt into a puddle of goo.* "Then what?"

"What else? Your father. According to him, you're off-limits."

So . . . he didn't want to upset Michael. Was *that* why he hadn't gone all the way with her? "Well, he'll never know what transpires between us."

"He will. I'll tell him."

What? "Blue—"

"I'm not going to hide it, Evie."

He had a freaking conscience. Great. "Then we'll tell him after we've found John. Not that there's much to tell," she grumbled.

"You complaining?"

"Well, yeah. Was that not clear? I thought that was clear."

Again his lips quirked at the corners. "How long has it been since you've had sex?"

"Why?" Could he tell she was out of practice?

"Let's call it curiosity and leave it at that."

Heat bloomed in her chest. "The last time, I was twenty-three," she admitted.

"And you're, what? Twenty-six now?" He nearly choked on his tongue. "Why? How could you go three years without it?"

"I was a bit of a wild child, all right, sleeping with any older university guy who'd pay attention to me. I was used *a lot*, and I started to feel dirty. At seventeen, I decided to wait for a meaningful relationship. That never happened, so from seventeen to twenty-three, I got good at being alone. Then, after Claire, I was looking to punish myself, I suppose, and ended up in some stranger's bed, disgusted with myself. After that, my body just sort of shut down."

He said nothing.

She nibbled on her bottom lip.

"Do you think less of me now?" she asked softly. *If he does, I deserve it. I'll do whatever it takes to earn back his respect.*

He could have teased her the way she'd always teased him. He could have called her a slut and a whore, or worse. But he did none of those things.

"I don't think less of you. I think more of you. You picked yourself up from a situation you despised. That takes a hell of a lot of strength."

He was a better man than she'd ever given him credit for.

His eyelids dipped to half-mast and he grinned. "Your body isn't shut down now, is it, princess?"

Completely out of character, she leaned down and kissed his forehead. "You were right, you know. I was so obsessed with your sex life because I wanted you to be a part of mine. I'm sorry I judged you. I had no right. I think I did it because I was miserable about my own past, and misery loves company."

An emotion shifted in his eyes, but she wasn't sure what it was. "I told you to stop apologizing."

"No," she added, ignoring his last words. "It's not shut down now."

Back to work. Before she broke down. She inserted the top half of one of the syringes inside the wound closest to his heart and squeezed out the contents. As he unleashed a stream of profanity, she did the same to the other wound.

"Has anyone ever called you Dr. Hodad?" he growled.

"No. And what does that even mean, anyway?"

"Hands of death and destruction."

"Ha! I like that name. You may continue to refer to me as Dr. Hodad." She cleaned his chest, then her hands. "You lost a lot of blood."

"This isn't the first time, and it won't be the last."

"You might need a transfu—"

"No," he said with a shake of his head. "Arcadians do not share blood, and human blood wouldn't help."

"Why don't you share blood within your own race?"

"It creates an unbreakable bond. Remember Dallas? He said the Arcadian king fed him blood to heal him. Now the agent is forced to do whatever Kyrin en Arr tells him to do."

Ouch. Like Blue, Evie would rather die than become a slave.

"Close your eyes and get some sleep," she said. She placed another soft, sweet kiss on his brow. "I can tell you're weaker than you're letting on because I can't feel your power."

He reached out and snagged her hand. "Don't leave."

She tugged gently at his earlobe. "I won't. I'll be here when you wake up. Because, bluestocking? There's no place else I'd rather be."

Blue awoke suddenly.

His body burned with desire, and he wasn't sure

why. At first. Then he realized he was in bed with Evie. Her back was pressed into his bare chest, his hand was under her shirt, his fingers splayed over her belly. Her ass was nestled against his throbbing erection.

He remembered how they'd gotten here. Pagan had shot him, and Evie had doctored him.

He remembered she'd confessed to not having had sex in three years. How she'd kissed his brow in a show of comfort. Twice.

Now he thought, *Screw trying to earn her trust. Screw everything. I'm taking what's mine.*

Blue nuzzled the back of her neck and slid his hand to her breast, cupping the perfect little mound, kneading—and hissing as her nipple beaded for him. "Evie. Wake up for me, baby."

A breathy moan left her, and she arched her back to stretch, pressing harder against his shaft. The pleasure . . . he groaned. Supplication for more.

"Evie. Now."

She stiffened. Then she rolled to her back and peered up at him, those velvety brown eyes clearing, becoming more alert—and finally heating.

"Blue." Not a question. A demand.

One he heeded. "We do this," he said. And that was the one and only warning he would offer. He grabbed her shirt by the collar and ripped the material down the center. Her bra received the same treatment.

She uttered no protests. Even helped him discard the ruined fabric.

He practically dove on her, slamming his mouth against hers, thrusting his tongue deep, taking, taking everything. She met him with a thrust of her own, her delicious taste sending him into a maddened frenzy. But then, she always had that effect on him.

Have to have all of her. Finally.

He sucked on her bottom lip, holding on to it as long as possible as he drew away, then lowered his head to suckle and nip at her nipples, to flick his tongue back and forth, back and forth, and even to bite. Her nails dug into his scalp, as if to hold him where he was.

Oh, baby, nothing can pull me away.

Her knees rubbed against his hips, as if she couldn't decide what to do with her legs. Then she planted her feet on the mattress and arched up, pressing her core against his erection. The increase of pleasure was almost too much, and yet, it wasn't even close to being enough. His sense of urgency deepened.

Despising their clothing, but not wanting to take his hands from her breasts, he used his power to remove his jeans and underwear, then hers, jerking the garments away with only a thought and tossing them to the side. The cool air electrified him, washing over him and sensitizing every inch of him, all the more erotic as heated skin met heated skin . . . as his shaft met liquid fire.

He nearly lost what little control he had left.

Evie groaned. "Blue. Now."

"Soon." This time, he was going to learn all of her. Do everything. Play.

He cupped her between her legs and purred his approval. "So wet, baby." He loved how aroused she became—and how quickly.

He teased her with a finger, and when she was riding it, trying to grind down on it, he fed her another one. All the while, her head thrashed from side to side. Her eyes were closed, her red lips moist and parted. He knew she was as lost in sensation as he was when he brought her close to the edge . . . then backed off . . . brought her close again . . . backed off.

"Blue!"

"Desperate?" He was. Sweat trickled from his temples. *Never been strung this taut.* But it was worth it to hear her moan and groan and beg. To watch her thrash.

"Ready."

"Not yet." He gave her a third finger, stretching her, this time preparing her for what was to come, and she gasped an unintelligible word. Her nails found their way to his back and scraped, drawing blood.

He'd wear the wounds with pride.

"Hurt?" he asked.

"A bit. But, ohhh. I *need* it."

A beautiful plea from the indomitable Evie Black. "You're going to give me everything."

"Whatever you want."

"*Everything*. You asked for it once. Now I'm demanding it." Unable to hold back any longer, he slid his fingers out of her. They both moaned at the loss. He wiped the wet across her lips and, as he bent down to lick it off, to kiss her deep and sure, he hooked her knees under his arms and positioned his shaft for entry.

"Yes! Please!"

He wanted to shove, hard and fast. He pushed in an inch. Then two.

So tight. So damn tight.

He gained another inch.

Then another, and another.

Panting, she stilled.

"Okay?"

"Feels so good. You're so big."

Killing me. "Gonna make it feel even better." He reached between their bodies, found her little bundle of nerves, pressed and rubbed until her hips began to rock.

"Yes!" she cried. "Oh, yes."

He thrust the rest of the way in, as hard and fast as he'd wanted, and she came instantly, arching her back and screaming his name.

He'd never felt anything as rapturous as her inner walls clenching on him. So perfect. "Tell me you can take a rough ride, baby."

"Yes. Please, yes."

Never get tired of hearing her say that word. He grabbed the headboard, pulled most of the way out of her, then slammed in with so much force the entire bed rattled. A picture crashed to the floor. And maybe his Arcadian powers had caused the furniture to levitate, because a lamp tumbled from the nightstand and shattered.

He would pay for the damage. Gladly.

He kept moving. In, out. In, out. The pressure must have mounted inside her, because she clutched at him, urging him to give it to her harder, faster. He couldn't have stopped or slowed to save his life. Never had he been so overwhelmed, so overcome. So taken over, where only pleasure mattered.

Here. Now. This woman. *Mine.*

His rhythm became brutal and punishing. Exquisite. Evie grabbed him by the hair and tugged him down for another kiss. The moment their tongues met, she climaxed again, and as her inner walls squeezed him this second time, he joined her, coming, coming so hard. He roared, giving one last thrust, feeding her that last bit of his release, until finally he collapsed on top of her, utterly spent.

He wasn't sure how much time passed before he realized he hadn't moved, that he could be suffocating her with his heavy weight. Gathering her close, he rolled to his side. Sweat formed a slippery layer over both of their bodies, and neither of them could catch their breath.

Thing was, he only wanted more.

Evie reeled. Sex had never been that good for her. Sex had probably never been that good for anyone, and she almost wished she hadn't experienced it. Almost. How was she supposed to let Blue go now?

For the first time in years, she felt no sense of dissatisfaction. Only peace. As though all of the pieces of her life had finally lined up correctly.

But that couldn't be right. Ultimately, no matter how wonderful Blue was as a person, he was bad for her. They would never want the same things.

Have to put some space between us. "I feel foolish for bringing this up now, considering my profession and my past, but in all the excitement I honestly never gave it a single thought. Although, that's not really an excuse, is it? I should be totally ashamed." And even panicked.

But she wasn't panicked.

His eyes twinkled merrily, as if he were fighting a laugh. "I think that's the closest you've ever come to rambling, sugar puff."

"Well, what I was *trying* to say," she continued, forging ahead, "is that I'm not on any kind of birth control."

"No probs. I can't get you pregnant."

Ever? "First, no probs? Seriously? Second, what about disease?"

"First, yes. That is what I said. No probs. I think we should abbreviate more. It's sexy. Second, I don't have an Arcadian disease, and even if I did, I couldn't pass it to you. Also, I'm immune to human disease."

"Well, just for your peace of mind, I don't have one. I checked."

He kissed the tip of her nose. "Thank you for telling me."

She sat up, pushed her damp hair from her face. "So . . ."

He arched a brow. "Is this the part where you try to kick me out of your bed? Sorry, hotcakes, because that's just not happening. We're snuggling."

Wait. What? Peering down at him, she said firmly, "We are *not* snuggling."

His bottom lip stuck out in the most adorable pout.

Was he teasing her?

He had to be teasing her.

Stupid, adorable man!

"So now that you've used me," he said, "you're going to abandon me?"

Gah! Guilt trip. "I don't really have a desire to snugs. With anyone. Ever."

He barked out a laugh. "Did you just say 'snugs'?"

Her cheeks flamed as she realized that yes, yes she had. "What. I was giving the abbreviation thing a try."

"You did good." Grinning, he said, "Have you ever tried to 'snugs'?"

Her eyes narrowed to tiny slits. "No."

There was a softening around his eyes and mouth, as if he'd just spotted a kitten in need of help out of a tree. He cupped the back of her neck and massaged. "Let's try it, then. You and me. We might like it."

She closed her eyes in bliss, even as she inwardly cursed him. This was the charming seducer thousands had fallen for, guaranteed. "'We'?"

"I've never done it before, either, and I want to see what it's like."

She would be the first? Bollocks! How was she supposed to resist now? "You're serious? Never?"

"Never. I took what I wanted and left . . . or forced the women to leave."

"And they put up with you?" she asked, incredulous.

"Of course. They even tried to come back for seconds and thirds."

"*Of course,*" she mocked. "But . . . why now? Why me?"

He shrugged, unabashed. "You smell too good, feel too good, and I'm going to want you again very, very soon. Might as well have you nearby and save myself the trouble of having to hunt you down."

She should resist. One sexcapade had nearly killed her. No telling what a second go-round would do. And what if she actually enjoyed the whole snuggling thing? She'd start craving it—and when it came to Blue, she couldn't afford any more cravings.

Who knows, maybe you'll get lucky and hate it.

True.

Her silence must have provoked him, because he said, "Don't make me caveman-up and club you over the head to get what I want."

She rolled her eyes. "Okay, all right. Fine. We'll do a little snuggling." She draped herself over his chest, and he enfolded her in his arms. His heart pounded against her ear, fast and hard, pleasing her mightily.

She wasn't going to hate it, was she?

"We can do this for an hour, and maybe, if you're lucky, I'll get a little handsy," she said. "But after that we need to go our separate ways, okay?"

He combed his fingers through her hair. "Nope. Not okay. I need at least six hours. And definite hand play. No maybe about it."

They were bargaining about this? Seriously? "Two hours," she said. "And I won't beat you to death."

"Eight. And you'll caress."

Bloody hell. "That isn't how you negotiate, Blue."

"My bad. Ten hours."

Just to be contrary, she twisted his nipple.

"Ow!" He pried her fingers loose and kissed her

knuckles. "Just for that, I'm not going to tell you how I ranked you."

She jolted upright and met his gaze. "You do not rank your women." A pause. "Do you?"

"Not usually. But this time I made an exception."

"I don't think you know how close you are to having your spine pulled out through your mouth," she said, waving her fist in front of his face.

He tried to bite it. "Did I ever tell you how sexy it is when you threaten me with bodily harm?"

"No. Because that would be ridiculous."

"It's not, and it's true." Expression serious, he said, "Now, back to your ranking. I've decided to tell you, despite the titty-twister."

She shook her head, dark hair dancing around her. "I don't want to know." After all, she'd lost herself in the pleasure of his mouth and his hands, and then his body; he'd had to do all the work.

"Too bad. Baby, there is no question, no doubt in my mind, that you are and forever will be . . . number one. Seriously. This," he said, waving a hand to indicate her slender curves, "should be outlawed."

She tried to maintain a neutral expression—encouraging him was wrong—but she couldn't suppress a smile. "Two compliments from you in one day. You must be losing your edge."

"Of course I am. I just blew a major load."

Her eyes widened. *Can't believe he just said that.*

He gave another wave, this one imperial. "Go ahead. Laugh. You know you want to."

She slapped a hand over her mouth, but it was too late. Laughter escaped.

His gaze met hers with a mix of pleasure and awe, his features softening. "I will never get tired of seeing you lit up like this."

Getting too serious! her mind screamed. And, just like that, her amusement drained.

He frowned, as if her mood change upset him. "What are you thinking about?"

"What's going to happen tomorrow? With Tiffany?"

"Don't want me to make a move on her?"

"No," she answered honestly. And crap. Too serious again.

Now he grinned, pleased. "Don't worry. I won't. You have my word. I will flirt with her to make it believable when she leaves with me, but it will never go any further than that. When I get her alone, I will use compulsion to get her to fall asleep."

"All right," she said with a nod.

"Wait. No making me promise? Or sign a contract in blood?"

"No. I believe you. I need no more assurance than your word."

Something bright bloomed in his eyes as he kissed her temple. "I don't know what to say. Evie . . . thank you."

If anything, she should be saying those words to *him*.

"Are you hungry?" he asked, switching topics with a speed that left her floundering. "I'm starved. So why don't I make us something to eat? Afterward we can shower and clock a few more hours in bed before we go to sleep." His voice went husky with desire when he added, "Then, come morning, I'll wake you up in the best possible way. Promise."

Wait. He expected to stay the night in her room? The *entire* night?

"Stay here. I'll be right back." Naked, he padded into the hallway, leaving her alone with a growing sense of panic. At last it had arrived.

Eighteen

$\sim$

*H*E HADN'T WORN A condom. To be honest, Blue hadn't even thought about wearing one. On some level, he must trust Evie more than he trusted any other woman. He knew she would never make claims about a false pregnancy as Pagan had. As countless others had. She was honest to a fault.

And now that he knew she hadn't complained about the lack because she had been as caught up in the moment as he had been, he only wanted her more.

He was grinning as he carried a tray of sandwiches into the bedroom, nearly let-the-world-crumble eager to see her splayed out, dark hair splashed over the pillows, pale skin flushed with the pleasure he had just given her, lips red and swollen from his kisses.

He'd never been a possessive guy. Today, that had changed. Evie Black belonged to him, and he wasn't letting her go. He was already addicted to her taste—the honey she smelled of. But now he knew her warmth, and her inner softness, and the sounds she made as her excitement built. He knew the feel of her nails in his flesh and her body moving against his, surrounding his, knew her smile afterward, the huskiness of her voice.

She's a treasure. My treasure.

Yes, he betrayed Michael.

Yes, he felt guilt. But he would make his boss understand.

What about tomorrow? The postgame party? Tiffany?

Evie understood. She trusted him, no questions asked, and the knowledge floored him. He didn't think he'd ever been this happy.

He wouldn't blow it. For once, Blue had drawn a line and he wouldn't cross it.

"Evangeline," he said, grinning as he stepped into the room.

She wasn't in the bed.

He set the tray on the dresser and strode into the bathroom. But she wasn't there, either. Frowning, he checked the entire suite. There was no sign of her, and her clothes had been picked up from the floor.

"Evie," he called.

There was no reply.

He raced through the entire house, checking every corner, every shadow, but she wasn't hiding anywhere.

Scowling, he stomped into her office and watched the security feeds, using the codes she'd given him. Within minutes he was seething. The little witch climbed out of her own bedroom window and scaled down the side of the house. As if he were a booty call she regretted.

Fury rained, a storm of ice and fire. His motions were jerky as he strapped weapons all over his body and dressed. She had a ten-minute head start. He'd have her back in bed in five. Whether he would spank her, lecture her, or seduce her, he wasn't sure. Maybe he'd do all three.

Why do this to him?

She wasn't the type to run away from her problems.

Or, hell, what did he know? Maybe she was. She still hadn't told him about Claire.

Outside, the moon was high and full, the sky a stretch of diamond-studded ebony, the air cool. The roads were deserted, the entire neighborhood at rest. Evie had gone north, so he took off in that direction, following the lingering trace of her sweet perfume.

She'd left prints in the ground, and they were deeper than a normal step. She'd been sprinting, her shoes pounding into the dirt. She was *that* eager to escape him?

Infuriated all over again, he rounded a corner just in time to watch Evie disappear inside an all-night grocery—and catch a Bree Lian dodging her steps, moving faster and faster, drawing closer to her heels. Blue lurched into super-speed, several yards away one minute, right behind the guy the next.

He slapped a hand over furry lips—and stabbed, stabbed. Spleen. Kidney. The Bree Lian's startled, pained howl was muffled as he fell to his knees. Blue dragged him into the darkened alley beside the building and slammed his knee into the guy's face, propelling him backward. Before he could figure out what was going on, Blue had a pyre-gun unsheathed and aimed.

"Why are you after the girl?" he demanded. "Who do you work for?"

Clutching his bleeding side, the otherworlder pressed his lips together in a tight, mulish line.

Blue picked him up with a single stream of power

and kept him suspended in the air. With another stream, he spread the Bree Lian's arms and legs, hopefully making him feel as if the appendages were going to be ripped away any second. Because they were.

"I'm not going to ask again."

The Bree Lian peered down at Blue with resignation. He had just realized he was going to die. It was only a question of how painfully. "Tyson Star."

Tyson? Not Gregory, the father? "Why?"

"I don't know. I'm never told why, only what to do."

"And what were you to do?"

"Pick up Miss Black and escort her to Mr. Star."

Where she would be beaten? Killed?

Fury stampeded him. "One last question. Have you seen a Rakan with the Stars, or heard of one's skin being sold?"

"No. The Stars are the most secretive family I've ever met. They'll assign different aspects of hired hits to different men, so no one knows the whole of what's going on."

Secretive, and smart.

"You've earned your death. I'll make it fast." He sheathed his gun, intending to take the guy out with his bare hands, when a noise caused his ears to twitch. He spun, a stream of bright azure light shooting out and nailing him in the chest. Every muscle in his body turned into stone, though his mind remained utterly aware. He heard the Bree Lian slam into the ground, no longer held by Blue's power.

His fury found a new target: himself. *Should have suspected the Stars would send more than one.*

A second otherworlder stepped from the shadows. A Cortaz Blue he saw guarding Star's country estate. The male was a few inches shorter than Blue, with dark hair, green eyes, and skin that looked as if it had been dipped in a honey pot. "I'm not sure how you pegged my partner, Mr. Blue, and I don't really care."

Blue let the worst of his emotions shine in his eyes.

The man wasn't impressed. "I only gave you a partial stun, so you'll be as good as new in a few hours. In the meantime, I'm going into the store and finding your girl. And she *is* yours, isn't she? A very surprising development, I have to say. You'll get to watch me have a little fun with her before I take her to see Mr. Star."

"Hmm. I don't think that's how this night is actually gonna go down." Evie's voice echoed through the alley as a stream of azure light erupted and slammed into the Cortaz.

Like Blue, he froze in place.

Then she shot the Bree Lain, freezing him, too, just in case he decided to fight.

Blue had never been so relieved to see a woman he wanted to strangle.

Evie, his beautiful, irreverent Evie, flipped the Cortaz off as she passed him, then stopped in front of Blue. "You are so lucky I'm on your side." She dug in her purse—that glorious, magical purse—and withdrew a ring with a big oval in the center. "This will counter the effects of stun."

Before she could stick him, her arms were grabbed, twisted, and pinned behind her back. The ring fell to the dirty ground.

"Good thing I came as an insurance policy," a gleeful voice said from behind her.

Still unable to move, Blue glared at the tall, muscular Arcadian spinning Evie and slamming her against the brickwork. It was like watching a horror movie in slow-mo. Every detail was in Technicolor. From the surprise on her face to the dust that sprayed from the building.

An indignant gasp left her.

Absolute, utter rage detonated inside of Blue. He drew all of his power into his core, letting it concentrate there, building layer upon layer.

"I'm giving you one chance to let me go," she gritted. "And then things are going to get nasty."

"I think they already *are* nasty." The Arcadian patted her body down, looking for weapons.

"Yeah? Wait till you see this." She slammed the back of her skull into his nose.

Bellowing, the Arcadian released her and stumbled away. She whipped around and punched him in the throat. As he gasped for air, she kicked him between the legs. He collapsed face-first, a writhing puddle of agony.

Blue released his grip on the power, and as it exploded through him, life twitched into his muscles, allowing him to trip forward. He grabbed Evie by the arm and drew her behind him . . . then whaled the Arcadian.

He punched, and punched, and punched. "You don't hurt her. Ever." Punched, and punched, and punched. Blood sprayed. Teeth flew and skidded across the ground.

› Soon, there was nothing left of the guy's face.

"Uh, I think he's dead now," Evie said. "You can stop and maybe we can go the hell home."

Blue jolted at the sound of her voice. He was panting, and he knew he had to look fearsome. Still, he straightened and jerked her into his arms, needing her close, if only to soothe the bestial rage inside him.

She offered no resistance. Even curled closer.

"I'm sorry, baby. I'm so sorry I let him get to you. He'll never harm you again."

"Hey, it wasn't your fault. I was so primed to get to you, I forgot to scour for a third hit man." Very gently, she began to pet his chest. "And you killed him real good, Blue. Watching you work was a real pleasure. My review will be glowing. He's not going to harm anyone ever again. Promise."

If anything had happened to her . . .

He wasn't sure what he would have done. Right now he was having trouble muting his emotions. Panic. Fear. Relief. Anger.

A long while passed before he felt calm enough to speak again. "You have a lot of explaining to do, young lady!" he snarled, pushing her away while maintaining his hold on her shoulders. *Dude. Maybe you should have waited a bit longer.* "Why the hell did you leave the house?"

She broke away with a single step back, and a rumble of irritation cut through his chest. "Do you really want to do this here and now? Some of our audience is still alive."

He turned and shot both the Cortaz and the Bree

Lian in the face. Yellow beams. Not azure. Death rather than stun. "Not anymore."

"Blue!" she said, and stomped her foot. "We could have interrogated them."

"I got all the answers I needed from them. So. I ask again. Why did you crawl out the freaking window, Evie?"

She threw her arms up in a what-did-I-do-to-deserve-this gesture.

"Well?"

"Several reasons," she said, raising her chin.

"Name one."

"I saw the guys lurking in my yard."

"And you didn't call for me?" he shouted.

"I didn't want to lose them, and, quite frankly, I needed a little time away from you. Time to think."

Inside him, the fury chilled, becoming far more dangerous. "Is that so? Well, then, take all the time you need, princess." He stomped away, never looking back.

Evie knew she'd made a mess of things.

Blue was in the guest room and she was in her room. They were like boxers in their respective corners. Sunrise would be the starting bell, and only one of them would be declared the winner.

I can't wait that long.

She had to make things right. Already she missed their easy banter. Their . . . friendship.

They really were friends, weren't they?

Wearing a tank and shorts, she marched down the

hall and into his room. For once he wasn't working. The lights were out, and she couldn't see jack, but she could feel the hum of his power.

"You awake?" she asked loudly.

"I am now," he grumbled.

"Good. You promised we'd have snugs and then you dare not deliver? Don't be that guy." She climbed into the bed and stuffed herself under the covers. Divine body heat enveloped her, and she shivered, her lust level rising quickly.

Though she pressed into his side, he didn't tug her any closer. "You aren't the only one in need of time apart, Evie."

Ouch. "I'm not used to this relationship stuff, okay? I've never even had a boyfriend. I've had boys that took advantage of a young girl desperate for someone's approval, guys that used me for a night and snuck away—and, yeah, okay, that always made me feel like crap and I suck for doing the same to you, and I'm sorry. I was wrong. And I know you told me not to apologize anymore, but it really does bear repeating. I was also wrong to judge you and call you the very names I called myself for years. Minus the 'he-' and '-man,' of course. You're a great guy, Blue, and it's throwing me off my game."

At first he gave no reaction. Then, with a sigh, he tucked his arm under her nape and rolled her into his side. She nearly wept with relief.

"You are not a whore or a slut," he said. "And I don't want to hear you talk like that ever again."

His vehemence thrilled her. Who was she kidding? Everything about him thrilled her. "I want to be with you while we're working this case," she admitted. "You and no one else. Not just once or twice, but every day, every night. I want us to be exclusive."

A pause.

A pause that scared her.

Rejection? This one would hurt more than any other. But she was a fighter and wasn't going to give up easily. Not this time. "You need space to think. I get it. Meanwhile, ask me anything," she said. "I'll tell you straight up. I'll even kick things off. Do I think this relationship is going to be easy? No. Do I think it'll be worth it? Yes."

No longer hesitating, he said, "What happened to Claire?"

She stiffened. Of course he'd go there. But she'd said she would spill, and so she would. "Three years ago, Michael assigned me a job, told me to pick a couple of agents to help with recon before I made the kill." The more she spoke, the easier it was to get the words out. "But I didn't want to pick a couple of agents. I wanted to do it on my own. I was so certain I'd succeed, and then I could hog all the glory."

He didn't say anything, but his arms tightened around her.

"Do you remember the Night-light Killer?"

"Yes."

"It was her. I narrowed down my suspects to two, did more recon on both, and decided it was one over the other. I was right—and I was wrong. I made my kill, and while I was busy patting myself on the back for a job well done, the other woman was doing recon on me.

The two were partners. I'd taken her best friend, so she waited for the perfect moment to strike and take mine."

Blue kissed her temple. "You don't have to tell me the rest."

Yeah, but the rest of the details poured out of her anyway, unstoppable. "I came home and found Claire in pieces. Blood everywhere. And on the television screen was playing a loop of the murder. In it, Claire screamed. She screamed so much and even begged for me to save her. Until the woman ripped out her throat. Then she quieted, and I wanted so badly for the screams to start back up because it would mean she was alive. My sweet, gentle girl alive."

"Oh, baby. I'm sorry. I'm so sorry."

Her chin trembled and tears trickled down her cheeks. "After that, I told Michael I was done with the agency, and I meant it."

"So you're not back on payroll once John is found?"

"No. I'm going back to the hospital."

"Do you like it there?"

"Yes."

"But not love?"

"I . . . don't know anymore."

"I think you love being an agent. You're so good at it."

"Thank you." But . . . "I'm not going to risk leading a criminal to an innocent ever again."

"You're wiser now. You know how to avoid—"

"No."

He sighed. "Okay, baby. Okay. Let's backtrack a little, then. You said you want to be with me as long as we're working on the case. What happens after?"

"Afterward you go back to your house and your life."

"And that means we can't see each other anymore?"

Her brows drew together in genuine confusion. "Doesn't it?"

"No," he said. "Not to me." Never had he sounded more determined.

"I know this isn't the deal with Tiffany, but one day the seduction of a target is going to be the only option open to you. And I'm not dropping the hammer of judgment on you or anything like that. I just know the kind of cases you're given, and I'm stating what I can and cannot accept from a boyfriend."

At first he gave no reaction. Then his grip tightened on her, almost bruising her, and she wondered what thoughts tumbled through his head.

"So . . . I called Michael," he said, changing the subject, "and told him to put a watch on Tyson Star if at all possible."

Disappointment hit her. She'd wanted assurances from him, she realized. "Good thinking. It's odd that the guy wants me. I mean, he wouldn't even meet with me when I toured Star Light. Talk about setting myself up for the perfect snatch-and-kill."

"Didn't want your disappearance linked with his business, I guess."

"All right, I'll give you that, but *why* does he want me?"

"I can think of two reasons. Either to please his father and help the guy nail Michael, using you as bait, or he's taken over the empire, since Daddy is hiding in the country, and as Michael's daughter you're now a liability."

Blue always seemed to home in on motive, something Evie always struggled with. She was great with gadgets but horrible with other people's reasoning. "Well, I'm sending Tyson a personal invite to the victory party. He'd better come."

"I have a feeling he will, since there's no way his sister will stay away—which is why I want *you* to stay away. You shouldn't make it easy for Tyson to get to you."

"Uh, that would be a big fat no. Besides, the party is at his hotel, and if you're right and he doesn't want to involve his business, he won't make a play for me while I'm there. It's the safest place I could be."

"Had a feeling you'd say that," he grumbled. "We need to get some sleep—after we have sex. Papa wants some loving. But I'll make it fast, because we've got a big day tomorrow."

"So kind of you." Feeling suddenly shy, she said, "Afterward are we going to have our snugs?"

"Try to get away. I dare you."

"Intruder. Intruder."

Blue jolted upright, instantly alert. Evie did the same, the covers falling to her waist. Sunlight slanted through the curtains, highlighting her beauty. Her tank was bunched under her breasts, revealing the flat plane of her stomach. She was blinking rapidly, trying to focus.

He'd been having the most erotic dream, his hands all over her body, his mouth soon following, when all of a sudden—

"*Intruder. Intruder.*"

That.

"Someone's trying to break in," she gasped. She jumped to her feet and raced out of the room before he could stop her.

Cursing, he grabbed the pyre-gun he'd shoved under his pillow. He pulled on a pair of boxer briefs that did nothing to hide the stiff morning wood he would have liked to introduce to Evie.

"Intruder" was going to pay. Severely.

He stalked into the hallway. The sunlight was brighter there, streaming through uncovered windows, filling the confined space. No sign of Evie.

Gonna spank that girl so hard. She'd left him behind like a damsel in distress.

Then she raced out of her bedroom, still in her tank and shorts. Her expression was all *Why are you just standing there?*

"They're in the kitchen," she whispered.

"'They'?"

"There's two of them."

"How do you know?"

"I checked the data stream from my room."

Blue moved to the stairs, descended quietly. Evie stayed at his side. He wanted to lock her in a room, keeping her out of danger, but couldn't bring himself to do it. She was a good agent—very good.

Last night, she *had* rescued him.

And afterward, in the dark of his room, she'd nearly broken his heart with her sorrow over Claire. Every day he fell a little deeper under her spell.

When they reached the bottom step, he motioned for her to branch to the right, go around back, and come in the kitchen through the yard entrance.

She nodded and took off.

He slunk around a corner, gaze scanning, ears listening. A woman's voice registered.

"—please turn that thing off. It's upsetting the baby."

Baby?

"I'm trying, sweetheart, I swear I am, but I've never encountered a system quite like this one."

A male voice.

One he recognized. Solo. Solo was here.

Running now, Blue burst into the kitchen. Solo had his back to him as he messed with the security box beside the yard entrance. The male immediately straightened, pulling a small blonde behind him with one hand and aiming a gun at Blue with the other. As soon as Blue's identity registered, he lowered the gun.

"You're alive," Blue said. He'd known Solo was alive—of course he had—and had even known the male was in the area, but that was the equivalent of a starving man stumbling upon a banquet—with raw, uncooked food. He'd needed to see his friend with his own eyes.

"I'm alive," Solo agreed.

"Dude." Blue strode forward, grinning from ear to ear.

The back door splintered open and Evie flew into the kitchen, pyre-gun raised and ready. Solo reacted just as he had before, protecting the blonde and lifting a weapon.

"Solo?" Evie demanded, arms falling to her side. "Bloody hell, man. Do you know how close you came to losing your head?"

"As close as you came to losing yours?" The male did *not* lower his weapon.

Having none of that, Blue used his power to force the gun out of Solo's kung fu grip, letting it hover just out of reach.

Solo frowned at him. "I wouldn't have shot her. I just wanted to make a point."

"No one's losing their head today," Blue snapped, swiping the gun and slamming it on the counter. "Especially Evie."

"Especially *Evie*?" Solo stared at him as though he'd just sprouted horns and a tail.

The little blonde jammed her hands on her hips. "If you're going to fight, let's make it interesting. Take off your clothes while I get the oil."

Evie slapped her gun beside Solo's. "Next time, come to the front door and knock, you bloody—*argh!*" Glaring, she pointed at Blue. "If he broke anything, it's going on your bill. And I'm charging double!"

Knowing Evie better now, Blue saw her through a new pair of eyes. She wasn't angry with Solo about possible damage to her home. She was scared about what could have happened—harm to her, to Blue, even the harm she could have done to Solo and his woman—and she was trying to purge the excess emotion the only way she knew how. Through her fiery temper.

He wanted to pull her into his arms so badly, he shook. And he would have done it, uncaring about their audience, if he thought she would let him. Right now she might just claw out his eyes and use the insides to spread on her toast.

"I'll pay the charges, whatever they are," he said, and Solo gaped at him.

"Good, because you owe me a new back door! A good one, too. Nothing mass-produced." She stomped to the security panel Solo had been screwing with and punched in a code, then rerouted some of the wires. The alarm finally shut off. "That just cost you an extra thousand."

"Why so much?" Solo asked. "That system is glitched to the max."

"Glitched? Did you say glitched?" Bombs exploded in Evie's eyes. She grabbed her weapon and was about to aim at Solo's chest—and probably go trigger-happy.

Mr. Judah had just crossed her line.

"It wouldn't shut off," Solo gritted.

"For a reason, you idiot," she snapped.

Blue took the gun from her. "Don't crap on her security system," he told his friend. "It's the best you'll ever come across." To Evie he said gently, "Did you hear me, princess? The best. And you know I don't lie."

Gradually she calmed down. "You're right. The best. I can't blame a layman for not recognizing genius when he sees it."

Can't smile. Solo was far from a layman.

Blue gave the baffled Solo a hug and a slap on the back. His friend gave him a slap as well and almost drilled him into the ground. Guy didn't know his own strength.

Without the taint of kill-or-be-killed aggression, Blue looked the warrior over. Same shaggy black hair he liked to cut with a blade, same electric-blue eyes—except they were no longer glazed with constant inner pain. They were almost . . . soft. Definitely happy.

"Where have you been, my friend? Why haven't you come to see me before now?" Blue gave the blonde with plum-colored eyes a thorough once-over. "And who's the babe?"

Grinning, Solo tugged the curvy little female close to his side. "Blue, I'd like you to meet Vika, my wife. Vika, this is Blue, my partner."

Vika waved at him. "So fantastic to meet you at last. I've heard such wonderful things." She was Solo's opposite in every way. Tiny, petite, soft, and pretty. And her disposition seemed to be sweeter than sugar.

"The dark-haired tyrant is Evie," Blue said, motioning to her. "She's my—" What? He pondered the best word to use. "—friend." No matter what, that was still true. Although, he wanted more. More of what they'd had last night. Sex and sharing. Cuddling. Waking up with her in the morning. And he could have it. She'd offered.

But she'd offered something with a definite expiration date.

He should be okay with that.

He wasn't.

"Now that the introductions are over, why don't you go put on some clothes, Blue," Solo said, and Vika giggled. "Then we'll talk."

"I'd be fine with you staying as is," the girl said.

He looked down at himself. Thinking about Evie had gotten him hard again. Wasn't that just freaking great.

He met Evie's gaze and realized she was now trying not to laugh.

Worth the humiliation.

"I don't know why you think this is funny, candy cane. You're in the same half-naked boat."

She gave him a double-birded salute before walking away, calling over her shoulder, "At least my flotation device isn't sticking out for everyone to see."

Nineteen

AFTER DRESSING IN A T-shirt and jeans, Evie called Michael to let him know what was going on. He couldn't wait to see Solo, and snuck over. Watching him jerk the agent into his arms filled her with happiness rather than the usual jealousy.

She was so happy, in fact, that she mixed up her favorite fruit smoothie and offered everyone a glass.

Blue brushed his fingers over hers as he claimed his portion, and tingles of heat and power nearly drew a moan out of her. She was hungry for him. More than hungry. Starving. They'd had sex a third time during the night, and she'd wanted a fourth in the morning.

Waiting, now that she knew just how perfectly he filled her, was . . . difficult.

Solo stared at his cup as if she might be trying to poison him, but Vika jumped up to give her a hug. "Thank you."

"Oh, uh, we're really going to do this?" Evie said, uncomfortable. "Even though we're strangers?"

The hug merely tightened. "We are going to be the best of friends. I just know it."

"Okay. Uh, sure. If that's what you want. But I have

to warn you, you might change your mind after you get to know me."

"She won't," Blue called.

Was he confident in Evie's charm, or just determined to force a friendship if necessary?

Vika urged her to the couch. Once they'd settled, she placed Evie's hand on the bulge in her belly. "I shouldn't be this big, but Solo tells me his race has accelerated gestation. Do you feel my sweet baby boy?"

"No." A baby, she thought. A family. Something she hadn't ever wanted for herself. Had that changed?

She thought for a minute, shrugged. Maybe. Not with Blue, though. She'd told him that he wasn't a forever kind of guy, that a case would come along and he'd have to do what he did best, and he hadn't denied it. But maybe later, one day in the future, she could start a family with a doctor at the hospital.

Yeah. Okay. The idea didn't exactly repel her.

Except . . . it was Blue her mind conjured when she thought of lying in bed with a man, his hand on her swollen belly, and little white-haired, lavender-eyed half Arcadians she saw toddling around her house.

Concentrating, she applied a little more pressure. But . . . nothing. "No," she said again, disappointed. "I think he went into hiding the moment he heard my voice."

"Are you taking a nap, angel?" Vika asked her belly. "Mommy loves you, oh, yes she does."

Evie scanned the room, wondering what the guys thought about the girl's baby talk. Michael and Solo were deep in conversation, though Solo, who sat on

Vika's other side, had his arm draped around her to massage the back of her neck.

Blue was staring at Evie with a strange look on his face.

"What?" she mouthed.

He shook his head, refusing to answer.

Confusing man.

The motion caught Michael's attention. "What was that, son?"

Without missing a beat, Blue said, "Solo, I believe you had some answers for me."

"Right." The otherworlder never stopped ministering to his wife. "By the time I reached New Chicago, I knew Michael was alive but playing dead. He'd paid a visit to Vika before I was able to find my way back to earth. What I didn't know was your location, Blue. I wanted you to be alive, but . . ." He cleared his throat. "That AIR agent, Dallas Gutierrez, had a friend trapped in the circus with me. I knew he was looking into Star, and I knew Star had been at the explosion site. I started following Dallas, hoping he'd make an arrest and I could strike. Then I saw him at Evie's, saw Evie drive to your house, and I began to suspect the two of you were working together. Then you went public, Blue, and I knew I'd been right. *Then* I decided to let things ride because I'd drawn AIR's notice, and they were coming in strong. I didn't want to put you on their radar."

"He took care of that himself when he smashed Dallas's nuts beneath his boot," Evie said. "So is AIR no longer after you, Solo?"

"No. Last night Dallas tracked me down and gave

me all the info he'd been able to put together on Star. Apparently, Star's planning to host some big fashion exhibit for his daughter's newest line. Golden Sunrise is what they're calling it."

Golden. Like John.

"When?" Blue demanded, his fury evident in every bulging muscle.

"Two weeks."

The color drained from his cheeks. "They've already done it, then. They've already skinned him."

Grim, Solo said, "Yeah. I figure she's making the clothes now."

Oh, John, no. According to Tiffany, two weeks was when he'd been scheduled for skinning. Not the actual show. The Stars had moved up their timeline.

Blue's power suddenly electrified the air, and furniture lifted off the floor and hovered. Vika gasped, scrambling closer to her husband.

"Blue," Solo and Michael said in unison, both using soft, soothing tones.

"Calm down," Michael added.

Words weren't going to do the job. Last time she'd used her body, and both she and Blue left the encounter satisfied—and alive. With an audience, that wasn't exactly an option. So Evie hopped to the floor, closed the distance, and slapped him. Hard.

Solo commanded her to back off.

Michael held out his hand to stop her from doing it again. "That's not how you handle him, sunbeam."

She crossed her arms over her middle. "You got anything to say to me, blueberry?"

He glared over at her as he rubbed his jaw—and, what do you know, the furniture settled back into place. "What was that for?"

"Don't act like you don't know. Now do yourself a favor and focus," she said, cruel to be kind. For sure this time. "I know you're angry, but break down on your own time. Your friend needs you to keep it together."

At first he gave no reaction. Then he nodded stiffly and said, "No probs."

Before she could stop it, a huge smile spread across her face. "Good. That's, like, totes amazeballs."

Blue actually laughed out loud.

"What's so funny?" Michael asked. "And why are you talking like that?"

"Nothing," they muttered in unison.

"And just because," she added.

She turned away before she made a (bigger) fool of herself and reclaimed her spot on the couch. Vika watched her with awe, Michael and Solo with suspicion.

Her heart drummed in her chest. Michael was going to be more ticked than she'd assumed, she realized. And he was going to blame Blue.

Blimey. She was going to be the dumb hobag stuck between an old rock and a very sexy hard place, wasn't she? And one day Blue would hate her for it—and he'd have every right!

Should have resisted him.

But now that the damage is done . . . there's no reason not to forge full pleasure ahead.

"Now, then." She cleared her throat. "We know Tiffany works from home. We also know that home has guards stationed at her door 25-8. We assumed that was because Star was determined to protect his daughter, but what if the men are there to protect the pelt?"

"I can sneak in," Blue said. "Steal it."

"There might not be any need," Evie replied. "If she attends the party, you can compel an invitation to her house. You wanted to leave with her anyway. And that way she'll make the guards wait outside as well as turn off any alarm she has, giving you free rein and an entire night to search unimpeded."

Blue scrubbed a hand over his jaw, his gaze locked on her. Expecting her to balk at the thought of him alone with the girl? Evie hadn't lied. She trusted him. His honor wasn't readily apparent at first glance, but it *was* there.

"All right," he finally said. "But if she doesn't attend, I'm going in after the party."

Where was his earlier confidence that Tiffany wouldn't miss out on a date with him? "Deal." And meanwhile Evie would go after Tyson Star with everything she had—charm, drugs, whatever was necessary—and try to get her own invitation. If he was holding John, he would suffer and beg for death before she finally ended him.

By the time this was over, *all* of the Stars would be dead.

No mercy.

"Remember Tyrese Cooper?" Michael said, switching gears. "I finally got him to detox. He's married, but he was keeping a mistress on the side. The mistress got pregnant and he served the wife with divorce papers. A few weeks later, the mistress came up missing. Then, a few days ago, pictures were sent to Mr. Cooper. In them, the mistress was in bed with different men. *A lot* of different men. To the untrained eye, she probably looked like she was enjoying herself, but there were signs she had been drugged and bound."

Possibly an abduction. Then . . . punishment? For her? Or Mr. Cooper? Or, hell, both?

"That's unconscionable," Vika said, her chin trembling.

The symbol of revenge . . . Had Mr. Cooper's wife arranged for the mistress to be hurt and the husband to bear witness? She was the only one with motive. But if so, she must have paid Star to take care of the revenge for her. That was the only reason Evie could think of for the male's involvement.

It was possible Star had been paid to take care of *every* victim. Even Michael.

"What do you know about the wife?" Blue asked.

"Only that I want one of you to chat with her when we finish up here."

"I'll do it," Solo said. "Fear makes people talk, and females tend to fear me."

"I think it's safe to say Star is in the revenge-getting business." Michael drummed his fingers on the arm of his chair. "Considering we were looking at seventeen victims before the explosion, we're now dealing with seventeen accomplices. Someone the victims knew must have contacted Star and paid him to do their dirty work."

"I was just thinking the same thing," Evie said. Great minds and all that.

Patting yourself on the back again? Ugh.

"All seventeen have managed to keep the dealings a secret," Solo pointed out. "No one's bragged. Do you know how rare that is?"

Yes, she mentally grumbled. But a *little* vanity wasn't such a terrible thing—when it was deserved.

"Probably out of terror," Blue replied. "They've seen what Star can do and don't want the same fate to befall them."

Evie jumped in, saying, "Plus they don't want to implicate themselves in a crime."

Blue smiled at her.

She smiled back.

Michael sucked in a breath, and they looked away from each other.

"So, who wanted you dead?" Blue asked her father. "Who would pay big bucks to have you killed?"

Michael didn't have to think it over. "We know Monica Gains, my former assistant, worked with Star, and I can only guess it's because she told me one of her kids was mine. I insisted on a DNA test. When she refused, I gave her the option of quitting or being fired. She quit."

"Wait. How many people have you slept with?" Evie asked. "No, don't answer that. I don't want to barf up my smoothie. If she quit, she no longer had access to your home. How did she set the bomb?"

"She was a familiar face, and I made the mistake of telling no one about her lies. My new assistant would have let her in without thinking twice."

Everything was beginning to come together. A woman looking for fast cash who'd once had access to the files Michael kept on the criminals he pursued. A woman who would have known just how to tempt a man like Gregory Star. A woman looking to hurt the man who'd rejected her.

"Well," Evie said. "What's our next move? Do we try to finesse information out of the Star children as planned?"

"Yes. But we take it to the next level. We inject them both with isotope trackers," Blue said. "That way we'll know where they go, when they go. Maybe they'll lead us straight to John."

Okay. That was a seriously genius move. *Embarrassed I didn't think of it myself.* "Why didn't we do this sooner?" The answer hit her in an instant. It wasn't standard procedure, and it was highly illegal.

But they weren't playing by the rules, were they.

"Never mind," she muttered.

Once in the bloodstream, the isotope would send out a traceable signal for the next six months. All that was needed was a computer and the right code.

Michael wanted to inject Evie when she first came to work for him, but she refused. Criminals could hack into the tracking stream and find her at any time. No, thanks.

"It'll take me a few hours to get the vials," Michael said.

"The party starts in a few hours," Evie reminded him. "Can you do better?"

"You don't rush quality tracers, princess. Besides, I don't mind being fashionably late," Blue said, his gaze once again locked on her, making her shiver. "After all, the party won't really start until I get there. I'm the belle of the ball."

I guess that makes me Prince Charming.

Twenty

EVIE STOOD AT THE entrance to the Star Light Hotel roof, greeting guests as they arrived for the party. Behind her, the moon was high and golden, a million stars twinkling from a sea of black velvet. There was no wind, the temperature warm and perfect.

Mother Nature hadn't wanted to ruin Blue's big night, she supposed.

Also behind her, past a half wall of mirrors, was a summer oasis. A large swimming pool in the shape of the number eight consumed half the space. Palm trees stretched toward the sky. A buffet table piled high with rare delicacies drew the biggest crowd.

Evie wore a glittery silver sundress with a black bathing suit underneath. Five-inch hooker heels took her from maybe-I'll-take-a-dip to I'm-already-soaking. Most of the invited guests had already arrived. The team, their families and friends. Season ticket holders.

Blue wasn't here. Did he have the tracers?

Tyson and Tiffany Star hadn't arrived, either.

The elevator dinged, signaling the arrival of another guest. She held her breath, hopeful. The doors slid open and she sighed with disappointment. And dread.

"Evie Black." Dallas Gutierrez stepped forward and grinned a seducer's grin. "You look stunning."

"I know. But thanks." He wore a perfectly tailored suit in the traditional black and white, his dark hair slicked back, his blue eyes bright. "A party crasher so soon. No wonder you didn't know the dress code."

"Like the ladies could really handle me in my swimmies." Leaning forward, as if sharing a secret, he said, "Did you notice? No man boobs."

She tried not to smile. Failed.

"By the way, you're welcome."

"For what?" she asked, arching a brow.

"My presence."

She rolled her eyes.

"Don't let him fool you. He's not a crasher, he's one of my plus twos." An elegant woman stepped up beside him. She had honey-colored hair and a beautiful face usually only seen in magazines. She wore a short red dress that displayed a belly rounded by her pregnancy.

"Noelle Tremain," Evie acknowledged.

"None other."

Blue spent a year of his life with this exquisite, elegant woman. But he never shared his true self with her, and Evie suddenly wondered why. "Congratulations on your recent marriage."

"Thank you. I felt really strongly that it was time I took a step up."

Meaning her husband was better than Blue?

Evie masked a scowl. "Who's the lucky guy?"

"Me," a gruff voice replied. A man with dark hair, green eyes, and the rough features of someone who knew his way around a bloody battlefield wrapped a gloved arm around Noelle's waist.

Why gloves?

"Hector Dean, meet Evangeline Black." To Evie, she said, "Dallas tells me we have a mutual frenemy."

Evie glared at Dallas. Yes, he'd had permission to spill the gory details about Blue, but he shouldn't have acted on it.

"Whoa. Cool down now, Miss Black, and keep your hands out of your wizard bag. I don't want to know if you've got another magic compact in there. Blue wanted her to know," he said, palms up.

"If that's so," Noelle interjected, "why did you tell me Blue was going to kill you for being the messenger, and I needed to protect you?"

Dallas threw his arms up. "Because that's also true. Hector, control your woman before she gets me killed."

"Don't think I will," Hector said.

Noelle beamed at him. "Anyway." She took Evie's hand, squeezed. "If you ever want to compare notes, I'll make myself available."

The trio sailed past her without another word. Good thing, too. Another ding sounded, and out stepped Blue. As usual, Evie's breath snagged in her throat. He looked edible—and it had been too long since she'd had a taste, feeding her addiction.

He sported a simple white tee that hugged his heavy biceps and rippled chest, and a pair of swim trunks that could have doubled as golf shorts. Casual and ready to play, but also ready for business.

His gaze swept over her and heated. Then his power

followed the same trail, and it was as though his hands caressed her, causing her nipples to harden and her belly to quiver.

Tonight, after he returned from Tiffany's and she returned from Tyson's—fingers crossed—she would sneak into his room. If he didn't sneak into hers.

"Evangeline, wow . . ." Another full-body once-over, his eyes lingering on all the places he liked to touch. He clasped her hand and kissed her knuckles, and she could only gasp at the heady sense of pleasure that flooded her. "You look gorge."

Can't laugh. "Thank you," she said with a regal nod. "If I didn't know you were abbreviating the word 'gorgeous,' I would think you were telling me I look like a ravine."

"Gorge *and* smart." His voice lowered. "The things I want to do to you . . ."

Can't fall into his arms. "Oh, yeah?"

He nodded—and then he snatched her purse and dug inside. "A wad of Chinese money. A handful of zip ties. Taco Bell sauce packets. An Immortals After Dark friendship bracelet. Six safety pins. A mini-Taze. And now a pen." He held a plain-looking ink pen in the light and pressed the end.

It wasn't a pen, she realized. A needle emerged rather than a ballpoint. In the belly was the isotope tracker.

"Perfect for my collection," she said.

Lavender eyes narrowed with determination, surprising her. "I thought you'd like it." He took her hand, much as he'd done the first time they'd met, and kissed her knuckles. "Forgive me, but . . ."

A sharp sting in her palm.

She frowned and jerked away from him. A tiny bead of blood welled just beneath her index finger—a needle puncture?

His expression was hard and intractable.

She lowered her gaze, saw last year's NOFL Super Bowl ring glinting from his hand. He'd never worn it before.

"What did you do?" she demanded quietly.

"What I had to do to keep you safe. You're welcome."

"Blue—"

The elevator dinged, saving her from having to form a reply—it would have been a death threat, no question. Because if she had to guess, she'd say he'd just used the isotope tracker on her.

He handed her the bag, expression cleared of all emotion. Aaannnd, out stepped—

Tyson and Tiffany Star.

Game face on.

Evie cloaked her rising anger with a blank mask.

Blue gave a megawatt smile to Tiffany, and Evie marveled that he'd ever been able to fool anyone with his acting talents. He did not look besotted, but determined. "I was just asking Miss Black if you'd arrived," he said to the girl. "And here you are, like a wish come true."

Tyson stiffened, but Tiffany offered a shy smile in return.

Evie felt no stirring of jealousy. And, strangely enough, even her anger drained. Blue was doing his best to find his friend, and he knew how badly a distraction could screw him up. Worrying about his woman—a woman being stalked by the enemy—had to be the biggest distraction there was.

So you're his woman now?

Well, yes. For the moment.

"You are all my sister has been talking about, Mr. Blue," Tyson said, with zero emotion in his tone. However, his eyes gave him away. Flames crackled in their navy-blue depths.

Tiffany cast him a nervous glance.

Evie wondered if the guy had ever gotten violent with her.

If so, well, she might just kick him while he was down. And he *was* going down, somehow. Like Blue, she'd brought a pharmacy in her rings. One held the truth serum, one a sedative, one an aphrodisiac, and one a big dose of mental-patient cray-cray. She'd use them all if necessary.

"Please. Just Blue." He took Tiffany's hand. "I've thought about you a lot since that day at the coffee shop, wondered if you were doing okay, and if I'd get to see you again."

The girl blushed, and honestly, it was kind of . . . sweet.

Almost feel sorry for her. Almost.

"A thousand times I've asked my father to meet you," Tiffany said. "I'm not allowed to date anyone that hasn't met him. But he's refused. I'm sorry."

"We'll find a way. No probs."

The phrase was a caress to Evie's ears.

Tyson ran his tongue over his teeth, reminding her of her job.

"I know this comes a little late, but welcome," she said to him. "I'm Evangeline Black, tonight's hostess."

The Star heir stepped forward and nodded in greeting. "Tyson Star."

"Ah. The illustrious owner of this amazing paradise." She swept her hand out to indicate the pool. "I was hoping I'd get a chance to speak with you."

"And I you." He hooked her fingers over his and placed a kiss on her knuckles.

She pretended to be charmed. He was a handsome man. Tall, like his sister, and leanly built. He was not in casual wear. Like Dallas, he wore a suit. He wasn't the type to relax, she would bet.

I can help him with that.

"Your staff has done a wonderful job," she said.

"We only hire the best."

How special for you. "Well, it certainly shows."

Blue and Tiffany wandered past the mirrored wall, whispering to each other, obviously flirting and, to any outside observer, seemingly lost in each other. Tyson watched, his shoulders squaring more with every step the pair took. A warrior preparing for battle.

Evie smiled at him, hoping to distract him. "It seems you're in need of a companion, Mr. Star. Come, and I'll introduce you to the rest of the team."

Blue was having trouble concentrating. Chatter and laughter rang through the night. Every so often someone would jump in the pool and warm water would splash everyone nearby, eliciting startled cries.

One of those cries came from Evie. She used the water as an excuse to escort Tyson to the edge of the roof, a secluded spot overlooking the lights of the city. The two stayed there for half an hour, talking. Tyson's gaze continually strayed to Tiffany. At one point he even tried to walk away from Evie, but she somehow convinced him to remain at her side.

Blue had never before watched the woman he was sleeping with flirt with another man. But then, Evie might be done with him. She suspected he'd injected her with the tracker.

Too bad, princess. We're together, and that's final.

How many women had watched him over the years, wondering about his affections? How many women had he left twisted up, angry, and frustrated?

Too many. He was done living that way.

Hello. My name is Blue and I'm a reformed bad boy.

He couldn't blame his current mood on jealousy. He knew what tonight's flirtation games were about. He knew Evie felt nothing but contempt for Tyson Star, and that she wouldn't do anything sexual. He knew she was doing this for John. For Blue. And he knew she could protect herself.

He blamed yearning. He and Evie couldn't be open about their relationship. They had to hide their affection for one another. Blue couldn't stand beside her and look at lights. Blue couldn't put his arm around her or kiss her in the moonlight.

He also couldn't leave the party with Tiffany until Evie convinced Tyson to take her somewhere else. Anywhere else. Otherwise, Big Brother would definitely try to stop Blue from leaving with Little Sister, and that would put unnecessary kinks in the plan.

At least Blue didn't have to entertain Tiffany while he waited. A few of her friends were guests, and they had swept her away to gossip about him—if he had to take a guess. He'd claimed a seat at an empty table to watch her . . . and all right, yes, to watch Evie. He was dividing his attention between the two.

Tyson ran his knuckles down the length of Evie's arm.

Blue stiffened. *When John is safe, I'll be removing those knuckles with a butter knife.*

"All alone?" a female said. "What a shame."

He recognized the voice and closed his eyes to pray for patience.

Noelle Tremain slid into the chair next to him. Light from the tiki torches bathed her, illuminating a pretty face he'd once wanted so badly to love.

In greeting, he nodded at her. "You're looking well."

"Don't be modest. I'm looking magnificent." She smiled coldly and waved at someone across the room. "Are you going to congratulate me on my nuptials and pregnancy or continue to glower at the owner of your team?"

She'd noticed. Damn. Others might have noticed, too. "Congrats," he said, facing her fully. "I'm happy for you."

"Are you? Really?"

This was long overdue, wasn't it? "Yes, I really am. I'm sorry for the way I treated you, Noelle. I never wanted to hurt you."

The coldness remained. "Well, you did. You were a

crappy boyfriend. Like, I could have shoved a dagger in your gut and no woman in the world would have convicted me of a crime. You were always trying to change me, and there at the end you even tried to forbid me from seeing Ava."

Ava. Her best friend. The two were practically joined at the hip. "Where is she tonight?"

"Out hunting with her vampire husband."

"That's right. I heard she tamed a feral vamp capable of stopping time."

Evie laughed, the sound dazzling, drawing Blue's notice. She was talking to Tyson, motioning to the elevators, but he was shaking his head no.

Only an idiot would refuse the raven-haired beauty.

There was a slight hardening of her shoulders, but she recovered quickly and reached up to toy with the ends of the man's hair. Any resentment Blue might have felt about the action evaporated as her emerald ring glinted in the moonlight.

That's my girl.

Wouldn't be too much longer now.

"Blue," Noelle snapped.

Noelle. Right. He forced his gaze on her. "Look, you were a job, meant to introduce me to the right people. I enjoyed your antics, I really did, but you were getting me in trouble. I'm sorry I tried to change you, I really am. You're wonderful just the way you are. You always deserved better, and I knew it, and that's why I incited you into breaking things off with me by telling you not to see Ava. My boss couldn't force me to date a woman who wanted nothing to do with me."

She surprised him with a smile. Small, short-lived, but undeniable. "I know I was a job, Blue. Now. Dallas told me what he learned about you, and everything fell into place. You're lucky I didn't find you that night, or you would have woken up with your balls stuffed in your mouth. You're also lucky I know how to extract promises from my darling husband. He would have done much, much worse to you. He's quite savage, you know."

"If he wants a go at me, he'll just have to get in line."

Rubbing her hands over her swollen stomach, she said, "When it comes to the women in your life, have you learned your lesson?"

"I like to think so, yes." He watched as Evie linked her fingers with Tyson's and pulled him toward the elevators. This time he offered no resistance.

When they disappeared around the mirrored wall, Blue pushed to his feet. "It's been nice chatting with you, Noelle, and if there's ever anything I can help you with, please let me know. But right now I have to go." He didn't wait for her reply but zeroed in on Tiffany.

Twenty-one

~~~~~

BLUE COMPELLED TIFFANY TO go to his car, then to sit quietly during the fifteen-minute drive to her house. She didn't even protest when he jabbed a needle in her thigh and injected her with the isotope, even though he might have used more force than necessary. *Hate this girl.*

One task checked off his to-do list.

He parked at the curb, studying the row of townhomes. They were tall, well-manicured, and semi-attached brownstones. Tiffany's was easy to spot, because there were two armed guards at the door.

"You will tell them you want me inside, that I will be spending the night, and they aren't to disturb us."

"Yes," she said, eyes glassy and voice monotone.

Couldn't be helped. He stepped outside, walked around, and opened her door. From this angle the moon wasn't as bright and the stars weren't as sparkly. Even better, the sidewalks were abandoned.

He threw an arm around her shoulders and walked her to her door. The guards watched him warily.

"I want him inside," Tiffany said. "He will be spending the night, and you aren't to disturb us."

If they noticed the lack of inflection in her voice, they made no comment.

She swept inside and Blue moved in behind her, closing and locking the door.

He tugged her into the living room, just in case the guards were listening through the metal. "Do you have any servants?"

"No. We're alone."

"What about your brother and your father? Will they be paying you a visit?"

"No."

Too bad. "Tiffany, you are tired. You will go to sleep now, and when you wake up, you will believe we had amazing sex." That way, if he needed to see her again, she would be more likely to agree.

"Tired," she said, then yawned. "Sleep. Sex." Her eyes closed and her knees buckled, but Blue caught her before she hit the ground. He found the master bedroom upstairs, a big, messy space with clothes strewn all over the engineered hardwood floor.

He set her on the bed, stripped her, and messed up the sheets to support whatever sexual tale her mind wove.

As he searched the entire home, he planted bugs in each of the rooms. He looked over the few pictures she had, those of her with her father and brother. Judging by the way Star senior smiled at Tiffany, he adored her—information that could maybe be used against him.

Michael didn't think Star was the type to cave to demands, but it might be worth a shot.

The townhome didn't seem to have any secret passages. What it did have was stacks and stacks of clothing, different rolls of fabrics, and device after device loaded with digital sketches.

He looked over a few of the sketches, searching for anything having to do with the Golden Sunrise line—and finding plenty. He fought for control as he read her notations in the margins.

Save discarded cutouts from shoulders and use for decorative edging on skirt.

Cinch the pelt here to accentuate waistline.

Possible to blend the Rakan with silk for softer feel?

Suddenly the front door crashed open. Multiple pairs of footsteps sounded.

Blue dropped the device and reached for his pyre-gun. Three guards turned the corner just as he aimed. He could have fired on the one in the center and taken out the other two a split second later. But there were more guards filing in behind the original trio. He could release an energy ring, shocking everyone in the vicinity, but then he would be drained.

Why risk that if he could talk his way out?

When the first three pointed pyre-guns at him, he held his hands up, all innocence.

"Mr. Star would like to speak with you," said the one in the middle. "The condition we find the girl in will determine the condition you leave in."

Well, well. Good thing he'd opted not to go with group electric shock therapy. "What a surprise," he said with a smile devoid of humor. "I'd like to speak with Mr. Star, too."

Footsteps echoed from the staircase. Then a man called out, "She's fine. Just sleeping."

Blue allowed the men to lead him out of the townhome and into a dark SUV. He hoped Tiffany would be left at home, alone; with his hand at his side, he quickly texted Solo, telling him to go and get her . . . but to be careful. Still, Blue doubted things would be that easy. Most likely, Star would have her moved to a new and private location, kept under a more vigilant watch.

One man slid into the front seat as two sandwiched Blue in back, weapons trained on him.

"Are you afraid?" asked Front. "You should be afraid."

"I'm hungry. Tiffany was a little wildcat, and I worked up an appetite. You got any snacks?"

Front glared at him.

The guy at his left watched him reverently. "Would you, I don't know, sign my shirt or something, Mr. Blue? I've been a big fan ever since—"

A look from Front shut him up. "We allowed you to keep your weapons per Mr. Star's orders. But that also means we have the right to defend ourselves if you act up." He stroked the hilt of his gun. "Please act up."

Blue smiled. "Another time, perhaps."

The rest of the drive passed in silence. When the car stopped in Star's driveway, he saw the entire area was illuminated by massive lampposts. Two other guards were waiting and opened the door for Blue to emerge. He did so without hesitation. Was John somewhere inside, and Blue missed him the last time he was here?

He scanned the foyer, taking note of every detail,

things he might have missed in his haste. The floor was marble and veined in gold. The walls were white and flecked with gold. Overhead, the chandelier looked like vines of golden ivy, with thousands of tiny sapphires and rubies blooming from the emerald leaves.

Clearly, Star had an obsession with gold.

Calm. Steady.

A frowning Gregory Star opened a pair of double doors leading inside his office. He was a little taller than Tyson, with salt-and-pepper hair, a slim build, and the features of a man who'd seen the worst the world had to offer—and caused a lot of it.

"Welcome, Mr. Blue. Welcome." He waved Blue over. "Come inside. Let's talk in private." Then he turned his back to Blue, as if he had no fear of what Blue might do.

Blue followed, *without* reaching for one of his weapons. Something to marvel over. But John's welfare came before rage and revenge.

The office was very much like Michael's. Dark leathers, massive desk, plush rugs, and hologram pictures of his children displayed on the walls.

Star settled behind the desk, and Blue plopped into a chair across from him.

"I don't like that you went after my daughter," Star said, hands forming a steeple in front of his face. "She's innocent in all of this, and doesn't deserve to be hurt."

Blue tsked. "Now, we both know she's far from innocent, and frankly I'm insulted that you'd try to convince me otherwise."

"So we're not going to pretend ignorance of the situation," Star said, nodding. "I approve."

"I'm so glad," Blue replied drily.

A fleeting smile, devoid of humor. "It took me a while to figure out that you are more than a football star, for which I'm deeply ashamed. I'm not usually so slow. But now, at least, I know you're part of a government-run black ops team."

"What gave me away?"

"My son sent men after Miss Black, hoping to force her father out of hiding. Those men turned up dead. And you, Mr. Blue, were spotted sneaking into her home soon after. So I asked myself, why would a playboy like you keep such a relationship secret? You wouldn't be intimidated by the thought of bad press. You don't care what people think of you. So I had to assume you weren't there for sex but for protection. How am I doing so far?"

"Quite well, actually." His reputation had finally served him well. Star had no idea Blue and Evie were romantically involved, or that Evie was an agent.

"Then, of course, there was the fact that you ran into my daughter, and bugs were found in my home. Yes. We found and destroyed them. And don't think to try again. As of a few hours ago I added an audible pulse to the inside of my walls. I don't know all the technical aspects, just that it will scramble any audio signals."

"Thanks for the warning."

Star nodded as if he was serious. "Then there was the fact that my daughter became obsessed with you. And when you two were next together, she acted like a robot." My men called me, concerned. You compelled her, I'm guessing?"

Blue shrugged.

"You know, you otherworlders might have your supernatural abilities, but we humans have our counters. There are drugs we can take to make us immune to Arcadian compulsion, though the side effects are terrible. I'd never thought it worth it. Until now. Also, I've seen you play. Seen the things you've done on the field, the power you've wielded. I've taken precautions against that as well. Try to expend your energy, I dare you."

He was careful to keep his expression neutral. His weapons were being stripped away, one by one. "Hurrah for you, doing what you can to protect yourself. But there are other ways to get to you."

A flare of irritation in Star's eyes. One that held an edge of cruelty. Here was the boy from the streets. The boy suspected of selling organs on the black market. The boy with the skills to peel flesh from bones.

"You are angry with me, Mr. Blue, when there is no reason to be."

"No reason to be? Are you kidding me? You bombed my boss and closest friends. And oh, yeah. Me."

"You and your friends were simply collateral damage. Michael Black's former assistant, Monica Gains, came to me. She said Mr. Black was a government agent and he was looking into seventeen disappearances now linked to my name. I was surprised, I admit. I considered Mr. Black an excellent business rival, but nothing more. She said we could help each other."

Michael had been right.

"I rarely ask my associates for motive, but in her case, since I would be attacking the New World Order,

I made an exception. Seems she had gotten herself into terrible debt, but your precious Michael wouldn't help her. Instead, he made things worse by taking away her only source of income. And after all her years of dedicated service. Shameful."

In his business, trust was everything, and Monica broke it. "So, when detonation day came, my friends and I were just in the wrong place at the wrong time."

"Exactly."

"But you decided to take advantage of the situation anyway. You sold one and took the Rakan."

Star merely blinked, curious. "What makes you think your friend survived the blast?"

So much for not pretending. "I've seen the sketches. I know what you're using him for, and I will not rest until he's home safe."

Star peered at him for a long while, silent, unaffected. "If I was worried about your involvement, Mr. Blue, you would be dead right now. But nothing I've told you can be proven, nor was it something you hadn't already figured out on your own. I've taken every possible measure to protect my investment, as well as myself."

"You're not infallible."

"Agree to disagree. Because, you see, Mr. Blue, if I die, your friend dies. I'm the only one who knows where he is. Without me, he will starve."

Blue bit the side of his tongue until he tasted blood.

"Try to take my children to offer in trade, and you'll find your friend's parts sold at auction. An arm here, a leg there."

"You would be condemning your children to death."

"And I would grieve, despise you, and do everything within my ability to secure my revenge, but I wouldn't be behind bars, and that's what would matter most."

How was Blue supposed to deal with a man this coldhearted?

"Speaking of my children, Tyson called me just before you arrived. He lives at the Star Light Hotel and he took Miss Black to his suite. He caught her snooping, making him wonder at her involvement in all of this. He's determined to punish her"—Star lifted a pyre-gun—"and you're going to be blamed."

Twenty-two

———❦———

*E*VIE MADE SEVERAL BLUNDERS. She had used the aphrodisiac on Tyson, and he had responded—just not the way she hoped. Lust had mutated into aggression, and he'd threatened to obliterate Blue, his need to protect his sister from the playboy far surpassing his need for sexual release.

Where she'd once thought the guy might have beaten Tiffany, she now knew otherwise. He worshipped the girl.

So, to counteract the aggression, Evie had used a small dose of the sedative.

She should have used more, but she hadn't wanted Tyson to (1) pass out on the roof before she could convince him to take her to his room, or (2) fall asleep the moment they reached his room, ruining any kind of interrogation.

Two guards had taken her purse before allowing her past Tyson's door, and she had been unable to think of an excuse to grab her "pen." Then Tyson had fallen asleep when they got inside, and she should have realized it wasn't a deep sleep, that with as small a dose as he'd had, he would wake up very quickly. Instead, she had used the time to paw through his things. He woke up, realized he had been drugged, and found her in his office. There was no talking her way out of the precarious situation.

Hands in the air, she walked around the desk.

He kept a pyre-gun trained on her. "That's close enough." He nodded to the pile of paperwork she'd just dropped. "Did you find anything interesting?"

Actually, yes. Confirmation of a drug habit he hadn't kicked (paraphernalia) and confirmation that the Golden Sunrise clothing line was set to debut in two weeks (invitations).

"Finally, nothing to say." His eyes narrowed on her. "You are a beautiful woman, Miss Black, and the time we spent on the roof made me question my decision to use you to draw out your father. But you have proved you are just like the man, and that means you must be eliminated."

She smiled sweetly and inched a little closer to him. "Being compared to Michael Black is a compliment. But you are just like Gregory Star, and that isn't."

His nostrils flared. "It is."

Please. It wasn't, and they both knew it.

A little closer . . . "What do you have against Michael, anyway?"

"He was going to try and lock my father away—or have him killed. Star Industries would have suffered. My inheritance would have suffered. My sister and I have endured too much to lose everything now."

Just a little closer . . . "Well," Evie said, unwilling to feel sorry for him for whatever he'd endured at the hands of Gregory Star, "let's see what I can do." She kicked out her leg and batted his shooting hand. Instinctively he squeezed the trigger, but with the motion he missed her and the bright laser stream blazed through the wall.

He was startled, unprepared, and Evie was able to slam her palm into his nose, spin to his side, and elbow him in the back of the head. He fell to his knees, hissing in pain.

She reached for the gun he still held, intending to wrench it from his grip—only to hear a familiar click. She froze.

"That's right, little girl." The harsh voice came from the doorway. "No sudden movements."

She glanced over, saw one of the guards who'd been posted at the front door pointing a gun at her heart, and two other men standing behind him.

Tyson shoved her away and lurched to his feet. His eyes sizzled with fury, and blood leaked from his nose. "Tie her," he said nasally.

The pyre-gun remained trained on her as the other two guards closed the distance. Her arms were bound behind her back with laser cuffs. Prickles of fear ignited in her chest, and her blood flashed cold.

"Have the guests left?" Tyson asked.

"Yes, sir."

"Then let's take her to the roof."

They were going to push her off, weren't they?

Evie struggled against her captors as she was escorted out of the suite and toward a private elevator.

"Go ahead. Scream," Tyson said. "No one will hear you."

The group entered the elevator and the doors closed, sealing them inside. She mentally calculated the odds of a successful escape. If she knocked out the guy on her left with a head butt, and closed the throat of the guy on her right with a swift kick, that would leave the one with the gun and Tyson. She would be shot before she got to either male.

Thing was, that wasn't any worse than what awaited her on the roof. So. She did it. Head butt. Guy moaned. Swift kick. Guy went down.

Except she wasn't shot. She was pistol-whipped on the side of the head. Sharp pain slashed through her, and stars winked through her line of vision.

The two guys she'd downed scowled as they stood, and when the doors opened, they roughly hauled her forward. Any hope that a guest had lingered evaporated. The entire area was deserted. Empty glasses littered the tables, and plates of half-eaten food waited on the ground. Floats drifted across the surface of the pool.

Tyson faced her, murder gleaming in his ice-cold eyes. "Here's what is going to happen, Miss Black. I have no taste for death, so I will be leaving you. These fine gentlemen are going to tie you to a chair and throw you in the pool. You will drown, and I'm sure it will be most painful. Then, when you are dead, they will remove the chair and the cuffs and throw you back in. Tomorrow morning, when the staff comes to clean, you will be found. Corbin Blue will be in the very chair we take from you, his brains splattered all over the stone. A tragic murder-suicide the world will never forget."

Don't panic. "A slight problem with your plan. Over a hundred people saw you leave with me."

"And that's what sent Mr. Blue into a rage. That's why he punched me, knocked me out, and dragged you away."

"But he left with your sister."

"Only to make you jealous. But as Tiffany will later recount, he ranted and raved about you, the rage getting stronger and stronger until he abandoned her with every intention of finding you."

Keep trying. "Do you really want my murder linked to your name?"

"No, but it will be a small price to pay to be rid of you."

Gah! "You'll never be able to capture Blue."

His smile was all kinds of evil. "It's already done." He nodded to the men before turning and striding away.

As she bucked and kicked, she was dragged to a chair. Though she landed a few decent blows, the men were eventually able to force her to sit. And when the cuffs were hooked to the back of the chair, she had to cease all movement. To continue fighting was to lose both of her hands.

Do you want your hands or your life?

In a few minutes she might not be able to have both. The chair was lifted and carried to the water. Her fear returned, making her tremble.

"How much is he paying you," she rushed out. "Because I'll triple it."

"Sometimes it's not about the money," one of them replied. "Sometimes it's just about the fun."

She was dumped into the pool, face-first.

The chair was metal, and heavy, and she sank fast, the chemically laced water stinging her eyes, filling her ears. The fear magnified, and panic threatened to overtake her. *Calm. Stay calm. Think!*

She kicked her legs until she flipped the chair to an upright position. She knew the men were still up there, watching, because she could see their shadows through the surface of the water and the strands of dark hair floating in front of her face.

Can't let them stop you. She angled her body forward so that she could stand, then walked toward the steps, the chair like a tortoise shell. If she could just reach the steps, she could climb out of the pool and breathe.

They'll just throw you back in.

Yes, but she would have more time, giving Blue a chance to find her. She knew he would. Knew he hadn't been captured. He was too strong, too smart. Too determined.

But all too soon, her lungs began to burn, burn so bad, and that burn spread to the center of her chest, then to her throat and nose. Darkness descended like a curtain over her eyes. Where were the steps? She couldn't see the freaking steps!

Desperate, Evie kicked and pulled at her arms. So she'd lose her hands. So what. *Breathe, have to breathe. Please. Please.* This couldn't be the end. Her last memory couldn't be one of defeat, knowing Blue would be blamed for her death, one way or another.

Suddenly, the water pressing in on Evie lifted and she was sucking in great gulps of air, her lungs practically weeping with gratitude. The chair fell backward, slamming her hands against dry concrete.

She'd made it to the steps? Climbed without realizing it?

Gradually the darkness faded and colors began to take shape. She frowned. She hadn't actually gotten out of the pool, she realized. She was still on the bottom—the water hovered *above* her. Like a cloud.

Strange muffled noises snagged her attention. She turned her head and saw Blue standing at the outer edge of the pool, his arms lifted high, as if he were holding the water in place.

She shook her head to dislodge the moisture trapped in her ears.

"—now! Evangeline," he shouted. "Climb out. Climb out now."

Yes. She struggled to get to her feet. Her legs shook more violently with every inch she gained, but she did it. She reached the steps. The moment she cleared the ledge, the water splashed back into the pool, a tidal wave, droplets spraying in every direction.

Blue rushed to her side and disabled the cuffs.

"Guards?" she panted, pulling her arms to her chest and rubbing her sore, raw wrists.

"Dead."

"Tyson?"

"Don't know." Blue jerked her into his arms, holding her tight. She didn't have the energy to do anything more than lean against him and accept his offer of comfort. "I haven't seen him, but the next time I do, I'm going to gut him."

The trembling in her legs migrated to her jaw, making her teeth chatter. "Not yet. Star will punish . . . John." He'd never forgive himself if Star hurt his friend for his actions. "How did . . . you find . . . me?"

"Isotope."

"Figured."

"Don't be mad. It saved your life."

"No, you did. Just . . . get me . . . home."

"Okay, baby. Okay. I'll get you home."

In the car, Blue turned the heat as high as it would go and aimed every vent in Evie's direction. Then he seethed. Fury was a living entity inside him. Fury directed at the Stars. At himself. Hell, even at Evie.

She almost died.

He kept remembering how he disabled Gregory Star with a ring of energy before a shot could be fired, allowing Blue to escape the house. How he used his super-speed to get to the hotel, then through the hotel, screaming Evie's name. The tracker had assured him she was in the building, but not where. He checked Tyson's suite, and found evidence of a struggle. He flew up to the roof as a last resort, not really thinking the male would have taken her back to the party, but not knowing where else to look.

Then he saw the men peering into the pool and laughing. Saw Evie at the bottom, fighting for her life. He used what was left of his power to tear the men into a thousand tiny pieces, at the same time lifting the water out of the pool.

As drained as he'd been, he almost hadn't had the inner strength to do it.

"I never want to find you like that again," he said.

Her trembling began to subside. "Trust me. A repeat isn't on my agenda."

He'd come so close to losing her. He just couldn't get past that fact.

The feisty, bad-tempered little vixen had become the favorite part of his day. He was happier when she was nearby. He was challenged. Satisfied. Horny as hell, pleasured as hell. He needed more of her. More time. More sex. More arguments. More surprises. More everything. He hadn't gotten nearly enough.

And the Stars had tried to take her away.

They had to die.

At last they reached one of his more luxurious safe houses and parked in the garage. "How are you?" he asked as he helped her into the living room.

"Better. Stronger already."

"In pain?"

"No."

Good. He stepped in front of her, and leaned down, getting in her face, scowling. "I want you off the case."

She pushed wet strands of hair from her cheeks and stared up at him as if he'd just lost his mind. Maybe he had. "Are you freaking kidding me?"

"No! I'm deadly serious."

"Well, too bad. I'm in this thing to the end."

The end? A poor choice of words. "You almost died tonight, Evie."

"But I didn't. Thanks to you and your dastardly ways—which I will forgive you for after you've begged for an appropriate amount of time. Or have written me a sonnet. Yes, that's what I want. A sonnet."

"Evangeline."

Sighing, she placed her hands on his shoulders. "I'm still here, and I'm still willing to fight."

He shook his head, refusing to back down. "You planned to go back to work at the hospital anyway. Why not go now rather than later?"

Her nails dug into him as she clutched his shirt. "What happened to me being a good agent? And why should *you* get to put your life at risk?"

"Because I—" *Love you.*

Did he?

Damn it. He did. He really did. The feeling was too strong to deny.

Her eyes widened as his implication became clear. "What? Say it."

Why not? he thought with a bitter laugh. *Why not put everything out there?* "Sex has never meant anything to me. It has always been a distraction. A pleasure. A means to an end. Until you. You make me feel things I've never felt before. I want to keep you around. I *need* to keep you around. I'm falling in love with you, Evie." Shitty phrasing. He wasn't falling. He'd already gone *splat* on the pavement.

No longer so brave, she backed away from him. "Blue."

"I've never said those words to another woman. Not even for a case. I can't lose you. And, Evie, I will be faithful, I swear to you. You will never have to worry about another woman. Not for any reason."

"Blue," she said again.

Going to turn him down?

Let's see if he could change her mind.

Moving faster than she could track, he picked her up and tossed her on the couch. She bounced up and down, and he fell on top of her, pinning her arms over her head.

"What do you think you're doing?" Evie demanded. This man had just rocked her entire world. *I think I'm falling in love with you.* He'd all but gotten down on his knee and offered her a ring, and she had no idea how to feel. Or deal.

What did she know of romantic love? Nothing!

Not how to give it, and certainly not how to receive it. Because receiving it would mean getting used to it. Needing it. Relying on it.

What would happen if it was taken away?

"I've relocated the battle," Blue said easily.

The battle over her right to stay on the case? Or . . . her heart? "As if turf really matters. You won't be winning."

"Let's find out." He smashed his lips into hers, his tongue thrusting hard, insisting on entrance, slamming past teeth, uncaring when she bit down to prove a point. Panting, he said, "I like it when you fight me."

Her, too. "Don't be nice about it. Fight back."

"Nice? No, not this time." He wasn't kind or caring as he stripped her of every piece of clothing. And he wasn't a gentleman as he stared at her breasts. He was a man possessed by raw, animal need. "Gorgeous. My mouth is watering for them." He lowered his head, and as the heat of his mouth enveloped her nipple he sucked, *sucked hard*, and she cried out, her hands tangling in his hair, tugging at the strands.

"Blue!"

He reached between her legs and worked her with his masterful fingers, thrusting in and out with savage force. "Let's find your sweet spot, baby."

He did something he'd never done before. He angled one of his fingers, almost hooking it, and a white-hot lance of pleasure shot through her. Her hips came off the couch and she clutched at him, gasping his name.

"Yeah," he said, clearly pleased with himself. "Right there."

"Yes!"

He rubbed her there, again and again, and the pleasure just kept coming. Soon she was writhing and moaning, trying to beg for more, but the words were utterly incoherent. He was edging her closer and closer to insanity, where nothing mattered but what he was doing to her . . . what he *would* do to her.

"You want me inside you," he rasped. He trailed kisses along her jaw, then her neck, then the curve of her breast. "Say it."

"Yes." A moan. "Want you. Please." As she spoke, she worked her hand between their bodies and clutched his massive erection. The tip was slick with evidence of his desire.

He didn't take the time to remove his clothing.

Maybe he was worried she would change her mind. She wouldn't; she was too far gone. He simply ripped open his pants, pinned her hands over her head, and slammed home.

Release came instantly for her, and she screamed, filled, stretched, shuddering around him, barely able to breathe. Floating, flying away as he hammered inside her, again and again.

The delicious brutality never ended. His control was shredded. He showed no mercy, and she was glad. She wanted none. She wrapped her legs around his waist and began to meet him thrust for savage thrust. Though she would have thought it impossible, her own need began to build again. Hotter. Stronger.

She grabbed his head and forced him down for a kiss. It, too, was wicked and without control, their tongues mimicking the motions of their bodies. Around her, she heard lamps and vases falling, shattering. She heard furniture toppling over. And she didn't care.

"Blue!" She broke apart at the seams as she shot straight into another climax. Satisfaction hit next, leaving her boneless.

This time he followed her, thrusting so hard, he actually moved the couch, inch by inch, until it finally banged into the wall . . . and everything stilled, the storm over.

He collapsed on top of her. "Evie."

Took a moment for her mind to kick back into gear. What the hell had just happened?

That couldn't have been sex. It had been too raw. Too primal. Utterly consuming. Powerful. As if she'd done more than give her body, despite the lack of fore-play. As if she'd given pieces of her soul.

Was she falling in love, too?

He rested his head just over her thundering heart-beat. "Did I hurt you?" he asked, his voice ragged.

"No."

"You were with me all the way?"

"I can't believe you have to ask."

He kissed the wild pulse at the base of her neck be-fore rising to his elbows and peering down at her. His gorgeous lavender eyes were dark with contentment and determination.

"Do you trust me?" he asked.

She traced the edge of his lips with a trembling fin-gertip. "Yes."

"Do you believe I'll be faithful to you? Not just for this case but for all others? No matter what I'm as-signed."

All? All! Were they talking . . . forever? "I . . . think so."

Disappointment replaced the contentment. "For now, that's good enough. I *will* prove myself to you."

She closed her eyes. "It's not a matter of proving yourself, bluejay. It's a matter of believing you won't grow tired of me."

"I won't grow tired of you."

How confident he sounded. "All right. Okay. We can try a real relationship. But things have to stay the same. We have to keep it a secret."

"Evie—"

"No. I don't want to be the reason you and Michael break up."

"We won't break up. We'll fight and make up."

She heard the doubt in his tone. "Maybe. But I know him, and he'll say things that he'll never be able to take back. You'll be hurt, and I'll be mad."

His expression softened. "He's a spy, Evie. He taught me everything I know. He's going to find out sooner or later."

"But—"

"No buts. Right now I have a reason to sneak over. Very soon I won't. How are you going to explain my presence?" He wound a lock of her hair around his finger. "Because I'm not sleeping without you."

Falling faster . . .

"I don't want to sleep without you, either," she admitted. "But. Yes, there will be buts. We'll tell everyone sometime after the case, as planned. No reason to distract our only backup."

"Fine. Once John is found, I'll give you a week. A business week, just to be clear. You aren't taking the weekend, too."

"Two weeks."

"Three days."

"You still haven't learned to bargain!"

"Two days."

"One business week," she said on a sigh.

He kissed her. "Agreed. Now, can we commence with the snugging?"

"No. More loving." She wrapped her arms around him and nibbled her way across his jaw. Lazy pleasure, that's what this was, and she was going to enjoy every moment of it. The fire no longer raged, it simmered with promise of things to come. "Solo will flip, you know. He hates me."

"Now you're grasping," Blue said, flipping to his back and placing Evie on top of him.

Mmm. The new position opened up a whole new world for her to explore. "Doesn't matter," she said, flicking her tongue over one of his nipples. "It's still a valid reason to me."

His hands tangled in her hair. "Well, then, he just doesn't know you."

"He'll try to talk you out of seeing me." The other nipple received the same spa treatment.

"And I won't listen."

Gah! He had an answer for everything.

"Any other objections?" he said.

She kissed her way to his navel. "You are so frustrating, coming up with intelligent responses."

"And you are maddening." There was an edge to his voice . . . a hum of desire. "Clearly, we deserve each other. Now, stop messing around, princess. You've teased me enough."

"Poor Blue. Needing your woman again? Sorry, ducky, but I've only just begun."

"Too bad. I want you to suck me."

"I will . . . if you're a good boy."

"I haven't been a good boy a day in my life."

"There's a first time for everything. Now, shut up and let Pudding Pop do her thing."

Twenty-three

*E*VIE SAT UP WITH a gasp.

After her brush with death, Blue suspected she would have a nightmare and hadn't let himself fall asleep. He was glad.

"It's all right," he said, urging her to stretch out beside him. "I'm here."

Trusting him, she curled into his side. He kissed her forehead.

The sun wouldn't rise for another hour, and darkness clung to the bedroom. In this secret hideaway, he would keep her safe, even from her dreams.

"So, what are we going to do?" she asked. "Now that we've both been nailed as agents, I mean."

He traced his fingertips along her spine. "We're going to place all three of the Stars in a holding cell and beat them until someone reveals John's location."

"I like it. First, though, we have to catch them. And, Blue, I wasn't able to inject Tyson. It was mission fail, all the way. I'm sorry."

"Don't worry about it. We'll track him another way. Who knows? He may be so cocky, he's still at the hotel, thinking he's secure."

"What if we beat them, and they still refuse to talk?"

A possibility. "I'll use compulsion. Daddy Star says he took a drug to counteract the ability, but it can't last forever." And if that failed, he'd think of something else.

"Well, it's too late—or early—to do anything now, and we're both in need of a recharge. So why don't you give Michael and Solo a call, update them on everything that's happened, and I'll draw us a bath."

"Deal."

She rolled from the bed and he picked up his cell phone. Solo answered on the first ring and Blue explained the situation. They agreed to meet in two hours.

"You sound shaken," the otherworlder said.

"Yeah."

"She means that much to you?"

In deference to Evie, he ignored the question. "Do me a solid and tell Michael what I told you."

"Sure."

Blue heard water pouring from the faucet in the bathroom and grinned. "I've got to go."

Naked, he strode to the doorway and crossed his arms. Evie was already lounging in the tub, honey-scented bubbles all around her. His body was conditioned to react to the fragrance and did so instantly, hardening.

"Someone can't get enough of me, I see," she said, and tsk-tsked.

"Someone doesn't deny it."

Pleasure flushed her cheeks. "How can he?" Her tone was droll. "His hard-on gives him away."

He barked out a laugh. The things that came out of

her mouth . . . good enough to eat. "By the way, we're hosting a meeting in a few hours. Which means, my sweet little apple bottom, that there's just enough time for us to have our bathtub playdate and eat breakfast. Off of each other."

"I like the sound of that." Her smile was seductive as he climbed in behind her. But when he tried to draw her against his chest, she slipped away to press against the other side of the porcelain. "Uh, uh, uh. Playdates require games."

"What kind of games?" Hot water lapped at his skin, making him burn that much hotter for her.

"Let's start with Man Obey Woman and go from there."

He snorted. "That's how we're going to do this, huh, monkey bear? You boss me around, and I come to heel?"

"Isn't that what we've been doing all along?" The steam produced a moist sheen over her beautiful face. The ends of her hair were wet, curling upward, around her nipples. "I thought that was what we've been doing."

"Funny."

Grinning, she ran her hand through the bubbles. "We're going to play Q and A. I've got questions, you've got answers."

"Very well."

She tapped her chin, saying, "Where to start, where to start? Oh, I know. Have you ever been totally, madly, deeply in love? You told me you've never said the words, but have you ever felt the emotion?"

"Other than with myself?"

She leaned over to twist his nipple. "I was being serious."

"Ow! So was I." He pried her naughty fingers loose. "No." A pause. He remembered the sweatpants and boxers from his first days here and stiffened, thinking of her mooning over some faceless guy—who would soon die. "Have you?"

"No."

Well, then. Murder was off the day's agenda. "Then why do you own men's sweatpants and boxers?"

"Because they're comfortable."

"Not from a previous lover?"

"No. Like I would really wear someone's inferior clothing."

Darling little elitist. He loved it. "What else do you have for me?"

She nibbled on her bottom lip, and he wasn't sure he would like what came next. "You told me we didn't have to worry about kids. Why is that?"

Okay. That he could handle. "I am, for all intents and purposes, fixed."

Her eyebrows drew together in confusion. "You had surgery? But what about your ability to heal?"

"I wasn't snipped like human males. A nifty little device was anchored inside my sac."

"It is reversible?"

"Yes. Why? Do you want kids?"

She shrugged. "Maybe one day."

His gaze lowered to her flat belly, and he thought about watching her grow big with his child. He went from wood to mega-wood in seconds.

Yeah. He liked the idea. "What's your next question?"

She thought for a moment. "What's the most romantic thing you've ever done for a woman?"

He reached through the water and latched onto her foot, lifting it to massage her arch. As she moaned in pleasure, he said, "I'm doing it right now."

"That's sad."

"Want me to stop?"

"Stop and I'll poison you with the shampoo, stuff your body in a garbage bag, and set you out on the curb for trash day."

Won't laugh. "That's quite a detailed murder plan."

"Well, I don't want to be caught, now, do I?"

He rolled his eyes and claimed her other foot. "All right, baby boo-boo. Getting serious now," he said, and she gulped. "You've been attracted to me since the moment you met me, haven't you? You've been carrying a torch for me all these years."

"Ha! I'm being completely serious when I tell you it was hate at first sight. After a double shot of lust."

He grinned. "Well, *I* was attracted to *you*."

"You were?" she squeaked.

He nodded. "Then you opened your mouth. 'Hate' is too mild a word for what I felt then."

She threw a handful of bubbles at him. "We've talked a bit about this, I know, but it hasn't changed. I'm not even close to your type. Look at these," she said, arching her back to cause her breasts to thrust up. "They're so small."

"I'm looking, and I'm thinking they're perfect."

"You're going to throw out your first lie? Over these?" She cupped them. "Maybe I'll get implants."

He went still. "I'm not lying, and you won't get implants."

"Maybe."

"If you do, I'll give the doctor who performs the surgery an implant of his own—my fist inside his chest. I will rip out his heart and drink his blood from his boots."

"You're serious," she said, gaping.

"Totally."

Grinning slowly, seductively, she crawled to him and straddled his waist. "That's a very sweet thing to say."

"Just being honest. And if you tell me you're okay with me getting a penile implant, I think I'll finally put you over my knee and spank you *so hard*."

She nipped his ear, her breath warm on his skin. "Darling, if you were any bigger, you'd tear me in two."

The endearment he loved. The compliment he savored.

The woman he adored.

He ran his hands over the perfect lobes of her ass. "Don't think I didn't notice the fact that you failed to protest the spanking."

"Sure, you can spank me . . . if I can spank you."

His own smile was slow. "Deal."

She arched a brow. "Not going to try one of your famous bargains?"

"Why would I? I'm getting what I want."

She laughed.

He loved when she laughed. "Okay, I have one more question before I forget I can use my mouth for talking." His fingers slid forward and wrapped around her inner thighs, closing in on her sex. "What do you think about tattoos? For or against?"

Shivering, she rasped, "Some are good, some are bad. Why?"

"I used to have a few, but the fire destroyed them, and I'd like to get new ones—but only if my snuggle doodle likes the idea." Two fingers inched higher. . . .

She licked her lips. "I remember now. You had those strange symbols around your navel."

Among other things. "And how did you know that, hmm? Did you use to stare at me, princess?"

She slid her hand down his stomach and curled her fingers around his shaft, drawing a moan from him. "One thing has never changed, Mr. Blue. You like to walk around without your shirt. But to answer your question, I'm now one hundred percent *for* new tattoos. On one condition."

He reached her center and drew his hands through her slick heat. "Yes?"

Her moan blended with his. "I get to pick one out."

At the moment, as her grip tightened on him, he would have let her do anything she wanted. "You want me to get a unicorn or a rainbow, don't you?"

"Don't be ridiculous. I want you to get 'Property of E.B.' right here." She ran her thumb from his base to his tip.

"Possessive, are we?"

Her eyelids drooped with carnal hunger. "Very much so."

He took her by the wrists and folded her arms behind her back. Holding her with one hand, he positioned himself at her core with the other. "Gonna make you so glad you said that, princess."

And he did.

Forty minutes before everyone was set to arrive, Evie thought. Another forty minutes with Blue.

She looked at the food she'd placed on the kitchen counter, thinking to cook breakfast, then looked at Blue. He sat at the table, watching her, fire crackling in his eyes.

Food—or Blue? There wasn't time for both. And there definitely wasn't time to eat the food off each other, as planned.

Blue, she thought a second later. Absolutely. She couldn't get enough of him, and she wasn't sure whether the rush of adrenaline just hadn't dissipated, or if she really was addicted to him and needed a fix—or, hell, if his earlier confession had permanently revved her to all systems go.

Maybe she needed him so much because she feared she would lose him all too soon. He'd said he wanted to be with her. Not just now, but later. He said he was falling for her and he didn't care what anyone else thought, and she was certain he meant it. At the time. It was easy not to care when there were no consequences.

If Michael fired him, he would lose his agency job as

well as his place on the football team. She could convince Michael to hire him back, no probs, but the damage would have already been done. Resentment would
have its claws in both men.

Or maybe her fear was unfounded. Michael ob-
jected in the beginning, but once he knew Blue was
committed to her, he might just give them his blessing.

Still. Maybe they should forget their bargain and
wait until they knew beyond any doubt whether they
did or did not love each other. That way they'd know
if the potential consequences would be worth the risk.

Could a man in the process of falling in love fall out
of love before the actual emotion was achieved?

Probably. Men in love fell out of it all the time.
Right?

And what about her? She had never felt this way
about any other male. The thought of losing Blue
nearly destroyed her.

"What are you thinking about, baby?"

She blinked and discovered he was no longer in his
chair. She turned, meeting his gaze. He crowded her
against the counter, his body heat enveloping her, his
power stroking over her, causing goose bumps to rise.

"You were giving me a come-hither look," he said,
cupping her cheeks, "and then you were frowning."

To tell or not to tell? "Just thinking about . . . feelings," she said, then cringed. "How mortifying. That
was such a girl thing to say."

"Well, you're a girl." He hefted her onto the counter.
"Wrap your legs around me."

She obeyed.

"Arms, too."

Again she obeyed. "Feeling bossy, Mr. Hammer?"

"Just tit for tat, snookums. And maybe I'm a girl, too, because I'm one hundred percent invested in this feelings conversation. So, what kind are we talking about? Confusion? Anger?" A pause. "Love?"

"Yes, Evangeline. What kind of feelings?"

Michael's cold voice echoed through the kitchen, and she gasped. Her father must have come in through the back door. He was clearly programmed into the security system; no alerts had sounded.

Blue stiffened.

Horrified, Evie jumped to her feet and gave him a little push to the side, hoping to urge him out of the room to save him from a confrontation. At least until she'd calmed things down. Because one thing became very clear as she met her father's gaze. Blue was right. Michael would not be giving them his blessing anytime soon. His eyes were narrowed, his color high. His hands were balled into fists.

Blue remained in place, shoulders back, legs braced apart.

A battle stance.

"Let me explain," she rushed out.

"Do you really think an explanation is needed?" Michael, who was dressed as a factory worker to disguise his true identity, looked at Blue. "I gave you everything, taught you everything you know, and only asked one thing in return."

"I realize that," Blue replied.

His tone . . .

He sounded miserable.

Sickness churned in her stomach.

"It's my fault," she said. "I came on to him. He was helpless against my potent seduction."

Blue scowled at her. "Don't lie. You're better than that. But yes, I was helpless."

"Don't talk to her like that," Michael growled, and took a menacing step forward.

As skilled a fighter as he was, he was still recovering from the blast. And Blue, with his Arcadian abilities, would always be stronger. Evie moved between them and held out her arms.

"Let's take a moment to talk about this," she said. "I'm an adult. Blue is an adult. What we do with each other affects no one but us. You never should have told him to stay away from me."

"It *does* affect me. It affects your life and my ability to—"

He pressed his lips together.

But she could guess what he was going to say. "You're more upset that you're losing your resident slut than about the fact that he might break my heart. Do you know how lousy that is?"

"I'm concerned about the loss of those particular talents, yes, but not more than I'm concerned about your heart."

In a show of comfort and support, Blue draped his arm over her shoulders. She was grateful, and it must have showed. Michael cursed under his breath.

She pinched the bridge of her nose. "Daddy, why are you here so early?"

Like Blue, he planted his feet. "I wanted to see you, to spend some time with you before we got to business." He held up a paper bag. "I brought you breakfast."

"Oh," she said guiltily. "I'm . . . sorry."

"How long has this been going on?" he demanded.

"Since I broke things off with Pagan," Blue said.

"Another woman scorned." Michael frowned at Evie. "Is that what you want for yourself? To be one in a line? Sunbeam, I hoped you would have so much more."

First, outrage hit her.

Then more outrage.

"Hold on a sec. You gave Blue those assignments, Daddy. You acted as his pimp. You didn't care that he had a girlfriend when you did it, either. You gave him orders and expected them to be obeyed. And he wanted your approval. Of course he obeyed."

"I had a choice, Evie," Blue said, resolute. "Always."

There was shame in his voice, and she didn't like it. "It's not what you did yesterday, darling. It's what you do today." She pointed a finger at Michael. "Did you tell all agents to stay away from me, or just Blue?"

A pause. A muscle ticking in his jaw. "Just Blue."

At her side, Blue stiffened all over again.

He'd just taken a major blow. Had just realized Michael judged him as harshly as Evie once had.

Oh, Blue . . .

He once told her that he *wanted* to be faithful. She realized now he wanted it more than anything. He grew up without the love of a family. He had John and Solo, but only during training and missions. He never really belonged to anyone.

She, at least, had Claire and Eden.

"Well," she said, "that's probably one of the stupidest things you've ever done, Daddy, and as I'm learning, you've done some pretty stupid things!"

He opened his mouth to reply.

"Shut up. Just shut up." She placed her hand on Blue's chest. "I could play this the way you'd like best. I could dump Blue and tell him it's because I don't want to stand in the way of his friendship with you, especially since we aren't even sure where this thing between us is going. But you know what? You don't deserve him. Neither do I, but I want him with every fiber of my being. Therefore, I'm keeping him."

"Evie—"

"No. You and the rest of the world might find this foolish, but I trust Blue. He's not going to take those kinds of mission anymore. Are you?" she demanded of Blue, glaring up at him.

Though there was still hurt in his eyes, there was also a glow of amusement. He shook his head. "No, ma'am."

"You and you alone have permission to call me anything you want—except 'ma'am.' The word makes me think of mom jeans, and I'd rather die." She turned to her father. "And you aren't going to offer those kinds of missions to him. You aren't going to be mad at him for disobeying your stupid order to stay away from me, either."

"But—"

"No!" She stomped her foot. "You're like a father to him. Act like it."

Michael's shoulders slumped.

"Now, then. Blue, put the food back in the fridge. Michael, sit down and give me my breakfast. Neither one of you is to say another word until I've decided what your punishments are."

"Our punishments?" they demanded in unison.

She raised her chin. "That's right. You've both put me in a terrible position. One of you was going to make a horrible mistake and ask me to choose. Isn't that right, Daddy? I was then going to have to murder you both in cold blood. Now, get silent and do what you were told."

"That still doesn't explain what I did," Blue said— *not* getting silent.

She kissed him without any hesitation. "You are making me fall deeper and deeper in love with you, and I'm furious about it, poppet, I really am."

Twenty-four

ONCE SOLO ARRIVED, THINGS moved quickly. Well, except for the one-on-one the guy insisted on having with Blue.

He pulled Blue into a hallway and said, "I knew there was something there, but I didn't know it was serious. Evangeline Black? Blue, you can do better."

"There's *no one* better." She was top of the line. Grade A. And she was falling deeper and deeper in love with him. He'd never let her take back those words. They'd rocked his world.

"You couldn't scratch your itch with someone else?" Solo persisted.

"It's not an itch," he replied flatly. "It's forever."

"So, what, you're going to marry the devil's favorite handmaiden now?"

Blue barely stopped himself from throwing a punch. *This is your friend. You love him.* "Watch how you talk about her, my man, or we will have problems. How would you feel if I insulted Vika that way?"

"I'd have to kill you." Shamefaced, Solo patted him on the shoulder. "I'm sorry. If you like Evie, that's good enough for me. I will never treat her with anything other than respect."

"Thank you."

"No need for that. Your happiness matters to me."

"I'll *never* be happy without her." Evie was wonderful. The way she stood up to her dad. The way she defended Blue and confessed her feelings. He'd never seen anything like it, and doubted he ever would again.

She accepted him. All of him. Past, present. Future.

He'd always hated being called a slut and a whore, and he'd always told himself that he did what he did for the job, that it was okay. To discover that Michael viewed him through the ugly veil of judgment . . . yeah, that hurt. But Evie hadn't backed down.

"All right," she said now, checking the scope on a pyre-rifle as he and Solo returned to the kitchen. "Are we ready to do this? I call dibs on the guys in the photos with Mr. Cooper's pregnant girlfriend."

Beautiful, savage female.

Solo had spoken to Tyrese Cooper's wife, and with a little . . . persuasion she'd admitted to paying Star to abduct and hurt the mistress. The mistress had since been found, alive, and returned to Mr. Cooper. All three had a long, dark road to navigate.

"More than ready." Once upon a time, Blue had refused to admit Evie was the type of woman he'd wanted. The type he *needed*. But she was. And he wouldn't change a single thing about her. "But I don't want you rushing into a massive free-for-all, princess."

"Duh," she said. "I seriously suck at fighting more

than one angry dude at a time. As I've proven. I'll be more help on a hill, picking off the idiots foolish enough to step within my sights."

That's my girl. "Let's go, then," Blue said.

They gathered all the weapons they could carry. Waiting for dark would give Star more time to hide. Or prepare.

They would take him, then his son, then his daughter.

In the car, Solo claimed the driver's seat, Blue the passenger, and Evie the back. No one spoke a word the entire drive, but that was okay. He knew that they were all thinking the same thing. No mercy.

About a mile from the gate, they dropped Evie off. Before she could clear the vehicle, Blue reached through the open window, grabbed her by the nape, pulled her close, and kissed her hard.

"Be careful," he whispered against her lips.

"No probs." Her gaze was grim. "But you, too. I mean it, Blue. You have no idea the fury I'll unleash on you if you allow yourself to get hurt."

"Get hurt, and delay our snugs time? No." He gave her another kiss before letting her go.

Leaving her was tough. He had to force himself to nod to Solo. The otherworlder drilled the pedal into the floorboard and zoomed to the gate blocking the public road from the private driveway. They emerged. As cameras watched their every move, Blue set a small bomb on the left side and Solo set one at the right.

They turned their backs, and *boom!*

The charge was small enough, and isolated enough, that he felt only a whoosh of white-hot air along his back and a slight burn on his neck and arms. As pieces of metal sprayed over the ground, he and Solo climbed inside the car and sped forward.

Armed guards rushed from the house, but Solo didn't slow. He'd taken control of the vehicle and disabled every sensor, allowing him to run into one man, then another. As they tumbled over the hood and screamed, the other males jumped out of the way.

When he reached the porch steps, he slammed the car through the front door. Bricks and other debris flew in every direction. Blue palmed his weapons as he got out. Moving faster than any gaze could track, he wove through the guards, shooting one, stabbing another. Shooting, stabbing. Grunts and groans sounded. Bodies fell to the ground, never to get up again.

He and Solo left no survivors.

They stomped inside the estate, alert, scanning for Star senior as well as any soldiers who might be lurking nearby. Blue's gaze caught the barrel of a pyre-gun peeking from around the corner of the far wall. He motioned to Solo, then launched forward, whizzing around, secretly closing in on the man.

A stream of yellow light sprayed at the other warrior. The fry setting, rather than stun. Solo dodged, but not quite swiftly enough. His arm was grazed by one of the flames.

Blue reached his target a second later and shot him in the temple.

"The others are running outside," Solo called. "Either they're afraid of us or they know something we don't."

An angry voice spilled from an intercom system. "They know something you don't."

Star.

While Solo searched for the reason the men had run, Blue ground his teeth and sought out the camera. There had to be one, and it had to be—there! In the corner, beside the entrance to the office. He glared into the lens. "You got something to say?"

"If you haven't already guessed," Star said, "I'm not there."

"Too bad."

"I thought we reached an understanding, Mr. Blue."

"We did. You tried to kill me and my woman, and I struck back."

A low growl echoed over the airwaves. "You murdered an entire contingent of my men and destroyed my home. Aren't you afraid of what I'll do to your friend?"

"Yes. But you should know, anything you do to John, I'll do to you. Twice."

"I do not appreciate threats, Mr. Blue."

Using his most insulting tone, Blue said, "I don't make threats, Mr. Star. I make promises."

"Bomb," Solo suddenly shouted. "Two minutes."

Blue leapt into action, moving to Solo's side and tugging him outside. They were at the gate by the time detonation occurred, but it was still a strong enough blast to knock them off their feet.

Blue was thrown into one of the fake trees, hitting with so much force he knocked the entire thing to the ground. A sharp sting in his side made him look down. A piece of metal protruded from his stomach.

Blood and his Arcadian power were hemorrhaging from him, draining him fast. He used what he could to lumber to his feet and check on Solo. The agent's cheek was badly cut, and crimson smeared the lower half of his face, but he was steady, unwavering.

"We need to leave before the authorities arrive," Solo said, even as sirens echoed in the background. "Or before Star sends more men."

Their car was in pieces, so they hoofed it deeper into the trees. Then, two yards before they reached the road, a group of Star's men stepped from behind the trunks, surrounding them—aiming pyre-guns.

Evie squeezed the trigger.

Pop!

Turned, aimed through the scope. Squeezed the trigger.

Pop!

Turned, aimed through the scope. Squeezed the trigger.

Pop!

Every time the *pop* sounded, another guard dropped—and very little was left of his head. Star's men soon figured out that anyone who dared raise a weapon against the Arcadian died.

Can't look at Blue. Can't run to Blue. Not yet.

If she looked, she would cry. That spike . . .

If she ran, she would give the enemy time to reach him.

The remaining men fired at the agents. Bright yellow lights erupted. Pretty. Like a display of fireworks. Blue and Solo managed to dodge, but Blue lost his footing and fell. He landed with a hard thump, the spike sinking deeper. He grimaced—and stayed down.

Dang it. She'd looked. And she was already crying.

With a roar, Solo collided with one of the males, and the two thudded to the ground.

His body expanded several inches. His skin took on a crimson glow. Spikes grew from the tips of his ears, and claws sprouted from his nails. Just then, he was a monster feared by other monsters, and yet the guards didn't run screaming.

As she picked off another of Star's men, she wondered if they were all under compulsion to stay and destroy. That would explain a lot. And it was possible. Star employed many different alien races, including Arcadians.

She peered through her scope, but the men were now being careful to remain in a state of constant motion. She could still hit a target, but it would take more time.

Pop!

Another went down. Only five more to go.

Solo disarmed one with his claws. A hand went flying—without an arm. Blood sprayed.

Four more to go.

Blue got to his feet, wavered. "Evangeline," he shouted. "Your three."

Understanding, she swept her gun to the right. A male had gotten down on one knee to aim a grenade launcher in her direction. She nailed him between the eyes, but it was too late. The rocket had been released.

She fell to the ground, hands over her head to act as a small measure of protection. Only, the blast never came.

Brow furrowed, she straightened and scanned her surroundings. Blue had caught the fist-size missile with his power. As she watched, he sent the thing high in the sky. There was an explosion of fire and smoke. Blue collapsed, spent.

Solo moved to his side and stood sentry, daring the three remaining men to approach. Evie steadied her rifle. *Keep it together.* One by one, as the males circled the pair, closing in, she introduced them to the grave.

Draping the weapon over her shoulder, she ran. Finally ran, screaming, "Blue! Just hang on. I'll patch you up, I swear I will."

When she reached his side, she dropped to her knees. His skin was pale. His lips were a scary light blue, doing justice to his name.

He offered her a weak smile—there was blood on his teeth. "Saved me . . . you, warrior princess . . . me, soldier in distress . . . storybook . . ." The rambling stopped as his head lolled to the side—and he died.

"Michael!" Evie shouted. "Help!"

Heart thundering in her chest, she rushed down the hall, clearing the way for Solo, who held an unconscious Blue in his arms. She managed to revive him on the drive over, but he crashed three more times. If she didn't get him stabilized, she was going to lose him for good.

Vika appeared in a doorway and gasped when she saw the bloody trio.

"In here," Evie said to Solo, barreling into her bedroom. They'd called Michael during the drive and told him to meet them at a safe house she used for medical emergencies. "Put him on the bed, and be gentle."

The steel pipe lodged between the slabs of muscle in his stomach had sunk so deep it now poked out the other side.

The moment he was settled, she leapt into action, gathering the supplies she would need. She might not be prepared to deal with massive burns, but this . . . this she could handle.

Keep. It. Together.

Michael raced into the room.

"You're going to assist me," she said, her voice calm despite her raging emotions. "The rod has to come out, but I can't remove it and stop the bleeding at the same time."

"I've done triage," her father replied. "I can do this. I won't let you down."

In the bathroom, she scrubbed up as best she could. She was trembling, and that wasn't good. She could do more damage to him . . . to Blue . . . her Blue.

Deep breath in . . . out . . . Okay. Yes. I'm capable. Cutting into people is practically my superpower. Her nerves began to steady as her adrenaline kicked in and her confidence revved back up.

Blue would come out of this. No other outcome was acceptable.

Blue cracked open eyelids that felt as dry and rough as sandpaper. A strange beep sounded in his ears.

Wherever he was, the lights were dimmed. His side ached.

"Hey," a soft voice said.

Evie.

The beeping quickened.

It had to be monitoring his heart rate, because the muscle careened out of control at the first indication that she was nearby.

She came into view, leaning over him, his own personal angel. Long, dark hair fell over her shoulder, curling at the end. Those big, brown eyes that dominated her face were filled with worry and relief. The heart-shaped lips he loved to kiss were . . . slightly blue? Why? Then his gaze snagged on the angry mark marring her pale skin, and he could focus on nothing else.

"Your poor cheek, baby," he said, reaching up. The tendons in his shoulder protested painfully, and he grimaced, but that didn't stop him from running his fingers across the wide bruise. "What happened?"

"You were in another explosion," Evie said. "A piece of metal tubing perforated your side, but we got it out. You lost a lot of blood, but don't worry, we didn't give you a transfusion. I remembered what you said." She smoothed her hands over his forehead.

"I didn't mean me. What happened to you?"

"Oh. Your power came back in a burst and knocked me across the room."

"What?" A sharp pain lanced through his middle. "What?" he asked more gently. "I did this?"

"You had no idea what was going on, so I'm not

going to hold a grudge. Seriously. Don't worry. I promise I'll only remind you of the pain I suffered on holi-
days and anniversaries."

She made light of it, and he wanted to hug her for
it, but he wasn't sure he would ever be able to forgive
himself. "I'm sorry, princess."

"Don't be. I mean it." She traced her thumb across
his jaw. "You're on the mend and that's all I care about."

He held her gaze for a long while, wishing he could
do more. He would rather be stabbed every day for the
rest of his life than do anything to hurt her. "How's
Solo?" he finally croaked.

"He's already up and around."

Good. Something to be relieved about. "Give me a
few hours. I'll be up in every way that matters, too."

He wanted her to grin. She didn't. She merely blinked
at him, saying, "How about I give you a few days? You
only got out of surgery yesterday." Then she dropped
away from him, flopping into a chair beside the bed.

Light from a side lamp spilled over her, allowing
him to see her more clearly. Glistening tears cascaded
down her face, and her teeth . . . her teeth were chat-
tering. The air was frigid, he noticed, and he frowned.

"Come here," he said, patting the mattress beside him.

She shook her head, and his frown deepened. "I
don't want to accidentally—"

"Come here," he repeated more sternly.

This time she obeyed without hesitation, stretching
out beside him and curling into his side, being careful
of his wound.

Her skin was ice, and he didn't like it. He wrapped

himself around her, willing his warmth into her body as she shivered. "Why are you so cold?"

"Remember when Dallas told us he was healed by the Arcadian king? Well, I called Dallas and told him I'd cut off his man junk if the king failed to give me any pointers. He told me open wounds heal better in frigid temperatures. Apparently, your planet is a frosty one."

Blue hadn't known that. He'd always lived here. "If you get sick because of this, I will finally give you that spanking you so richly deserve. And I won't let you give me one in return."

She humphed. "You wouldn't be able to stop me."

"Want to bet?"

"Darling, did you hear the part about speaking to the Arcadian king? I also asked him where your most sensitive parts are so I could have you on the ground crying for your mommy in seconds."

He swallowed a laugh. "All you're doing is turning me on." He loved waking up to this woman. Loved holding her. Loved comforting her as she comforted him. He just flat-out loved *her*.

Totally, madly, deeply. Weren't those the words she'd used?

Somehow, she had become his everything.

Challenges rocked. He'd always preferred the missions and games he'd had to work hard to win. And Evie had certainly made him work for every milestone. But, oh, when she surrendered a few yards, there was nothing sweeter.

"I believe I've noted the fact that everything turns you on," she said.

"When you're involved, yes."

She chuckled—but the humor soon morphed into gut-wrenching sobs.

Reeling, he held her close. He had never seen her break down like this, and it tore him apart. "Pooh bear?" he asked the moment she calmed enough to hear him. "What's wrong?"

"I'm sorry," she said, sniffling, wiping her tears away with a shaky hand. "I've been running on adrenaline, and now you're awake, and, well, it's crashed, and my emotions are getting the better of me."

He kissed her temple, relieved. "Thank you for taking care of me."

She nodded, her cheek rubbing against his chest, the friction sending a lance of pleasure straight to his groin. "I would do it again in a heartbeat," she said, "I really would, it's just . . . I'm coming to need you too much. If you had died . . . I wasn't sure what I would have done without you."

The words . . . yeah. He wasn't going to let himself get emotional about her declaration, but . . . yeah. This woman.

My woman.

She loved him, too, totally, madly, deeply, whether she realized it or not.

"What I feel for you scares me, too," he admitted. "I've never felt it before. Obsession and addiction, as if my identity is now forever tangled up in yours."

"You don't mind?"

"No. You are such a self-contained woman, it's difficult to get past your barriers. But I made it, and I *want* you to need me the way I need you. I don't want to be alone in this thing."

A pause. Then: "You're really right there with me?"

"I am." And he wouldn't change a thing.

"Blue," she whispered, kissing his chest just above his beating heart.

"I want you, baby. *So much*."

"We can't."

"We aren't. You are."

"Well, well. I like the thought of that. Finally, I'll be the one to do all the hard work." She gently pulled at his pants, stripping him. Then she sat up in the bed and discarded her own garments.

As golden moonlight spilled over her, she straddled his waist.

The contact electrified him, wet heat pressing against his length.

"I love seeing you like this," he said. "You are the most beautiful creature ever created, Evangeline Black."

"No. That would be you." She cupped her breasts and leaned down to him, offering him a taste.

He licked one, then the other, then blew on both, watching the nipples pearl. "Love these little darlings."

"Mmm," she moaned. "Love them more."

"With pleasure." He flicked his tongue over a beaded tip, then sucked, then licked again, always savoring. She gave another moan and ground against the long, wide length of his shaft. "So perfect, baby, so perfect." He reached back and curled his fingers around the bars of the headboard. "I will never get enough of you."

She turned her attention to his mouth, kissing him, feeding him passion and pleasure, nipping at his lips while sliding up and down along his erection—so warm and wet—her hands all over him, learning him, driving him insane, her hunger feeding his own, already an undeniable force, and peeling away all sense of self.

There was no Blue without Evie.

"You ready for me, baby?"

"So ready."

"Then take me."

She rose to her knees and placed him at her entrance, then, slowly, she sank down. He had to fight the urge to surge up, going deeper, all the way.

"Feels so good," she groaned.

"Someone needs a vocab lesson. It feels amazing."

A smile lifted the corners of her lips, a powerful smile, feminine. "Oh, yeah?"

He practically vibrated with a hunger only this woman could induce. "Yeah."

"Tell me if I hurt you." She lifted before she'd worked herself all the way down, only to slam back with all of her strength; his hips arched automatically.

Yeah. Yeah, like that.

"Again," he rasped. "Please. I can take it."

She did, harder and faster, and she didn't stop. She found a rhythm and rode him, lost, wild, taking all that she wanted, all that she needed, and he loved every moment, always rising up to meet her, uncaring about any momentary pain, giving her all that he was, all that he had; and when she screamed with the force of her release, his own poured forth, the pleasure too much to bear.

She collapsed on his chest, out of breath and damp with perspiration, and, hopefully, too exhausted for dreams. She drifted off to sleep and he rolled her over, cleaned them both, then curled into her side.

For the first time in his adult life, he felt as though he'd found a home.

Twenty-five

~⌖~

THE NEXT DAY BLUE sat at Evie's desk with Evie in his lap. "There she is," he said, tapping a red dot on the screen. "Tiffany Star."

Evie frowned. "The dot tells me nothing."

"She's in a remote part of Vermont."

"Then to Vermont we go."

If they were lucky, the Star boys would be there as well. If not, they would deal.

During Blue's recovery, Solo had gone after the son on his own; but, like his father, Tyson had already gone into hiding.

"How soon can you be ready to go?" he asked.

"Thirty seconds. I just need to grab my purse." She hopped off his lap—he wanted to pout like a child—but returned in only ten seconds, her bag in hand.

He checked the contents, smiling when he found a small bottle of ranch dressing, duct tape, dice, a pair of panties, a man's bow tie, and other things he couldn't identify.

"No weapon?" he asked.

"Please." She snorted. "Everything in there is a weapon."

Love. This. Woman.

"We'll take Michael's jet," she said, and he noticed she gave a little shudder. "It's got, like, warp speed, so we can be there in an hour."

Why a shudder? "I'll call Solo and tell him to meet us at the airstrip."

Thirty minutes later, the three of them boarded the jet and settled in the plush, dark leather seats. There was a dining table, a bedroom in back, and three four-by-four cages for carting criminals. Luxury and business at its finest.

Blue sat next to Evie. She grew pale and tense, and even squealed when the engines started up.

"You okay?" he asked her.

"I hate flying," she grumbled. "It's stupid. Planes are stupid. And *we're* stupid for climbing inside this death trap!"

Distraction time. "Look away, Solo," he said, leaning in to place a kiss at the base of Evie's neck. "Things are about to get freaky."

She pressed her lips together, but it was too late. A giggle escaped. And when he made growling noises against her skin, as if he were the big, bad wolf, she outright laughed. *Better.*

"Do you know how hilarious it is that the indomitable Evie Black is afraid of flying?" he asked.

She slapped at his arm. "You take that back, Corbin Blue! I'm afraid of nothing."

"Except joining the Mile High Club. Right, baby?"

That earned him another slap. This one packed a little sting. "Maybe I'll join—with myself."

"Mmm, don't tease me like that." She hadn't noticed that they'd hurtled down the runway and launched into the air, he thought with a smile. "Especially since this stupid plane comes with a bedroom."

Looking at Solo, she hiked her thumb in Blue's direction. "Has he always been like this?"

"Incorrigible? Always." And then the warrior did something that astonished Blue. He winked at Evie.

A stamp of approval, right there.

His grin was wide.

"So you two are really together," Solo said.

"Yes, but I'm considering breaking up with him," Evie replied.

Blue shook his head with mock pity. "I'd just win you back. You know it's true, so why even waste the time? You're helpless against my immense charms."

She rubbed her temples as if warding off a headache. "How did his other girlfriends put up with him?" she asked Solo.

"He was never like this with his other girlfriends" was the soft reply, and Evie faced Blue, her eyes wide.

He shrugged. It was true. He could be himself with her, no secrets in the way. No fears.

With a contented sigh, she nestled her head against his shoulder.

When the jet landed, he almost wished they'd had to go a greater distance. Holding her was a sweeter pleasure than having sex with another woman.

The cabin was twenty miles away, and once they reached it, Blue realized it was smaller than the blueprint made it seem, and decrepit-looking, hidden in a thick cluster of real trees.

A single light spilled from the only window Blue could see. A window leading into the living room. There were no guards outside patrolling the area, which meant there had to be trip wires on the ground.

Well, okay, then.

Evie anchored her night-vision goggles in place and attached a laser sensor over the lens. As she searched for any place the ground might have been disturbed, as well as any glowing red lines to indicate that an invisible security fence was activated, she quietly said, "The entire area is surrounded. There isn't a clear spot anywhere."

He took the goggles and looked for himself. Every red line was computerized with a signal meant to scan body heat and weight, as well as bone structure, and decide whether or not the invader was animal or man—no matter how quickly the creature moved. Once a determination was made, weapons—probably guns—would pop out of secret locations, all stripper from a cake deadly.

"I can get in without detection," Blue whispered. "You two stay here and shoot anything that comes out without first shooting a flare."

Solo nodded and took off for the other side of the house.

"Plug your ears, baby." Blue pulled the pin on a scrambler grenade and tossed it through the wires. Then he closed his eyes and covered his own ears. He knew the exact moment the grenade detonated. A surge of electricity lifted the hair on his arms. A piercing ring made his brain want to jump out of his skull. Anyone within a mile radius would experience the same reaction.

Couldn't be helped.

One.

Knowing he had only five seconds before the scramble failed and the lasers kicked back on, he sprinted forward, moving as fast as his feet would carry him.

Two.

He reached the front porch and dropped to his stomach, removing his mask and palming two pyreguns. Aimed.

Three.

A tall, muscled—and armed—male opened the door and peered out, frowning. He rubbed at his ears.

Four.

Blue didn't have to squeeze the trigger, because a yellow blaze soared past him, slamming into the man's chest. *Thanks, baby.* The guy dropped to the ground, already dead. The beam fried his heart to a crisp.

Five.

"Henry?" another man said.

The ringing stopped.

Blue popped to his feet and launched forward, through the door, barely missing the reengagement of the lasers. He scanned the home, taking everything in at once. The living room had three other guards in it. Two were watching television. One was striding toward the fallen Henry, his expression concerned.

Pop. Pop. Pop.

All three died as quickly as their friend, this time courtesy of Blue.

A search of the premises revealed no other guards. Just Tiffany in bed, her blue eyes wide as she pressed against the headboard, her hands trembling as she aimed a pyre-gun at him. She squeezed off a shot as Blue approached, but he dodged, and the blaze soared over his shoulder. He was on her the next instant, rolling her over and tying her hands behind her back.

She bucked, far stronger than she appeared, but still Blue managed to subdue her easily enough.

"Stop fighting," he said. "You're not going to win this."

"No, Blue. No. Don't do this."

Begging won't help, honey. "I'm taking you hostage."

"You don't understand." Her struggles renewed, but they were just as ineffective as the others. "Please," she said. "Don't do this. You'll regret it."

"I'm not going to kill you." *Yet.* Pressing her into the mattress with one hand, he withdrew a syringe from his pocket with the other. "Right now my plan is to use you as a bargaining chip. Your father has something I want, and you're going to get it back for me." Star claimed he would not trade, but they would soon put those words to the test.

"No," she sobbed. "You don't want to take him on. Just leave me here. Walk away before you tumble straight into his trap. It's the only way you'll survive."

Blue paused. Her words . . .

Those of a frightened captive, sure. But there was something else at work here, it seemed, something far more desperate than he was used to seeing from those he'd wrangled over the years.

He didn't have time for a conversation but found himself flipping her over anyway, placing a knee in her stomach to hold her down and training a gun on the doorway, just in case they had any unexpected visitors. He also kept the syringe ready to be plunged deep into her neck.

She was fully dressed, he noted. T-shirt, jeans, and tennis shoes. The tennis shoes looked odd on her. Too casual for the girl he'd come to know, the white canvas somehow out of place when paired with the bright colors of the rest of her clothing.

Watery eyes beseeched him. "Walk away. Leave Tyson and me alone."

"I can't. What do you know of your father's plans for John, now that I'm coming in strong?"

She pressed her lips together in a thin, stubborn line.

"I'm going to find out one way or another. You can make it easy on yourself and talk now."

"No. I can't," she whispered, her features tormented.

"You can." Drawing on his compulsion, he said, "You will."

But she shook her head, making him think her father had given her an injection of whatever made him immune to the ability. "I won't. You don't understand."

"Enlighten me."

She closed her eyes, and a tear beaded from the corner, cascading down her cheek. "I'm not a horrible person. I'm not. But he's going to make me become one, and I don't want to become one, but I will, there's no other way, because I can't survive on my own, don't want to survive on my own."

Enough babbling. He wasn't getting any answers out of her. Frustrated, he jabbed the needle into her vein with a little more force than he'd intended, watched as her eyes closed and her head lolled to the side.

He double-checked her vitals before hefting her over his shoulder. When exiting the front door, he disengaged the lasers outside and fired a flare into the night sky.

Evie and Solo raced over to him.

"Got her?" Evie demanded.

"I do."

Hauling her to the plane was easy. Locking her in one of the holding cells was satisfying.

Once they were in the air, Blue called Michael to tell him everything was set.

"I'll find a way to reach Star and let him know we've got his baby girl," Michael said. His tone wasn't as affectionate as it used to be, but it wasn't laced with disappointment or anger, either.

Progress.

"I want to know what he says." Blue paused, then offered: "Something's off with Tiffany. She knows something, but I couldn't get it out of her."

"Whatever it is, we'll find out. Time is on our side now."

Blue scrubbed a hand through his hair. "Yes. You're right. See you soon."

"Wait," Michael rushed out just before he disconnected.

Curiosity and dread warred. "Yes?"

There was a crackle of breath. "Listen, I know I haven't been supportive of your relationship with my daughter."

Understatement.

"I'm . . . sorry about that. You make her happy and that's all that matters. Just . . . take good care of her."

Shock hit him as his gaze found Evie—his gaze always found Evie. His heart seemed to beat for her, and her alone. She sat in front of Tiffany's cage, waiting for the girl to wake up, determined to have a little girl talk. Every moment in her presence was a gift.

"I will," he vowed. Just then, he thought loving Evie was what he'd been born to do.

Twenty-six

*T*IFFANY WAS STILL SLEEPING when they reached New Chicago. And she was still sleeping when they carted her to a cage in Michael's underground room at the boathouse. Nothing roused her. In fact, she was still sleeping an hour later.

"Go home," Michael finally said. "Eat. Get some rest. You're all operating on pure adrenaline. She'll be here in the morning. Or afternoon. Whatever."

Solo took off to be with Vika—where he'd left her, no one knew.

Blue and Evie weren't far behind. They stopped to pick up a bag of Evie's things, then drove to his safe house and fell into bed, exhausted.

When her phone rang, however many hours later, bright light slanted through the curtains. She groped for the cell perched on the nightstand.

"Hello?" she rasped.

"Sorry, sunbeam, but I need to speak with Blue," her father said, "and he's not answering his phone."

"Hang on." Groggy, Evie tried to hand the cell to Blue, who was curled tightly around her body, holding her as if he feared she would slip away.

"Put it on speaker," he muttered. "I like where my arms are."

She pressed a button. "You're on, Daddy."

"I sent a message through certain underground contacts, letting them know I have Tiffany. They let Star know. He called me but refused to talk about terms. He wants to talk directly to you, Blue."

"All right. We'll be there as soon as possible."

"Also, Tiffany has woken," Michael added. "I spoke to her at length and even used Evie's truth serum, but I got no answers out of her. She's definitely had some improvements since you last saw her."

Blue stiffened. "Well, then, we've been asking too nicely. Might be time to change that."

Evie hung up and set the cell on the nightstand. She dug through her bag, picked the purse she wanted, and filled it with everything she thought she might need. A golf ball, a pair of glasses, a coaster, a Rubik's Cube, three tubes of lipstick, all in a different shade, and a package of freeze-dried ice cream.

"More weapons?" he asked, startling her when she realized he was standing behind her.

"Yeah. When I fit my fingers into certain grooves in the golf ball, it's activated, and poisoned smoke will fill the air. You can breath it in, and that's fine, but if it comes into contact with your eyes, you're in trouble. And the Rubik's Cube is actually a bomb. Line up certain colors, and you get to watch a room go *boom boom*."

Grinning, he tugged her into his embrace for a quick kiss. "You are too adorable for words."

"Uh, Blue. I hate to break it to you, but I think

there's something wrong with you if you find a girl with weapons of destruction adorable."

"*So* adorable. Or should I say 'adorbs'?"

She punched his arm, but inside, she was as giddy as a little schoolgirl.

The boat ride proved uneventful, for which she was grateful. She used the time to get her focus off Blue and what he made her feel and onto the Stars and John. The entire ordeal was almost over. There was finally a light at the end of the tunnel.

Her father was in the spacious living room, cleared of all but a table piled high with weapons, a lounge chair, a few computers, and now a cage. Tiffany was trapped inside. Dirt and tears smeared her cheeks, and her shirt and jeans were ripped and wrinkled. There were angry cuts running the length of both of her arms, and one across her neck. She looked nothing like the elegant woman Evie saw at the victory party.

Tiffany paled when she spotted Blue, stood, and curled her fingers around the bars of her cage. "You'd be wise to leave," she said, a tremor in her voice.

"You'd be wise to give us the answers we seek," he snapped, "before I make use of the tools on the table. That happens, and you'll pray for death. But you won't get it." He looked to Evie. "You want to watch me work, princess?"

"Would love to, Mr. Hammer." He deposited her in a chair at the computers, kissed her, kissed her again, and stalked to Michael, who waited at the table, cleaning a dagger.

"Where's Solo?"

"On his way," Michael replied. "I have Star's number, if you want to call him."

He smiled coldly at Tiffany. "Yeah. Let's get him good and scared about what I'm going to do to her."

Blue was so ready for this to be over. He wanted to move into Evie's officially, or move her into his place. He wanted to take her on a date. Their first. He wanted to ask her to marry him.

Yeah, he realized. He did.

He wanted her to wholly belong to him. To be his family.

He wanted her ensconced in every part of his life. And he wanted to be ensconced in every part of hers, whether she did a little agenting or went back to the hospital as she'd originally planned. He wanted to romance her so hard she offered her heart on a silver freaking platter.

He just plain wanted.

Michael held out a cell phone. "You'll need this. And you'll also need to stop staring at my daughter."

He blinked into focus, only then realizing he'd switched his attention to Evie.

She offered him a knowing—wicked—smile.

He winked at her, then shifted his gaze. Tiffany sobbed quietly.

He hardened his heart and dialed Star's number.

Two rings in, the male answered with "Well, well. Someone finally remembered he's at war" in lieu of a greeting.

"You know we have your daughter and you know what we want. Let's not play games."

"Mr. Blue," a low growl crackled. "Where is she?"

"Somewhere you'll never find her."

"You don't want to do this. I will kill your friend and send you the pieces."

"Despite the money you would lose?"

"Oh, yes. I've done more for less."

Blue's laugh was devoid of humor. "I could say the same. You hurt John any more than you already have, and I'll do the same to your little girl. In fact, as soon as we hang up, I'll take her fingers and make myself a real pretty necklace from the bones. Or maybe I'll remove her skin the way you removed John's."

A hiss of fury.

"So, where does that leave us?" he finished casually.

Silence dominated the line for several seconds. "I suppose you want to trade."

"I do."

"And you would trust me to keep up my end."

"Of course not. I would *force* you to keep up your end."

Another hiss. "I want to talk to her first. Proof of life."

"That's great, wonderful. I'll let you. Just as soon as I've spoken to John."

"I thought you'd say that. Sadly, he's not in the mood to speak right now. However, if you'll glance at your screen, I'll show you a video of him."

Dread filled Blue as he lowered the phone. An electronic notebook was held up, displaying that day's paper. Then the notebook was removed, and a small concrete room came into view. The walls were gray. There was a bed—a gurney, really—with a huge red lump in the center.

A red lump that was . . . that was . . .

Blue nearly hunched over and vomited. That red lump was clearly John. He was a mass of meat and blood, without a single inch of skin to protect his insides. His mouth was parted in an endless, agonized scream he probably didn't have the strength to unleash.

The scene vanished, and Blue shoved the phone back to his ear. His hand was shaking. "You'll pay for that," he croaked. "I will make sure you pay."

Evie came up beside him and wrapped her arms around his waist, offering comfort. He was glad. His knees were knocking and his head swimming with a rage his body couldn't seem to contain. He was on the brink of cracking and he hadn't even realized it.

"My turn," Star said stiffly.

Blue kissed Evie's temple before stalking to Tiffany's cage. He held out the phone and pressed Speaker. "Say hello."

"Are you all right, darling?" Star asked.

Tears beaded in her lashes. Gaze locked on Blue, she shook her head no, her lips smashed together as if she didn't want to speak.

"Answer him out loud," Blue snarled.

A heavy pause as the tears rolled down her cheeks. "Y-yes, Daddy. I'm all right."

"Good." The tenor of Star's voice had changed. From concerned to commanding. "Then do what I told you to do. My men are already in place."

Click.

Blue's brow furrowed in confusion.

"I told you that you'd regret this." Tiffany closed her eyes, tremors rocking her entire body. She breathed in and out, as if trying to calm herself, before bending down and removing one of her shoes. She fit her fingers into grooves at the sides before tossing it in the center of the living room. That done, she grabbed a small silver hook resting at the toe of the other shoe.

Trying not to panic, Blue shook the bars. "What did he mean?"

"My brother found the isotope tracker Miss Black meant to use on him, and figured you'd used one on me," she said softly. "A little hacking proved him right. My father has been tracking me, too. He knows where I am. He's known all along. His men are waiting outside the perimeter. And now it's too late. I have to do what he told me. I have to punish you for embarrassing him. Have to show his clients he can deliver whatever he promises. If not, *I'll* be punished. And if not me, then Tyson. I don't want either of us to be punished. I'm sorry."

He believed her and knew something terrible was about to go down. He'd brought Evie into an ambush and hadn't had a clue. Some agent he was. "How many men? What's the plan?"

Tiffany's smile was sad. "He said to tell you that you began this way, and so you'll end this way."

With that, she tugged on the hook, and a black cloth pulled free. A cloth she spread over her entire body.

This way, she'd said. The shoe. The covering. Blue put two and two together.

Heart slamming against his ribs, he shouted, "Bomb!" and whipped around, diving on top of Evie. They crashed onto the ground just as the shoe bomb detonated.

White-hot heat blasted through the room, lifting him up and ripping Evie from his arms. He landed with a horrible smack, his lungs without air. Smoke was so thick he felt as though he were drowning in it. Debris rained in every direction. Pieces of wall here. Computer parts there. Fires, fires everywhere.

Coughing, Blue staggered to his feet. His leg throbbed. He looked down. His pants had been scorched away. A bone protruded through his skin. Whatever. He stumbled through the smoke. "Evie," he shouted.

Please be all right. Please be all right.

He found her in the next room and fell to his knees at her side. No. *No!*

She wasn't all right.

Her body lay at an odd angle, her spine clearly severed. There were gashes on her cheeks, blood all over her beautiful face. One of her eyes was swollen shut. The other was glassed over as it tracked his motions.

"Blue," she said, and a crimson river flowed from the side of her mouth. "You okay?"

"Shh. Shh. Don't talk, baby." He wasn't too late. He could fix this. He had to fix this.

He ripped apart what remained of her shirt and flattened both of his hands on her chest, then closed his eyes. In his mind, he saw his very essence sweeping through her, through blood and muscle and bone, trading what remained of his health for every one of her injuries.

Inside, he felt his cells bursting, his tissues ripping,

his bones snapping. It hurt. Oh, it hurt. Then his legs went numb. His arms stopped working. His heart stuttered into a warped beat as if it had been nailed into his chest wall by his ribs and couldn't escape. He fell to the side, barely able to breathe.

Worth it.

Because, a second later, Evie sat up. The swelling had left her face. The gashes had stitched together. She looked over at him and cried out with dismay.

"Blue! No, no, no." She pressed her fingers into the pulse of his neck. "What did you do? *Why* did you do it? You idiot! I will never forgive you or myself if something happens to you."

"Well, I for one am glad he did it." Tyson Star stomped into the room, the smoke parting as he pointed a gun at her face.

A roar brewed in the back of Blue's throat, but he was too weak to release it. He tried to gather the strength to put himself in front of Evie, to shield her, but he couldn't. Frustration and fury battled for supremacy.

"Stand up, Miss Black," Tyson commanded. He had two black eyes and a cut in the center of his nose.

Courtesy of his last run-in with Evie?

"No," she said with a shake of her head. She raked her gaze over Blue, as if she meant to start tending him here and now, despite their audience. "I have to—"

"Evangeline," Blue gasped. "Please. Do what he says." In a few hours Blue would heal. Maybe faster, if he could get his hands on someone. Someone healthy, that is. Blue could drain their strength, taking it into himself as easily as he'd taken Evie's injuries. All she had to do was stay alive until then. Once he was strong enough, he would tear Star's world apart and she would never be threatened again.

Tyson switched his aim, the barrel now pointed at Blue. "Listen to your man before I kill him."

Evie jumped to her feet. "Okay. Okay. I'm up. But you listen to me, you miserable little worm. Anything you do to him, I will remember and I will revisit upon you a thousand times worse."

He smiled smugly. "Dead women can't follow through with their threats."

Four men marched into the room. One carried an uninjured Tiffany. The other three were empty-handed.

"Where's the father?" Tyson snapped, the smugness gone. "Michael Black."

"Either his body is buried under the rubble or he was able to run. Again."

As he pondered what to do, Tyson flicked the tip of his tongue over an incisor. "Two of you search the surrounding area. If he's out there, he's injured. There will be a blood trail. I don't want to leave anything to chance. Not this time."

Two of the men rushed out.

To the remaining, empty-handed guard, he said, "Carry the football player to the van." He glared at Evie and grinned. "I'll take care of the girl."

Twenty-seven

*E*VIE WOKE UP TIED to a bed.

Her first reaction was confusion. Then memories surfaced. She had been with Blue, and he had been on the phone with Gregory Star. Tiffany had cried, and there had been an explosion. Evie had been hurt, unable to move. Dying. Cold, so cold. Then Blue had loomed over her, and heat had filled her, and the pain had vanished. Yet he'd fallen over, suddenly pallid, his features pinched with pain.

She wasn't sure what happened. Unless . . . he took her injuries into himself?

Maybe. The wonderful, beautiful idiot!

Then Tyson appeared.

Tyson. Yes.

He must have drugged her. She fought as a large male hefted Blue over his shoulder, unconcerned about the warrior's broken spine. A hard hand pressed a cloth into her nose, and her body went lax. Darkness descended.

Now her fight-or-flight response kicked in, and, as always, fight won. She jerked against her bonds until the skin on her wrists and ankles was shredded and blood dripped from the wounds.

Not helping the situation, girl.

Panting, she sagged against the mattress. Took stock. She was trapped in a room of utter luxury. There was a chandelier overhead, thousands of crystals glinting in the light. The walls were papered with slightly yellowed lace. Clearly an older home. In the Western district, maybe. An affluent "don't ask, don't tell" part of town.

The door opened, hinges groaning, and Tyson strolled in. He wore a business suit and had his hair slicked back, not a strand out of place. His gaze immediately sought her. "Good. You're awake."

Anger rocked her. "Where's Blue?"

"What? No worry for your father? We haven't yet found him, you know, so half of our forces are out there looking. But don't get any ideas about trying to escape while we're so divided," he rushed to add, realizing he'd said more than he should. "As weak and puny as you are, you'll never be able to take on all of us."

Weak? Puny?

Trying to save face for the nose job I gave you?

She couldn't worry about her father. It would cloud her thoughts, compromise her instincts. Besides, he could take care of himself. "What do you plan to do with Blue?"

"Me? Nothing." Tyson removed his jacket, revealing the pyre-guns sheathed at his sides. "Your man made a mistake challenging my father. He'll make sure Blue understands that before he kills him."

Have to escape. Have to save him. "What are you going to do with me?"

There was a pitcher of water on the dresser. He poured himself a glass and drained the contents. His features were pinched as he said, "To be honest, I haven't figured that out yet."

He wasn't as hard-core as his father or he would have hurt her already. She could work with that.

If possible, establish camaraderie. "Will you cut me loose, at least? Please. I don't have any weapons. I don't even know where I am. There's nothing I can do to you while I'm this weak, and nowhere I can go."

He ignored her, lifting her purse. "I remembered the weapons you had in the last bag, so I thought I'd find a treasure trove in this one after I peeled it from your unconscious body. Instead, all I found was toys." He sneered. "Just one of many mistakes you've made."

Each one of those toys will drop and sock you, boyo. "What can I say? I'm easily bored."

"That's because you had a rich, pampered childhood. Unlike Tiffany and me, who were punished for every wrong we ever committed, real or otherwise." He poured another glass and brought this one to her, placing the cup at her lips.

She drank greedily, desperate to wash the soot from her throat. When she finished, she licked her mouth and, to relax him, offered a small smile. "Thank you."

"You're lucky I decided to keep you," he said tightly, "rather than let my father do what he wanted to do to you." He set the cup aside and traced his knuckles along her jaw.

She flinched from the contact, acting the part of the frightened little lamb.

A muscle ticked under his eye. "I'm not a bad guy, Miss Black."

Okay. Screw camaraderie. A statement that grotesquely wrong couldn't be ignored. "Your father has kidnapped and killed innocent people. He removed the skin of a living man. He bombed two of my father's homes. This time you helped him. So, yes, you're a bad guy."

He scowled down at her. "Is this the part where you try to convince me to help you prove I'm nothing like the man who sired me? Well, let me save you the trouble. No one challenges my father, and that includes me. I've never bucked the system, for myself or my sister, and I certainly won't do it for you. A pretty woman whose sharp little tongue ruins everything."

Only a strong man could truly appreciate a strong woman. "Tyson," she said, once again going for frightened little lamb.

His scowl morphed into the semblance of a smile. "Bet you wish you'd been nicer to me over the years, huh?"

With that, he strode from the room, shutting her inside.

Over the years?

She'd encountered him at a few parties, she was sure, but she couldn't recall being rude to him specifically.

You've been rude to everyone.

Okay. True.

There was no clock, so she couldn't track time. She only knew an eternity passed. Her stomach growled. Her bladder filled and began to hurt. She worried about Blue, about what was being done to him. Had

Michael been well enough to follow Tyson here? Was her father aware she had the isotope in her blood? That he could track her the same way Star tracked Tiffany?

Maybe not. But if Tiffany was here . . . He could track *her*.

Would Star really be that stupid, though?

Finally, Tyson returned. His eyes were bloodshot, his clothing wrinkled. There were lipstick stains on his collar, and he reeked of smoke, alcohol, and sex.

"I'll be nicer to you," she said with as much eagerness as she could muster. "Please. Just free me. I have to use the bathroom."

"I know you'll be nicer, Miz Black. You've had time to think and you've realized it'll be better for you to make friends with me and do whatever I tell you." Smirking, he stumbled to her side and untied her, surprising her.

Don't leap into action. Wait. Plan.

He remained at her side, rather than offering to escort her to the bathroom. She rubbed at her wrists. Was he too drunk to remember her major badassery skills? Or did he think the threat over Blue would keep her docile? Yeah. That one. Typical bully move.

"What time is it?" she asked in an effort to keep him relaxed.

"Midnight. The time for lovers," he said with a leering grin.

Gah! Gonna play that game, were they? "Is Blue here? In this house?"

"Still worried about him? How sweet. Well, you'll be happy to know he is indeed here, and he's alive. Barely.

We wanted you close to him, just in case we needed to convince him to behave." His gaze bored into hers. "But I'd be better off killing you, I think. I can't ever let you go. You know too much."

"Know too much? Me? Nah," she said. "Besides, I'd never tell."

"Liar," he said, and slapped her.

A trickle of blood ran through her mouth. Her eyes narrowed on him. "Do *not* do that again."

"You are known for your brutal sense of truth, and yet you dare lie to me? When I hold your fate in my hands?"

"You're right. I do know too much, and I will tell. But I'm going to hurt you real bad first."

"Doubtful." His head tilted to the side as he studied her. "I left a club full of women desperate to warm my bed. For you. Last time we were together, I was too concerned for my sister to feel much for you. Now I don't want to have what I've already had when I can have something new."

Plan: kill him, find Blue.

Done.

"What did you have in mind?" she asked. "I'm assuming you'll beat me if I refuse."

To kill him: rip out his larynx? Yeah. That would work. It was satisfying (for her), and quiet. Any guards posted outside the door would remain unaware.

"You're assuming correctly." His eyes brightened with triumph. "But I'll even throw in a bonus and let you earn medical treatments for Blue."

Wanker. "Such as?"

"First up, you're going to suck me off, and in return I'm going to have someone realign Blue's spine. See how kind I can be?" He stood and stalked to the dresser, though he never took his gaze off her. His fingers toyed with the button on his jeans. "What do you think?"

"I think I want to decline," she said with a sugary-sweet smile. "If I'm being honest."

His grin bloomed all over again. "I almost hope you do decline. Because my next order of business will be to go down and break Mr. Blue's spine in other places."

Go down.

So. Blue was downstairs, and she was up. A priceless piece of information.

For dramatic effect, she shuddered. "All right. Okay. We understand each other," she said, and threw her legs over the side of the bed. As she walked forward, she pretended her knees were trembling, and staged a trip. Then she crawled the rest of the way.

He seemed to like her fear, proudly squaring his shoulders when she reached him.

She slowly lowered his zipper.

"If you bite me," he said, gripping the hair at her nape in a hard, intractable fist, "you'll end up needing a wire for your jaw."

"No. Please. Anything but that." Too much? "Are you a screamer?" she asked softly.

He softened his stance, saying, "Only if you're good."

"Oh, I'm very good." She pulled his pants and underwear down to his ankles. His erection bobbed in front of her face. No wonder he had such terrible rage issues. Little Ty-Ty had been teased in the school bathroom, hadn't he?

"I'll be the judge of that. Now do it," he gritted, as though in pain.

With pleasure, she thought.

She balled her hand and punched his sac as hard as she possibly could. He doubled over and, lightning fast, she rammed her other hand into his nose, breaking it a second time.

As blood spurted, he opened his mouth to bellow, but she slapped a hand over his lips, silencing him. Forget the larynx thing. She had a better idea. He stumbled forward, tripped over his pants, and landed on his knees. She popped up and grinned.

And then she kicked him in the back of the head with so much force he immediately crumpled into a wilted heap.

Just for fun, she kicked him again. Then, working fast, she rooted through her purse and found two of the tubes of lipstick. With a little fancy finger work, the tubes were transformed into mini pyre-guns. Yes. Like Swiss Army makeup.

Killing was out, and torture was in. She dragged the motionless Tyson to the bed and, through sheer grit and determination, got him up on the mattress. He could be leveraged. After engaging the laser cuffs on his wrists to keep him in place, stuffing his mouth full of tube socks, and punching him again just for funzies, she removed his weapons.

The guns she couldn't use. They were programmed

to his ID and useless for everyone else. But she found a switchblade and claimed it as her own.

Up next: bladder relief.

When she stalked out of the bathroom, life was worth living again.

Now for the tricky part of the plan. Getting to Blue.

Were there guards stationed outside the room?

Probably.

She draped her purse around her side, opened the door, and peeked out quickly. Wow. Empty. Tyson had been that sure of himself. There were three other doorways before the hallway curved. Tiptoeing, she walked to the first door, listened. No sounds. She peeked inside. A bedroom. Furnished, and clean, as if no one had been inside in a very long time. Or ever.

The other two were the same.

So the guards didn't live up here. A blessing. No one would be sneaking up on her.

She moved to the top of the stairs and paused, peering down a small alcove into the living room. There were ten armed males. Most had their backs to her. Some gazed out the windows, watching for intruders. Some paced between the living room and kitchen. Two sat in front of a wall of screens, probably watching the security feed.

Evie lay on the floor and dug through her purse, setting the Rubik's Cube and the golf ball at the ledge, and anchoring the glasses on the bridge of her nose. The lenses sealed off her eye sockets, preventing any air from penetrating. Then she placed both guns in position.

Deep breath in . . . release . . . she pushed the cube and golf ball over the ledge with her chin. A second of normalcy, then . . . *boom!*

A violent gust of heat blew her hair all around her shoulders. Smoke thickened the air and debris rained. Men screamed. Not only did the glasses protect her from the poison, they also allowed her to see past the smoke. She focused on the men still standing, running this way and that, and squeezed the triggers of her guns. Two bright streams of yellow light pierced the chaos, hitting her targets. They slumped forward. Her next two targets went down just as easily.

A few of the men seemed immune to the poisoned air that should have swelled their eyes shut, and turned toward her, searching for the source of the gunfire. Now that she'd thinned the herd, she had a little more room for error. So she just started firing. Down, down, down men fell. The last one managed to whip out his gun and shoot in her direction, but the miasma distorted his aim and the blaze soared just over her shoulder. She felt the sear of the flames but not the sting. Then he, too, was dead, and she was standing.

Hold on, Blue. I'm coming for you.

Twenty-eight

A COMMOTION BEYOND THE CELL diverted Star's attention from Blue, and the man frowned at his daughter.

Tiffany sat on a stool in the corner, watching everything that happened. She wasn't happy to be there. Her eyes were swollen from crying, her cheeks red with tear tracks, and she whimpered every time her father hurt Blue. But Star had told her to stay and "learn the family trade," and so she had stayed.

"Go find out what's going on," Star commanded.

"Yes, sir," she replied dutifully, and tripped from the cell.

Blue was happy to see her go. He was strapped to a table, unable to move, and the extra set of eyes pissed him off. So did his failure. He hadn't managed to steal Star's health.

Now he was waiting for his body to heal on its own.

The spacious cell had no bars, only concrete walls and a door. It reminded him of the room he'd seen in the video, the one with John. There was a single light, a too-bright halogen bulb, hanging overhead, and his bomb-sensitive eyes burned as if they'd been set on fire.

Was Evie nearby?

Star faced him. "Ready to continue?" he said with a sigh, waving a scalpel in the air. "You should have walked away when I gave you the chance. Now I'm going to treat you to the same procedure I treated John to. A procedure I learned years ago while living on the streets. Did you know that? How poor I was as a child? Sometimes I had to kill for my dinner, and not just to steal what someone else had. People do terrible things when they're hungry."

Do not comment. Make the monologue last.

"I know, because terrible things were done to me." Star's hand tightened on the knife.

Won't feel sorry for him.

"I learned to protect myself, though, and always went back for revenge. Now I help others who can't help themselves. It's a public service, really."

"You also hurt innocents." The words slipped out.

Star shrugged. "Is anyone ever really innocent, Mr. Blue? No matter our age, we've all hurt someone in some way."

"Some of us are sorry about that."

"That doesn't make the pain go away." Back on topic, he said, "Your flesh is battered and bruised and won't fetch me any money, but it will make a nice trophy for my case. You've caused me considerable trouble, Mr. Blue."

"You deserved it," Blue gritted.

"For defending my empire? If anything, I should be commended. I couldn't let you come along and cause my clients to doubt my capabilities. Couldn't let them wonder how I could possibly punish their enemies when I couldn't punish my own."

A twitch in Blue's fingers.

Movement?

He tried again. His finger rubbed against the plastic blanket spread out underneath him. Finally! He'd begun to heal. His power wouldn't be far behind.

Can't grin.

He grinned.

Star narrowed his eyes. "I would have injected you with painkillers so that you wouldn't feel the worst of it, but I'm recording this to show to anyone who thinks to come against me in the future, and I'm going to need you to scream. I'll start with your toes and work my way up. Afterward I may or may not put you out of your misery. You'll have to beg. John did."

"I'm going to enjoy killing you." Come on. *Come the hell on!* Another twitch, this time in his wrist.

"No need to be rude, Mr. Blue. Especially since I control the fate of your girlfriend as well as your friend. Instead of hurting her in front of you, I did you the courtesy of placing her in the care of my son. He'll make sure she experiences . . . pleasure."

A tide of rage spilled through him, and his shoulder twitched. "How sweet of you."

"Yes. It was. And now for your pain." Star hunched over Blue's left foot and slid the tip of the blade just underneath his skin.

Blue's nerves were in the process of coming back to life. He felt the sting and hissed in a breath.

Star worked slowly, dragging out the terrible sensations. Finally he straightened and brushed his bloody hands together for a job well done. "The first toe is finished. Now for the second. The secret is in the angle of the wrist. Too far this way and you'll tear. Too far that way and I'll take muscle, too."

As the blade slid underneath the nail of the second toe, Blue's entire leg jerked to avoid the pain.

"Steady now. I'll call the guards in to restrain you further if I must."

A white-hot lance rode the waves of every nerve in his body, and Blue cried out. He'd never felt anything so terrible, and his rage grew. John experienced this. For hours.

"So dramatic," Star said with a nod. "Keep it up."

The blade began to move, and Blue waved his fingers. They were his to control again. He turned his head left, right, the bones popping. Good. No problems there, either. He bit the inside of his cheek to stop another grin.

His power hadn't returned, but he was back in the game.

He had one chance to do this. Only one.

He closed his eyes and drew what strength he possessed into his core. Then, arching his back, putting his weight into his shoulders and elbows, he jerked at the straps confining his wrists. The material snapped apart.

Frowning with confusion, Star straightened.

Blue jolted upright and fit his fingers around the man's neck, squeezing. Drawing from the man's strength and health, his muscles began to plump; Star's began to wither.

Eyes wide, Star desperately tried to pull away and, when that failed, remembered he was holding a scalpel and stabbed Blue in the neck. Blue experienced a sharp sting, felt a warm spurt of blood.

But only a few seconds later Blue healed and the injury appeared on Star.

The man's blood filled Blue's hands and slicked his skin, and he lost his grip. Star clutched his neck and stumbled away from him, gasping for breath.

Blue yanked at the ankle straps, then stood at the side of the gurney.

Star fell to his knees, his strength depleted. Still, he managed to whip a gun from the back of his pants and aim. "You stay right where you are, Mr. Blue, or I'll kill you."

"The time for orders is over." Lunging, Blue swiped the weapon out of his hand and turned it, pointing it at his opponent's heart. "You were saying?"

Suddenly the door burst open and Evie raced inside, dragging Tiffany behind her. She took one look at the scene and cried out with relief. "Blue! Thank God!"

"Evie." Somehow, his smart, intrepid woman managed to escape Tyson on her own. Of course she had. And, rather than saving herself, she came looking for him.

I have the best taste in women.

"The guards are dead," she announced. "All of them.

There could be more outside the home. I couldn't tell. Get the answers we need, kill him, and let's go."

He swallowed a laugh. How easy she made it sound.

"Tyson," Star gasped.

She smiled evilly. "Resting upstairs—for now. If you don't tell Blue what he wants to know, well, I'll let you fill in the blank."

"If you hurt him . . ." the male growled.

"Oh, trust me. I'll hurt him. The broken nose and destroyed ball sac were just the appetizers."

Tiffany covered her mouth with her hands. "Not Tyson. Please, don't hurt Tyson."

Distracted by her, Blue didn't realize Star palmed a second gun. One he aimed at Evie. He tapped at the trigger, and a stream of yellow light shot out.

Evie dodged, barely escaping.

Furious now, Blue aimed his own weapon at Star. "You shouldn't have done that."

He, too, tapped at the trigger. Intending to harm irreparably, but not to kill. Not yet.

With a shout of denial, Tiffany jumped in front of Star, acting as his shield, taking the flames into her own body. Her heart fried instantly, her eyes widening as her knees buckled. She tumbled to the floor.

"No!" Star shouted, horrified. "No!"

Blue leapt into action, kicking the second gun out of the man's hand, then grabbing him by the shirt to lift him off the ground. His legs dangled in the air.

"We both know you're not going to kill me," Star gritted, his grief for his daughter vanquished by self-preservation. "You won't find your friend without me."

Eyes sparking with electric energy, Blue shouted, "Where is he?"

"Not here," Evie interjected. "I've checked every room in the house and every room downstairs."

"You need me," Star said, gloating.

Blue's fury knew no bounds.

He had another choice to make, he realized. Take Star with him and lock him up, as originally planned, leaving the filthy piece of trash alive in the hopes that he could somehow force the man to tell him where John was being kept. Or he could kill him, let off a little steam, and pray he would find his friend on his own.

It wasn't really a choice, was it?

Blue patted the man down, found three daggers, a vial of some kind of poison, and a bag of pills. He threw everything aside. Removed the man's shoes, then his clothes, leaving him in his underwear.

Humiliation burned Star's cheeks. "This isn't going to get you the answer you seek."

"It's not meant to."

He tied Star's hands behind his back, then shoved him forward. Evie trailed behind him.

"I used one of the guard's cell phones to call Solo," she said. "I left it up there and turned on so he could track the signal. He should be here—"

Boom!

The entire underground shook.

Overhead, footsteps pounded.

"—now," she finished.

"We're down here!" Blue shouted.

Solo descended the steps, his bones enlarged, his skin a deep crimson. He was breathing heavily, ready to kill everyone in his path . . . until he took one look at the stripped Star and ground to an abrupt halt.

"Won?" the warrior asked, clearly confused.

Blue nodded, a wave of pride washing through him. "We won this battle. Thanks to Evie."

"Not just me," she said. "Blue and I were a team."

He kissed her temple.

Some of the red faded from Solo's skin. "Your father is upstairs," he said.

"Tyson's up there, too. Someone needs to haul him away before I return and kill him. He's still excellent leverage." Evie raced past Blue and then Solo, and Blue wanted to call her back, because he didn't want her far from his side, but she was well able to take care of herself, wasn't she. He let her go.

As Star looked over the monstrous Solo, he trembled with fear.

"He thinks he can keep John's location from us," Blue said.

Solo cracked his knuckles, and despite the lessening of his monstrous visage, his claws were still so long they sliced into his palms, drawing blood. "I would love a chance to change his mind."

Star raised his chin. "You might scare me, but you won't break me. You have no idea the things I've had to endure over the years. Worse creatures than you have had a go at me and failed."

Trying to gain pity?

Please.

Blue kicked him in the backs of his knees, sending him crashing into the concrete floor. Then Blue pushed him the rest of the way down, to his face, and pressed a bloody foot into his neck. "That's enough out of you. For now, at least."

Evie came back down the stairs, grinning from ear to ear. She stomped on Star to get to Blue. "Michael's good," she said, jumping up and down with happiness. "Badly bruised, but he's got all his parts and they're working, so I can't complain."

"What happened to him?"

"He made it into the forest outside the cabin, evaded the men hunting him, and called Solo." She twisted to eye the warrior in question. "When *I* called you, you didn't tell me you knew where we'd been taken and that you were on your way."

Solo shrugged his wide shoulders. "For all I knew, you were under duress. I didn't want anyone to know how close I was."

"Forgiven. I guess." She focused on Blue and her grin returned. "We did it. We really won."

His chest constricted. Oh, how he adored this woman. "You okay? Was anything done to you?" From the looks of her, she hadn't been hurt, but he needed to hear the words directly from her.

"No. I'm fine, I promise. You?"

"Better every second." He increased the pressure on Star's neck, and the man gasped for breath. "If Star had been smarter, he would have realized you were the greater threat."

Beaming at him, she cupped his cheeks. "You keep

saying stuff like that and it's going to go to my head." After kissing him, she said, "So what's next?"

He nuzzled her nose. "Now we get to a secure location and have our chat-up with Star."

Since Michael could officially come back from the dead, everyone was able to congregate at his house, in the basement. The dungeon, Evie liked to call it, where multiple cells awaited, as well as torture devices stained with the blood of past victims.

She watched as Blue and Solo took turns interrogating Star. She'd never seen two men more focused, driven, or—to be honest—cruel. But they had to be. It wasn't until the end, six hours later, when there wasn't much left of Star, that the male who'd caused so much death and destruction finally broke.

He'd proven to be immune to compulsion and truth serum but, ultimately, not to pain. Blue and Solo were merciless, cutting off Star's fingers and toes one at a time, then removing hunks of his skin the way he'd done to John, and then . . . She shuddered. She didn't want to think about what they did to Star after that, but it worked.

Star spilled his secrets, along with everything else.

Evie stayed with Michael, keeping Star alive while the boys rushed to the address they were given. A place Star reached through underground tunnels in his country estate. As soon as she got a call saying John was in custody, unconscious but alive, she pulled the plug on Star's life support.

He died soon after.

Tyson had to watch it all from a cell. Now he sobbed quietly in the corner.

Finally, it was all over. The mission. The worry. The guilt. Over.

Evie and Michael hugged and, okay, both of them cried tears of joy.

"I'm sorry," he said into her hair. "For everything."

"I know. Me, too."

"I love you, sunbeam."

"I love you, Daddy."

After that, Evie drove home. She didn't know if she'd see Blue that night or not.

She should have known she would.

He arrived a few hours later, still covered in soot and much more blood, his clothing torn, his feet bare but healed.

Honestly? He'd never looked better to her. He was there, he was alive, and he was with her.

He stalked into the bedroom, jerked her into his arms, and buried his face in the hollow of her neck. She immediately wrapped herself around him, thankful that, despite the horror of the circumstances, they'd come together, they'd opened themselves to a relationship, and they'd fought for it. Fought for each other.

"He's going to live," he said. "John's going to live."

"I'm so glad."

"We took him to the medical facility where your father was held those first few days. I want you to . . . Evie, will you take over his care? They're stabilizing him tonight, but if you could visit him in the morning . . .

if you could make sure he's receiving the best . . . I just . . ."

"Of course I will," she said. "You don't even have to ask. I'll call in the best Rakan specialists. I won't let anything happen to him, and I'll make sure everything possible is being done for him."

"Thank you. Thank you so much. I don't know what I'd do without you, princess."

"I'm glad about that, too, because . . . Blue? I'm not falling in love with you anymore. I'm there. I'm so in love with you I'm sick with it. I just thought you should know."

He froze, even stopped breathing, as if he couldn't bear to disrupt the moment. "I wanted you to love me. Wanted it so bad, because I love you, too, Evangeline Black. I love you so much, it's pathetic. I'm whipped. Head over heels. Obsessed. Possessed. I'm thinking about having you permanently glued to my side."

He loves me, too!

Joy swept through her. She wasn't sure how she'd won the heart of the world's most notorious playboy, but she was glad that she had. "I'm strangely okay with being glued to your side," she said. "I even know a surgeon who'd be willing to do it, if the price was right."

He gave a hoarse laugh. "I'll pay double if he'll make sure our parts are lined up properly. That way I can just stay inside you for the rest of our lives."

Dirty-minded man. She loved that, too! "Come on. Let's get you cleaned up, fed, and rested. I could use a nap myself. That way I'll be at my best when I visit John." She led him to the shower, stripped him, pushed the right buttons, and waited as the mist cleaned him.

Afterward, she drew him to the bed. Then, as he'd once done for her, she went to the kitchen and dug up some food. Wearing only a robe, she straddled his lap, facing him while they ate. He received the peep show of a lifetime.

"By the way, if I wasn't clear with the whole surgical, stay-inside-you thing, we're getting married," he said, "and our prenup is going to stipulate that you have to do something like this every day."

Married? Yes, please! She wanted this man legally bound to her. "Do you seriously think I'm going to let you have a prenup? I want everything you own, including your soul."

"Princess, it's already yours. To prove it, I want to do a human and an Arcadian ceremony. One with vows. One with blood. And before you start to panic on me, you won't be a slave like Dallas is to the king. I will take your blood, too, and it will bond us. You will age slower, like my race, so I won't have to live a single moment without you."

Slowly she grinned. "You, Corbin Blue, are a sappy, sappy man."

"But you love me anyway."

"I love you always."

He squeezed the tops of her thighs. "Since I'll be Mr. Evangeline Black, you have to wipe out my bill."

"I will . . . just as soon as you pay it."

"Can I get a discount?"

She thought for a moment. "Well . . . I think you once mentioned paying in orgasms."

"This is true."

"Then no discount. You'll pay every cent."

He laughed. "Good."

"Anything else we need to cover before you knock out a few dollars?"

"A few dollars? Ha! A good orgasm is worth thousands. But, yes, one more thing to cover. You once told me you were done with agenting when the case was over. Is that still the plan?"

"I . . . don't think so. I liked getting back in the game, I admit it. But I also like being a doctor. So I'm not sure what I'll do."

"Maybe you can do both. I mean, you managed both with me. Every time I did something stupid, you were right there to patch me up."

"True." She nibbled on her bottom lip. "Yeah, I like the idea of doing both. Of working cases and patching agents."

He toyed with the ends of her hair. "Thank you for everything. For being you. For saving me in every way."

Warmth flowed through her. "You saved me, too. You gave me your strength and took my weakness, and as much as I love you for it, I will seriously hurt you if you ever do it again. I would rather die than lose you."

"I *will* die if I lose you." He traced a finger down the center of her robe, widening the lapels, revealing more of her breasts. "You are so beautiful," he said. "So sweet. So soft. So perfect. So utterly mine. You could have done so much better than me, but I'm glad you didn't."

A slow grin spread across her face. She would never tire of his compliments. He made her *feel* beautiful and sweet and soft and perfect. "Silly man. I happen to think you're the best there is."

"Yeah?"

"Oh, yeah."

"You're making me question your intelligence, panda bear, but that's okay, because I've always liked ditzy women."

She gave a fist pump toward the ceiling. "Finally. I'm officially your type."

His fingers wound around a thick lock of her hair, not stopping until he reached her nape. He pulled her down for a kiss, and when that wasn't enough contact, when the heat sparked between them, he rolled her onto her back and loomed over her.

"My type is Evie Black. Everything I like revolves around *you*. You're the best thing to ever happen to me. And before either of us takes another case, I want to whisk you away for the best vacation of your life. Sun, sand, and mandatory nudity. Then maybe I'll spend my billions buying the world for you."

"I'm on board with everything but the present. I'd like something I don't already own, please."

He snorted.

She had never thought she would end up with a guy like him. Had anyone suggested it, even a few months earlier, she would have laughed—and then maybe pulled a gun. But Blue burst into her life, infiltrated every aspect of it, and definitely turned everything upside down while he chased away the darkness inside her and ushered in the brightest of lights.

"Actually, as long as you're with me," she said, "I have everything I need."

He grinned and challenged, "As long as I'm *with* you . . . or *in* you?"

She laughed, the sound genuine and tinkling like bells, surprising her. When had she become such a girl? "I'm greedy. How about both?"

"I can get on board with that." He fit his hands on her hips. "So let's get started, shall we?"

"Working with Evie Black combines my two favorite things. Starting my day with her . . . and ending my day with her."

—CORBIN BLUE

"I guess I'm like fungus. I grow on you."

—EVIE BLACK

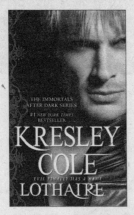
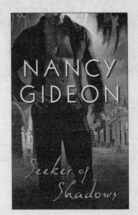